THE EDITOR

ALSO BY STEVEN ROWLEY

Lily and the Octopus

STEVEN ROWLEY

The Editor

A Novel

G. P. Putnam's Sons
New York

PUTNAM

G. P. Putnam's Sons
Publishers Since 1838
An imprint of Penguin Random House LLC
penguinrandomhouse.com

Copyright © 2019 by Ten Wry Wolves, Inc.
Penguin supports copyright. Copyright fuels creativity, encourages diverse voices,
promotes free speech, and creates a vibrant culture. Thank you for buying an authorized
edition of this book and for complying with copyright laws by not reproducing, scanning,
or distributing any part of it in any form without permission. You are supporting
writers and allowing Penguin to continue to publish books for every reader.

LIBRARY OF CONGRESS CATALOGING-IN-PUBLICATION DATA

Names: Rowley, Steven, author.
Title: The editor : a novel / Steven Rowley.
Description: New York : G. P. Putnam's Sons, [2019]
Identifiers: LCCN 2018042427| ISBN 9780525537960 (hardback) |
ISBN 9780525537977 (epub)
Subjects: | BISAC: FICTION / Literary. | FICTION / Family Life. |
FICTION / Historical.
Classification: LCC PS3618.O888 E35 2019 | DDC 813/.6—dc23
LC record available at https://lccn.loc.gov/2018042427

International edition ISBN: 9780525542995

Printed in the United States of America
1   3   5   7   9   10   8   6   4   2

Book design by Francesca Belanger

For my parents

In short, there's simply not
A more congenial spot
For happily-ever-aftering than here
In Camelot.

—*Camelot*, lyrics by Alan Jay Lerner

THE EDITOR

THE QUARANTINE
A Novel by James Smale

The room was warm, too warm, Russell thought, to share with a dead body, but no one seemed concerned. Guests wore their coats cinched tight at the waists, as if taking them off would obligate them to stay. In the back of the room a giant silver percolator was brewing coffee, and there was another kettle for tea. His mother, having had three cups black, did laps around the room like the women who exercised inside the Pyramid Shopping Center—mall milers, they called them—somehow connecting with anyone in her path and simultaneously avoiding everyone.

"Look at her," Russell said, watching his mother's path from his vantage point by the casket. "When this is over I swear I'm going to lock her in a room."

"Who?" Sean tried to follow his brother's moving gaze.

"Mom."

"Mom? Why?"

"Why?" Wasn't it obvious? She's all they had left. He tugged at his tie. "Is it warm in here?"

"Very."

Russell ran his hand across the closed casket; his father had it worst of all, stuffed inside in the suit he hated and wore only to church. Or maybe he had it best. If only Russell could give his father some air. "She has to answer some things."

Sean offered his hand to the Speighs as they approached and gave him and his brother, the sons of Dick Mulligan, a solemn nod. "Thank you for coming."

"Dick was a good man," Mr. Speigh said, his nose twice the size it once was, not from the lie but from age. "It's a shame what he d—"

". . . what *happened*," Mrs. Speigh corrected, tugging at her husband's arm. No one wanted to say it out loud.

"Your father had some of my tools . . ."

"Of course," Sean said. Eventually they would clean out the garage.

"Another time, Arthur." Fed up, Mrs. Speigh gave her husband a full yank, pulling him toward the door.

Sean waited until their old neighbors were out of earshot. "What things? What does Mom have to answer?"

"Questions! She has to answer questions. Without circling the room, without walking away. Face-to-face. It's time."

"Now? You think now is the time. In the wake of . . ."

In the wake of, well, this wake.

"YES."

"And how will she answer them, these questions, locked in a room."

Russell stared at his brother, his eyes red, cried out, but overrun with inspiration. "I'm going to lock myself in with her."

And that's when the idea for The Quarantine took hold. As his mother, on her umpteenth lap, passed the table with the cups and the saucers and decided they needed restacking. As Sean removed his jacket and rolled up his sleeves like a politician hitting the campaign trail. As his sister, Fiona, held everyone's hand and listened as the same drab stories were told again and again and again. As his own head throbbed with torment and heartbreak. A quarantine. Russell wouldn't go home, back to California. He would stay in Ithaca, secured inside a room with his mother until there were no more secrets, until they knew each other as well as two people could. As two people with the same blood should. It was the only way he could make sense of the gunshot that took half his father's face.

It needed to shatter everything.

Dreams

February 1992

• ONE •

She moves quickly and with purpose, threading the tight corridor between a hedge maze of cubicles and the string of office doors. Her stride is serious; I have a thousand questions, but the snap to her step suggests I should select only one. Maybe two. Nope, *one*. I try to take everything in, to remember the details—I'm going to want to recount them later, to relive this in my head—but we're moving so fast. I see paper. Lots of paper. And push-pins, I think, colorful ones, tacked directly into the cubicle walls, holding calendars, schedules, memos, and important lists (more paper!) in place. Marketing stand-ees announce titles as *Coming Soon*, and a parade of book covers framed like art hang evenly spaced on the walls between door-frames, following me down the hall as if I'm viewing them through a zoetrope.

"I'm sorry, where are we going?" Just like that, my one question wasted. And I hate that I apologize. I have been invited here and I need to act like I belong before they figure out that I'm the wrong guy. An imposter. A dupe.

Without looking back, she says, "Conference room. End of the hall." Then, with barely a pause, "Would you like some water, James?" The sound of my name startles me. Hers is Lila. She told me, by the bank of elevators, where we were introduced. My agent's assistant told me it was Lisa, but that's typical Donna. Thank goodness Lila introduced herself before I had a chance to call her by the wrong name. That would have really started things out on the wrong foot. Lila has blond hair, but not so blond that you can't take her seriously. I really like her shoes.

"No. No water, thank you." I can't imagine walking this fast with a glass of water and not sloshing it everywhere, on my sleeve, or—heaven forbid—down the front of my pants. "I'm sorry I was late." Another apology, but this one is warranted.

"You were five minutes early."

Was I? "I'm usually ten minutes early, so in that sense I was late."

Lila ushers me inside the last room at the end of the hall. "Here we are. Conference room." She stares at me, and for the first time I notice her clothes are impeccably tailored. She's serious for a beige girl. That's what I've heard people call a lot of young women in publishing. I'm not fond of the term; it reeks of an unnecessary sexism. They're called that, beige girls, because they wear understated monotones and sweaters to match. But this girl (*woman!*) is a different animal. Power beige. Like a café-au-lait color, or camel or ecru.

"It's nice," I say, about the conference room, which is stupid. It makes me sound impressed, like I've never seen such a room before, and of course I have. I've worked at pretty much every office in Midtown in a never-ending string of toxic, depressing temp jobs. This conference room is exactly like any other conference room, with a bulletin board, a whiteboard, a phone in the center of a long table (at least I think it's a phone—it looks somewhat like a light-up game I had as a child), and a set of dry-erase markers.

"It serves a purpose." Her enthusiasm is considerably less than mine.

Yes, *conferencing*. For some reason I try to sell her on it. "It has everything. Even a window." Then, as an afterthought, "Anyone ever jumped?"

"Out the window?" She is appalled. I can tell. She tucks her hair back behind an ear while pursing her lips.

"It's just . . . I can imagine these meetings get a little . . . I mean, I know I'm feeling . . ." *Fraught?* Power Beige is just staring at me. "I'm sorry." I cringe. My third apology inside two minutes. "You're not interested in my twaddle."

For the first time in our incredibly brief relationship, she perks up. "I'm interested if you're going to jump out the window."

"I promise I'm not going to jump out the window."

She exhales. Disappointed? Perhaps. "Why don't you just have a seat, then." We've officially run out of things to say.

Silence.

Which I abhor.

I pull a chair back from the table and start to sit and then stop. There's a loud ringing in my ears similar to the one I would get as a kid after swimming endless summer hours in Lake George. "I always thought I'd be more of a pills person."

"More twaddle?" There is the vaguest hint of a smile. She's joking with me, letting me know to relax.

"Ha, no. It's just, I don't like it when other people have to clean up my messes." Talk of suicide has gone on so long, it may be professional suicide. To change the subject, I try to steer us toward business. "So, my manuscript. You've read it?"

"I have."

I replay that last bit in my head; it doesn't sit right. "Not that I think my manuscript is one of my messes! I just wanted that to be clear."

"It was. Clear." Lila picks up a dry-erase marker from the table and sets it on the lip of the whiteboard. In doing this, she softens slightly. "And even if it wasn't, that's an editor's job sometimes. To clean up."

"And you're interested? In being my editor?"

"You ask a lot of questions."

"It's nerves, I guess. I tend to . . ." I make a motion with my hands like I'm vomiting words. Lila grabs the corner wastebasket and holds it out for me. She smiles again, this time more broadly. I decide I like her; she has the ability to play along.

"No," she responds.

"Oh." I can feel the heat in my cheeks.

"You're here to meet with someone else."

"Oh my gosh. I'm sorry. I was told by my agent's assistant to ask

for Lila. Well, she said Lisa, but she can't read her own handwriting."
I'm going to have real words with Donna for putting me in this predicament.

"James, it's okay. I set up the meeting for you and this editor."

"And he liked it? The editor I'll be meeting with?"

"She."

"Sorry." Apology number four! I wince. This must be some sort of
record.

"Take a deep breath. We're not really in the business of calling
writers in to personally tell them how much we didn't like their work."

A wave of relief. "No. I don't suppose that's the best use of anyone's time."

"It's easier to do that in a letter."

"I received plenty of those," I say, before realizing how unvar-
nished that truth sounds. "Well, not *plenty*. A normal amount." Pause.
"Lila." I use her name as punctuation, unsure if it sounds like an exclamation point or a period.

She pulls the chair out farther and pats the back of it. "It won't be
long now. If you'd like to have a seat."

I sit before I get myself in any more trouble, and she leaves the
room, closing the door behind her. I swear I can hear her chuckle on
the other side before heading off down the hall.

Alone, I rifle through my bag to make sure I have a copy of my
manuscript, should they ask to see it. I do. I walk over to the window
and press my forehead against the glass to look straight down at moving vehicles that look like Matchbox cars. SPLAT. That would do it.
I cross back to the phone. What was the name of that game? Simon.
There's one visible button, and without thinking, I push it. It beeps
loudly and I jump, but then there's a dial tone. I push the button
again, quickly, and it stops. I pray the commotion doesn't summon
Lila. She would not be pleased.

I've been a writer for ten years. Since I graduated college. Or
maybe it's twenty-five years. Depending on when you start counting.
My mother had an old Swiss Hermes typewriter when I was growing

up; I have no idea where she acquired it or why she had it, but it was a thing of beauty to me. It was robin's-egg blue and came with a lid that clamped to the typewriter itself, turning it into a stylish, if heavy, attaché. The keys clacked and the bell dinged and I always pulled the lever for the carriage return like I was casting the deciding vote in a crucial election.

"You're not writing about me, are you?" I remember my mother asking, when I was only seven or eight years old. Like many of her questions, she delivered it more like a command.

"No," I would say, and at the time that was the truth. My stories were small, trite, about cats and the neighbors with the horse stables and a pond in the woods that wasn't much more than a puddle. But I felt they carried literary heft once they were typed. To me, typing was akin to publishing. I lived for that typewriter, and I would agonize when the ribbon became twisted, or the keys stuck, and I needed my mother's assistance. She didn't prioritize typewriter repair the same way I did. When I would point this out to her she would roll her eyes and say, "One day you can tell your therapist." She said that about a lot of things. But instead of getting a therapist, I became a writer. Instead of telling one person, I aspire to tell the world.

I rearrange the thumbtacks in the bulletin board on the wall into a peace symbol before having a seat. At least I think it's a peace symbol. It may be the Mercedes-Benz logo. I often get those two confused, so I get back up to undo my work in order to keep my mind on track.

I had some early success. As a writer. Two short stories published in two different literary journals. With typical youthful naïveté, I thought it would always be that way, but, of course, it wasn't. I took odd jobs to pay bills, convincing myself the whole time that these jobs provided life experience—essential to a writer who wants to have something important to say. But I don't have much insight from these experiences to share other than how to make coffee and remain invisible in a room full of people and battle a growing depression. It's been years now since I've had anything published, so long that I wonder if it's still acceptable to call myself a writer. That thought in itself is depressing, so I sit. Someone, an editor, is finally interested in my work, I remind myself, and I have to make the most of this nibble. I have to turn it into a bite.

Then I have to turn that bite into a sharklike chomp.

As soon as I'm settled in the chair the door opens. A woman enters, immediately turning her back to me so that all I can see is her slender frame and that she is a brunette and tall. She closes the door, taking pains to do so as gently as possible.

I scramble to my feet, knocking a knee against the table with a deafening whack. And even though I want to scream out in pain, to sink back into the chair and massage my leg, when she turns around and I meet her gaze, I stop. And then, strangely, I begin to bow.

Because . . . because . . . I don't know the protocol.

I don't know the rules of conduct in this situation.

But I no longer feel any pain. I don't remember that I have knees, that everyone has knees or what knees are even for. I'm completely mesmerized by her hair, blown back and resting gently on her shoulders, and a demure smile both shy and radiant. I look down at the ground as if I've dropped something, convinced when I look up again it will be someone else, a look-alike, perhaps, a woman who molded her style after hers.

But when I look up it's still . . .

It's her.

· TWO ·

It's you. I almost say it out loud.

She's immediately recognizable. Her posture, her eyes—there is no mistaking her. Of course I know who she is. But that's an understatement. I try to breathe. Have I not been breathing? In fact, it's perhaps the biggest understatement in the history of understating things. Which on its face sounds hyperbolic, but in this case I don't think it is. It's not even whatever falls just shy of hyperbole. Embellishment? Overstatement? No. It's a simple declaration of fact.

Because *everyone* knows who she is.

Now I try to remember how to breathe. What is breathing? The process of moving air in and out of your lungs. It involves the diaphragm? Something expands, something collapses, the blood gets what it needs. Oxygen in, CO_2 out. My inner dialogue is as deafening as it is dull.

"James," she says. "Lovely to make your acquaintance." Her voice is breathy, impossibly feminine, even in her . . . I try to attempt some quick math . . . *late fifties?* She's wearing dark slacks. A cashmere pullover. A jacket. It has shoulder pads. Chanel, maybe. Something distinguished like that. I'm not good with designers or labels. Daniel would know. He knows these things. She's very still and her gestures are small, her arms stay close to her body; it's as if she's spent a lifetime trying not to make sudden, attention-grabbing moves. When she steps farther into the room, she glides with a seamless light-footedness.

"I'm Jacqueline," she says, somewhere between the French and American pronunciations. That voice! Is it real? Is it really addressing me? She holds out her hand and I watch as my arm rises reflexively (lifted, perhaps, by an invisible bouquet of helium balloons), and as my hand reaches out for hers, I try to say something, but words fail me. That's not good for a writer. She looks at me quizzically before moving her hand the rest of the way to meet mine. We shake. Her skin is soft. My only thought is that she uses lotion. "You are James, aren't you?"

I blink. My own name somehow passes my lips. "James." I manage another word. And my last name. "Yes. Smale."

She smiles and our hands drop back to our sides. "Very good. And you were offered something to drink?" She pulls back a chair for herself but hesitates before sitting.

"Not anything strong enough for this."

"I'm sorry?" Her apology has an airy lightness; it's not clumsy like mine. It's less an expression of regret and more a cue for me to make yet another apology myself.

"No, I'm sorry. I may be in the wrong place. I was told by Lisa to wait here for an editor regarding my manuscript." It's a sentence, but it ends on an upswing, impersonating a question.

"Lila," she corrects. *Goddammit, Donna!* "You're in the right place."

I look at her, because it feels like I'm on one of those hidden-camera shows that are becoming increasingly common because they're cheap to produce. "Are *you* in the right place?" I say it hesitantly.

"Oh, yes. My office isn't very accommodating, and closing the door for privacy just makes it seem that much smaller. I thought we would both be more comfortable in here."

I can't hold it in any longer. "You're Jacqueline," I say, although my pronunciation is entirely American. "Jacqueline Kennedy."

"Onassis."

"Onassis. Right. And I'm . . ."

"James Smale. How nice of us to recap." She offers another shy smile.

"Yes. I guess we've covered that ground already. And, *believe me*, it's very nice to meet you. I'm just not sure what we're doing here.

Right now. In this room." And then, to drive the point home, I say, "Together."

She takes a seat and motions for me to do the same, so I pull back my chair and sit and she reaches out and rests her hand on top of mine. It's motherly, calming. She's wearing a distinctive bracelet that rattles softly like a tambourine. "James, I'm the editor who liked your book."

My entire life I've been waiting to hear someone at a New York publishing house say these words. But in the thousands of ways I may have imagined this moment, not one time did it look anything like this. Tiny fireworks are exploding in my head like it's the Fourth of July. For some reason I can't take my eyes off her earrings, which are pearl. "This is a lot to take in. Maybe I should have accepted that glass of water."

"Of course." She pats my hand twice and then stands. "I'll get it for you."

I start to protest—I can't have the former First Lady of the United States fetch me a glass of water—but she's already gone. *Am I crazy?* I scramble to pick up the phone, push the button for the dial tone, but who am I going to call? Lila? Even if I had her extension, wouldn't I just be humiliating myself further? What's more, she's obviously enjoying this, wherever she is. She could have prepared me—that would have been a small act of kindness—and yet she didn't. This is not off to a good start. I retreat to the corner and do ten jumping jacks, a coping mechanism I've developed for writer's block: ten perfect jumping jacks and blood moves to your brain (in theory, at least). Was my agent really not in on this? He's a practical joker, the type that likes other people to squirm—it helps, I guess, in negotiation. But would he do that to a client? Would he do that to me? I barely finish my jumping jacks when Jacqueline—*JACK-well-in? Zhak-LEEN?*—returns, holding a glass of water. She doesn't notice me at first in the corner.

"Ah. There you are," she says. I cross back to my chair and she hands me the glass. "I thought perhaps you had jumped out the window." She nods at the view and I lean in to make sure I heard her correctly, then laugh, probably too hard. Should I explain why that's so funny?

I hold up the glass of water as if to say "Cheers," then down most of it in several gulps, and she gestures for us to retake our seats.

"All set, then?" she asks.

I nod and watch her position herself gracefully in her chair, cross her legs, and pull herself in toward the table. When I take my seat, the chair unexpectedly drops several inches and I have to fuss with a lever underneath to bring it back to a proper height. Flustered, I try to say something, anything, to mask this awkward spectacle. "My middle name is Francis."

"Beg your pardon?"

"Francis, my middle name is . . ." I slow to a stop like a windup toy whose crank has run down.

Jacqueline Onassis studies me; I watch her eyes sweep across my face. After an interminable silence she says, "Bobby."

"Yes, sorry. That needed some prefacing. My middle name is Francis. After Robert Kennedy. I'm . . . I don't know why I'm saying this. Your time is valuable. I will focus." Deep breaths. "I can't believe you read my book."

"I read it twice," she says. She says nothing about my predicament with the chair as I fidget underneath and somehow sink farther, in a second humiliating display.

"Twice?" I try to sound nonchalant.

"Does that surprise you?"

"I'm still getting used to your reading it once." I finally master the chair's mechanics and lock it in a respectable raised position. I pull myself into the table and take another sip of water.

She flips through some notes on a pad of legal paper, and I wonder if they are notes about me, about my book. I strain to see, without looking like I'm straining to see; I'm dying to know her every thought. "It's quite difficult to put down. Once it gets going."

"A friend told me it's slow to start."

"Not slow. Deliberate. In order to deconstruct the American family, you must work diligently to construct it."

"That's what I said!" I brighten, and for the first time feel like I find my footing.

"I'm wondering if we could discuss the book, the two of us." The way she adds "the two of us." Persuasion. Just us. Alone in a room. Is she doing this on purpose? Is she luring me in only to lowball me with an offer? How can I think of business at a time like this? Whatever she's doing, it's artful. I'd be happy to sit here and talk books—my book, any book—until the afternoon is gone.

Until all of the afternoons are gone.

"I would be honored."

"*The Quarantine*," she says. It's an almost out-of-body experience to hear the title of my book in her unmistakable voice. I can hear the word's Italian origins, the way she says it. *Quarantina*. Forty Days.

"Yes."

"Did you live through such a thing?"

"An actual quarantine?"

"An isolation."

"With my mother?"

"With anyone."

"No. Not as such. Not formally."

Jackie nods. "How did you come to it as a framing device?"

I take a deep breath. "We all feel isolated, don't we? At one time or another?" *Does she? Oh, God.* "People yearn to connect—it should be easy, and yet it seldom is. That's true with my own mother. We talk, often past each other, somehow unable to convey meaning. It's fantasy, I suppose. Putting two characters in tight quarters. Eventually they can't avoid saying the things they desperately need to say."

She scribbles a thought on her pad. *Scribble* is the wrong word; I doubt she's careless with anything. "And that . . . fantasy, you call it . . ."

"I wasn't going to get my actual mother in a room for any length of time."

"That led you to write a novel."

"I didn't set out to. I considered myself more a writer of short stories. I thought I might have one published in *The New Yorker* one day, like many of the writers I admire. Updike. Cheever. Mavis Gallant. *Dreamed* I might, not thought." Ugh, *thought* has an element of presumption. I bite the inside of my cheek to slow myself down. "So, one of the early chapters in the book? The one after the service? With the argument over pie? That's the one I wrote first. When I finished it, I imagined this, finally, was my *New Yorker* story. And then I showed it to a friend, who encouraged me to write more." I pause here, expecting her to interject; she looks at me, poised and unblinking. "I realize now how unsatisfying it would have been as a short story. That it was inherently . . . incomplete."

"What a delightful note to receive as a writer. *More.*"

I smile at her like a child asking for juice.

"And you. Are you . . ." She checks her notepad. "Russell?"

"The character in the book? I'm not *not* Russell." *Check yourself, James. Now is not the time to be cute.* "He is a version of me, I suppose, in that we are both seeking and searching—yearning to understand."

"I would love to know more about the mother."

"What would you like to know?"

"What would you like to tell me?"

Afraid this is some unanswerable riddle, a test I'm doomed to fail, I revert to her previous question. "If you're asking if she's *my* mother, she would say no."

"Has she read the manuscript?"

"No." As soon as it comes out of my mouth I realize just how harsh it sounds on its own, so I say it again, softer this second time. "No." And then, because it's a point of contention between us, I add, "Not even once."

Jacqu—Mrs. Onassis taps her pen twice on her notepad. "Why not?"

"I wish she would. I suppose she's afraid of what she'll see."

"I saw something quite lovely."

My eyes are growing wet. Mortifying. It's a little early in the year to pass it off as allergies; I blink twice in an effort to stop it. "I thank you for saying so, but it's almost beside the point. She doesn't want to be written about."

Mrs. Onassis sets her pen down. "Well, your mother's in good company there."

"I suppose so," I say, smiling so that she knows I understand she's referring to herself.

"So why did you choose to write about her?"

"I'm not sure I did. Choose. I thought I would have endless stories. Deep, complicated, rich narratives that had profound things to say. I started a half-dozen novels centered on characters I thought would jump right off the page. But after numerous starts and stops they all seemed kind of flat in comparison to the most complicated character I knew."

"Your mother."

"My mother." I glance down at the pad between us and it reminds me of the terror of blank pages. "So, desperation, I guess?"

Mrs. Onassis raises an eyebrow. "Well, I think you've observed her quite eloquently. I admired her."

I look down at my nails and am embarrassed to see it's been a while since I've cut them. I quietly move to sit on my hands.

"Since I'm not asking her, I'm asking you—is she your mother?"

"Absolutely." And then, since I'm also deeply protective of her, I add, "A carbon copy. One that I can place just outside our relationship and stretch and mold and make malleable. Get inside. One that serves the novel, I hope. And one that I can possibly come to understand."

Mrs. Onassis makes additional notes and I wonder if she's writing down what I'm saying, which fuels my self-consciousness. Are these thoughts worth recording? When she looks up she asks, "One you can come to set free."

Your mother's in good company. Sitting across from someone so well known, I can't help but conjure a slideshow of every image I have of her, that every American has. The iconic moments, the idyllic portraits. Any one of them is imposing; together they are irrepressible. I try desperately to clear them from my mind—to focus on the woman in front of me—but in person she's no less an artfully framed photograph: stoic, quiet, still. The exotic bird, caged for voyeurs like myself. Have I done that to my mother? Cataloged her in snapshots? Confined her to a lifetime of observation? "One I can come to set free. I like that."

A man with a beard and wide tie opens the door, startling us both. "Oh, I'm sorry, Jackie. I didn't realize anyone was in here."

"That's quite all right," she says, and the man quietly closes the door. It's all so normal—he calls her Jackie, he sees her every day, they probably sit in staff meetings—I want to call after that man just to make sure he knows who his coworker really is.

I take advantage of the interruption. "May I ask *you* a question?"

"I would be happy if you did."

"Why am I here?"

Laughter. It's almost indescribable, the feeling of making her laugh. Like somehow all is right with the world, even if this laugh is at my expense.

"Are we speaking existentially?"

"No, no. Despite how my question sounds. I'm genuinely asking."

"Why are you here, as opposed to another author?"

"Why my book?"

Mrs. Onassis flips back the pages that are folded over the binding of her legal pad and sets her pen down on top of it. "Well, books are a journey. And I'm always excited to embark on a journey I haven't taken before. So I wanted to meet you, James."

"Thank you."

"I found your book to be very mature for a first effort. I have some ideas, if you are open to hearing them."

"Of course."

"Ideas that would strengthen the work and amplify the book's central themes. It's a wonderful setup, and there's work to be done on the ending, but we can fix all that. In short, I would like to acquire this novel for publication. It is my sincere hope that you're willing to work with me."

And just like that, I've completed the slow climb to the top of a roller coaster. I'm about to experience the first drop and people all around me are clutching their hats and sunglasses and screaming in both fear and exhilaration and my mouth is open to scream as well, but no sound comes out. The feeling is so intense I have to look down to make sure my chair hasn't collapsed again.

"James?"

I close my mouth in a vain attempt to appear sane. "It would be an honor to work with you."

"Would you like to take some time to think about it?"

"Should I think about it?"

"My father always advised me to sleep a night on important decisions."

"My father had no such counsel."

"Well, if I may." The way she asks permission suggests both a timidity and a deliberate command in steering our conversation. "It's a rare editor anymore who is more . . . well known, shall we say, than her authors. So, immediately, there's that to consider." She pauses, as if to make sure I'm following. "It would also mean you saying 'no' to me when you believe I'm wrong. Do you think you could do that?"

"Oh, no."

She leans back, hopefully amused. "Is that a joke?"

I have to think about it. "Perhaps. A lame attempt at one rolled in the truth. I could learn to."

"Make a joke?"

"Say no." It feels like a little rapport we're building. Daniel's heart is going to stop when I recount this bit for him later.

"I would like us to have a conventional editor/writer relationship. And that means I'll stand up for the things I believe in strongly, and you'll stand up for the things you believe in strongly. And we'll debate until there's a victor."

For a brief second, I picture us going toe-to-toe in a boxing ring, performing the most delicate pas de deux, me too afraid to ever throw a punch. "I would like that too. For us to have a normal relationship." No boxing gloves. "Although, it might knock my friendship with Eleanor Roosevelt down a peg." I say the *roo* in Roosevelt like in *kangaroo*, as that's how Dustin Hoffman says it in the movie *Tootsie*, and it always makes me laugh. Mrs. Onassis, however, doesn't. Laugh. "Another joke," I clarify.

"You must have more questions for me."

I do. I have eleventy million questions, but synapses are firing, or misfiring—if synapses even fire (or misfire)—and all that comes out is one of those passing non sequiturs that are embarrassingly easy to access in moments of great awkwardness. "How tall was Charles de Gaulle?"

She cocks her head, like I've started speaking in tongues, before finally emitting a laugh. "How tall was . . . ?" She stops to give it some thought. "Tall."

"I don't suppose that's the kind of question you had in mind."

"No, it was not."

"I didn't want to be obvious."

"In that you've succeeded."

"I'm sort of a Francophile. I love Paris. Which sounds dumb now that I say it—I mean, who doesn't love Paris. But here you are and you've met Charles de Gaulle."

"Well, he was very tall. He . . ." She starts to say more, then stops. She studies me, scanning my eyes to see if I can be trusted. She proceeds, but does so with caution. "This is neither here nor there, but I suppose I will follow your lead and be unexpected. He struck me as somewhat sad. He rode with President Kennedy and me through Paris, and when we got out of the car I remember thinking of Shelley's *Frankenstein* monster. It was something about the way he moved, slowly, deliberately, and the streets were lined with villagers. I tried my best to be charming. At the time I was very focused on bringing the *Mona Lisa* to the United States—it had never been on loan before to a foreign nation. I wanted to be bright, sunny, for my mission. As for the monster himself, it was hard to pierce that sadness."

I'm struck by her answer, the way she attributes *Frankenstein* to Shelley—in case anyone listening would miss the literary nature of the reference; I want to linger on it, but there are so many other things I want to know. About today, and every other day. About history. About the world and our place in it. About everything she's witnessed. About why she says "President Kennedy" instead of *my husband* or *Jack*. But I can't delve into any of that so I simply ask "Were you successful?"

"In getting the *Mona Lisa*? Oh, yes. I can be quite persuasive when I want to be. Even to monsters." This time she winks.

I understand that in being allowed to ask questions I'm being further persuaded. But I can't stop. "How long have you worked at Doubleday?"

"Fourteen years." She crosses her hands in her lap. "And several at Viking Press before that."

"That's probably more in line with what you were expecting."

She dips her head in agreement.

"And you have an office? In this building?"

"I have an office here, down the hall. It's a regular size and stacked high with manuscripts. I get my own coffee and wait in line to use the copier, same as anyone else."

"And, this is embarrassing. But what do I call you?" *Is there a title for former First Ladies?* "Ma'am?"

"I think Mrs. Onassis would be appropriate, if you agree."

I nod. I've been nodding a lot in this meeting, overwhelmed to find all the right words.

I lean in, set my arms on the table, and join my fingers. "And you want to work together." I should feel awkward for retracing so much ground, but surprisingly I don't.

"I see great promise. The work needs polishing, if I may be blunt, but now that I've met you I'm confident we will accomplish good things together."

My cheeks grow flushed and I start to sweat and it dawns on me that we could be spending some real time together, beyond this meeting, beyond today. And if she opened up to me about Charles de Gaulle, even momentarily, she might open up to me about much, much more. That maybe she sees me as some sort of kindred spirit. That we might become . . . friends. My brain marches ten steps ahead of me and I do all within my power to reel it back.

I see Mrs. Onassis glance at the clock on the wall, and it's obvious from that one small signal that our time is almost up.

"So." It's that awkward moment at the end of a first date. "What do we do now?"

She stands and offers her hand and I leap up to take it. We shake. I lean in, just a little bit, just enough to absorb her intoxicating presence a heartbeat longer; her hair smells like perfume and also, surprisingly, of cigarettes.

"Why don't I have a conversation with your agent to work out the details. And then the hard work begins."

I laugh nervously, realizing how difficult—crushing, even—it might be to hear real criticism, constructive though it may be, from this woman. When she lets go of my hand, I desperately try to think of anything to prolong this good-bye—clamber to name other mid-century heads of state and devise pressing questions about them. Alas, my mind roars only with the flat hum of an ocean, a momentous sound for a consequential occasion.

"We will be in touch."

I open the conference room door for her, as any gentleman would, and as quickly as she entered my life she is gone.

THREE

I manage to stay collected until I reach the bank of elevators, even though I can feel everyone's eyes on me as I walk down the hall, back through the paper and push-pins and cubicles and past the framed book covers; I trip and pause only when it hits me that my cover will perhaps one day be among them. Miraculously, I get an elevator to myself for four floors, leaving just enough time for me to self-defibrillate before the doors reopen and three chatty coworkers enter the elevator and join me for the rest of the ride to the lobby, complaining the whole way about a new brand of powdered coffee creamer that leaves a residue in their mugs. I wonder if they have any idea what just happened. I'm curious if they can glimpse my secret, if they can smell it on me, my own residue, and the coffee-creamer conversation is a cover. I try to smell myself, to see if there is some trace of Jackie's perfume, or, better yet, some faint whiff of American decorative arts from her White House restoration, leather or oils or fine upholstery. It occurs to me they think I'm crazy, a man in a corner with a stunned expression, smelling himself for any trace of 1962.

Does Jackie (surely she's not Mrs. Onassis in my thoughts) drink office coffee with powdered creamer out of a foam cup—does she like it, or just choke it down to fit in? Does she talk about her weekend in dreamy terms ("How was your weekend, Mrs. Onassis?"; "Fine, I reframed the Chagall and then got some sun in Belize")? Or is she just one of us, stretching her lunch breaks when spring is in the air, stealing uni-ball pens from the supply closet to use at home.

When the elevator reaches the ground floor I let the others off first, then push through the lobby and revolving door, almost forgetting to exit on Fifty-Second Street. The sharp February air enters my lungs and jolts me like a shot of ice-cold vodka. I line up in front of the first hot dog vendor I come to, even though I don't eat hot dogs; when I get to the front of the line I pretend not to have my wallet and continue toward Times Square as I start to replay what just happened.

I lied to Jackie in our meeting, about how I came to write about my mother. Because it was a choice, even if I said it was desperation. We were once close—very close—and slowly as I grew older we were not. She blames me for the end of her marriage, for my father. She never said so explicitly, but honestly how could she not? My father was a difficult man, older, not just from another generation but from another time. He never knew what to make of me. He certainly didn't approve of me, my sensitive nature, my creative ambitions, my wanting to live in the city, my insistence on being myself. He called me foppish once, and I think we both knew it was a placeholder for another derogatory *f*-word. My mother spent a lot of time running interference. I think she thought she was doing what was best—shielding me from him—but it cost my father and me any chance at a real relationship and she paid a price for it too.

I retreated into adolescence; a casual observer would say I was barely there as my parents' relationship crumbled. But I was everpresent, lurking in the shadows, an aspiring writer already reading Tennessee Williams, fascinated by human behavior. I mastered the spell of invisibility, at least as much as a powder keg could. I knew instinctually I was the catalyst, the spark for the fury around me. I dimmed my light as long as I was able, but gunpowder is made to ignite—especially when that gunpowder is repressed teenage sexuality. The explosion was not something the three of us survived.

After they divorced, my mother withdrew and she became a mystery for me to unravel. A more patient son might have waited for this to self-correct. I could have led by example as I grew into the man I was meant to be, been a beacon for truth that somehow lit the way. But the more closed off she became, the louder the invitation was to unscramble her; I would pursue, she would retreat—it became an endless, vicious loop. Eventually I chose fiction as a way toward fact. It was inevitable that she would become my subject.

"I'm writing a book about Mom," I remember telling my sister, Naomi, when I completed a particularly inspiring writing intensive. It was a three-day workshop and I came out feeling the time for a novel was now.

"Oh, God. Why?" was her response.

It was so obvious to me. "Have you met her? C'mon. *Why not.*"

I thought I could show my mother how much I understood her, how grateful, in fact, I was for everything she had sacrificed for me. My brother Kenny told me there were certain questions about Mom that were just going to remain unanswered, and the sooner I accepted that, the happier I would be. He was able to make peace with it. Naomi was able to go about her life just fine. But a child wants to be close to his mother, and I was forever the baby. I think Kenny and Naomi felt that by not kicking the hornet's nest, they would be just close enough. Not so for me.

I started writing and I didn't stop. I was obsessive, writing for an audience of one. I stayed up nights, wrote through lunch breaks, and canceled plans with friends. Daniel had to remind me to eat, and even at times to sleep. Nine months later, right on cue, I delivered a novel I called *The Book of Ruth*, after the mother character, despite the heavy-handed allusion to the Hebrew text. Because of the Jane Hamilton novel I settled on a new title, *The Quarantine*, after the self-imposed isolation (literal and figurative) at the heart of the book.

Did I say any of this to Jackie? No, because I lied and said it was desperation. Although, wasn't it? Just not desperation for a subject, desperation for something else. Reconciliation. Repatriation. *Damn.* Why wasn't I better prepared for this meeting?

My agent!

Allen sent me walking into the lion's den with no warning of the lioness. I pass a pay phone by a Sbarro pizza and empty my pockets of their contents. I fish dimes from a pool of pennies and subway tokens, then pick up the receiver, making as little contact with it as possible. How many drug dealers and prostitutes and (worse) tourists have used this phone before me today? I dial my agent's number, which I memorized after our first meeting. The phone rings three times before his assistant picks up.

"Donna? It's James Smale. Could you put Allen on the line?"

Donna laughs. "He said you'd be calling."

I hate being obvious (should I ask *him* about former French presidents?), but there's no way around it. "May I talk to him, please?"

"How was your meeting with Lisa?"

"It was Lila, Donna. Her name was Lila." *Actually, that wasn't her name at all.*

"I can never read my own chicken scratch. Anyhow, he's on another line."

"Have him hang up!" I'm shouting, but I can't tell if it's from excitement or from the din and chaos around me.

"What? It's hard to understand you. Where are you? Do you want me to interrupt him?"

It occurs to me he might be on with Doubleday, that the call might be about me. "No, no!" I say, both to her and to someone who has just approached with a cigarette, harassing me for a light. "Just have him call me. I'll be home in twenty minutes."

I hang up the phone and turn around to see a black man dressed in drag as the Statue of Liberty approaching, torch in the air and all. "Give me your tired, your poor, your huddled masses, honey," he says.

I smile and think of the last line of the poem, which has stuck since I learned it in Mrs. Chaddon's sixth-grade class. "I lift my lamp beside the golden door."

"That's right you do, baby," he says, before disappearing into a tour group wearing green-foam Statue of Liberty visors exiting the Sbarro.

A bus stops at the red light in front of me with the high-pitched squealing of poorly maintained brakes. I glance up at the people on board before noticing that the bus sports a tattered poster for Oliver Stone's *JFK*, released in theaters this past Christmas. The poster is faded and torn, as if some drunk NYU student tried to pry it off for his dorm room wall and abandoned the theft halfway through.

I can hear my heartbeat in my ears. I just met a woman in a conference room who is also somehow everywhere, even in the image of a tattered American flag draped over Kevin Costner's face on the side of this bus.

It's impossible to reconcile.

Across Seventh Avenue, I spot a mother holding her child's hand. Her eyes dart from one potential danger to another, and she places her other hand on the boy's shoulder so as not to lose him—that single touch a time machine for me. My first ever visit to this neon circus, I think I was seven. My parents decided to drive us into the city from our sleepy upstate home so we could feel the energy, walking us all the way up Fifth Avenue from the Empire State Building to Central Park. On the way back to the car, my father charged forward, insisting that Times Square was a sight everyone should see. Kenny and Naomi were teenagers, able to withstand the bustle of the city and seemingly unfazed by it all. But my mother held me so tightly, at times I thought I might bruise.

"Keep up, Aileen. The boy's fine," my father bellowed. And then, "What we should really do is see the subway. A marvel of urban transportation." Those were the things that interested my father, tunnels and bridges and trains.

But I didn't want to go underground, like rats—I could barely breathe above; I looked desperately for patches of sky. I glanced to my mother for help, prayed she would never let go, and she leaned down and whispered in my ear the words that would one day change my life: "You know, all the great writers live in New York." And just like that, the city transformed from menacing commotion to inviting possibility.

In eight years of living here, I've lost the sensation of my mother's excited whisper and firm grip. Times Square came to mock me—symbolic of the dismissal I faced trying to make it as a writer. It was every rejection letter, every failed job interview, every face that chuckled when I revealed my dream, every horrible, soul-crushing temporary job. It led to my hating New York. Hating myself. I never felt the same energy of that day again.

Until now.

I count to ten to just "feel the energy," giving my father at least that much, then blow into my cupped hands to warm them. *Gloves!* I have gloves. I find them in my coat pocket and put them on before scurrying west across Forty-Ninth Street. I have to get home to Hell's Kitchen. I have to get home to tell Daniel and to be there when my agent calls.

I have to get home before I wake up.

• FOUR •

I bound up the steps of our five-story walk-up, two at a time from floors one through three, then individually until I reach the top. On the fourth-floor landing, my messenger bag swings forward and I almost eat one of the steps that leads to our door. It's then that I realize just how grungy our building is, the stairs thick with years of grime and grease from whatever unpleasant bits of the city people track in on their shoes. I brush myself off, but not the troubling realization that we really do live like this. It's not at all suitable to entertain these new circles I may be traveling in. When I reach the apartment door, it's locked. I mean, of course it's locked. Even though this is David Dinkins's New York, we're not animals. Usually I have my keys in hand, but I ran up the stairs too quickly to retrieve them. I reach in my pocket and pull out a crumpled gum wrapper. Please tell me I wasn't chewing gum during the meeting! I check my mouth. No gum. Breath not great, but no gum. This brings some small relief. I find my keys, but it takes me three attempts to open the door.

Inside, Daniel is lying on the couch.

"I was hoping that was you. I thought we were being burgled." Daniel is the type of person who says "burgled" instead of "robbed," and he's not even a writer—or a lawyer. He directs theater. I stare at him, his maddeningly thick hair and dark features, unsure of what to say. Not what to say so much as how to begin to say it. Also because my heart is pounding from my sprint up the stairs and I taste something coppery and I may be having a stroke. "You're not going to believe this." He gestures toward our nineteen-inch television. "There's another one."

I start to catch my breath. "Another one what?"

"Another bimbo. It was just on CNN."

"Another one?" Strike that. I don't want to get engaged in conversation about politics, something I don't particularly care about at this moment.

"I think this is the end of his campaign." Daniel looks up at me and notices my chest heaving. "Jesus. Did you run up the stairs?"

And that's when I break into a huge, cat-who-ate-the-canary kind of grin.

"What?" Daniel has this look on his face that I love. I remember he made it on our first date, maybe even in response to my smiling devilishly at him. Brown eyes wide, lips slightly parted, hinting at the whitest teeth behind them, one of his pronounced Latin eyebrows slightly higher than the other. Five years later, that look still slays me.

I shrug and grin more. I must look like the Joker. Or at least Jack Nicholson.

"You're not going to defend him, I hope."

"Clinton? Nope." Then I burst out laughing. It's orgasmic, like a release for the whole day.

"What, then?"

Daniel and I met when we were both trying to get rush tickets to the Broadway revival of *Cabaret*. I made a crack about Joel Grey getting top billing for playing the emcee. I mean, he had won an Oscar for the role, but he was still the emcee. Daniel overheard me gripe and said it was like reviving *Grease* as a starring vehicle for Doody and I laughed. I had noticed him earlier on line for the box office and wanted to sleep with him the moment I laid eyes on him. It was the way he jumped up and down while pleading for a ticket, any ticket, like a dog on its hind legs, begging for scraps. We were unsuccessful that day but left far from empty-handed.

I snap off the TV.

"I was watching that," he protests.

"It's CNN. It's on all day." I take off my gloves and my coat and throw them on the chair. "I think I sold my book."

Daniel stares at the blank TV screen until that sinks in. "Wait, you what?"

"Well, the offer will go to my agent and I'm sure there will be some back-and-forth and we'll have to come to some agreement on terms. He may be on the phone with them now. Did Allen call? And there's work to be done on it still. Hard work, she called it. On the ending, mostly." I bite my lip. "But . . . *yeah*. I think I sold my book."

Daniel's legs swing around and his feet plant firmly on the ground. He pushes himself up with his fists and hovers just over the couch, preparing to leap up if necessary. "To a publisher?"

"To a doorstop salesman." If it's going to take him so long to catch on to this bit of the news, the rest of it will be a Sisyphean task of explanation on my part.

"Obviously to a publisher. To a *good* publisher?" Daniel doesn't leap, but at least he stands. "Who?"

The grin is back. This is going to knock his socks off. "I sold it to a *giant*."

"A giant," he says skeptically.

"That's right."

"A *literary* giant?"

"A GIANT giant."

Daniel crosses over to me and puts his hands on my shoulders, concerned. I peripherally glance down at his hands. "Wait, I've heard this before," he says. "You sold your book for a handful of magic beans."

Daniel is going off the deep end. *"What?"*

"And we no longer have a cow. But I shouldn't worry, because you're going to grow a beanstalk!"

"No. Stop it. Not a *giant*. An icon. But I'm sure she hates that word. She's a really big person."

"Like, obese?"

This is coming out all wrong. "Okay, I'm ready to move on from this part. Jackie. I sold my book to *Jackie*!"

Daniel thinks on this for a minute. "Karen's friend? The lesbian who works at *Reader's Digest*?"

"KENNEDY. Jackie. Kennedy."

He freezes. *Finally.* The reaction I was looking for. "Oh," he says, quietly. But he's still not quite there.

"Oh . . ." I repeat. And then I coax, "Na-ssis."

Finally, magic happens. In unison: "Jackie . . . Kennedy . . . Onassis."

It's just like out of a movie, us saying it together: a scene that would strain credulity but would still be an audience favorite and get high marks in test screenings.

"Get out!" Daniel removes his hands from my shoulders and pushes me in the chest. Hard.

"Ow."

"You're kidding."

"You just punched me in the sternum."

"Jackie fucking Kennedy."

"Onassis. Except I don't think that's her middle name. And she says Jacqueline, but like in the French pronunciation."

"You're joking."

"*Non, non,*" I say, mustering my best French. "*Je ne . . .*" I can't think of the word. "Joke *pas.*"

He looks at me, scrutinizing my face, just as he did the first time I told him I loved him, to see if I am recklessly toying with his emotions or if I'm indeed telling the truth. He scans my eyes, perhaps to check if my pupils are dilated in the throes of some drug-fueled hallucination. At last he smiles, a recognition that I am of sound mind, just as he did upon *I love you.*

"Oh my God! When do you meet her?"

"I just came from there."

"From where?"

"From meeting her. At Doubleday."

"Her office. You just came from there." This is two steps forward and one step back. I try to be patient; it took me time to catch on to all this and it happened with me in the room. "You just entered our apartment door, coming straight from Jackie fucking Kennedy's office."

"Yes. Well, no. A conference room. Her office was too small."

"Her office is too . . . *small*."

"That's what she said, yes."

"She's the widow of Aristotle Onassis, who was, for a time, the richest man on the planet."

I fail to make the connection. "So?"

"She could probably buy Doubleday. And the building it's in. But you're telling me her office is small?"

I see his point, but I can actually answer this one. "She doesn't want to buy Doubleday. She doesn't want special treatment."

"She told you that?"

I try to recall our exact conversation. She said something along those lines. And could she buy Doubleday? I seem to remember something about Onassis's daughter getting the money. "We didn't go over her financials or anything. It's all kind of a blur, to be honest."

"But you know this because you just came from there."

"Exactly."

"And you had a meeting—not in her office, which is small, but in a conference room, where she made an offer to buy your book."

"It took me a while too. You're doing great." Daniel rolls his eyes. He thinks I'm being patronizing, but I'm really not. I'm being sincere. So I wrap my arms around him, nuzzle my face in his shoulder, and excitedly scream.

"Did you just spit on my shirt?" He stretches the fabric for evidence.

"Daniel! Focus!"

He returns his attention to me. "So. What did you talk about? You and the former First Lady."

"I asked her about Charles de Gaulle."

"The airport?" Daniel peels me off of him.

"The French president." I bang my head against his shoulder several times, embarrassed.

"As in how he's doing? Because I think Charles de Gaulle is dead."

I laugh, because that's the man I fell in love with. The man who makes me laugh every night before we fall asleep holding hands. "I asked if he was tall." I kind of throw my hands up as if to say, *What else are you supposed to ask her about?* and also, *I know!* in recognition of my own ridiculousness.

"You asked her a question that rhymed?" Daniel is incredulous.

"I don't think I phrased it as a couplet."

"But it was about the physical stature of the former president of France."

"I couldn't think of what else to say!"

"And that's what popped in your mind. Not 'What do you do in your spare time? Is that an original Oleg Cassini design you're wearing? Do you have any shirtless pictures of your son?'"

"Who is Oleg Cassini?"

"My point is—"

"Your point is clear," I interrupt. "But what else are you supposed to say to someone who wants to publish your book?"

Daniel takes a lap around our minuscule living room. Since the couch and the coffee table and the TV and the one accent chair we found on the curb near Ninth and Forty-Third take up most of the space, he basically turns in a very tight circle, careful not to trip on the edge of the oriental rug, which is folded in half because it's too big for the room. When he stops he says, "What I don't get is *why*. Why does she want to publish your book?"

I mime a dagger going into my heart.

"Oh, come on. I don't mean it like that. I've read your book. I love your book!"

"But you can't imagine anyone wanting to publish it."

"In fact, I can. I just didn't think she published fiction."

"It's a memoir. Sort of. Just fictionalized."

"It's a novel, genius, and I didn't think she did that."

"What did you think she did?"

"I don't know. Art books."

I blanch at the thought, but I don't know why. If you asked me yesterday what kind of books Jackie Kennedy published I would have had no idea. I had only a vague recollection that she even worked in publishing. Today I have no sense of her list either, but I'm feeling oddly defensive of it.

"You know," Daniel continues. "Coffee-table books. Like on the history of tatting."

It's infuriating at times, the things he knows. In the middle of our worst arguments he'll produce a fact that makes me want to hit him in the face with a shovel.

Daniel can read my bewilderment. "Lacemaking."

"The history of lace?" The idea is almost absurd.

"The history of *making* lace."

I glare at my boyfriend. "You frighten me."

Daniel does another turn in place, the way a dog might before lying down.

"Well, I don't know what to tell you other than she's interested in publishing my book. We're going to work on it. Together."

Daniel chews the inside of his cheek. "And what if she wants to change it?"

"I imagine she will want to change it. That's her job. It's called editing."

"But what if she wants to change it and you don't agree with how she wants to change it, but you can't say anything because she's Jackie fucking Kennedy?"

"You've really got to stop calling her that."

"I'm serious. What if she wants to set the story on Cape Cod?"

"You could try being excited for me."

"What if she wants to set the story on Cape Cod and add schooner racing as a leitmotif because that's what she and Ethel did off of Nantucket."

"She and Ethel discussed leitmotif?"

"No. Raced their . . . lady schooners."

I want to laugh but also bang my head against the wall. "Please don't say 'lady schooners' again."

"But . . ."

"She doesn't."

"You just know."

I nod. I don't know how else to explain it to anyone who wasn't there. We talked a little about characters and relationships and motivation, and I know we will talk more. And even if we hadn't, we definitely discussed my ability to tell her no.

Daniel finally relents, his engines out of steam. "Well, congratulations. I mean it. Bravo." This time he hugs me.

"Thank you." This is what I've wanted. I grip him tight. His T-shirt smells like dryer sheets from the fluff-and-fold we splurge on sometimes when we have money. But more than that. It smells like him. Daniel breaks the hug first to look me square in the eyes and I bite my lip to avoid a toothy grin.

"You had me going there for a moment," he says. "The bit about Charles de Gaulle was a nice touch."

Huh?

"Can you imagine if you ever did meet her and that's what you asked?"

"I did meet her and that *is* what I asked."

Daniel laughs. "Is Charles de Gaulle tall? Was he on the ball or off the wall? Did you two break bread on the National Mall? Tell me, Jackie, is the frog the opposite of small?"

I punch Daniel in the arm. Normally when I do this it's meant to be playful. This time I'm not so sure. "I asked that for my mother. She used to talk about the presidential visit to Paris like she was there and not stuck in rural New York with three children under the age of ten. I knew she would love whatever the answer was. Oh! And there's a whole story about the *Mona Lisa* that I can't wait to tell her."

"Your mother . . ." Daniel says.

"You may remember her. You've been introduced on numerous occasions."

"Your mother, who has adored the Kennedys for most of her life."

Oh, shit.

"Your Irish Catholic mother whom you wrote a not entirely flattering, although, to be fair, not entirely unflattering, book about? The one who named you Francis? The one who will have a book about her edited by Jackie Kennedy?"

At least he doesn't say "fucking" this time.

And then it hits me. As frustrated as I have been with Daniel for not immediately getting it, there are layers to this bonanza that even I have yet to process. I'm still scooping my chip through the top layer of a fourteen-layer dip. There are thirteen more layers of mush and fattening sludge to get through before I reach the bottom. As I chew on that image I realize it's a horrible metaphor—with each passing moment, I feel more like the dip, in another sense of the word.

"Come here."

Daniel motions for me to step closer, but I'm frozen in place.

"Come. Here."

I take two steps in his direction and he hugs me again, this time for real. "You really did this. You really met Jackie Kennedy." He pauses, the truth now undeniable. He cups the back of my head, massaging my scalp.

"I thought you didn't believe me."

"I do now! It's written all over your face. You bastard." I can feel him smile, his cheek pressed against mine. "I'm so proud of you."

He squeezes me even tighter.

"What's more, I think this is a terrific marriage."

"You don't believe in marriage," I say, halfheartedly. I'm hundreds of miles away.

"I don't believe in monogamy and the subjugation of women, but I'm not so worried in this case."

"Gee, thanks."

"This could be a great *creative* marriage." He leans back to see if I'm paying attention. "You've worked so hard. Been so disciplined. This is your moment. I'm really happy for you." He musses my hair. "Seriously, though. How are you going to tell your mother?"

"I don't know." I'm certain the words fall out of my mouth, but in my head I just say *Fuck, fuck, fuck, fuck, fuck,* over and over again until my mind goes dark.

• FIVE •

I wake to the sound of my mother crying. I grasp and find one of the buttons sewn on the mattress, the one that I cling to when I wake from nightmares of monsters grabbing my feet, but the button fails to provide familiar comfort for a simple reason—I've never heard my mother cry. Not like this. And it's more frightening than any demon.

"Mom?" I call, but no one answers.

I study the contents of my bedroom in the morning light to distract myself. I can see my dresser and my toys and the needlepoint fire engine my grandmother stitched. The curtains flutter and float on the breeze sneaking in the open window. I know where I am and I know my name and that I am seven years old and I'm comforted by at least that much. Still, I feel apprehension, bordering on anxiety—what news could this crying possibly bring?

I look down under the bed like I always do to make sure it's safe before planting my feet on the floor, and slowly slink out of my room. My mother is in the living room chair where my father usually sits, smoking a cigarette. She's watching our small TV while clutching a mug, as she does in winter when she wants to warm her hands. The news people on the screen seem especially somber, more so than usual. The volume is low and I can't make out their words, but their expressions need no interpretation.

"Mom." I say it again, real quiet this time, in case I am not supposed to see this.

I fidget with the snaps on my pajama pants, grasping for an activity so that I'll appear casual when I am eventually seen (and I *will* be seen). I count the seconds, as I somehow know they are the precious foundation of a future important memory; the more seconds I can

count, the stronger the memory will be. There won't be many. My
mother has eyes on all sides of her head.

... nine ... ten ... eleven ... twelve ...

"You should be getting dressed for school." Her head remains perfectly still, encased in a cloud of dancing smoke.

I remove my hand from the snaps of my pants and take a step
closer, looking at the thick, brown carpet the entire time, imagining
it a sea of mud. Or quicksand. I quickly lift my feet just to make sure
I still can.

"Go on, Francis," she says, encouraging me again to retreat, to get
dressed, to leave. Sensing that I am not only disobeying her but am
actually advancing, she sets her mug on the TV tray, ashes her cigarette, and wipes her eyes with the backs of her hands in a vain effort
to transform this crying stranger back into the mother I know.

I place one foot in front of the other, carefully, deliberately, heels
touching toes every time, each foot docking with the other before I
attempt any further forward motion. I can smell the acrid smoke of
my mother's cigarette and I inhale it deeply, inhale her. Eventually I
am beside her. I grasp the arm of the chair, afraid to reach out for her,
afraid, given her strange trance, that she might dissolve into ash like
her cigarette from even the faintest human touch.

"It's Bobby." She starts sobbing. I'm startled by how much sobbing
looks like laughing. And by how the way she tucks her head into her
arm makes her look like one of the preening swans that used to visit
our duck pond. "They got him." I wrack my brain trying to place this
Bobby, and discern just how close he is to us. *They got him?* I'm not
even sure what that means. Did a van pull up alongside him? Is he a
cousin or a family friend? If they got him, were we somehow in danger of being snatched too?

I look closely and can spot where tears have dripped and stained
the sleeves of the blouse that covers her spindly arms. I want to lick
them, her tears, like our dog Casper did mine the night my hamster
died. I remember how loved I felt in that singular moment, puppy
lashings covering my salty face, both rough and soft like the

finest-grained sandpaper from my father's workshop; I want nothing more than for my mother to feel this loved too. But just as I work up the nerve and I can feel the smallest tip of tongue cross the threshold of my lips, my mother inhales so deeply on her cigarette that I can hear the paper and tobacco crackle; somehow it's the loudest sound in the room.

She exhales her words. "They killed him just like they did his brother."

Nothing my mother ever said has stopped me so cold. This was not grief I was witness to, it was rage. I want to ask who "they" are, who is doing this killing, but I know better than to open my mouth. I want to know how people could be so angry or violent, but I know not to form this thought in words. Not right now. The only way to coax more information out of my mother is to stay silent and let her volunteer it. I delicately trace the five freckles on her forearm; I have them memorized. They are stars, the makings of a constellation filled with stardust and matter that holds the answer to every question that could ever be asked. You just have to be quiet enough to listen, so I put my ear to her arm.

She stubs her cigarette in the clay ashtray I made for her in Scouts, giving my handiwork her full attention as if soaking in its imperfections, its mottled shape and uneven glaze. She then turns to me, startled to see me leaning against her, and stares at me this time, taking in my imperfections, the excuses she would have not to love me if I were someone else's son.

"Remember his name. Robert F. Kennedy. He was a good man."

His full name does not help me place him, so I stare at the television, hoping the images will help. Most of the pictures are of chaos, and they move too quickly to clarify much of anything.

"Who is he?"

My mother thinks about how to answer. "He was Irish like we are Irish. He was Catholic like we are Catholic." She clutches the cross that she wears around her neck. "He represented a hope that the future would be good. Now I don't think I understand the future at all."

She kisses me on my head, as if to wish me luck in these unknowable times, and I lean in, trying to get her to do it again. But she doesn't say anything else for so long, I think the conversation is over. Then, out of nowhere, she adds, "You share a name with him, in fact."

I think of my name, James Smale, finding no overlap.

"Francis. You have the same middle names."

"Dad gets mad when you call me Francis."

"Your father gets mad about a lot of things."

"I like Francis," I say, my ability to suck up to my mother knowing no bounds.

"Your father's name is James and he wanted you named after him. But I chose Francis, and so it became your middle name." She starts to quiver again, but this time she doesn't break. She gets up to turn off the television and I hear the hum of static and then nothing. Silence, except for the twittering of birds by the feeder outside and the faint singing of chimes. I want my mother to stop crying, but I also know that when she feels sad I am the only one who can comfort her—and that means maybe getting out of going to school today.

So I remain perfectly still.

· SIX ·

I t's been like two minutes."
The silence on the other end of the line is so absolute, I swear I can hear my mother's refrigerator hum. My first instinct was to wait, to tell her about Jackie in person, but I knew in my gut this was news that wouldn't age well. The best thing to do was to get it over with, rip off the Band-Aid and come clean. I drank half a bottle of merlot for liquid courage, then picked at the $5.99 price sticker while having a staring contest with the phone; eventually I blinked and dialed. When she picked up she said she was glad I called, having just had an uncomfortable exchange with the neighbor over a rapidly growing tree encroaching over her property line. When she finished recounting that, I asked after Domino, her overweight cocker spaniel recently diagnosed with canine diabetes (unsurprising, I suppose, given he's named after the yellow bag of sugar). Domino's responding to his medication, she said, but he has to go outside more often to pee. When we exhausted all possible topics of conversation, I dropped my news like I was carpet-bombing Baghdad in Desert Storm.

I check my watch. "Three minutes. It might help if you say something."

The first time I ever mentioned the book to my mother, more than a year ago now, I had already finished a draft. I had an unexpected lull between temp assignments and I drove out to see her. Naïvely I thought she would be curious to know everything about it, so I printed her a copy at the shop near our apartment and had it spiral-bound—the presentation was a nice throwback to the stories I once typed on her typewriter. Instead, she diligently sliced a tomato as I told her about the undertaking, explained the inspiration, and described the long hours I put into the endeavor. When I finished, all she said was, "Have some tomato," and she pushed the cutting board my way.

"I don't want any tomato," I replied. I wanted a reaction to the fact that I'd written a book. *A book!*

"Well, this is dinner," I remember her saying, "I wasn't expecting company."

"Dinner is a tomato?"

"Yes."

"That's not dinner even if you weren't expecting company. I thought we could celebrate."

I'll never forget the look on her face, pallid yet outraged. "Celebrate what?"

Celebrate what. And that sums up where we've been ever since.

I'm about to switch the phone to my other ear and check my watch a third time when my mother finally speaks. "I don't know what you want me to say." If I'm not mistaken, there's panic in her voice, but maybe it's just surprise.

"You should at least read it."

Another long silence.

"You're still not going to read it?"

"What difference does it make if I read it now?"

I'm confused. "Do you not get this? It makes a difference to me."

"Well, I just assume not."

"You're being crazy." I don't mean to be accusatory, it just comes out.

"How wonderful for you. Now you can tell Mrs. Kennedy I'm crazy and mean it."

"You think I told her you were crazy and *didn't* mean it?" I smile because it's a clever line, though I'm aware my mother can't see my smile over the telephone. I swirl the remaining wine in my glass; shame sets in as I watch it slow and then fall still. I know my mother's not in the mood for jokes.

"I have no doubt you meant it."

"I didn't tell her you were crazy."

The clanging of pots and pans. She's always doing some ridiculous task when I call. Today's project, it seems, is emptying the cupboards. "Maybe you didn't say it in those exact words."

"Maybe not in *any* words. I don't think that you're crazy, so it's not something that's in my head to tell." When speaking on the telephone, it's easy to conjure the mother I know from the past, when we were close. Her voice sounds much as it always has, at least since she gave up smoking. I like to think she's frozen in time, and that's mostly true; she looks to me the age she was when I was maybe fourteen— not young, far from old, with a kind of natural, easy beauty. The only difference: Her hair has gotten lighter over the years, dyed, perhaps, to mask the gray. I wonder if she's all too aware of time passing, self-conscious about aging, but I could never ask. Certainly she doesn't see herself through the same softening filter of nostalgia. And I'm sure it's much harder for her to look at me and imagine I'm still fourteen.

"People are going to read this now. Is that what you're telling me?"

I clear my throat. "My novel? I hope so. Which is why it's important you read it first."

"They're going to read that I stood on the table and made up words to 'Carol of the Bells' when I burnt the Christmas ham."

"So you *have* read it."

"Naomi told me."

"Naomi told you," I repeat, imagining this conversation between her and my sister. "Well, you did stand on the table and make up words to 'Carol of the Bells' when you burnt the Christmas ham. Or new words. 'Carol of the Bells' already has words." I can tell by her silence she thinks I've wandered into the reeds. "And you conducted an invisible orchestra with a wooden spoon."

"Then how is it a novel!"

I have to push past this because we can't litigate every scene from the book she may or may not have heard of secondhand. Certainly not over the phone. "Dad had just . . . Forget it. You are not insane. You are a human being. It was quite beautiful, that moment, and I wrote it that way. What does it matter if strangers read that?"

"Mrs. Kennedy is not a stranger."

I'm momentarily puzzled. "Are you *friends*?"

"She read that I stood on a table and waved a wooden spoon."

"Yes, she read that." And then I add, although I don't know why, as it certainly doesn't help my cause, "Twice."

I'm in my own kitchen now, with no recollection of getting here— when I first dialed her I was down the hall. With the cordless pinned between my shoulder and my ear, I reach for a box of croutons and pop a handful in my mouth.

"What are you eating?" she asks.

"Croutons." When I swallow I add, "It's nonstop glamour over here." It is glamourous now, though, in my mind. *Starving writer* is far more chic than *starving office temp*.

"Croutons," she repeats disapprovingly, but after the tomato incident I doubt she eats much better. We should get together more often; between us, we could almost make a salad. "I can't believe you let her read those things," she finally says. "About me."

"About Ruth Mulligan, a fictional character."

"Based on me, Aileen Smale."

"She doesn't know you."

"She knows you have a mother."

"I assume she does not think I was immaculately born!"

My mother aggressively exhales. I've skirted too close to blasphemy.

I hear a cabinet door close and all I can think is that she should sell the house. That I've moved on, and she needs to also. Naomi came closest to convincing her a couple years ago, introducing her to a Realtor friend. "It's too big for you," we all told her. But she got skittish and we backed off. I remember I cried at the time, because I was so ready to say good-bye. I'd been ready for a good while.

"Everyone's going to know that it's me."

"Everyone who?"

"Everyone who reads it."

"So what!" I fail to see what the big deal is; I would be honored if someone wrote a book about me. "I think people who buy books have a firm grasp on what *fiction* means."

"Write what you know. Isn't that what they say writers do? They write what they know. You know me, therefore she *is* me."

I'm almost impressed with her logic. *"Res ipsa loquitur."*

"What?"

"Never mind."

"What."

I sigh. "It's Latin. The thing speaks for itself."

It's surprising to me that this is now her concern. When I asked her to read it the first time, she was quite adamant that the mother character was not her.

"It's not about me," she had said at the time.

"It's not?"

"No. And you know how I know? Because you don't know me."

It was the ultimate slap to the face. A son a stranger to his mother— how could he have written an entire book about her? A mother, a stranger to her son—she had let herself be observed but never seen.

Naomi was our mother's defender at first. When I called to complain, she told me, "You would feel differently if things were reversed."

"If I exposed something of myself?"

"That's right."

"You don't think there are pieces of me on every page of that book? What do you think writing is?"

I remember she paused, not awkwardly, but like she was genuinely giving it thought. "I don't think I ever considered it."

At least I had ushered one ally over to my side.

"I don't know why you're so worried," I say to my mother now, when we've been quiet so long I almost forget we're still on the phone. The box of croutons is empty. "Nobody's perfect. I think people will recognize that."

"Certainly not in this family."

"In *any* family."

"I don't—" My mother stops. "It too late now."

I consider the world's imperfections. Not even the world's, our family's. The way everyone has tacitly agreed to leave so much unspoken. Everyone, that is, except me.

"I don't want to be written about. Let's leave it at that. Good night, James."

"Don't you even want to know what she said? Mrs. Kennedy?"

The sound of another cabinet door closing and then things go quiet again. I'm almost certain I can hear her click off the kitchen light. "I want to go to bed. I'm tired."

"It's worth adding two more minutes to your day." I almost add "promise," but it's not a promise I'm certain I can keep.

"I'm not tired from the day. I'm tired from forty years of my children."

"Your children haven't kept you up in years."

"And yet here you are."

I plow forward before she can hang up. "She said she admired the mother. She said the reason she responded to the book so strongly was because she admired the character at the heart of it." I let that sit before emphasizing, "She was saying she admired you."

I can hear my mother breathing, the labored way she used to when we were young and a migraine headache was bearing down. "And you believed her."

There's a click and then the line goes dead.

SEVEN

My agent's office occupies a small suite on West Fifty-Ninth Street. It's cozy and dim; the wooden shutters are kept mostly drawn and the office is lit with Tiffany table lamps, giving it a soft glow. It has the requisite characteristics of what you think a literary agent's office once was, and still should be: someplace where you'd like to curl up with a good book and read. And you could find plenty of them—books—as the walls of the main room where Donna sits are lined with dark walnut bookcases crammed with endless titles. The rest of the office is littered with stacks of dusty newspapers, old copies of *The New York Times Book Review*, and past issues of *The New Yorker*. Sometimes I have to move papers out of a chair just to sit down.

Donna usually greets me with the enthusiasm of a poodle who has been left home all day. Most of Allen's business is conducted via phone and fax, as his clients are spread across the country; I don't think they get many visitors. But when I walk through the door, the office is quiet and empty, and I jump when the door closes behind me.

"Allen?"

No response. I take a precursory look at Donna's desk to see if there's any paperwork with my name on it. I don't see any, and head farther into the office, nearly tripping on a box from UPS. Usually I can hear Allen on the phone, but it's so quiet I start to wonder if this idyllic agency setting isn't also an exemplary place to stumble on a body or two. *Mrs. Peacock in the office with the quill pen.*

"Allen?" I ask again, this time a little louder.

I hear motion in his office and I freeze (is the killer still here?), and then Allen peeks his head out the door. "I thought you were Donna."

"Nope. Just me."

"Come here." Allen waves me into his office and shuts the door behind me. He starts unbuttoning his shirt.

"Did you spill something?"

"No." He looks me square in the eyes.

"Allen . . ." When he has the shirt all the way undone, I put up my hands like I'm fending off an attack. "No, no, no, no, no."

"Just look at this."

I jam my eyes closed. "I'm grateful for everything you've done for me, but . . ."

For my own safety I lift one eyelid just enough to peek. He slides his shirt off his shoulders, revealing a surprisingly broad, muscular frame.

"Allen, I'm flattered, it's just . . ."

Out of the corner of my eye I see a flash of red; curiosity gets the best of me, so I open my eyes fully. His back is battered and the color of a rich cabernet.

"Is there bruising?" he asks.

"Jesus, what happened to you?"

"Reggie." Allen excitedly nods his approval.

I lower my voice to a whisper. "Should I call the police?" I make a quick scan of the office for weapons. Do I have it in me to three-hole-punch an attacker?

"No, no. Of course not." He slips his shirt back on and starts buttoning.

"Was this part of a negotiation?" I'm thoroughly confused and maybe a little impressed, as I'm left to wonder if Allen would really go to the mat in this way for his clients.

"Reggie's this guy. In Chinatown. I pay him to do that."

I'm appalled but also fascinated. "Beat the shit out of you?"

Allen's eyes swell with pride. "I got in a few good hits."

Of course the writer in me wants to know everything, but he's already crossed behind his desk to move on.

"So, contracts," he says, tucking his shirt into his pants. He looks under a stack of papers.

It's been six weeks since I first walked into Doubleday. Allen did his part and negotiated a fair deal on my behalf. I'm not sure if Jackie has real sway, if the book is indeed good, or if they let her buy whatever she wants to keep her from taking her prestige elsewhere; when Allen told me the official offer came in I had to sit down. It wasn't the money (the advance isn't much to speak of), but the fact that Jackie came through. That this wasn't a dream—it was really happening.

When the contracts arrived, Allen messengered a copy over to me and we spent a good hour or two dissecting it over the phone. He pointed out where he was able to do well for me, and also what were industry-standard terms. When I felt I understood the agreement as best I could, I made an appointment to sign.

"*You* ever met her?"

"Jackie?" he asks. "We spoke on the telephone."

"In person, I mean."

"Sit down, sit down."

For once there's an empty chair, but I have to push a few manuscripts on the floor aside so there's room for my feet.

"Not one-on-one like you, hotshot. But back in the day when she was first at Viking. I knew Tommy Guinzburg, the publisher. We'd do business together and he'd invite me to the office when he knew she'd be there. She's tall. Surprising, right?"

"She was mostly sitting down."

Allen guffaws. "I wish I could have seen the look on your face."

"Yeah, well. You were no help."

"Listen. I didn't want you to be in your head. Remember our first meeting? You're very engaging, but you can get in your own way." I shake my head in protest even though he's got me pegged. The first time we met I was trying to make a joke about his credentials and mispronounced the word *emeritus*. After that, I was tripping over my tongue for the entire conversation.

"Bygones, right? I got the two of you in a room together."

"You're quite the yenta."

You can tell Allen's still pleased with himself; he chuckles, forming a slick grin. He leans back in his chair, then grimaces and bounces forward.

"Bruises?"

"Yeah. That's going to smart for days. Anyhow, I don't even know why he hired her. Tommy. She had no experience. Her Rolodex, I guess. Thought she could bring in some big books as an acquiring editor. I think he offered her something like two hundred bucks a week. I'm not sure the whole experience was even worth that."

"Why not?" I'm fascinated.

"The relationship only lasted two years before it blew up in his face. She quit over some two-bit novel they did about the assassination of Ted Kennedy."

"You mean Bobby?" I'm confused.

"No. Ted. It was some alternate-history sort of thing. She sent him a letter of resignation in the middle of the night. The middle of the night! The book was in poor taste, but still. Meanwhile, for those two years? Chaos." Allen looks all over his desk and finally produces a pen. "You have to put it in context. She was enticingly available to the public for the very first time. She had an office, regular hours. Their poor receptionist had to field every whack-a-doo who stepped off the elevator wanting to see her. People would show up with a ream of blank paper and demand a meeting like they were the next Mario Puzo. Meanwhile, phones ringing off the hook. Mike Wallace on one! Barbara Walters on two! Some housewife called like clockwork for a daily report on what Jackie was wearing. One man showed up, and when he was refused an audience he said he was wrapped in dynamite! Tommy himself had to intervene and talk the man down. Ha!" He reads the shocked expression on my face. Clearly, I'm not finding this as funny as he does. "Ah, well. You'd have to know Tommy."

"So, what happened?" I hesitantly ask.

"Bah." Allen dismisses my concern with the wave of his hand. "There was no dynamite."

I roll my eyes. "Is it still that crazy? Do I need a flak jacket?"

"Oh, no. She got down to work and disappeared. Novelty eventually wore off." Allen hands me four copies of the publishing agreement and the pen.

"So I'm not nuts, then. To sign these?"

"You may be nuts, kid, but not for signing these."

I flip the top contract open to the final page, which is tabbed "sign here." I pause, wondering if I should do something special to mark this occasion but decide it's best not to stand on ceremony. I put Allen's pen to paper and . . . nothing. It's out of ink. I shake the pen and try again. Nada. "I hope this isn't a sign."

"Oh, come on." Allen rummages through a drawer. "DONNA!"

"I don't think she's here."

"You celebrate yet?" He pats himself down to see if there's a pen in his pockets.

"Nope. Waiting to sign these."

"Family happy?"

"I've been keeping a low profile. Superstition." I cross my fingers on both hands to emphasize the point before remembering that some consider that bad luck.

Allen looks up at me. "Your mother?"

I put my finger on my nose. "I don't know what she thinks. She hasn't read it."

"What do you mean she hasn't read it?"

"I asked her to read it, she gave me a tomato."

"She threw it at you?"

"No, just offered it. To eat. I asked her a second time and she said she'd still rather not."

"Rather not what?" Allen conjures another pen, removes the cap, and hands it to me. It's a promotional giveaway from a paper supply company in New Jersey and the top of the pen has bite marks. It feels anticlimactic, to say the least. I imagine if Jackie were the one to countersign these agreements (and not some business-affairs person) she would do so with an elegant fountain pen. I guess we all work with what we have.

"Read it, I guess. But I suppose she'd rather it not exist at all." I hover the pen above the contracts and my hand shakes. Allen notices my hesitation.

"It's a loving portrait," he says.

"It's an *honest* portrait."

He chuffs. "She'll come around. If not, now you've got a spare."

"What, who—Jackie?" My face turns as red as Allen's back.

"Editors are mothers of sorts."

I'm annoyed the shutters aren't more open so that I can stare dramatically out the window onto Fifty-Ninth Street. This is my last chance to do the right thing by my mother. Yet would that be the right thing for me? Is the mark of adulthood putting others first? Or is it standing behind your own vision, your own work, your own view of the world? Beads of sweat form on my forehead and I have to wipe my brow.

My hand still trembles, but I manage to sign all four agreements. I stare at my signature, barely recognizing it as my own. My name looks foreign. Like it's not mine but my father's—someone else who let my mother down. I thought this would be fun, I thought I would want to remember this moment, but in truth I just want to move on. "When do we get paid?"

"First check upon execution!" Allen takes the contracts from me and I place the pen in an empty mug, which I'm hoping is a pencil jar and not the remnants of his morning caffeine. He flips through the agreements to make sure everything is in order.

I suddenly see the wisdom in paying someone to hit me. I even consider asking Allen for his guy's number. If I'm indeed causing my mother pain, wouldn't some in return be rightful penance? And even if not, I already feel like the wind's been knocked out of me—perhaps a few swift punches could knock it back in. I lean forward and put my head between my knees.

"You okay, kid?"

"Thought I dropped something." I don't tell him I'm suddenly nauseated.

"One for you, one for me, two for them. I'll have Donna send them over this afternoon. Whenever Donna returns from Donnaland."

I sit up as he stacks the contracts, fastens them together with a binder clip, and slides them into a large envelope. "We good?"

I nod, unable to say anything more.

"One more thing." Allen thrusts a piece of paper with a phone number in my direction. "Your new mommy wants you to call her."

EIGHT

I t's two minutes before five o'clock when Lila guides me back down
the long hallway that leads to the conference room, her coworkers
packing up to go home. I try to make eye contact with everyone,
smile to diffuse their annoyance. I can read the stress on their faces.
*Who is this arriving just as we are leaving? Do I have to stay? Will I miss
my train?* Lila keeps her usual pace; had we not met before, I would
feel she, too, was itching to leave. She probably is, but Lila has only
one setting: rushed. This time when we hit the conference room
we bear a sharp right, down another hall, toward, I assume, Jackie's
office.

"Do you want coffee?"

I can picture the coffee mugs washed and put away for the day and
the kerfuffle it would cause if I said yes. "No, thank you." And then,
because I can't help myself from babbling around Lila, "Caffeine
makes me jittery this late in the day." I don't want to say what we both
already know: I'm jittery enough already.

A young, fair-haired man, handsome, maybe twenty-five, approaches us while pulling on a blazer in a windmill-like fashion I
imagine members of a varsity rowing team do. He locks eyes with me
like we're cruising for random sex in an out-of-the-way park, and
while unnerved, I can't look away. I've spent years wanting to belong
in these halls; glancing down would send the wrong message.

"Oh, hey." Lila stops us. "This is Mark. He's Mrs. Onassis's new
assistant. Mark, this is James Smale." Lila punctuates my name with
an air of disinterest.

"James Smale," Mark says, shaking my hand while trying to place
my name.

Lila rolls her eyes, I hope at Mark and not at me. "Jackie's new acquisition."

"Right." Mark clasps his other hand on mine, they are soft and warm.

"Acquisition?" Like I'm some antiquity she's acquired on an exotic foreign trip? "I guess we'll be working together."

"I look forward to it." Mark lets go of my hand, but not before he winks. Thankfully, Lila doesn't see that, her eyes might roll fully back in disgust. He walks past me and we both turn back for one last look. I'm one who feels invisible more often than attractive, so I'm almost giddy when I see him smile at me. Not to say Daniel doesn't do his best to prop up my self-esteem, but he's obliged to; the return date on me has long since passed and he doesn't have a receipt. But was this flirtation? Or just aggressive friendliness. I stumble forward to catch Lila. Whatever that was, I don't have time to process it.

We stop in front of a door that's only slightly ajar.

"Here we are." Lila raps on the door three times. *Loudly.* I would have knocked gently, with decorum; I'm instantly horrified. I turn to protest, but she's already gone.

"Found it!" The unmistakable voice rings out from inside the office.

I knock again, quietly this time, and open the door a few more inches. "Mrs. Onassis?" I peer around the open door into the office and see no one. I bite my lip just in time to keep from saying "Jackie." I peek farther into the room and find her standing by a bookshelf in the space behind the door. "Oh, hello again," I utter awkwardly. I realize I have no idea what's going on and hope for my own sake that what she's found isn't a manuscript more intriguing than mine. "What did you find?"

"A book I brought from home. Come in, come in." She ushers me inside her office and I push the door closed most of the way behind me. I have the good sense to leave the door cracked, enough, at least, so that I can't be accused of doing something untoward; it feels inappropriate to be entirely behind closed doors with her.

The office is not what I would call small, although it's decidedly not palatial. It's quite nice—comfortable, even. There's nothing that would have prevented us from meeting here when we were first introduced. I'm wondering now if she didn't select the conference room as neutral territory to put me more at ease, and I feel empty-handed suddenly, a gentleman caller without flowers or wine or chocolates.

"So nice to see you again, James."

I can feel myself blush. "You as well."

Jackie steps over several boxes (books, I'm guessing), which, in her skirt, is no small feat of gymnastics. They seem out of place, these boxes, uncharacteristically messy, but upon closer inspection her shelves are at capacity with manuscripts and galleys. There's a painting of a dancer on the wall that looks like it could be worth a good deal of money, but I don't know enough about art to be sure. I half expect her desk to look like her husband's from the Oval Office, but instead it's a Formica-topped eyesore that looks more like it might belong to a junior-high science teacher. The desk itself is covered in more manuscripts, weighed down with decorative glass paperweights.

Jackie holds the book up with both hands before circling behind her desk to take a seat. "I thought this would be just what we need for our working together tonight. Have you read the poet Constantine Cavafy?"

I glance at the book—his collected works. "No, I haven't." I wait for her to sit behind her desk before taking a seat in one of her guest chairs. I want to appear well read (and if there was homework for this meeting, I want to have done it), but this particular poet might be a little too obscure to fake a passing knowledge of.

"He's not widely read in the States. My second husband introduced me to his works and he fast became a favorite. He has a poem, 'Ithaka.'"

"The location of my book," I say, although these must be very different Ithacas. I'm doubting that any poet named Constantine wrote about central New York.

"I'm wondering if it might be a good title for your novel."

"Ithaca?" I'm momentarily disheartened. Not that I'm overly invested in my own title, but that the time has arrived to get down to work. I already miss the part where we fawn over me and the book. Can't we have several more meetings like that?

"Though we generally try to avoid publishing titles with negative onomatopoeic sounds . . ."

I chew on that for a second. *Ithaca.* "Ick?"

"It makes the marketing department frown."

Is she pulling my leg? There's an uncomfortable pause and then I laugh politely, but not too much, in case I've misread her. I look around the office for clues that will put me at ease. Something that I recognize could belong to anyone, to normalize our interaction. The truth of the matter—it's all rather conventional. It's an office, like any other.

"So why Ithaca?" Jackie resumes. "Why set the book there?"

"Oh," I say, the question snapping me back. "I grew up there. Well, a microscopic town just outside. So when people ask me where I'm from, that's what I say." Daniel's voice fills my head. "You don't want to change it to Cape Cod, do you?"

"I beg your pardon?"

I shake my head slightly. "Someone told me that you would . . . never mind. Nothing. It's small, Ithaca. Exotic-sounding, perhaps. I like the Greek name. I think it evokes the book's underlying tragedy. But otherwise, there's nothing special about it. Like the characters themselves, at first glance. They're unremarkable. On the surface they could be any mother and son. But I find simple can be . . . quite complicated."

"Oh, so do I. You only passingly refer to the name of the town in the manuscript. It got me thinking that you might mean it as more of a state of mind. Or a state of being. Does that make sense?" Of course she must know that it makes perfect sense, but phrasing it as a question sets me up to agree. Perhaps a skill she's used in the past, asserting her own ideas by involving others.

"It certainly does."

Jackie looks like she's about to say something and then stops. She thinks again before picking up the book. "I've marked the page. I don't have my glasses. Would you do the honors?" She opens the book and hands it to me. It takes a moment for it to sink in that she's asking me to read.

"Happy to."

"Just the last few lines."

I fumble with the book, almost losing her place, until I manage to get a good grip. I scan down the text of the poem, looking for just the right place to jump in. *"Ithaka has given you the beautiful journey."* Already I feel a lump forming in my throat so I read quietly until I get to the very end. *"And if you find her threadbare, Ithaka has not deceived you. Wise as you have become, with so much experience, you must have always understood what Ithakas mean."* I glance up at Jackie and she's looking just past me, as if considering the meaning again for the very first time. "That's . . . *wow*," I say. I left my apartment early to walk here, gathering courage along the way in the invigorating March air, desperately dreaming up intelligent phrases and casual topics of conversation to use as filler, should our dialogue sputter. And yet, all I can come up with is "wow."

But it is remarkable, especially if Ithaca is not a town or a place or a state of being, but a person, a mother, a soul. Indeed, she has not deceived me; somehow, I must have always understood that.

Once again Jackie opens her mouth to speak, then stops. But this time she plows forward without any further hesitation. "I have a thought."

"Oh?"

A grin spreads across her face, hinting at the woman one always suspected lay just beneath the decorum. She opens her desk drawer, pulls out an expensive-looking bottle of rum, and plunks it on her desk. The alcohol sloshes, creating a rippling meniscus.

"This was a recent gift from one of my authors after a trip he took to Barbados."

I'm not sure I'm following. "Rum was your thought?"

"Close," Jackie says. She stands, lifting the rum to inspect it. She pulls her shoulders back as if not to let the heavy bottle topple her forward. Allen was right—she is indeed tall. "Daiquiris."

David Letterman recently aired a Top Ten List of Least Popular New York City Street Vendors and the number-one entry served "Stunned Mouse in a Dixie Cup." I don't know why that comes to mind now, except that it became a punchline between Daniel and me (What would you like for dinner tonight? *How about stunned mouse in a Dixie cup!*) and—talk about stunned—even I wish I could see the look on my face right now. "Daiquiris." I scramble out of my chair; when a woman like Jacqueline Onassis stands, a gentleman does too.

She reaches back in her drawer and pulls out what miraculously appears to be simple syrup. I'm beginning to think this particular drawer is a magician's hat. "Don't tell me you're a teetotaler," she says.

I struggle to remember if *teetotaler* means someone who is on, or off, the wagon. "No. Far from it. I just don't usually drink daiquiris."

"That's because you don't usually drink with me." She notices me standing. "Sit, sit. I'm going to collect some ice."

Jackie places her hand on my shoulder as she squeezes past me and out the door. Alone in her office, I lean forward and grab the rum. It's hard not to think she's putting me on. I hold it up to my nose, and not only does it contain alcohol, it may be one hundred and fifty proof. Do I know her to drink? Are there photos of her drinking? Magazine profiles that mention the habit? If I were her, there's no way I could not drink. *Should I put a stop to this? Is this a bad idea?* I have just enough time to place the bottle back on her desk before she returns carrying a little silver platter with several limes, a knife, club soda, and two glasses with ice.

"What else do you have in that desk? A coconut tree?"

"Don't ever underestimate me."

"I wouldn't dream of it," I say, and that's the God's-honest truth.

"I think you will like this. It's distilled from molasses instead of sugarcane." She adds a healthy pour of rum to each glass and a more conservative amount of simple syrup. Whatever it is that she's doing, she's quite adept at doing it. Then she slices several limes and squeezes as much juice as she can into each glass; I can see the tendons in her sinewy arms. "I had to borrow these earlier from the cafeteria ladies."

Good God, she's been planning this all day. "I hope they didn't mind." *Should I point out they won't be getting them back?*

"Oh, they like me." She repeats the process with another lime, then tops each glass with a splash of soda. "On my first day here— this goes back a while now . . ."

"Fourteen years?" I try to recall her résumé from our first meeting. Jackie pulls a silver letter opener from a pencil cup and gives each cocktail a good stir.

"That's right," she says. "Back then, no one—and I mean *no one*— knew how they were supposed to behave in my presence. If I got into the elevator, people would get out. If I walked down the hallway, people would turn around and scramble in the opposite direction. If I went to the breakroom to pour a cup of coffee, people would panic and hand me theirs."

"That sounds . . ." I grasp for the right word. "Lonely."

Satisfied that each cocktail is well mixed, Jackie gently taps the letter opener on the rim of one glass and it makes the most perfect chime. She picks up the tray and holds it out for me as if she's the most overqualified spokesmodel ever to be hired on a game show.

"Thank you," I say, accepting a drink. I hold it firmly in both hands by my lap, even though the ice makes it uncomfortably cold to the touch.

"It was. Devastatingly lonely. It was like I had the plague. After several weeks of this nonsense, I decided to head down to the cafeteria for lunch. Of course, everyone put their trays down and got out of line in front of me and disappeared from sight. It was horribly embarrassing, because the last thing I wanted was anyone thinking that I felt entitled to go to the front of the line. But it's not like I could tell them to hop back in line—they had evaporated! Anyhow, this one lunch lady, a rather robust woman, urged me to the counter with an exaggerated wave and bellowed, 'WHAT'LL IT BE, JACKIE?'"

My easy laughter catches me off guard. "So, what was it?"

"Tuna fish salad, if I recall." We both laugh. "I don't suppose everyone was fond of my being here. But after that, things were different. Better." Jackie leans in to the memory, taking a full beat before coming back. "In case that story didn't do it for you, consider this your lunch lady."

I hold up my drink and we clink glasses with good cheer, this long story a toast of sorts to our new relationship and the work we hope to accomplish together. "To Ithaca."

"To Ithaca," she echoes.

I take a sip, and the drink is . . . tart, citrusy. Only a little pulpy. A few of these would be downright dangerous.

"How does it taste?"

"It's . . . sly."

"You're lucky you're here this week. Last week I was keen on acquiring a book of cold blended soups. Lila and I tried a few of the recipes. As it turns out, after gazpacho there aren't many cold soups worth a damn. Have you ever had cream-of-cashew soup? Cold?"

"I haven't had the pleasure."

"Believe me, there's no pleasure to be had. Unless you like wallpaper glue."

I grimace, then gesture toward the Cavafy book, and she gives me permission to take it. I open to the marked page. "Ithaka referred to in the feminine, like she is mother herself. You must have always known what Ithakas mean."

Jackie makes a rich sound like an exquisite piece of chocolate is melting on her tongue. "And those are just the last few lines. Beautiful, isn't it? Take that book home with you and read the rest."

"It's remarkably . . . apropos." But have I always known? Is my book some sort of misadventure to understand something that, deep down, I already know?

"Inspired by Homer, if I'm not mistaken." Of course she's not mistaken.

"The return of Odysseus home," I say, grateful this time for something more intelligent to say. "Homer, I've read."

"The maturity of the soul as we all travel home is, I think, all the traveler can hope for. I want you to think of that, especially in the context of your manuscript's ending. I think that's where the bulk of your work lies."

"The ending."

"The last third of the book. I have a clear picture of who your characters are at the start of the quarantine, but I don't know exactly who they are at the end. To each other, to themselves."

"I keep thinking of our first conversation. How you said books are journeys."

"That's right."

"But . . ."

Jackie rests her chin on the back of her hand. "What is it?"

I hesitate, not sure how I can say this. "I'm sorry. I haven't worked with an editor before. I don't want to overstep."

"I tell my writers our conversations are privileged. Like doctor and patient."

"Lawyer and client?"

"Priest and parishioner. Confession only if you want." Jackie raises her glass.

"I was just thinking if my book is in part about motherhood, that's a journey you have taken."

"One that has given me some of my most sublime moments. But your book. Yes, it's about motherhood, but through the eyes of a son. And I haven't been one of those."

"I suppose that's true," I concede.

Jackie takes a long, slow sip from her glass. "I want to see real growth on the page, how the events have changed them, particularly the son. You have a remarkably fresh voice, so I know you have it in you."

My drink is going down too easily, and I can feel the rum rushing to my face, coloring my cheeks, creating a blessed hollowness between my ears, allowing me not to pass out. "I can taste the molasses."

Jackie narrows her eyes, scrutinizing me. "It's hard for you to hear a compliment."

"I don't suppose I've received enough compliments to know."

"That was wonderful deflection. The molasses."

"Another compliment?"

"Another deflection?" She takes one more sip, then sets her glass down on a coaster. "You can taste it, though, I'll give you that. Especially when you know that it's there."

I place the Cavafy book on the corner of her desk and inspect what's left of my drink.

Jackie refocuses. "Before we get to the ending, tell me more about your mother."

I burst out laughing and am immediately embarrassed, covering my mouth with the back of my hand.

"Oh, heavens. I sounded like your analyst."

I'm fascinated to know if she's familiar with the language of therapy. It wouldn't surprise me, and yet it's hard to imagine her vulnerable enough to seek help. But as much as our conversations may be privileged, I'm sure the privilege of probing conversation flows only one way. "What would you like to know?"

"Was she always sad?"

"No" is my first answer. But then I have to think—*Is she sad?* "I don't think so. Perhaps. Are we talking about Ruth? I'm afraid I'm a little confused."

"There's confusion in the character." She leans forward to retrieve the glass from my hand, and I barely loosen my grip enough for her to take it. If it weren't for the condensation from the ice, it might not have wiggled out of my hand at all. "There are several moments where you get close to expressing something real, and I think you pad your observations with what I guess are fictional details and it keeps you from hitting some of the harder truths."

She pours more rum into my glass. "Not too much," I say. But as she refills my drink I think, *To hell with it. You know? If we're going to do this, let's do this.* Let this be the grand marshal in a parade of lunch ladies to come.

"Tell me something true," she says.

"About my mother?"

"Even if it has nothing to do with the book."

I think about this and how not to further betray her. She'd already be horrified if she were a fly on the wall right now. *Do I tell Jackie my mother resents me for her being alone? That she took my side once, and it cost her her marriage? That even though it was the right thing to do, in the moment she probably didn't envision how long life would be in the wake of it? That we're barely on speaking terms right now?* "I don't think my mother got much of what she wanted out of life."

"She has her children."

"That's true, but hardly anything else."

"Does anyone? Get what they truly want."

The question strikes me as odd, borderline offensive, even, from someone who has lived such a fascinating life. I need more alcohol for this. "Well, no. I would imagine that's rare. But I also don't think she was given the tools to ask."

"That's true for a lot of women our age." Jackie steps in front of her desk to hand me my drink. She stands and leans elegantly with her legs crossed and one hand on the desk, looking like the perfect line sketch a fashion designer might make while dreaming up patterns for clothes. "I feel for her."

"That's good. As a reader, I hope that you would."

"I'll try over the course of our working together not to sound like your analyst. Writing it, I'm sure, was therapy enough."

"If I hadn't written it, I think I might have gone insane. Or become a Republican. Something horrible."

Jackie laughs in such a way, not heartily but genuinely, that I want it to be my validation forever. "You remind me of my son."

I can feel my face turn beet red, so I look down at my feet. They look cloddish in large, heavy shoes, the opposite of her narrow, elegant heels. "Don't do that."

"Do what?"

"Acknowledge that I have difficulty accepting compliments, then lay the biggest one of all on me and expect me to be okay."

Jackie waves her hand over her drink, wafting in some of the aroma. "Perhaps this round is too sweet."

"Deflection!" This is the rum talking. "Are you not comfortable with compliments either? Could this be something we have in common?" I take a victory sip.

She shakes her head. "You didn't compliment me."

"The heck I didn't."

"A compliment for my son is a compliment for me?"

I nod enthusiastically, and I can tell this pleases her. She moves behind the desk to retake her seat. "He failed the bar exam multiple times, which I'm sure you know if you read the *Daily News*." I can feel her utter sense of pride in him, as if this were self-depreciation.

I sink back into my chair and chuckle. I do remember the headlines: "The Hunk Flunks." That must have stung. But, still. I can't believe how much fun I'm having. I can't believe how much my outlook has changed in a matter of weeks. I can't believe that this is my life now. It feels resurgent, sparkling with possibility, like I've made some sort of comeback from an exile I hadn't deserved.

"I think my lunch lady is working," I confide.

Jackie sips from her cocktail and her eyes sparkle with thousands of secrets. "I think mine is too." When she finishes, she sets her glass down and holds out the silver tray to collect mine. Another magical moment ended too soon, and we're on to something new. "Now," she says. "Let's get down to work."

Go Your Own Way

July 1992

⋅ NINE ⋅

When I land at Boston's Logan Airport, I have only a few minutes to collect my bag and race to catch the shuttle bus to Cape Air's small terminal for the flight to Martha's Vineyard. The Cape Air plane is disconcertingly puny, what my father would have called a puddle-jumper. There are seats for ten passengers, five on each side of the aisle, plus a jump seat for the crew. The flight attendant places us according to weight to balance the plane; this is done discreetly as not to offend, but the end result is obvious. I'm seated across the aisle from a woman who indubitably comes from money, and I wonder if she knows Jackie, if they are neighbors on the island or on the board together of some local environmental organization to save the eroding dunes. We smile politely and say hello, but she doesn't ask my business, which disappoints me because I'm dying to volunteer the information: I'm going to visit my editor.

Three weeks ago, Jackie sent the latest draft of my manuscript via courier marked with her edits. As mild and polite as she can be in person, taking careful consideration of my feelings as both an artist and someone younger and less experienced in the publishing world, she was just the opposite on paper. Paragraphs, sometimes pages, were crossed right out with margin notes that screamed CUT! VERGING ON MELODRAMA! TRITE! And then other parts were circled; UNDERWRITTEN! SHALLOW! GIVE THE READER MORE! My heart sank as I flipped through the pages; I had thought the latest draft addressed many of her original concerns from our earlier talks, but there were still a number of sticking points—particularly with the ending. I gave myself a week to calm down. When I reached her via phone to discuss her notes, she informed me she was working from her home on Martha's Vineyard and invited me up to work through them.

So here I am, onboard what's basically an enclosed hang glider, waiting for runway clearance to take flight.

The midsummer morning is warm; the sun beats off the tarmac and through the plane windows, heating the entire cabin. It feels like we are ants under a child's magnifying glass—at any moment we might burst into flames (this is not an image you want while sitting in a fuselage). I roll up the sleeves of my linen shirt as the two outboard propellers start to spin. I look back to see if there's an indication we might receive drink service, but signs do not point to yes. We pick up speed down the runway and take off over Boston Harbor before banking to head south toward Martha's Vineyard and Nantucket. This is the smallest plane I've ever been on, and I'm amazed at how you feel every rippling current, how your stomach rises and falls with each dip and change in air pressure. I have a magazine in my messenger bag, but I don't have any interest in even pretending to read it—the view out my window of the Massachusetts coastline is far more interesting. The ocean is an emerald green, in contrast with the sparkling aqua-blue swimming pools that dot the shore—they seem almost Caribbean by comparison. I'm finally offered a small bottle of water, which I take but don't drink; there's no bathroom on board and my bladder is already full.

My mother and I have spoken only once since I told her about Jackie. I called her when I cut myself shaving and the bleeding wouldn't stop. I felt lightheaded (more from queasiness than blood loss), and without really thinking I picked up the phone; that's how ingrained it is to always want your mother.

"I'm bleeding," I said when she answered.

"From what?" My mother's trademark detachment rang through.

"The ear. Not the ear. Just under the ear. The part where the earlobe connects to the jaw. I don't know what that's called."

"Domino, down." My mother's dog yipped and then stopped, probably silenced with a treat. "I meant, what did you do."

"Oh. I cut myself shaving."

I could tell from her silence she wondered what it was I thought she could do from two hundred miles away.

"Anyways. I thought you could keep me company while I bleed out."

My mother groaned. "I have a hair appointment at eleven."

And that was the end of our conversation. No mention of the book. No questions about my life or any of the wondrous things happening. Nothing about Jackie. No real concern about my medical emergency, although my mother knew me well enough to know there was no serious call for alarm. (A therapist friend called these "bids," my calling home with extravagant takes to get a reaction. But my mother had my number; she was maddeningly patient, never raising her paddle, passing my lot on to other, more excitable auction-goers.) This is where we are, this stalemate our new home.

I would have loved to share this trip with my mother. She would have hated this flight and in fact may have refused to board it, offended by having her weight silently gauged. But she would have loved to spy on Martha's Vineyard, to see firsthand the places and names that she's read about in following the Kennedys over the years: Nantucket, Hyannis Port—even Chappaquiddick. Several months with no communication is not that unusual in our relationship. It's not the norm, but it's not unheard of. We've done this before. Still, there's a weighty sadness to our current silence; this is not merely a period of us being too busy or too lazy to speak. I have defied her expressed wishes—what else is there, really, to say? Calling to announce I had been invited to Jackie's beach house to work on the book would only rub it in.

The airport on Martha's Vineyard is centered on the island, in a clearing of some forested acres, and our landing is surprisingly smooth. There's a single, quaint-looking tower, and the airport building itself has a cottagey feel. When we deplane onto the tarmac, I'm immediately overcome with the smell and grit of salty air. I have the address for Jackie's place near Gay Head, but since I feel wholly

incapable of saying Gay Head without snickering, I tell the taxi driver
I hire to take State Road to Moshup Trail (the specific directions she
had given me).

I'm nervous, my heart rate increasing in synch with the cab's me-
ter. With these latest edits I can feel my esteem with Jackie slipping;
if I don't play this hand correctly, I could have created this mess with
my mother for nothing. I instruct the driver to drop me at the top of
the driveway, as I don't want to intrude on the family's privacy by
having him drive past the gate and up to the main house. Once again,
it's impossible to know the protocol. I pay him the fare with a generous tip (on the off chance he knows who lives here) before retrieving
my suitcase and walking down the quiet road, double-checking the
address I have folded in my pocket. The drive is lined with trees and
the air is filled with a symphony of chirping insects that sounds like
both a concerto and a warning. There's a turnoff on the right side of
the road, but I continue straight, even though I'm not sure that's
correct. I'm sweating, from the July heat or from nerves or from both,
and I fish for a Kleenex in my other pocket to wipe my forehead.
After a quarter-mile or so I round a bend and come to a clearing and
I can see what looks to be a main and guesthouse. There's a large pond
behind both, and I think maybe the ocean beyond that—it's hard to
tell from my vantage point in the driveway, everything feels so vast.

I spot a sturdy woman with graying hair and she calls out to me
as she shakes a scatter rug in the driveway. "Hello?"

"Hi there. I'm James. I'm wondering if I'm in the right place." I
look around like I might recognize something, although what I'm not
sure. I'm certain there's no mailbox that says KENNEDY.

"You're looking for . . ."

"Jackie," I reply without thinking.

"You're looking for *Mrs. Onassis*," the woman says pointedly,
studying me with some degree of skepticism.

"Yes." I cringe. I'm barely down the driveway and I've already offended. "Mrs. Onassis."

The woman hesitates, as if deciding whether I should be sent packing. She gives the rug another shake and I step back to avoid a small cloud of debris. "You're the writer?" She waves me in closer.

"That's right." I used to say it apologetically before this all began, like I was admitting something embarrassing or bad. It's a real gift Jackie—*Mrs. Onassis*—has given to me, to be able to say that I'm a writer with pride, the stress of the current edits notwithstanding.

"She said I should be expecting you."

"And here I am." It's meant to sound charming, but out loud it sounds condescending. Quickly I add, "Stunning. Martha's Vineyard. Very scenic."

It's clear from her expression she doesn't know what to make of me. "How was your flight?"

"Short." I smile expectantly, looking back and forth between the houses, trying to get the lay of the land. "Is Mrs. Onassis around?"

"She's resting. I'm to set you up in the guesthouse and she will see you for dinner." She reaches for my bag, but I pick it up before she's able to and attempt a friendly smile. We amble together over to the smaller house as a gentle breeze picks up. "I'm Joan," she finally offers.

"James Smale. It's very nice to meet you. You work for Mrs. Onassis?"

"Seven years now."

"This is our first book together," I volunteer, hoping it will inspire some pity. By the way Joan grunts her response, I can tell she thinks that much is obvious. We reach the guesthouse, which, while smaller than the main house, is still considerably sized. "This is all for me?"

"It is. Although you probably won't need the run of it. There's a bedroom set up for you on the second floor."

"Is this where . . ." I stop myself, knowing my question is inappropriate.

"Is this where . . . ?" Joan asks.

I blush, unable to think of a good lie. "Is this where John Junior stays?" I look bashfully at Joan, who says "Mmm" in response, as if that's all that needs to be said on that topic.

"Well, thank you. I certainly don't need all this space, and I promise not to make a mess of it."

"There's a pitcher of iced tea in the fridge. Brewed it this morning. Mrs. Onassis will see you for dinner in the main house at six."

"Thank you, Joan." I hope it's at least okay that she and I be on a first-name basis.

Joan opens the door for me and I step inside. She hesitates before closing the door. "A piece of advice?"

I nod. I need all the advice I can get.

"You're in someone's home. Remember that. She invited you, but that doesn't mean you should suddenly be overly familiar. She's very private. Be respectful."

"Yes, ma'am."

"She's trusting you with an invitation."

"Yes, ma'am," I repeat, showcasing my ability to be respectful. Joan is a bit of a killjoy.

She looks at me again to see if her advice is sticking. When she decides that it takes, she turns and repeats, "Dinner's at six. Don't be late." I'm about to say that I wouldn't dare when the screen door slams behind me and I jump. I get the sense she did that on purpose.

The house is decorated simply but impeccably. I set my bag down on the floor to stroll freely throughout. There's a deliberate beachlike, Ralph Lauren feel to it all, despite the European accents that are scattered throughout. Beside a comfortable and welcoming worn-in living room sofa is a rustic French country accent chair next to a Danish mid-century side table. The art is nautically themed, with masculine, stormy hues, seascapes with skies the color of gunmetal. In the kitchen, a collage of family photos hangs near a Shaker dining table and chairs. Somehow it all ties together: American with European, museum-quality art with family photographs, turn-of-the-century artifacts with mid-century furnishings. It's effortless in the way only someone with great style and taste could curate. Upstairs there's only one bedroom with the door open, obviously meant for me. I set my bag in there and plop down on the bed.

I immediately want to call Daniel. Sleeping in JFK Jr.'s quarters is, for red-blooded homosexuals, at least, far more exciting than a night in the Lincoln Bedroom. More than that. It's an outright fantasy. But it's not clear he would answer the phone. We had a small argument before I left, Daniel and I, and I'm not really sure what sparked it. He seemed annoyed about the trip; at first I thought he was hoping to be invited, but he finally revealed that he was concerned about what it would do to my mother.

"You should call her," he said.

"I did," I replied, tugging at my ear where the cut used to be.

"And she's okay with you going?"

I didn't understand why I needed her permission, so I lied and said, "She's fine."

He didn't really believe me, but the whole thing was over before it began. Still, I don't like it when we lock horns. The list of people who are currently on speaking terms with me, it seems, is shrinking rapidly, and Joan seems unlikely to be added as a confidant.

I look at the white ceiling (which I'm sure isn't white, but rather some color with a name like Edwardian Linen or Lustre), imagining others who have stayed here before me: celebrities, politicians, writers, bon vivants. It's impossible to nap, so after an hour or so of trying I return to the kitchen for some iced tea. I pour myself a glass from the pitcher and decide to stroll down to the waterfront. I step outside into the gauzy afternoon light, and a little breeze tousles my hair. The screen door again slams behind me.

There's a path along the pond, which, if I remember correctly from Jackie's invitation, has an Indian name like Squibnocket; I follow that path around the pond's western end until I reach the ocean, stopping only once to skip a few stones across the rippling water. I reach the dunes and remove my boat shoes and roll up my pant legs. I carry the shoes with me like I would at the Jersey shore, even though it's probably safe to leave them in the sand. I look up and down the coastline and there are only a few other people in sight, and none within shouting distance. A man waves and I wave politely back as a few sandpipers run feebly between us toward the outgoing tide.

It's so beautiful, unencumbering—I'm tempted to strip off all my clothes and run naked into the water. A baptism of sorts into a new life, with all the cares of my previous existence washed away in the salty waters of the Atlantic. Just me, naked and pure.

But of course I don't.

Instead I look out across the ocean, toward the United Kingdom, toward Ireland, from whence the ancestors of our two families came. One family who was the very image of the American Dream, whose children rose to the highest ranks of power before that dream morphed slowly into a nightmare. The other who never dared to dream big enough, too bogged down by the rules to ever truly get ahead, a family that produced timid offspring who lived through their own quiet ordeals. I wonder how far the horizon is, how far I can really see. Although, if maps are to be trusted, I'm not looking at Ireland at all, but rather at Portugal, or maybe France.

I scrunch my bare toes in the warm grains of sand. It feels like I'm standing in the sands of an egg timer, the firm beach slowly falling into another chamber beneath me. I feel a sudden urgency with time, about not having enough of it to make things right with the book, with Jackie, with my mother. But the beach is a seductive mistress, so I pivot east, hoping to make it as far as the cliffs at Gay Head before I have to turn back for dinner.

◆ TEN ◆

I'm on the front steps of the main house at six o'clock sharp, having showered after my walk and dressed properly for dinner in a white shirt and J.Crew slacks, which the catalog described as an apropos Nantucket Red. I check that my shirt is properly tucked and straighten my belt before knocking gently on the screen door. It rattles in its frame like the door of our family farmhouse, warped slightly from the sun or the rain, and I'm instantly transported to my childhood. It sounds so much like the door I grew up with that I half expect to hear my mother's voice call out.

"James? Is that you?"

Of course, it's not my mother.

"Mrs. Onassis?"

"Please, come in."

I open the door and Jackie strides forward, flipping through a small stack of mail. In my mind she holds handwritten letters, as she's too ethereal in this airy setting to be weighed down with solicitations or bills. She's wearing navy pants and a white silk T-shirt with a cardigan draped over her shoulders in the way certain women like Lauren Bacall do in magazines but you rarely see in real life. I'm surprised that she answers her own door with a casual "come in," as if that were in any way safe. I wonder why Joan doesn't guard the door padded like a baseball catcher to absorb possible intruders.

"How was your trip?" she asks, and we hug politely. I don't dare pull her too close or too tight; I imagine her with porous bones like a bird.

"Easy. Quite nice."

"Excellent. Welcome to Red Gate Farm. Allow me to give you the nickel tour."

The main house is decorated much as the guesthouse is, with a slightly more feminine touch. There are books in every room, and I wish I could spend hours quietly perusing her library, studying the titles to see which spines are cracked, if only to feel closer to her. I know that she is famous for once giving a televised tour of the White House ("the Diplomatic Reception Room is right this way"), but this has a quiet informality that is hardly reminiscent.

"Your home is lovely," I say, but it comes across like a line instead of a spontaneous remark.

"That's very kind of you to say."

We make small talk until dinner; I describe my view from the plane window like I'm some sort of cultural anthropologist from *National Geographic*. She retains perfect focus on me like she hasn't herself taken this flight a thousand times, and I feel like the belle of an invisible ball. The meal is Atlantic cod with some sort of balsamic reduction over rice and *haricots verts*.

"Will Mr. Tempelsman be joining us?" Mr. Tempelsman is Maurice Tempelsman, her suitor of several years. In our brief time working together I've heard her make reference to him as her companion, her "Belgian," and once even jokingly as "Mr. Kennedy Onassis."

"He is in Europe on business. I hope my company will do."

We both smile, recognizing the ridiculous nature of the comment. Out of sheer curiosity, I would love to observe them together, to see how she behaves with a man (momentarily forgetting that I am one), but I'm relieved not to have to make more small talk and grasp for polite questions about Antwerp. At the table, Jackie enlightens me in some of the history of the island. Before it was a summer home to affluent and well-known families, the island was home to the Wampanoag people. English settlement began in the seventeenth century and the island was brought into prominence by the whaling industry in the 1800s. She knows everything about everything, or so it seems, and the details that shade her lesson are remarkable.

"Have you ever heard of a Nantucket sleigh ride?" she asks, half-way through the meal.

"I can't say that I have."

"It's the resulting tow a whaler received after harpooning a whale, before it would tire and die."

"You're kidding!" I'm tickled by this bit of information. "That's delightful."

"I imagine not for the whale."

I laugh. "No, I imagine not."

There are no actual vineyards (I ask), nor have there ever really been; the island was, however, at one time covered with wild grapes. There was a secessionist movement in the 1970s; some of the flags from that campaign still fly over the island. She's so thorough in her knowledge and enthusiastic to share it, I wonder if there will be a test. She could easily have a second job as an island tour guide if she wanted it, or work for the chamber of commerce—a delightfully comical image in and of itself.

We each have a glass of chenin blanc with dinner; I sip mine slowly so that I'm not tempted for more, mindful of Joan's advice. (Despite the daiquiris we consumed in New York, perhaps she's right—a home visit requires extra decorum.) It's only after we consume most of the meal that talk turns to the book.

"So, James. We need to talk more about your ending."

"I knew it was inevitable." I set my fork down, annoyed at the book as if it were in the way of our relationship instead of being the reason for it.

"You're letting the mother off too easy."

Given where my mother and I currently are, it's difficult to imagine being harder on her. I must flinch, because Jackie eases off the gas pedal.

"I keep thinking what power a talented writer has."

"Did *you* ever entertain being a writer?" I ask, trying to obfuscate the fact that I clearly haven't accomplished what she was hoping with this draft.

"My mother thought I had the temperament, but I find the process painstaking. It takes me forever to draft a letter; I don't know how I'd ever manage a whole book." She takes the napkin from her lap and places it on the table before folding her hands under her chin.

"It is painstaking," I agree. "Painful, at times."

Jackie narrows her eyes. "Yes, but through pain comes great art."

"I won't flatter myself by thinking you're speaking of my manuscript." This is, after all, a woman who has seen and had access to the world's greatest antiquities.

But without so much as a pause she asks, "Why not?"

I chew on my lip as the profundity of such a simple question washes over me. Why am I not in the running to create something substantial? Why do I so easily discredit my own work? "Why not," I say, a declarative statement in place of the question.

"It seems to me you're capable. I believe in what writers can do. And I believe in you."

"I always thought there was magic in being an editor." I can feel myself blushing again, heat racing to my cheeks. "Compliments," I say, a callback to our last meeting.

Jackie nods, then gazes down at her plate. I'm beginning to recognize real patterns: I look away when complimented, she looks down when the subject of conversation. If this keeps up, we could spend the next few days avoiding eye contact entirely. "It *is* special. To find something in a manuscript that you recognize as familiar truth, but also as wisdom you're hearing voiced in a new and articulate way. It's why your manuscript stood out to me. You opened my eyes to something, James. A fresh truth. And I think a lot of readers will feel the same way."

I swallow the last of my wine.

"But you're being too protective. Of your mother. It's admirable, I admire it. I would want my own children to be as protective of me. But it comes at the book's expense." This is easier to digest than her edits on the printed page. It helps that the note comes wrapped in another compliment, further seduction, getting me to see her side of things. "You come into the quarantine . . ."

". . . Russell comes . . ."

"Pardon me." She smiles. "Russell comes into the quarantine with reasonable grievances, with a list of things to accomplish. Right at the outset you establish two central questions. *Who is she,* your mother, *Who am I,* you."

I start to protest and say "Russell" again, but it's embarrassingly clear what she's saying. "They remain unanswered."

"Not just who they are at the outset of the novel. Who do they become? What have they learned?"

"The maturation of the soul," I say, returning to Homer. "I struggle with my obligations."

"When writing fictional characters based on real people?"

"To the truth."

Jackie gets up from her seat across the table, crosses around to my side, pulls out a chair next to me, and sits. She rests her hand on top of mine. "Do something for me as you write."

"Anything. I'll take inspiration where I can." Her hand on mine has a vertiginous effect, doubling the potency of the wine; I feel a little woozy.

"Think about the difference between curing and healing." I must have a puzzled expression on my face, because she says, "How to explain what I mean," and then sits very still while she thinks. "Do you know the story of Isis and Osiris?"

I shake my head no. "Did one of them fly too close to the sun?"

"That was Icarus. Osiris was killed in a fight with his brother Set. Quite violently, in fact—he was cut into pieces and spread throughout Egypt. His wife Isis searched everywhere to collect the pieces and put him back together. In doing so, in burying him whole, she believed his spirit would be eternal."

"You're not suggesting I hack my mother into pieces." I reach for the low-hanging joke.

"On the contrary, you already have. I'm asking you to put the pieces back together."

I want to disagree, but then I remember we've already established—I've already admitted—that my relationship with my mother was the main impetus for writing the book. I decide to be honest with her. "I guess I'm not sure how that explains the difference."

Jackie sits back and runs her hands through her hair as she thinks, piling it on her head and letting it drop. "Don't tell your story to change something about the past; the past is inherently unchangeable. There is no cure."

"And yet there's a powerful temptation to rewrite it." I feel instantly foolish—look who I'm telling this to.

"But that's not the goal of the quarantine. Is it?"

"No."

"It's to find a way forward. So, instead, I want you to focus on healing. Remember, and then assemble all the lovely bits. Like Isis did. To truly remember, I believe, is to heal."

"Remember on the page."

"Exactly. I think the hardest thing to dramatize, without being cliché, is the love a mother has for her children. And you've done that. Not as a mother, not as a parent at all, but as a child, which I think is even more impressive. And let me worry about editing you." She taps the table with her index finger. "Do not edit yourself."

I try unsuccessfully to stifle a smile.

Jackie cocks her head. "What is it?"

"I just can't help but think you'd advise me differently if this book were about you." I keep my ears perked for Joan, wondering if she will materialize and rap my knuckles or simply chide me tomorrow for each instance where I've overstepped.

"This book *is* about me." Jackie takes my hand again and we share an intense stare. There's part of me, deep in the recesses of my addled brain, that wonders if I'm not being somehow conned. But I can't quite figure out, short con, long con, what the swindle would be.

"It's hard. This work."

"Hard truths can drive people apart. But great art can bring them back together."

I try desperately to repeat everything she's said in my mind so as not to forget. I will need to access all of it when I sit down with the manuscript again.

"Now," she says, standing and letting go of my hand, "I can't wait to see what you come up with, now that your shackles are removed."

"Yes, ma'am."

She collects my plate and I start to protest. "No, allow me. Please." I look around again for Joan.

Jackie brushes me aside and disappears into the kitchen, I can hear her setting dishes in the sink. Being here in her home makes everything simultaneously more normal and more surreal. A woman is doing dishes in her kitchen. *Normal.* Jackie O. just cleared my dinner plate. *Surreal.* I'm not sure which reality to plant myself in: Island resident shares local history; national treasure dispenses insight on writing. Either way, she seems much more human away from the heightened setting of New York.

"Oh, and one more piece of advice?" she calls out from the kitchen.

"What's that."

"Be like Fred Astaire."

"Romance Ginger Rogers?" I holler, confused.

Jackie pokes her head back into the dining room and raps her knuckles gently on the doorway. "Don't let the hard work show."

ELEVEN

When I return to the guesthouse, I pick up the phone and call Daniel collect. It takes four rings for him to answer and, while I'm sure he doesn't, it seems in my head that he pauses before accepting the charges.

The operator hangs up and we're alone. I listen to the electric hum for a moment, thinking there are secret messages in the static, and then I say, "Hi."

"Hi," he says back.

And then silence.

"We just had dinner. I thought I would call."

"Collect, I see. She's not springing for you to call home either?"

"I'm a guest. In someone's house."

"She must have really burned through that Onassis money."

I pull the receiver away from my ear and stare at it in annoyance before resuming the conversation. "Daniel. It felt like the right thing to do." I'm certain she would not have minded—I'm all but positive she wouldn't have even seen the bill—but there's an element of wanting to retain my privacy. She knows enough about me from the book.

"How's the house?" Daniel asks.

I pause and then, because it was such a perfect setup, say, "What. A. Dump." I swear I can hear him smile on the other end of the line. "Hey, what's that from?" Of course we both know what it's from: It's the opening of *Who's Afraid of Virginia Woolf?* We can quote the play endlessly to each other. I'm not really asking—that's literally the next line in the play. So I repeat it. *"Hey, what's that from?"*

"You want to do George and Martha now?"

"WHAT'S IT FROM, FOR CHRIST'S SAKE?"

Daniel laughs, for real this time, and all the tension between us melts.

"You expect me to remember *all* the pictures?" he says, finally playing along.

We don't ever remember the exact words, but we do our best to paraphrase. "Not every last epic . . ." I continue on about it being a Warner picture and Bette Davis having peritonitis. We both break into laughter and it feels good—erotic, even. This is the kind of phone sex we have, reciting Edward Albee. I debate pressing further, going on about Bette Davis trying to apply lipstick with her peritonitis and smearing it all over her face, but decide to quit while I'm ahead.

"It's nice, the house."

"I'm sure it is."

"Have you heard of a Nantucket sleigh ride?" It occurs to me Daniel might delight in this bit of trivia.

"No. Is that some kind of sex act? What are you two doing out there?"

"What? Oh my God. No."

"What is it, then?"

"I'll tell you when I get home. How was your day?"

Daniel sighs. I hate it when we're even slightly out of sync. Most of the time he makes perfect sense. Not just the words coming out of his mouth but how he feels in our house, how he fits in my life. It's so natural having him there, his presence often as unremarkable as my having a left arm. Only at times does such intimacy strike me as odd. Only late on restless nights do I lie awake wondering if he is some sort of pod person who might molt his human form and devour me. Only when he goes on one of his screeds about relationship constructs or the myth of monogamy or heteronormative paradigms am I tempted to rummage through all the pockets in his closet, through his books, looking for underlined passages and clues, through his bedside drawer for hidden pills that keep his alien lizard form from emerging. I think this paranoia stems from being my mother's son, the assumption that everyone is guarding secrets.

"I didn't get the gig. You know, the off-Broadway thing," he finally relents.

"No! You were perfect for that."

"Apparently not perfect enough."

I want to reach through the phone and hug him. "They will regret this. You'll see. The reviews will be terrible and they will pan the direction and the whole mess will close in previews."

"We don't have to dwell on it."

My heart breaks for him and I reflect back on our earlier argument. "You know how suddenly this happened for me?"

"The right opportunity will present itself, yeah, I know."

"It's true! Rosalind Carter could call you tomorrow to stage her life story."

"They already made a musical of *Peanuts*," he says glumly.

"Do you want to do more George and Martha? Bette Davis comes home from the grocery store?"

"Bette Davis is a grocer?" he replies, but our game fizzles.

We finish our conversation and say good night; when he hangs up I listen to the dead connection, where he somehow only seconds ago existed, and reluctantly set the phone back on its cradle. I'm not sure how we are and where we leave things. Better, I think, than before our call. Still, when I replay our conversation it's like watching a VCR tape when the tracking is just slightly off—our mouths are moving, but the picture sputters and the right words aren't coming through.

I walk outside. I'm instantly enchanted by the warm night breeze. It beckons me down the path toward the beach, and as soon as I get twenty feet from the house I regret not having a flashlight. When we were kids we would rent a camp in the Adirondack Mountains, and at night my dad would bring us down to the boat dock and we would lie on our backs, looking up at the stars. I'd never seen the night sky so bright.

"No light pollution," my father would say, as he set his camera on the tripod to try to take a long-exposure photo of the Milky Way.

It was the first time I ever heard anyone refer to light as pollution. It seemed antithetical to me, even then. A contaminant, maybe—even that was a stretch. But pollution? No flashlights were allowed then either. We could count only on guidance from the summer moon.

I creep past the pond, heel-to-toe, careful not to veer off the path. Twice I hear something rustling in the reeds and have to remind myself that there are no alligators in New England. This is only momentarily calming; I have no idea what other secret monsters the Vineyard harbors (or Jackie attracts). I pick up my pace until I feel the hard sand of the trail give way to the soft, cool grains of the beach. I realize only now I'm not wearing shoes. I take ten more steps and flop, exhausted, onto the sand. Not exhausted. Depleted.

The beach is dark in all directions. All I can really see is the bit of surf illuminated by a thin sliver of moonlight and a few flashing beacons out on the water to guide boats. If only they were there to offer me similar direction. On the far horizon creeps the faintest glow; or maybe it's my imagination. I'm facing south, away from Boston, so if my eyes haven't betrayed me it just might be the never-dimming lights of Manhattan.

Back at the house, I rinse my sandy feet in the tub and fetch the manuscript from my suitcase. I free the pages from the rubber bands that bind them together and lay the first chapter out on the bedspread in two rows of five pages. When I finish I lay the second chapter out page by page on the floor. On the far side of the bed there is just enough room for the third chapter, and so I lay chapters four and five down the hall. Chapter six runs down the stairs. Soon the entire book is laid out across the guesthouse. If Joan were to walk in here, she would think I'd gone mad, that I was no longer the collected, promising young author of a book but instead the crazed, eclectic scribbler of a manifesto.

Here it is, my mother in pieces. It's my job now to answer the questions, to put her back together. Not just to write beautiful prose, but to lay bare the naked truths of our relationship. Who am I. Who are you. How are these answers entwined? Seeing the manuscript laid out in this way, being able to walk from page to page, from beginning to end, I am suddenly able to see the book as a journey. One whose steps I need to retrace.

One whose end still needs illumination.

✦ TWELVE ✦

We sit on the front porch of the farmhouse, careful not to let the curls of peeling paint scrape our bare legs while a stiff night breeze shakes all the leaves in the trees, making them flutter like bats against the cobalt sky. It's spooky for an August night. Wind like this usually waits for the haunting chill of October, but we're grateful for it—both of us. The rustling trees fill the gaping silence.

"Fran," my mother starts.

"That didn't go . . ." I don't know how to finish this sentence. *Well? As planned?* How did I think it would go?

In the distance, crickets. You can just make them out in the shrieking wind, and I chuckle at both their literal and metaphorical presence. It strikes me how loud silence can be, or maybe it's the distant echo of my father's roaring disapproval. He's a quiet man, until he's not.

My mother stands up and walks into the house, the screen door slapping its wooden frame behind her. I'm stunned. Were we done? Was this over? Did she walk away just as my father had? The driveway looks queer, so empty at night without my father's sedan. Where did he go? Is he coming back? There's a pressure in my chest, a deep weight that's compressing my lungs into my diaphragm, slowly draining them of air. Is it possible to have a heart attack at seventeen? I try to breathe deeply, to return my lungs to their original size, but it feels like I'm a noodle-armed weakling wielding a mallet, trying in vain to win a prize in a carnival strongman game while onlookers stare and laugh. Watching the weight approach the bell but never able to make it ding. How did this happen? Why did I push? Why was any of this so important to me? Why did I want so desperately to ring a goddamn bell? To prove that I'm a man while declaring myself, in my father's eyes, at least, unmanly? I've lost all sense of self.

The screen slams again, sharply announcing my mother's return. She holds two open bottles of beer and hands one to me as she retakes her seat. The bottle is cold in my hand. It stings; the sensation is welcome, but is this something we do? I slap a mosquito away from my neck and then massage the skin where Scott's lips had just hours ago been, before we were interrupted by my mother—the catalyst for this whole chain of events. She would never have said anything to my father, but I didn't want her to have to live my growing lie, and I didn't want to avoid her gaze for the foreseeable future not talking about something we both already knew.

"I thought we could both use it," she says indicating her beer, before taking several sips.

"Aren't you worried about the message this sends your under-age son?"

She gives this some genuine thought as we watch an unfortunate insect meet the bug zapper. "I don't worry about you."

This is, of course, a lie. I am the baby. On top of that, a mama's boy. All she does is worry about me. And tonight I've given her a thousand new reasons.

I clink the neck of her bottle with mine, the way I've seen adults do, before taking a long, malty sip. I let it roll around in my mouth before swallowing. I've had beer before, at Sabrina Holcumb's party and such, but—I don't know—only when it was an adrenaline rush. Not when I've given any thought to how it fits with my palate. The bitter aftertaste reminds me of the way the neighbor's horse's saddle blanket used to smell when I was allowed to brush him.

My mother starts and then stops. "Your father . . ." What is there really to say? "It's probably all my fault."

"Don't do that."

"What?"

"Make excuses."

"He thinks I raised you to be too . . ." She struggles with the words and I want to help her find just the right one but I don't. She picks at the label on her bottle until it's peeling just like the paint on the steps. "How do you know, Fran. I mean, how do you know for sure?"

I think about the weight of Scott as he laid on top of me. The taste of Scott. How his breath felt against my collarbone. How alive I felt and how I might have exploded, literally burst into a quadrillion particles of nothingness had my mother not interrupted us. But how to put any of that in words. "You just know."

My mother shakes her head. Not in denial, but in acknowledgment that she doesn't understand how the world works. Yet, unlike my father, in this instance she doesn't seem scared by what she doesn't know. For this I want to reward her.

"Do you know how I learned you were beautiful?" I ask.

My mother laughs and puts her bottle down. "You had to learn?" She jokes like this to mask her shock—I'm not sure that I've ever called her beautiful out loud.

"Well . . . yeah, I had to learn."

Silence. And then curiosity gets the best of her. "How did you learn?"

"Do you know the way scientists discover new planets? Extrasolar planets?"

"Extrasolar . . . ?"

"Planets that are too far away to see."

She looks at me, befuddled.

"Astronomers look for distortions in the gravity fields of larger objects nearby they *can* see."

"How do you know this?"

"Because I read. Anyway, that's how I learned. I couldn't see you were beautiful myself, not at first, you were my mother. But I came to recognize the way other people behaved around you. The way they fawned or tripped over themselves just a bit. A distortion in the field."

My mother does her best to take this in, but even I know it's a lot to process, so we sit and wait for a large gust of wind to die.

"It's kind of like that. Tonight. How I'm sure. On some level I've

always known, but it was confirmed by others around me." I wonder
if she understands what I'm getting at, but in truth I'm not entirely
sure I understand it myself. Scott, for one. The other boys in my class,
the meaner ones, who somehow had the magic ability to see who I
was before I even could. The girls who were my friends, who took me
in as one of their own. Even my mother herself, who understood on
some level I was delicate and called me by an equally delicate name.

"You're almost grown, Fran."

I stare at my bottle and wonder why she says "almost." Didn't she
just hand me a beer? Shouldn't the way I held my ground against my
father suggest I had fully become a man?

"And?"

"But," my mother corrects; she abandons the rest of her thought
to the prevailing silence.

"Do you love him?" I ask.

"Your father?" Without thinking she says, "I chose him."

What an odd non-answer. What does it mean? Chose him when?
Chose him for what? Over whom?

It is only then that I notice the faint sounds of The Carpenters'
"(They Long to Be) Close to You" coming from the record player.

"They're playing our song," I say to my mother.

She leans in and brushes my shoulder with her own. "I put the
record on when I went inside."

I have the urge to cry because it's clear to me now that the most
beautiful things in life are also the most fragile. Like Karen Carpen-
ter, a girl drummer with a voice that sounded like pale blue light. I
look over at the empty driveway. My father stormed out. Maybe for
good. Do I want to cry for that? Or the fear that my mother may
disappear next?

"Fran. There are things you don't understand."

I turn and glare at her, angry at first, as if she's telling me I don't
know myself, or that the proclamation I made tonight is not true. But
I can tell by the way her head is turned, slightly down, slightly away,

that if I'm not understanding something it is through no fault of my own. "What do you mean?"

"I wouldn't know where to begin," she says. "It's not your fault."

With the right amount of teenage bluster I announce, "I didn't think it was." I sit there and stew in the lie.

"It's not your fault," she repeats, because she always knows when I'm lying. "There are things you need to know."

I'm not certain I want to know what she has to say, but tonight I am not backing down. "Tell me."

"Not tonight." She puts the beer bottle to her mouth and seems to consume half of it. When she sets it down she says, "I'm afraid for you."

"Because of Dad?"

"I'm afraid that you won't be happy."

"I'm afraid none of us will." I don't really know what I mean by that, other than the world feels like a scary place. And even if the country didn't have its own problems, there are plenty of people hell-bent on making life miserable for people like me. I take a long sip of beer, tilting my head back to let the ale slide straight down my throat. "I'm scared," I say, but I'm not sure exactly what I'm scared of. Of growing up, I guess. Of leaving home, of leaving my mother, of having to stop being Francis. Of having to become James.

My mother brushes the hair off my forehead. "You remind me of someone."

I look up at her expectantly, the way a young child might, wanting his mother to fix the world and take all of his pain away. "Who?"

"Someone," she says, as if that's any kind of answer. But in some weird way it is.

I am someone indeed.

• THIRTEEN •

When morning comes, I send word to Jackie through Joan that I found inspiration in the night and ask, if it's all the same to her, could I spend the day working; Joan returns with a fruit plate, a buttered English muffin, a pitcher of coffee, and a message from Jackie that that would indeed be fine. I don't open the door any wider than I have to for Joan; I don't want her to see the mess I've made with the manuscript and lecture me again on being familiar. Also I'm worried about the tornado of pages that could result from even a mild dawning breeze. I pound cup after cup of coffee, trying my best to recall every detail from a different time, every oddity, to tug at every emotional thread. I pause when working on chapter three—something about the father in this part doesn't sit right.

I catch a glimpse of Jackie from my bedroom window. She glides across the lawn dressed in a floral silk robe and yellow bathing cap, carrying a towel and a little white jar. When she reaches the pond she drops the robe to reveal a simple black one-piece bathing suit. It's hard to see her every move from this distance, but she appears to open the jar and slather its contents carefully on her arms, then legs. Lotion? Sunscreen? Cold cream, perhaps. As always, she's so graceful in this task, like an egret walking the saltmarsh, I wonder if this is not a daily routine. I admire her poise even when she thinks no one is watching. Or maybe it's instinctual for her to think that someone is *always* watching. When she's finished, she tests the water with her toes before slowly disappearing into the pond's depths. I watch her bathing cap bob along the surface of the murky water for a few minutes before I break myself from my trance and return my attention to writing.

At one o'clock I open my front door and there is Joan, as if on cue, holding a tray of charcuterie. The incoming sunlight bifurcates my work in two.

"Jesus, you scared me."

"Compliments of you-know-who."

I crane my neck around the corner of the house to perhaps see if you-know-who is near, just as Joan snakes her head around me, trying to get a sense of what exactly I'm doing inside. I see no sign of Jackie; she's either still in the pond or back in the main house. "Thank you, both."

As politely as I can, I close the door.

After lunch, I flag down Joan as she's plucking weeds from a flowerbed and ask to borrow the bicycle on the front porch; I'm in desperate need of fresh air. I pedal unfamiliar roads with purpose, as if they will cudgel my brain. Instead of bringing clarity to my work, the mental break from my own family provides the opportunity to daydream about belonging to another. The wind in my face and the way my hair sweeps first across my forehead and then back, coupled with my aviator sunglasses, makes me feel positively Kennedyesque. This fantasy is a trap, of course, but one I can't help but indulge; I sit even higher on the bicycle seat and pedal a good quarter-mile without holding the handlebars.

When I stumble upon the Chilmark Public Library, I go inside and look up books on Jackie's life on the Vineyard; they have several on the shelves, including a book with high-gloss photos that capture my imagination. I'm particularly taken with one snapshot where she is holding hands with her children. After an hour of this I'm overtaken with a sense of profound shame. *What am I doing?* Simply coming here is a betrayal of sorts; now I'm exacerbating my own disloyalty by, what, comparing two incomparable women and letting one come up short? These children in the photo are not me. There are no answers here. I put the books back on the shelf and bicycle furiously around the island, getting lost and finding my way back again.

At around five o'clock I fall asleep splayed out over chapter nine—I wake up with one of the pages cemented to my cheek and another partially crumpled under my hip. I open the cabinets in the kitchen and find an open bottle of scotch, pour myself a healthy slug, and eat three small triangles of bread from the charcuterie plate that have dried into makeshift toast points. I turn on a few scattered lamps and work for another hour.

At seven I call a taxi, then ring the house to tell Joan that I'm going out for a bit. I'm not sure this is allowed—am I imprisoned here?—so I ask if she needs anything from town; she seems to brighten from my consideration and tells me that she's fine and it's just as well, as Jackie is not feeling quite herself. I can tell Joan is relieved that I'm fending for myself instead of her awkwardly having to entertain me or fix me a meal. I walk up to the main road and wait for the taxi there. I ask the driver about restaurants in town and he says the Outermost Inn is local and nice. I like the clever wordplay as well as his description and tell him to take me there; he warns me that in the summer you often need reservations weeks in advance, but there is another tavern that I could get into, no problem, and it's within walking distance from the inn. I direct him to the Outermost anyway, deciding to take my chances.

The inn is a rustic estate with weathered clapboard siding and white trim, and the soft light from inside looks welcoming. I do my best to charm the host, but indeed they are booked up for the night. I ask if I can sit at the bar, but he is not able to accommodate. He too suggests the tavern down the road. I'm tempted to ask if he can make an exception for a guest of Mrs. Onassis, but I immediately think better of it. He says I can have a drink in the bar area, but there's no seating, so he won't be able to serve me food. I enjoy a scotch and soda while standing among better-dressed parties waiting for their tables and listen to snippets of people's conversations. I smile as patrons pass by me, unable to successfully engage with anyone except to exchange a few pleasantries. I leave the inn reluctantly; a woman near the exit is eating a bowl of mussels in a white wine sauce and it looks exactly like what I am craving.

The road is gravelly, and there are very few cars. I can hear the pounding of the ocean surf, but I can't see the water over the tall dune grass. My path is lit from the three-quarter moon and the occasional streetlamp, and the very last bits of sunlight on the western horizon. It's quiet, other than the surf; the cawing gulls must be done scavenging for the night and have gone wherever they go.

The tavern is a short walk, and it too is a welcoming oasis, but in a rowdier fashion than the inn; I can hear the guests erupt in laughter from a good distance. Inside, the place is lit somewhere between dim and bright, and the entire reddish wood interior is covered in framed black-and-white photos of the tavern and the island from the 1960s and 1970s, all hung slightly askew. A waitress tells me to sit anywhere I like, and while there are a few open tables, I take a seat at the bar; sitting alone at a table feels conspicuous. The menu doesn't have mussels with white wine sauce; in fact, there's not much of a wine menu at all (unless you count RED or WHITE as a menu), so I order a fried clam plate and a draft beer. I figure the opposite direction is the best way to go.

"You visitin'?"

"Pardon?" I turn to the woman next to me. She's a hard forty, dressed in a short denim skirt and magenta tee with some sort of ruffled cap sleeve and brown boots boasting embroidery. She sits with her legs crossed, sipping a bottle of local beer, looking like an extra in a movie—a Hollywood version of what a local might look like.

"You vis-it-tin'." She says it slow, like I'm hard of hearing.

"Yes. From New York."

"I could tell. Next time get the lobstuh roll. It's bettah than the cla-yums."

The bartender slides a pint of beer toward me and I raise it in a toast. "James."

"Deb." She taps my glass with her bottle. "You stayin' in Gay Head?"

I choke on my first sip of beer. How do people ever get used to saying that? "With some friends," I answer, deciding to count Joan as more than an acquaintance. "How about you. Here year-round?"

Deb nods. "Up island." She points heavenward, a direction I'm guessing she thinks is north. "Eighth generation."

"What's that like?"

"Uncomplicated." She smiles; her teeth are a smoker's and there are deep crow's feet around her eyes. "No, I like it. It gets quiet in the wintah. I do odd jobs. Make ends meet. In the summah it's easy-ah."

I nod and focus on my beer. "Seems like a good place to be from."

"Why, you from the city originally?"

"New York, but upstate." I point at the ceiling for emphasis.

Deb shrugs. "What brings you here?"

I think about that. Directly, a cab and then my own two feet. Indirectly? "I don't know. I guess I'm a little bit lost."

She looks at me suspiciously. Didn't I just say I was staying in Gay Head? How lost could I be? "That's what's good about living on an island. Few-ah wrong turns you can make. Eventually you always hit the ocean."

It's both comforting and frustrating how literal she is. "Not lost, lost. I guess I mean . . . I feel a little out of place in the world."

She lets that sink in while taking a swig of beer. "You and everybody else."

"I guess." *Does everyone else feel that way?* I can hear Jackie making an editorial note if she were to read a transcript of this scene: OVER-DRAMATIZING. I think about what I mean and how best to express it, then the silence grows awkward and I decide to change the subject. "You ever seen anyone famous?"

"You mean like a Kennedy?"

I laugh nervously, like she's on to me. But I guess on Martha's Vineyard, *Kennedy* is the go-to name.

"That's what everyone wants to know," she says. "You tourists are all alike."

"I'll bet," I say, just to play along.

There's a long pause. The bartender appears with a cardboard plate of fried clams, french fries, a mound of coleslaw with a crinkle-cut pickle slice balanced on top, and a dinner roll. He drops it down in front of me.

"That was fast," Deb comments. "You even fry that up fresh for 'im?" she yells at the bartender, who turns and playfully gives her the finger.

"It's okay," I say. "I'm so hungry I'd eat anything." The smell of seafood and grease is nearly intoxicating. I stab a few of the clam bellies with a plastic fork, and indeed, in this moment, they taste as good as anything I've ever had.

"Yeah, I seen 'em," Deb says. "Kennedys. John Junior once and a bunch of the cousins. Jackie shops at Alley's. I seen her there once or twice."

"What's that like?" I'm further taken with the idea of Jackie as a local, as a mere mortal. *She washes her dishes* and *grocery-shops, too?*

"You a reportah?" Deb is suddenly on the defensive and looks me over for telltale signs like a notebook or a hat with a press card.

"No. Nothing like that." Although *something* like that.

"People leave her be. It's just sort of the island way. She's been through enough, you know." Deb thinks about this while she kills her bottled beer. She gestures for the bartender to bring her another, before looking at me and deciding I need another one as well.

"It's on me, though," I tell her, and she salutes me in response. It's the least I can do for her company, which I feel a sudden urgent need for.

"I think that's why they like it here. People leave 'em be."

I study my dinner companion. I used to think my mother was Jackie's opposite and wondered how Jackie could possibly look at her and recognize any of herself. But the simple truth is, my mother and Jackie are in many ways alike. Deb is the true anti-Jackie. I use the pause in conversation while we wait for our beer to shovel more clams in my mouth. When the bartender returns with our beer, Deb squeals like a delighted weasel.

"Did you want me to have a french fry?" she asks, popping one in her mouth without waiting for my reply.

I laugh while she chews. And then I laugh again, trying to imagine Jackie doing the same, inviting herself to eat off someone else's plate. *"Did you want me to have a haricot vert?"*

"Oprah. Oprah was here."

"Here?" I ask, pointing at the floor to indicate the tavern.

Deb looks at me like I have three heads. "No. On the island. I ain't seen her though. Just heard that she was."

"That's a good one. Sighting, I mean."

"Yeah, but I didn't see her."

"Still," I say.

"Why you so interested? You probably see famous people all the time in New Yawk." Deb immediately turns her attention to a man eyeing the jukebox.

I do see plenty of famous people in New York. Harrison Ford waiting to cross a street in the West Village. Gene Hackman entering the Brooks Atkinson, where he was starring in *Death and the Maiden*, and similarly Alec Baldwin in Times Square following a performance of *A Streetcar Named Desire*. Jerry Orbach at a liquor store on Ninth Avenue. All kinds of people, all kinds of names. Even Jackie doesn't seem out of place. But I'm fascinated by her existence outside of Manhattan, how she maneuvers in a world of Debs, how she negotiates her way around us normals. Maybe that's a kinship Jackie feels with my mother—or at least Ruth Mulligan, the woman she knows from the pages of my book. A woman who tiptoes outside with trepidation, not because paparazzi are lurking but because she is uncomfortable being noticed at all.

I'm not quite sure what to say, so I just mutter a simple truth. "New York is different."

Deb sips from her longneck, and after a moment of contemplation says, "You said a mouthful." It's as if she's remembering a particularly distasteful trip where she had her purse stolen stepping off a bus at

Port Authority before being forced to sit through a matinee of *Cats* and watch the Red Sox lose at Yankee Stadium.

I finish my clams; the last few are room temperature but still tasty on a summer's night. Deb asks me what I'm doing with my time on the island. I almost say "Working," but I know that will invite more questions than I want to answer, so instead I say, "Kicking around."

"You should drive out to Chappy, see the east side of the island."

"Oh, yeah?" I assume she means Chappaquiddick.

"Yeah. While you're ovah there you should stop at Mad Martha's for ice cream. Bring your friends you're staying with so you can get the Pig's Delight. It's twelve scoops and tons a toppin's."

I laugh. The image of Jackie, Joan, and myself attacking the Pig's Delight with three plastic spoons is delightful. "We'll see. I'm not sure my friends would eat all that."

"Your call. Fun though. I used to scoop summahs there when I was young."

It's only now that I wonder if Deb is maybe hitting on me. If she is, she's getting the hint that I'm helplessly oblivious.

"You want any more fries?" I offer. "I'm not going to finish them."

"Nah. Soggy now anyways," she says. "I'm gonna go put somethin' on the juke." She places her hand on mine and leans in for a last word. "Enjoy the island. If you ever feel lost, just take a right."

Just take a right. It's so simple it's almost profound. I settle the check with the bartender and thank Deb for her company.

"Catch you around, *tourist*."

I try one last limp fry, then push my plate back so I won't eat any more. I swivel my barstool to study the tavern's other diners, or, more aptly, drinkers. It's an entirely different crowd than the Outermost's— everyone looks like they're having genuine fun. Before I decide to leave, I scan the room for Deb and find her in the middle of the dance floor by herself, swaying to the music. I watch her for a minute. She's clumsy, slightly off the beat, tripping over boots that are perhaps too big for her. No one else is watching.

As I head for the door I make out her distinctive squeal when her song comes on the jukebox, but it's not until I'm in the parking lot that I recognize it as Billy Joel's "We Didn't Start the Fire."

JFK

BLOWN AWAY

WHAT ELSE DO I HAVE TO SAY?

❖ FOURTEEN ❖

Joan arrives with breakfast again, this time with an invitation to the main house for dinner, which I eagerly accept.

"How was last night?" she asks.

"Good. Fun. I tried to get into the Outermost Inn."

Joan scoffs, at me or at the inn, I'm not sure.

"I ended up at the tavern down the road."

"Did you get the lobster roll?"

"Clams."

"You should get the lobster roll next time."

"So I hear."

I ask how Jackie's feeling, to make sure that she's up for seeing me. Joan looks over her shoulder and then leans in, as if trading a state secret.

"She's fine. They had a tribute last night on the teevee. For Bobby."

"The Convention." I groan, having completely forgotten that the Democratic National Convention was unspooling at Madison Square Garden back home. I want to kick myself for being so obtuse.

"I think she wanted to watch it alone." It means a lot that Joan is starting to trust me. I haven't really seen her interact with Jackie and I know nothing about her life; is it too much of an assumption to think that Joan gets lonely?

"I'm surprised Mrs. Onassis wasn't invited."

She cocks an eye as if I'm the dumbest man on the planet.

"Of course she was invited," I correct myself.

"Probably why she's here, so she could say honestly she'd be out of town." It's so obvious to me now: She's a prop they would trot out for the entire party, the entire country, to fawn over.

"Dinner, then," I say, setting the tray down so I can close the door. "Thank you."

Over melon and scones, I give thought to my mother as a young woman. Who she was, what she wanted—before she was a parent. The resulting image is both a gorge and a bridge; I feel closer to understanding her heart, while other, tangential mysteries deepen and feel unsolvable. When lost, I hear Deb's words: *Take a right.* I'm not sure it helps; there's something just out of reach.

At eleven-fifteen, I catch a glimpse of Jackie's yellow bathing cap bobbing across the Squibnocket. In the grass beside the path I can make out her robe and the jar of cream, and I start to get a real sense of ritual. This time I don't watch for long; it's her practice, not mine.

I nap in the midafternoon. At five I shower and dress in the other nice outfit I packed and cross the driveway to the main house. The sound of the gravel under my feet sounds much like my father crunching the ice cubes from his empty scotch glass. It's a rare thought of him, and it catches me off guard.

"James?" I hear Jackie call my name before I'm even on the porch. "Good evening."

"You're right on time," she says, and waves me in.

I enter the house, gently closing the screen door behind me.

"I was hoping you'd join me in a cocktail."

"I would never say no to that." Sitting on a silver tray on the sideboard are two double old-fashioned glasses filled with a light cranberry drink and garnished with lime wheels. It seems she is definitely in the mood for company again. "No daiquiris?"

Jackie hands me a glass. "When in Rome."

"Cape Cods."

She raises her drink in my direction. "I hear you've been keeping busy."

"Yes. Writing. Rewriting. I have to thank you for inviting me here. To the island. The change of scenery has given me fresh perspective."

"This place has always had a similar effect on me."

"I can see why." I make an all-encompassing gesture, taking it all in.

"I'll be excited to see your new draft," she says.

"I'll be excited to see it too." I chuckle. A change in scenery doesn't guarantee me an ending; I'm waiting on a bit of writerly magic.

"These are the moments, helping writers find their inspiration, that I find so rewarding as an editor."

"Is that why you got into publishing?"

"One of the reasons."

"I think a lot of people wonder."

"Do they?" Jackie seems genuinely surprised.

I follow her to the living room, which has a large picture window that overlooks the pond. The chair where I sit is comfortable and white, as is most of the rest of the seating. The coffee table looks like it's assembled from the timbers of old ships, perhaps here on the island. The rug is a faded yellow with a simple stripe. The room is unfussy, and yet I'm very aware of not spilling my cranberry drink.

"I suppose people speculate on how it's fashionable for wealthy women to work, or for working women to be wealthy. I've heard it all."

"What do you say? To the naysayers. If you don't mind me asking."

Jackie holds her glass to her lips without taking a sip. "I don't say anything at all."

She seems entirely at home. Relaxed. Her hair is pinned on one side, away from her face, as if she were caught halfway through doing it. The light of this magic hour gives her a pinkish, youthful glow.

"I have a question," she says, changing the topic. "Have you given thought to the book's cover?"

"I know I have my ideas, and I'm also curious what your art department will come up with." I tuck one leg under me, careful not to touch the chair with my shoe.

"I'm very interested in design, as you may have surmised. Especially the design of my books. I can spend hours on the smallest details. The look of a book is very important, I think." And then sheepishly she adds, "It can drive some of my coworkers mad."

"I suppose it could."

"But I've found the only way to be happy in life is to love and be good at your work. Don't you agree?"

I look down at my drink, struggling with what she is saying. If I pull my punches to protect my mother, or go out of my way to avoid telling the story that I want, I'm not being good at my work. If I'm not good at my work, I won't ever be happy. My eyes sting, from the ocean air or holding back tears I'm not sure. "I just want to write. It's all I've ever wanted to do." I pause to chew on my lip. "How did things get this complicated?" A gust of wind rattles the window and I hope that query is lost in the bluster.

"I had a thought last night."

"Tell me." I'm desperate still for any more guidance.

"When's the last time you've seen your mother?"

The question catches me off guard. "In person?"

Jackie nods.

"I don't know. Last fall? It's been a while." It's only when I say it out loud that I realize how awful it sounds. But in refusing to read the book, it feels like she's the one closing the door on knowing me as I am now. How are we supposed to sit down and share a meal?

"I think you should go home, James."

"I just . . ." I stop and look out the window. How do I respond without sounding callous? "I don't know what that would accomplish."

Jackie sets her drink down on a coaster and turns in my direction. I can feel her eyes on me, waiting for me to look back at her. She doesn't speak until she knows she has my full attention. "Every mother has a story."

I feel myself chewing on my thumbnail but make no effort to stop.

"Ask her about hers. You don't have to use it. Just listen. Let her talk, and listen. I wouldn't be surprised if the ending you're looking for is somehow in there."

I nod and look at my lap. I think I've known this all along. The block in my writing is directly related to the block in my relationship with my mother. The characters are stalled, because the two of us are on hold. But a trip home requires real thought. And as grateful as I am for advice, I'm ready to move the topic off me. "I still think you should write. Your story. The things you've seen. People would be very interested."

"Oh, I would never waste time writing such things when there are beaches to be walked."

"Do you think of your obligation to history?"

I mean it only as a question, but it sits between us as an accusation and the room stands perfectly still. Or maybe my meaning is more pointed; I feel pushed and it's a clumsy attempt to push back. Either way, I think furiously how to backpedal—whether to outright apologize or try to pass it off as teasing. Just as I'm about to take the question back entirely, she answers. "I believe I've filled my obligation to history."

Dinner is salmon, wild rice, and Brussels sprouts (*choux de Bruxelles*). Everything is delicious, if portioned a bit small. I already know I'm going to have to forage for a late-night snack.

Our conversation remains thankfully light; we discuss our favorite books. "*East of Eden*," I say without hesitation. I explain how it's a book I relate to endlessly, even if the California dustbowl is a far cry from my own roots in rural New York. I'm fascinated, like Steinbeck, by the subtle differences in meaning words can have, in this case the Hebrew word *Timshel*, which, while thought to have meant *thou shall*, when retranslated in Steinbeck's novel by Chinese scholars comes to mean *thou mayest*. In that slight difference—destiny vs. free will—exists the fate of all mankind. "What about you?"

"Oh, I have many. *Gone with the Wind* when I was a girl. Now? It depends on what day you ask. I suppose today, Jean Rhys's *Wide Sargasso Sea*."

"That was conceived as a sequel, of sorts, to Brontë?"

"A prequel, actually, to *Jane Eyre*."

I can recall the basics of the plot, a woman loving a domineering man, but not all of the shading. "I read it in college. I'm trying to remember the particulars."

Jackie lifts one shoulder and looks just past me, deciding how much to share. It's obvious to me that this is about as intimate a conversation as one could hope to have with her, and I can almost see Joan warming up on the sidelines, ready to pounce. "It's about, in part, the unequal power between men and women. Especially in marriage."

I'm dying to know which of her relationships the book evokes. Since the Sargasso Sea itself takes up a great swath of the North Atlantic, perhaps the novel bridges both marriages, just as the Atlantic connects North America with Europe, the two continents of her unions. I'll have to look up when the book was published to see if that lends a further clue.

"Do you have a someone?"

I place my fork gently on my plate and pause for a moment in uncertainty. I assume she knows I'm gay; the narrator of my book is not actively heterosexual, and I'm hardly the spitting image of a quarterback. But to say so out loud is like coming out to my mother all over again—I'm the scared teenager sitting on a front porch. Yet I am an adult and there's no avoiding a direct question, potentially making a fool of a woman who has shown me nothing but grace.

"I'm prying," she says apologetically.

"No, not at all. I have a Daniel."

I look for a reaction, but she doesn't blink. "Is he handsome?"

"He is."

"Is he kind?"

"He is."

Jackie twirls her hair with her index finger and swallows the last of her wine. "Well, you know what I always say. Never marry, never mix your money."

I laugh, and this time, with all apologies to Joan, I just can't hold it in. "Says the woman who married twice, once to the world's richest man." It's the boldest thing I've ever said to her and I hold my breath as Jackie considers this charge.

"The other time to the world's most powerful. Don't you forget that." She rises from her chair, picks up a folded newspaper from the sideboard, and swats me across the back of the head. "Come along, smarty-pants."

"Should I clear these?" I ask, indicating the dishes.

"Leave them." She is already gone.

I hear the television, and when I reach the living room Jackie has resumed her seat on the couch. She tucks her legs beside her, propping herself against the right arm of the sofa, sitting not unlike the famous Little Mermaid statue in Copenhagen. It's the last night of the Democratic Convention and Al Gore is making an impassioned plea to Perot voters to remain involved (and presumably vote for the Democratic ticket), despite their candidate dropping out of the race.

"He looks so young," Jackie says wistfully.

"Mmm-hmm." I wonder if she realizes that part of the appeal of youth, of this ticket, is the throwback to her and her husband. Does she look at old photos of herself in the White House and think the same thing? Was she even thirty when she became the First Lady? Was she no longer young when she did? Or was she forever young until a fateful day one November, when a whole country seemed to age overnight.

Al Gore finishes his speech and there is brass music, but where it comes from I don't know. People clap in unison and wave CLINTON/GORE signs. Tipper appears onstage in a royal blue dress and, while I'm not certain, I think I see Jackie cringe. The Gores kiss and wave and they cut to Hillary Clinton in the crowd, who's so obviously ready for the warm-up act to step out of the spotlight that she might race backstage to yank them with an old-timey vaudeville hook.

Newscasters speak in voiceover about Gore's résumé, and their thoughts on the effectiveness of the speech. And then conversation turns to Bill Clinton and soon a biographical video starts to play across the screen.

"Have you met him?" I ask.

"Bill Clinton?"

A photo of Clinton shaking John Kennedy's hand as part of some boy's curriculum for future leaders splashes across the screen. It was smart of the campaign to include it. To tie Clinton and JFK together.

"Apparently, I met him in the Rose Garden."

"Have you met him *recently*," I clarify.

"Oh, yes."

I can picture him now, as someone who idolized her husband, much as my family did, coming to her to seek her blessing, to kiss the ring as if she were an imposing godfather. I'm watching this pageant with someone who still holds incredible sway over Democratic politics, and I imagine it's for other men, straighter men, like watching the World Series with . . . ? I don't even know how to finish that comparison. It's like watching the Academy Awards with Katharine Hepburn. Straight men will just have to extrapolate.

"Do you like him?"

"Do *you* like him?" Jackie lobs the question right back at me.

"I do," I admit, hoping against hope this is not a wrong answer.

We watch the video for few minutes more before Jackie says, "I've papered his war chest on several occasions."

I look up at Jackie with a curious expression.

"That's not a euphemism!" she protests, when she reads my face. Then she laughs. "Well, I guess it is for giving him money. But not for anything else."

When the video fades, Bill Clinton appears onstage and gets a rock star's reception.

"He's a natural," I say.

"A little too natural."

I know she's heard the rumors of infidelity, they addressed them on *60 Minutes*. I puzzle over how much of her first husband she sees, why she chose to support him, and how much she sympathizes with Hillary. Whereas she suffered indignities in silence, the Clintons give joint interviews—the job of political good wife now even harder.

We sit silently for most of the speech and I move only once to adjust myself in the chair. At times I want to cut in with a comment or an observation, but Jackie is watching the television screen with such scrutiny that I don't dare interject. Is she as taken with Clinton the man? Clinton the politician? Is she mournfully lost in the memory of seeing her own husband on such a stage, remembering the night he himself became the Democratic nominee? I study her Little Mermaid and I see her desperately wanting to live in another world too. Not at Madison Square Garden, but in a parallel world where the promise of Jack and Bobby was fully realized.

About two-thirds of the way through the speech, I hear Clinton say, *"Them, the minorities. Them, the liberals. Them, the poor. Them, the homeless. Them, the people with disabilities. Them, the gays."*

I sit straight up in my seat. Did he say "gay"? "The gays"? Has a presidential candidate ever acknowledged gay people in such a prominent way? I lean forward, resting my chin on my hands, listening intently as Clinton continues.

"We've gotten to where we've nearly them'ed ourselves to death. Them, and them, and them. But this is America. There is no them. There is only us."

"YES." I say it out loud, and for the first time Jackie turns to me. Just when I think I might be in trouble for speaking out of turn, she raises an eyebrow and nods as if to say *not bad*.

"One nation, under God, indivisible, with liberty and justice for all."

"This is good," Jackie says, and then we're silent again until the very end of the speech when Clinton name-checks John Kennedy. Not heavy-handedly—in fact, it's quite graceful. *"As a teenager, I heard John Kennedy's summons to citizenship."*

I keep Jackie in my peripheral vision, imagining the looks she endures when much of the history she witnessed—or made—is mentioned.

"That America was the greatest nation in history because our people had always believed in two things—that tomorrow can be better

than today and that every one of us has a personal moral responsibility to make it so."

The speech crescendos with a call and response and I know that it's coming to a close. Or it would be if I were writing it; no writer worth his salt would put a rejoinder in the middle. Clinton pauses and bites his lower lip. Where most politicians would be relieved that such a task is behind them, there's a twinkle in his eye that suggests he's almost sad it's done. That he doesn't want to deliver the last line, that he doesn't want it to end. Fortunately for him, and I believe for us, it's hard to imagine this is the tail end of his time in the spotlight.

"My fellow Americans, I end tonight where it all began for me—I still believe in a place called Hope. God bless you, and God bless America."

The auditorium goes wild and balloons fall, and Hillary appears onstage, followed a moment later by their daughter, Chelsea, and the Gores, and then, belatedly, the Gore children too. Fleetwood Mac roars through the hall as the opening chords of "Don't Stop" start to play. The crowd is eating it up and there's confetti and signs and straw hats—where do people who aren't in Dixieland bands get so many straw hats?

"Well," Jackie says, "that about does it."

"What did you think?"

Jackie struggles for something to do with her hands in one of the only moments I've seen her appear inelegant. "I think the country belongs to your generation now."

I try to take that in. The baton being passed. The mantle of responsibility.

Maybe it's adrenaline from hearing a soaring speech, or from being here; for the first time in a long time I feel ready for what lies ahead. Even if that means facing my mother again and making peace with what keeps us apart, whether or not we can heal it.

To do that, I have to go home.

I watch as Jackie swings her feet to the floor and then rises to turn off the television. "I'm going to get us both some sherbet."

Lost in thought, I realize she's already out of the room before I can speak. "That sounds delicious!"

There's a gentle, constant sadness she exudes, but I find it comforting. Familiar. Here is a woman who in some of this country's darkest hours taught a nation how to mourn. But being here with her now, listening to her rummage in the freezer for frozen dessert, I wonder if she herself ever fully healed.

Yesterday's Gone, Yesterday's Gone

November 1992

• FIFTEEN •

In a scene straight out of a movie, I race across Fifty-Third Street toward Fifth Avenue from the copy place near my house to get my completed manuscript to Jackie before Doubleday closes for Thanksgiving. It wasn't my plan to cut things this tight, but the copy place had a toner issue (whatever that means) and it took twice as long for me to print. And then the register tape jammed, so I finally just threw cash down on the counter and told them to keep the change. A casual observer would diagnose me suicidal the way I'm racing through city streets at dusk; when I can't plow into traffic without facing certain death, I jog in place like a runner who doesn't want his heart rate to slow while waiting for the light to change. I make it most of the way in one piece before skidding on a jettisoned museum map outside of MoMA like it's a discarded banana peel.

When I reach the building, my trailing scarf gets caught in the revolving door, and for a flickering second I imagine suffering the fate of that dancer from the 1920s (what was her name?) whose scarf caught in the open spokes of her car's rear wheel. I can picture myself crumpled on the floor between revolving glass door partitions, manuscript pages raining down on me like prize money inside the cash booth on *Beat the Clock*. (*Isadora Duncan!* That was her name.) But the door plows forward and so do I and before I know it I'm in the lobby, making awkward eye contact with the security guard who would have been tasked with retrieving my strangulated body. I sign in, the same as I've done maybe a half-dozen times over the past few months, and catch an elevator to the Doubleday floor just as someone is exiting.

The receptionist is packing up and I wave and say, "Happy Thanksgiving."

"Big plans?" she asks.

"Going h-home." The word gets caught in my throat. "You?"

"Same. Enjoy!" She waves me through and points the way, even though she knows I know where I'm going. *Enjoy!* I laugh to myself; if only a trip home were that carefree. I proceed down the hall with the cubicles and the framed covers, doing this weird trot that's faster than a walk but slower than a run, bank a right at the conference room, and proceed directly to Jackie's office. Her door is closed, but her assistant, Mark, is sitting at his desk in the hall.

"She in?"

"James." He smiles at me and I'm confronted by his perfect teeth. "You just missed her."

I slump to my knees dramatically and the manuscript lands on the edge of his desk with a thud.

"Oh, relax," Mark says, unimpressed with my theatrics.

"I told her I would get this to her before the holiday," I say, grabbing a piece of scrap paper and jotting down a phone number.

"She'll be in tomorrow."

"*On Thanksgiving?*" I'm appalled. And then saddened at the thought of her not having holiday plans.

"James. It's Tuesday. Thanksgiving is the day *after* tomorrow."

Not knowing what day it is can be one of the hazards of working from home. "I raced . . ." I breathe in deeply to get oxygen into my lungs.

"Yes, you did."

"Eleven blocks."

"I can tell."

"For nothing."

"You won't have to come back tomorrow." It's more a statement of fact than an encouragement to look on the bright side.

But he has a point. At some hour tomorrow I would have certainly realized it was not Thanksgiving and done this all again on a day when the offices were all but certain to close even earlier. How many days in a row can one dash through the streets like a maniac and not get hit by a bus? "Well, anyway. Here's a number where I can be reached over the holiday." I slide him the scrap paper with my mother's information.

"I'm just shutting down for the day. Any interest in grabbing a drink?"

"With you?" I say it out of surprise and not disgust, but Mark gives me the finger anyway. I laugh. His hair forms this one sandy curl that swoops down over his eyebrow. "Sure." This could be a welcome distraction from the growing agita I feel at the mere thought of Thanksgiving dinner with my family.

I wait while he collects his things and wonder if this is appropriate. Surely he's asking me to drinks as a young man working in publishing; knowing writers is a smart way to advance his career. Yet he's only a few years out of college and he's working as an assistant to Jacqueline Onassis, so he probably already has some connections—it can't possibly be a job you get having your résumé blindly selected from the slush pile. So if he's well connected, with a guaranteed career trajectory, is this something else?

"Where to, hotshot?" he asks.

I look at him, really look at him. He's handsome, for sure—blue eyes, strong chin, rigid nose—but his best feature just may be his confidence.

"Forty Four?" I suggest the bar at the Royalton Hotel, but almost cringe as soon as it comes out of my mouth. I find dimly lit hotel bars erotic, and since I don't know what Mark's intentions are, it feels like playing with, if not outright fire, a modest flame. A smarter idea would be a well-lit bar without top-shelf booze, filled with tourists, that doesn't have floors of bedrooms piled above it.

"Great." I guess he likes hotel bars too.

We walk together, and the fall air is crisp and I can tell it's one of the last few nights I will be able to get away without a winter coat. I ask where he went to school (Brown), and then a bit about Rhode

Island and his family. His father ran for Congress as a Democrat in a heavily Republican district and put up respectable numbers (he lost by eight points less than the candidate in the previous cycle), making some Democratic higher-ups take notice. I wonder if this is how Mark got his job (Democratic higher-ups certainly have a line to Jackie), but asking outright seems rude, like I'm questioning his own credentials; I would never want anyone to think I achieved anything because of *my* father.

Forty Four, while not empty, is not buzzing with the usual after-work crowd. People, it seems, are already splitting town. We order our drinks at the bar and find a small table tucked in a quiet corner with plenty of shadow for cover. Mark gestures for me to sit down first, which makes me feel like I have more years on him than I actually do. My drink, a hickory old-fashioned, contains an ingredient called black dirt apple jack, which reminds me of Jackie's father Black Jack Bouvier (a nickname I learned from *A Woman Named Jackie*, a biography I checked out of the library). Mark sips some concoction with gin and ginger beer.

"What's it like?" I ask.

"Working with her?"

I notice he says *with* her instead of *for* her. If that's his natural confidence or the arrogance of privilege and youth, I don't know. "Yeah."

"I don't know. You work with her too."

"That's different."

"Yeah. I've never been to the *Vineyard*," Mark says, punctuating that very difference. I laugh nervously, but he pushes on, saving me from having to spill any secrets. "What's it like? Her phones are busy. Everyone wants to talk to her. You have to know who to let through and, more important, who not to."

"I can imagine."

"I remember once I transferred President Nixon through to her desk thinking it was some other Dick."

I laugh. *Dick.*

"No, I didn't mean it like . . ." He slaps my knee and I bite down on the inside of my cheek so as not to react. "Someone else *named* Dick, one of her authors, and when she picked up the line she was stuck. I don't think she hates anyone as much as she hates Richard Nixon. I got in so much trouble for that." Mark pauses and sips his drink. "This is all just between us, right?"

"Of course," I say, kicking his foot gently. I study the wide wale of his corduroy pants and the way his cuff bounces with my nudge. I'm not sure what prompts me to do this, the bourbon or the black dirt apple jack or his confidence with me. Or I'm lying to myself and it's my own newfound confidence, from my new identity as author— even in quiet moments like this, my book's publication likely still the better part of a year away. In either case, I want him to know he can trust me.

"Because officially, Mrs. Onassis doesn't hate anyone. She's too busy for that."

"She's above the fray."

"Exactly." Mark looks over his shoulder to make sure no one is within earshot. "I mean, she really is. She works very hard. She's edited nearly one hundred books."

I look over Mark's shoulder as well. "You worried she's here?"

"The Carlyle is more her style, but you never know."

"Should we come up with a code name?" I ask.

"Sometimes, to friends, I call her Jo. Just, you know."

"Joe?" Giving her a blue-collar man's name seems almost too coded.

"Her initials. J-O. It's less show-offy."

"Ah." Now it makes sense. "Ever share a drink?"

"With Jo? Once. Not bourbon though," he says, indicating my glass. "She doesn't like it."

"Hmm. Do *you* like it?"

Mark reaches over and takes a sip of my drink without breaking eye contact. He shrugs. "It's all right. Not my drink." I look down at my glass where his lips just were and wonder if they touched the same spot as mine.

"Do you think Jo's always wanted to work? That she would have

pursued a career earlier if she could have? I think about that sometimes. The *why* of it all." Our eyes are fixed on each other. "Is this
weird? I have no one else to talk with about this stuff."

Mark waves off my concern. "Oh, I know she would have. Worked.
In fact, I think someone said she brought up the idea when she
was married, but Onassis forbade it. Mediterranean men." Mark
shudders with a mild disgust that makes me laugh; he's like a child
repeating a grown-up phrase he heard without actually understanding
the meaning.

"Date a lot of Mediterranean men at Brown, did you?"

"Ha ha," he says, but then genuinely laughs too.

I should not encourage this, but it feels good to have a man treat
me as someone who matters, for my work. Mostly, it's nice to have
Jackie in common with someone, to share her just enough to have a
friend to gossip with about the absurdity of it all.

"You know, there are a lot of gay authors in her stable. A lot of gay
men in her life," Mark says.

I cock an eyebrow. "Stable."

"Giddy-up." He takes a long sip of his drink.

"Why do you think that is?"

"I don't know. We're sensitive."

"Ha," I scoff. "Speak for yourself."

"You don't think you're sensitive?"

"I don't think of myself as particularly sensitive, no," I reply.

"There's a four-hundred-page manuscript on my desk that says
otherwise."

My face grows flush; I can actually feel the reddening of my
cheeks. It's embarrassing to be read so completely by someone so
young. If he can see through me, Jackie certainly will. I think of her
reading this draft and feel dread.

"There's a book, in her library, in her Fifth Avenue apartment.
Have you been? To 1040?"

"Not yet."

"Just the *Vineyard*," he says, shaking his head. "Well, I've only been to deliver stacks of manuscripts and occasionally mail, so I'm not showing off." Now he's concerned with grandstanding. "Anyhow, it was entitled *The History of Homosexuality.* Or something like that. It jumped out at me as out of place."

"I got that book. At orientation. I never cracked it."

Mark leans in, squeezes my calf and says "Ha," then crunches on an ice cube until it's gone. "I mean, who would read such a book? Most people either like homosexuals or they don't. I've never heard of anyone researching the subject to decide if they should."

I look down at my leg where he touched me. The modest flame is in need of containment. "Maybe she did, like gay people, and what she was researching was *why*."

Mark shrugs. "Maybe."

"You still find that weird."

"I don't know. I guess not that weird. She has a book on everything. I'm sure she likes books more than people."

"Even gay ones," I agree.

"Gay books?"

"Gay people."

We laugh, although the idea of her preferring books to people is not an overstatement. We blather on about titles we've read and publishing in general, and as we near the end of our second round, Mark asks, "What are we doing here?"

"You suggested we grab a drink."

"I did?"

"You did."

"That was bold." He laughs, but I get the sense it's not particularly bold for Mark. "Do you have a boyfriend?"

I lean back in my chair and swirl the last of the watered-down bourbon in my glass. I take a few seconds before answering. Since I told Jackie about Daniel it seems unwise to tell Mark something different. "I do."

He shrugs. "Good. I wouldn't want you to get attached." He curls his lip like Billy Idol.

I do a quick calculation of the number of rooms in this hotel: Eighty, ninety, maybe? Plus another dozen or so suites and penthouses? I wonder how many are currently occupied and how many are host to people having sex right now. It's early still. Seven-thirty. Probably only a few, if that. People engaging in a quickie before going out for the night. Are any hotel guests having sex with someone other than their professed partners? These are the thoughts that make hotel bars so erotic, this is the math that made coming here a bad idea.

"Should we get the check?" Mark asks. His directness is unnerving.

"I think that's a good idea," I say. But maybe for a different reason.

When the bill comes, I pay, even if Mark is sitting on mountains of family money, or even if Doubleday would have picked up the tab, and excuse myself for the men's room.

The bathroom has just undergone the sort of New Age redesign that requires one to orient oneself upon entering. Normally bathrooms are intuitively laid out. Not in New York. Not anymore. I was in an empty men's room recently with a wall of running water and a circular trough in the center of the room. That's it. I wasn't sure if I was supposed to urinate on the wall and wash my hands in the trough or relieve myself in the trough and run my hands along the trickling waterwall. Eventually a man exited a hidden stall and proceeded to wash his hands in the trough, so I took initiative and peed on the wall.

Since what I'm really here to do is splash some cold water on my face to bring me to my senses, I'm glad when the sinks present themselves as sinks and not basins of plumbing mystery. The cold water is rousing, so I repeat the action two or three more times. What am I doing? *Nothing.* I look up at myself in the mirror and am almost surprised to see my reflection, water slaloming down my face like tears. I realize now, working on this latest redraft, how much I've felt like a ghost. Alone. Writing is an inherently solitary endeavor, immersing yourself in another world, either make-believe or in the past—in my case, a confusing combination of both.

I love Daniel. I'm not unhappy. I finished my book. I'm not a ghost. Not really.

So why does it feel so charged to be seen?

I reach for paper towels and dab my face dry, and when I look up I see Mark's reflection in the mirror walking toward me from the urinals, zipping up his corduroys. I flinch.

"Jumpy," he says.

"I thought I was alone."

"Well, you're not."

To prove his point, he steps closer so we're only inches apart. I don't want to feel any heat, I don't want to feel *anything*, but I do. I start to sweat in my blazer. Flustered, I ask, "Did you wash your hands?"

"Is that really what you want to ask me?"

I can feel blood . . . moving . . . where it shouldn't. "I don't know what I want to ask you." I wish desperately I could do my jumping-jacks thing, since it always helps me to think, but that would require a monumental feat of explanation. The visual is funny, and I emit a small, nervous chuckle.

"I thought one of the advantages of older men is that they knew what they wanted."

"I'm thirty-one."

"Yeah?"

"That makes me older men?" This is breaking news to me.

Mark leans in and hugs me tightly and eventually I hug him back. He's thinner than Daniel—scrawny, almost—and it feels strange to hold him. The side of his face presses against mine and it feels electric, sexual. It's smoother than Daniel's scruffy one, softer, younger; he reminds me of a boy I loved in college. I look at the restroom door, almost willing it to open, begging for our privacy to be interrupted, but quickly realize I'm on my own to stop this.

After a good thirty seconds I wriggle him off me. "Okay."

"Oh, relax," he says, letting go. I'm souring on this as a catch phrase. He turns on the faucet to wash his hands.

I pivot away from the mirror and adjust myself in my pants,

uptucking like a seventh-grader desperate for his classroom erection not to be seen. "We don't have to make a big deal out of this."

Mark looks at me with pity. "Is it a big deal?"

"No, no, I guess not." I lean against the sink, wishing I could click my heels three times and be home safely with Daniel.

Mark leans across me to reach for the paper towels and his arm brushes against my chest; I expect a shock of static but it doesn't come.

"You're not going to tell Jo, are you?"

"God, no." I spit the words out so quickly I almost choke. I look around to see if anyone else has walked in, to see if any of the stalls are occupied.

Mark gives me a puzzled look, *She's definitely not in here.*

I want him to disappear. I don't want to have to say good-bye, I don't want to have to ask him about his holiday plans, I don't want to chitchat about the manuscript, about business, about his family in Rhode Island. I just want this to be done.

"Should I walk you to the subway?" I offer, praying he'll say no.

"Nah, I'll cab it."

Cab? I should have let him pick up the bill. "Okay."

"Happy Thanksgiving, James." He leans in to hug me again, but I take the opportunity to shake his now-clean hand instead. He rolls his eyes.

"Happy Thanksgiving, yourself."

I turn back to look in the mirror, as if it will tell me what the fuck just happened, and in a moment he is gone.

◆ SIXTEEN ◆

Our rental car smells like fast-food grease, and as we pass exit after exit along the bleak highway, it's all I can do to not grab the wheel from Daniel and point the car in the direction of the nearest drive-thru—if only to settle my stomach. The interstate is bleak and lined with bare and colorless trees, their bark tinged with a gray frost that matches the ghostly sky. Trees get thinner when the weather turns cold and I get fatter, craving nothing but the non-nutrition whose negative effects I can hide under bulky sweaters in winter. The drive to my mother's house near Ithaca is usually just under four hours, but we hit a good deal of traffic in Jersey City on our way out of town; the toll road is faster more often than not, but apparently not today. We hit more traffic at the I-80/I-81 interchange—not surprising, still annoying. Now we're making good time, but I'm restless, not so much hungry as bored.

"Want food?" I ask Daniel.

"No, you?"

"No, not really," I say, admitting defeat. "You okay driving?" We switched seats when we stopped for coffee and a donut, but I'm not sure how long ago that was.

"Yup."

I think of Mark and the electric aura around him. What this drive would be like if he were here now. I'd be behind the wheel (he strikes me as the kind of privileged city kid who boasts of not knowing how to drive), while his hand would be creeping up my thigh on its way to doing something unsafe at interstate speeds. I pull my coat over my lap in case I get hard.

"You nervous?" Daniel asks.

"Huh?" I worry at times he can read my thoughts.

"About seeing your mother."

"Oh." *Phew.* "Need you ask?"

I was surprised when Kenny called a few weeks back to see if I was coming home for Thanksgiving. He said he hoped so—that Ellen and the kids were looking forward to seeing me.

"Didn't you hear?" I had asked Kenny.

"Hear about what."

"Mom and me. We're kind of going through a thing."

"She hasn't said."

"Huh."

"Other than to ask if I knew if you were coming."

Naomi called too, a few days later, asking if Daniel and I were coming for Thanksgiving.

"I think so?" I had said, the heaviest emphasis on the question mark.

"C'mon. Even big-shot authors get holidays."

Given that my brother and sister both called, it seemed obvious that this was another of my mother's orchestrations. That she wanted me home for Thanksgiving but was too proud to make the call herself. At least this is what I led myself to believe, what gave me the courage to pick up the phone to call her and accept her non-invitation. That maybe she wanted to work toward resolution too.

I remember she answered only after the machine picked up and I felt self-conscious at the thought of our conversation being recorded.

"Kenny called. As did Naomi. Daniel and I would like to come for Thanksgiving, if that's still all right with you."

"The turkey is seventeen pounds."

This was the kind of response you often got from my mother. Is it a yes? Is it a no? Is it conversation? Obfuscation? Deflection? It is merely information. There will be enough food if you decide to come. You have to be fluent in my mother to know what it really means: *Suit yourself.*

I lean in to Daniel to read the fuel gauge; it's still half full. Or half empty. It feels like it's been at half something for a while. I stare at the dashboard until the odometer ticks off another mile, then sink back into my seat. A white car with Ohio plates in desperate need of a wash passes us on the inside lane. "If Ohio added another *h* it would be a palindrome."

"With a double *h*?" It sounds weird the way Daniel says it. *Aitch.* How can it take five letters to pronounce one?

"No—Ohiho. Oh-i-ho."

"Oh," he says, realizing. And then, "So?"

"Don't you think it would be nice to have a state that's a palindrome? And why not Ohio? I mean, what else does it have going for it?"

"It's the Buckeye State."

"Yeah, but what is a buckeye?"

"It's like a horse chestnut."

But what's a horse chestnut?, I want to scream. But then he would answer, and I already know what a horse chestnut is and what I want him to explain to me has nothing to do with nuts at all. Unless you count the cluster of nuts I'm related to.

"Oh-i-ho," Daniel says. "The Palindrome State."

"Now you're talking."

My thoughts turn to Jackie; she's been ever-present since I delivered the manuscript to her office forty-eight hours ago. I imagine her reading the latest draft and my stomach churns. I had intended to go home over the summer, Labor Day at the latest, to spend time with my mother as Jackie suggested, but an invitation never came. I knew instinctually if I invited myself I would get my mother on her highest guard, so I let it be. Truth be told, I also knew it wouldn't be as simple as just showing up on my mother's doorstep. Jackie made it sound so easy, but in the weeks after my visit to Martha's Vineyard, I realized I had no idea what was supposed to happen when I got there. Then deadline after deadline passed and it seemed easiest to just fudge another ending.

"Putting a *t* at the end of Tennessee also makes that state a palindrome."

Tee.

Daniel looks up from the road and stares at me for an alarmingly long time. "I don't think that's even remotely true."

I gesture for him to look back at the road before he kills us, and then when that doesn't work I snap my fingers. "Tennesseet," I say, when I'm comfortable that his attention is back where it should be.

"It's missing a couple of *n*'s," he says. *Enns.* Daniel doesn't usually take everything I say so literally when we're goofing around; perhaps he's nervous about this homecoming too.

Traffic slows around a bend heading into the low afternoon sun and Daniel applies the brakes.

"I'm sorry," I say. "I'm being weird. I think I'm more nervous than I let on."

"I know."

"You do?"

"You're not that hard to read."

I look at my boyfriend and feel genuine relief that he knows me as he does. Why do I waste even one minute imagining Mark along for the ride, when everything I need is right here?

Daniel applies the brake even harder, as traffic comes to an abrupt halt.

"Do you ever think about dying young?" I'm always most aware of news stories about highway fatalities around the holidays, maybe because they seem even more tragic.

He looks at me as if he'd like to take back that comment about my being easy to read. "You trying to get rid of me?"

"No, nothing like that."

"Good."

Though it's true, it has been on my mind recently. Mortality. I think it's all this time spent with Jackie, with her pushing me to find resolution, finality, an ending.

"Wait," Daniel protests. "Do you think *you're* going to die young?"

"No, I'm going to live a very long time."

"Oh, really."

"Yeah. I'll probably live to be one hundred and eight. Of course, by then you'll be gone and I'll be with someone much younger."

"So they can change and feed and bathe you. Romantic."

"Very."

Just like when I entered the world. My blood flow will slow and I'll probably lose my words and my ability to speak, to write. My identity. I will have no idea who I am anymore, and will have only strange faces around me and I will scream and wail until my next basic need is met.

"My life, the palindrome," I observe.

"Your life the palindrome." Daniel nods, impressed.

· SEVENTEEN ·

Daniel offers to go inside first and break the ice and I tell him not to be silly—I am not going to hide from my own family. I hang back anyway, under the pretense of unloading luggage from the trunk.

"Smooth," Daniel says, as he returns from the front door to grab our bags. He sees right through my ploy.

"What?" I say, innocently.

He rolls his eyes.

Kenny's wife, Ellen, greets us at the door. "I thought I heard a car." She has a dish towel flung over her shoulder and looks like she's been working all day in the kitchen of some holiday movie made specifically for a women's cable channel. She's approaching forty and retains all of her good looks, even if her body has softened slightly from carrying two boys. I set our things down in the mud room.

"You did and *here we are*!" I say the last part louder for my mother's benefit, like how you would make a lot of distinctly human noises while walking in the woods during hunting season so as not to get shot. Confused by the volume of my voice, Ellen shoots me a weird look before pulling us in for a hug. I like Ellen, always have. She was crazy competitive before she married Kenny and had the kids—she played field hockey at some women's college—and when we used to stay up late nights playing cards or board games she would fight like hell to win. Now she does her best to set an example of sportsmanship, but it's easy enough to access her inner competitor with just two glasses of chardonnay.

The smell of roasting turkey hits the foyer. Daniel and I exchange looks; we are both in dire need of a good home-cooked meal. Food lately has been whatever American-looking crackers they have at the Korean market and slices of pizza from the place on the corner. Unless cheese is a food group, we are desperately malnourished.

"It smells fantastic," Daniel compliments.

"Well, turkey's just about to come out of the oven; then we'll put the sides in. Dinner should be in about an hour. Give you time to say hello to everyone and have a drink."

"And Mom?" I ask, peering around the corner into the kitchen, looking for any sign of her, fully prepared to duck back from enemy fire.

Ellen looks at me while slightly shaking her head. "Your mother's putting on a sweater."

She used to make glorious meals, my mother, so it seems odd that Ellen is at the helm today. My mother wasn't a gourmand, but she kept our family happy and well fed and I used to love to help her. The kitchen itself has changed very little since I left for college. The dishwasher is still marigold, as is the stove. The fridge is now white; the one that matched the other appliances gave out around the time I graduated. (When it died, she was angered about having to toss groceries that should have been discarded years prior. "Salad dressing doesn't go bad. Raspberry jam? I don't think so.") The wallpaper is coming up at the seams, and the linoleum refuses to stay tucked under the radiator in the one corner. If my father were around he would fix that with his hot-glue gun. There's a burnt smell that always seems to linger, the result of years of abuse of the oven's self-cleaning function. I know this room like the back of my hand, right down to the Charles Chips cookie tin on the counter that, sure enough, is still there.

Before I can fix that drink, I'm tackled by three nephews, the oldest of whom is six. William and Zachary are Kenny's boys and Aaron belongs to Naomi; all three are like small cheetahs learning to take down an aging gazelle. My only hope in getting them off me is a plan—dragging them to some watering hole with the hope that I can hold my breath.

"Uncle Daniel is here too!" That's an easier tactic.

The boys freeze, focus their sights on Daniel, and pounce with coordinated precision. Daniel lets out an excited yell as he's tackled, then trudges slowly into the living room with William on his back and dragging the other two, who are clutching his legs. Domino jumps and barks and nips at their heels, her pudgy body taxed by all the excitement. Daniel looks back at me and smiles. In another life he would make a great dad; he loves this family chaos.

Naomi passes them on her way into the kitchen and yells, "Just steer clear of the dining room!" She selects a cube of cheddar from an appetizer platter and pops it into her mouth. "We're eating off of the good china today."

"Fancy."

"We have our own china room now, like at the White House."

"Naomi," I say, part protest, part greeting. I squint my eyes and am surprised to recognize some of my father in her. "Or, should I say, the Honorable Naomi." I haven't seen her since she was appointed mayor of her small town.

"Ugh. You and Kenny are both the same. It's not a big deal. Everyone on the council takes a turn."

We hug, and Kenny appears from the living room, where he's been watching the game, and we high-five on his way to the fridge. We look more and more alike with each passing year, even if I'm a few inches taller.

"Either of you want a beer? Madam Mayor?"

Naomi turns to me like *See?*

"Did you buy the beer?" I ask.

"Yes."

"I'll have wine."

Kenny shakes his head. "Your generation and your craft beers." He opens the fridge and selects a Michelob, leaving me to fend for myself.

"We're the same generation, you and I. As I'm sure you're aware."

Naomi throws a cube of cheese at me, then pauses to take us in.

"Look at the three of us. In this kitchen. When is the last time it was just the three of us?"

Ellen, at the sink peeling potatoes, coughs.

"Oh. Sorry, Ellen," Naomi says. "Didn't see you there." She shrugs at me and winces.

"That's all right, don't mind me. I was just cooking a multicourse holiday meal for all of you."

Kenny kisses his wife on the cheek, then crosses back to the fridge to grab a second beer. "Daniel will have a beer with me."

I nod. "If you can unearth him from the pig pile of nephews." I reach for the cheese. "Mom hiding from me?"

"She went upstairs to change," Kenny says.

"Change into a mother that talks to her son?"

Naomi puts her arm on mine. "Lower your hackles. Everyone's doing their best." She reaches behind Ellen, gets me the biggest wineglass in the cupboard, and fills it with a generous pour.

I swirl the wine in my glass, smelling it as it comes to a rest.

"*I* brought the wine," Ellen says. "It's safe."

With an exaggerated sigh, Kenny retreats to find a compatriot in Daniel.

"Where's Paul?" I ask. Naomi's husband had yet to say hello.

"Stuck in Minneapolis. His flight home last night was grounded for weather."

"Thanksgiving in Minneapolis. Jeez." I've never been to Minneapolis; I'm sure they have fine Thanksgivings. But no one wants to be stuck in an airport hotel away from their family for the holidays.

Or do they? I have a sudden urge to grab Daniel and escape for a quiet Thanksgiving with Paul in Minnesota.

"Not everyone gets to travel to Martha's Vineyard for their work." Naomi shoves me playfully. "Oh, I almost forgot. Someone called for you." She rips off the top sheet of a notebook by the phone. "Mark?"

"Mark called?" My body stills. "What did he want?"

Naomi reads her message. "Something about Joe. Do you know a

Joe?" She hands me the paper. Written in her handwriting is *Joe says you didn't do it.*

So there it is. Jackie has read the new draft and she's seen right through me. My face grows hot and there's a hollow ringing in my ears. It's like being busted by a favorite teacher for turning in sloppy work.

"Well, you're turning red," Naomi says. "Who's Joe? What didn't you do?"

I grasp at the air for a quick lie. "A friend. I was supposed to leave a book for him to read, but I forgot." This is a terrible turn of events. I can't let this stand. There's no way I will be able to be even remotely present this weekend with this information hanging over my head. I feel a strong urge to defend my work, explain my choices. If I could just, I don't know, talk to her.

One of the boys screams from the other room. "Knock it off, nerds!" Naomi yells.

"You call them nerds?"

She shrugs. "They like it." Another scream. "I said knock it off!"

"Actually, do you mind if I . . . ?" I point to the phone mounted on the wall.

Naomi stomps out of the kitchen; the boys are going to be sorry they roused her ire. I grab the phone and pull the cord around the corner into the sitting room so that I'm alone. The room used to be filled with family artifacts but is strangely devoid of anything personal, as if staged for a catalog photo shoot. I quickly dial Jackie's office, not remembering until I get her voicemail that of course she's not there. "Mrs. Onassis, it's James Smale. I wanted to tell you a few things about the latest draft. You might have some questions and I thought I could . . . clear them up. I left the number with Mark. Thank you."

I hang up with the sinking feeling that I'm just digging a deeper hole. I gently place the phone back in the cradle and take a few deep breaths. With Naomi gone, it's just Ellen and me and sudden pockets of empty spaces. I fold the message from Mark and put it in my pocket. "Want some help with the potatoes?"

Ellen stops peeling and turns to me. "Your brother's very proud of you. We both are. I hear you've been getting some flack around here. So I wanted you to know that."

I make a fist in my pocket, crumpling the phone message. "I haven't been getting much of anything, flack or otherwise. But thank you for saying that."

"Well, we think it's very exciting. I told all my friends at work and they're all going to buy the book."

"Now all I have to do is finish writing it." I clench my teeth for show.

"So," Ellen starts, her eyes growing wide. "What's she like?"

"Jackie?"

I select a carrot stick from the appetizer tray and run it through some dip. Mark told me once that Jackie eats carrot sticks at her desk that she brings from home. I was convinced at the time he was making that up. Did she pack them herself? Wrap them in foil? Roll them in a damp paper towel and seal them in a sandwich bag? The idea of it was so immediately disarming, I thought it had to be some sort of shtick. *Carrot shtick.*

"No, the Queen of England. Unless you've met her too."

I laugh. "No. Not yet, anyway." I wink at Ellen. "She's nice."

"C'mon. Bank tellers are nice. Pharmacists are nice."

"Fine. But I don't concede the point—she *is* nice! But she's also . . . I don't know. She's all the things you think she is. It took meeting her a few times before my head came down from the clouds and I could even form an opinion. It's her voice that's hardest to get used to. It's like listening to history. But we've established a good working relationship. Alcohol helped."

"You drink in front of her?" Ellen drops her peeler.

"We drink together."

"Really."

"I think we're . . . friends." I'm showing off a little bit, but it's also not untrue. After my trip to Martha's Vineyard, she gave me a copy of Isak Dinesen's *Out of Africa* with a little note ("Another favorite of mine"). Just last month she closed our telephone conversation with "Heal, heal," reminding me of my mission for this new draft, and I barked like a dog and she laughed and told me I always brightened her day. We don't talk all the time, but she's there when I need her or have a question, and it's a nice feeling that she takes my calls. (I'm a "dick" that Mark will put through.)

"Oh my God. You're famous."

"Well, that's a word on a sliding scale."

Jackie and I met for dinner once at an Italian restaurant on the Upper East Side and were seated at a secluded table away from most of the other diners. It made me wonder if someday I might have some small recognition, money or notoriety of my own. I can't always tell if I like Jackie solely for who she is, or if I like being with her for her access. Obviously, I like her. But I'm not entirely sure if I'm happier to be adjacent to her celebrity or if I want some small slice of fame that's all mine. I used to think I wanted to be famous for my writing, but there's a loneliness she exudes that makes me wonder if it's not worth the trouble.

"Who's famous?" My mother enters the kitchen, toying with the gold chain that hangs over her turtleneck, trying to drag the clasp around to the back and the cross around to the front. Her hair is freshly done, or set, or whatever the proper word is for women her age; it's an ashier blond than it was when I saw her last.

"No one," I say, desperate to change the topic. I shoot daggers at Ellen and to her credit she drops it, but not before she mouths the word *proud.* "Happy Thanksgiving," I say to my mother. "Thank you for having us."

She lets go of her necklace and hugs me the way you might a homeless person who unexpectedly embraces you—with enough distance between us not to get anything on her. "You look . . . tall."

"Haven't grown."

"Maybe it's your shoes."

"I took them off in the hall."

My mother looks at my stocking feet, deciding whether to concede. "Well, anyway. You look good."

"Thank you. So do you." But the truth is she looks *small*. She has loomed so large lately, an ever-present character in my head, it's almost a shock to see her standing in front of me. "And everything smells delicious."

"I don't know about *that*."

"Well, it does."

My mother approaches the cheese tray and straightens it so that it is perpendicular to the edge of the counter. "How was your drive?"

"Uneventful. A little traffic around the interchange, but otherwise fine." I nervously pick at the corner of the countertop where the Formica overhang is loose, like I'm playing the strings of a harp.

"Well, you're here. You look good. Something is obviously agreeing with you."

I don't want to remind her that, despite the message in my pocket causing fresh agony, I've had a good year. That even in the throes of deadlines and rewrites and the pain of revisiting family anguish, there's a peace and a pride that comes from doing what you love. I also don't have to; I know it's front and center on her mind. "Thank you. I have a lot to be thankful for."

"We all do," my mother says. Certainly she means having her family healthy and safe under one roof, her children all now having found some success in their chosen fields. Yet she says it without pause or reflection; it makes me think this is a woman on autopilot, playing the part but not entirely living it.

"May I talk to you for a moment?"

I lead my mother into the dining room. The table is beautifully made, a perfect mix of highbrow place settings and turkey-day kitsch. My grandmother's china and her own gold-rimmed wedding crystal (the same goblets she mixes with Spode dinnerware at Christmas) offset by a dried gourd centerpiece and ceramic pilgrim salt and

pepper shakers whose Puritan faces are painted with surprised expressions like sex dolls. We turn to face each other and I notice my mother's necklace clasp is still not quite where she would like it.

"Here, let me help you." I slide the clasp behind her neck and then
rest my hands on her shoulders. I take a deep breath. "I'm really
happy to be here."

"I'm really happy you came." She averts her eyes.

"Are we good?"

"What do you mean?"

Sigh. "Do we need to talk about anything."

"James, I'm fine."

"A lot has happened this year. I'm here to talk about it, if you'd
like to."

"I think we've talked enough."

I wish Jackie could be here to witness this. *See?* I would say. We've
hardly spoken at all! Every mother may have a story, but good luck
getting mine to tell hers.

"I'd like to have a nice meal," she continues.

I let go of her shoulders and drop my hands to my sides. I notice
handprint-turkey artwork placed on everyone's chair. "We used to do
those, you and I."

"We used to do what?"

"Traced our hands and drew turkeys."

"I did those with the boys last weekend."

"That's really fun," I say, but I'm not sure really what I mean. You
used to be fun? I used to be fun? Life used to be fun.

"Aileen!" We jump. It's Daniel. He's broken free of the nephews
and has appeared in the doorway holding his Michelob. He approaches my mother and gives her a gentle hug. I laugh, as his hugs
used to be more encompassing, more bearlike, until it became clear
they terrified her.

"Hi, Daniel. Happy Thanksgiving."

"Happy Thanksgiving to you." He gives her a peck on the cheek.
Together they head back to the kitchen.

"Which pot has the neck?" I see Daniel head for the stove before he disappears from view.

"It's there somewhere," my mother calls after him. The first Thanksgiving I brought him home he innocently took inventory of each saucepan on the burners and freaked out when he found the turkey neck my mother was boiling to make gravy. Ever since then he's been fascinated by this tradition.

I look at the table and notice one setting missing a salad fork. I open the hutch drawer to fetch another, remembering as I always do when my father had built the entire unit by hand. He was protective of his workshop, a hidden room in the back of the barn. He and Kenny would spend hours in there, discussing the purpose of each woodworking tool, the plane, the radial saw, the different grades of sandpaper. I tried at times to join them but always felt profoundly out of place. I didn't like the screech the tools made, the burning smell that would linger after he cut a piece of wood, or the haze of sawdust that seemed to permanently hang in the air. I'm sure he read my disinterest, but I would have overcome all of it to feel the least bit included.

"You must be so proud of James," I hear Daniel say from the kitchen. I snap back to attention, place the missing fork on the table, and B-line for the kitchen to head off any trouble. Daniel winks at me to acknowledge he knows he's stirring a huge pot of shit and then pops two cheese bites into his mouth and hungrily swipes a stalk of celery through the onion dip. I would wring his own neck and boil it if he weren't so adorable.

"I'm proud of all my children," my mother replies, without looking anywhere near the one child of hers standing in the room. Autopilot. A written line from a play only she has the script to.

EIGHTEEN

After the meal we sit in bloated silence, moving the last bit of scraps around on our plates, the clink and scraping of silverware amplified by the lull in conversation. Everyone sits in quiet contemplation of another bite, an additional dollop of something with butter or gravy, but no one dares—the realization quickly sinking in that even one more mouthful is not possible without us exploding one by one like characters at the end of a *Monty Python* sketch.

"I can't sit on this any longer. We're all playing it cool, like it's not really going on, like this is just like any other Thanksgiving, with normal family news, like which kid did what in whose school. But I give," Kenny says. "What's she like?"

I'm tempted to offer a cool "Who?" but I know better. "My editor?"

"Yes, your editor." Kenny playfully snarls.

"Jackie," I say, as if anyone at the table needs help catching up.

"Is that what you call her?" Kenny is shocked.

"That's her name." And then, realizing how obnoxious I sound, I add, "I call her Mrs. Onassis in person. People afford her that respect."

"She's *nice*," Ellen says, mocking my earlier description.

"Ellen," I protest. I sneak a sideways peek at my mother, who is folding her napkin into some intricate swan.

"She's *not* nice?" Kenny is confused.

"She's nice," I say. "Really very nice."

"And you've met her," Kenny attempts to clarify. "In person. More than once."

"He's been to her house!" Ellen exclaims.

"Oh, that's right. Did you steal anything?"

"Kenny!" Naomi pretends to be horrified.

"Not the family silver! Just a little something. Like, you know, a pen, a hand towel. A souvenir."

Daniel places his hand on my thigh just under the tablecloth, him telling me to stay calm and to be honest and proud. "Yes. I've met her. No, I didn't steal anything. She's my editor. We work together closely. And I call her Mrs. Onassis—"

"Not *Jacqueline*?" Ellen interrupts, teasingly.

"The way she pronounces *Jacqueline* is sort of two-thirds French, one-third Mid-Atlantic English. I don't dare attempt it, I'd tie my tongue in knots."

"Zhaq-well-enn," Naomi tries, but ends up shaking her head.

"That's Katharine Hepburn," Daniel scoffs.

Everyone laughs but my mother.

"Remind us never to play Celebrity with you," I add. More laughter.

"What's Celebrity?" Kenny asks.

I pout and look at my brother. "Poor Kenny."

Ellen chimes in. "With the little pieces of paper. Remember? I beat all of you that one Christmas!"

I look at the three bottles of red wine that litter the table. Two bottles empty, one has a splash left. I hold it up, offering it to Ellen, who declines, before pouring its contents into my glass.

"So, back on topic." Naomi is having none of this distraction.

"There are other topics," I insist.

"No, there aren't. So what does that make you?"

"What do you mean?"

"What is your relationship?" Naomi clarifies. "Are you *friends*?"

"I don't know. Colleagues?"

"James is being modest," Daniel says.

Getting nowhere with me, Naomi turns her heated attention to Daniel. "Have *you* met her?"

"Oh, yes. We had her over to our apartment in Hell's Kitchen. We sat at our little table near the airshaft and played Uno until the sun set. I made empanadas!"

Everyone laughs again; even my mother seems to acknowledge him. I look around the table. Kenny is still drinking beer. *The rest of us managed to kill three bottles of wine?*

"No, I haven't met her," Daniel continues. "James keeps her all to himself."

"You gotta give us something," Kenny continues. "I mean, I once met our congressman at a local Bar Association thing, and Naomi met the mayor . . ."

Naomi stops him. "I *am* the mayor."

Kenny shushes her. "But this is in a whole other league. And, plus, Dad had that letter."

"The letter!" Naomi exclaims. "I forgot about the letter."

"What letter?"

"You don't remember the letter?" Kenny asks. I shrug, so he continues. "Dad had a letter. From President Kennedy. A letter of . . ."

Naomi completes his sentence. "A Letter of Recognition of Service."

"That's right," Kenny continues. "From his time with the Rotary. Remember when he raised all that money for the hospital and they bought those things? You know, for ambulances."

Everyone looks at my mother for clarification. She speaks quietly, without looking up from her lap. "Portable defibrillators."

"That's right. You know those things. Clear. Boom!" Kenny puffs his chest out in demonstration. "They're standard now, but back then they were new. And as head of the Rotary Club, Dad raised the money to buy like three or four of those things and President Kennedy sent him a Letter of . . ."

"Recognition of Service." Naomi tosses a dinner roll at Kenny and it lands with a thud on his plate. She reaches for another before realizing that our mother is watching and drops it back in the basket. *Conduct unbecoming of the neighboring town's mayor.*

"Right. He was so proud of that thing. Showed it off to everyone. Twice if you were Irish. Or Catholic. If you were both you would never hear the end of it! Had the Seal of the President and everything.

Embossed. Remember that, Naomi? Every time he would mention the Seal of the President you would clap your hands together like flippers and bark like a seal."

For added effect, Naomi does exactly that. "Does the sister still smoke pot in the book?"

"Ugh. And the brother's such a slob." Kenny looks at me, dejected.

"I'm thinking of running for the legislature. I really wish you would take that out. Oh, God, and now *she's* read it? My political future is doomed."

"Relax. Even our president-elect has smoked pot," Daniel says, coming to my defense.

"Yeah, but he didn't inhale!" Kenny bursts into laughter, and this time Naomi can't stop herself from throwing another roll; it beans Kenny right in the head.

"Stop throwing rolls before the kids see you!" Ellen covers the bread basket with her napkin.

"Where is that letter? Dad's letter." Kenny looks at our mother, who freezes like a statue. Fortunately, Kenny breezes right past her. "So you see, you have to give us something more than just 'nice.'"

My mother rests her folded napkin swan on the table and its neck droops like it's injured or diseased. She stands to clear the dishes.

Naomi snaps her fingers. "Sit."

My mother glares at Naomi in a test of wills, then responds like an unwillingly obedient dog. Domino, however, full from table scraps and napping in the corner, stands up and yips.

"Francis is telling a story," Naomi says, as if that will soften the bark of her command. She looks at me, delighted with her recall of Francis. Once my mother settles back in her chair, Naomi instructs me to continue.

I gulp the last of my wine and set the glass down on the table, and turn it in a circular motion three times. The sudden employment of a long-dormant name makes me feel like my mother's protectorate again, like I want to stand up for her now. She shouldn't have to hear any of this if she doesn't want to. I look up, to Daniel first and then around the table, for backup. I find none. My eyes land last on my mother.

"Yes, Francis," she says through gritted teeth. "Continue."

I shove my hands into my pockets and take a deep breath. I squeeze the phone message from Mark in my right fist. *You didn't do it.* I begin slowly, gathering the courage to power through. "In one of our first working sessions she made daiquiris."

"Whoa, whoa, whoa." The whole room erupts.

"Daiquiris?" Kenny asks.

"Yes. But not the, you know, syrupy kind that you would get on one of those cruise ships Kathy Lee Gifford sings about. A simple version with rum and lime."

"She made them," Naomi asks.

"Yes. She had the rum in her office."

"She did not," Naomi disagrees.

"You're pulling our leg!" Kenny protests.

"I swear! It was a gift from another author." Everyone looks to their neighbor to see if they believe me. "We work, mostly. But we talk about things too. Life and relationships and even politics, sometimes. We watched Bill Clinton accept the nomination together."

"At Madison Square Garden?" Kenny is impressed. "Did you have a private box?"

"No, no, no. On TV at her house on Martha's Vineyard."

Kenny slaps his forehead as if to say "of course," while my mother looks absolutely indignant.

"You talk about relationships? Like, her marriages?"

"No, other relationships. Like she knows about Daniel." Daniel leans back in his chair, impressed with himself, and makes a motion like he's shining an apple on a nonexistent lapel. "Familial relationships. Fathers and mothers." I pause, knowing I should stop, but more words drip off my tongue. "Mothers and sons." I bite my lip and look over at my mother, who further seethes. "I would never push and ask her much that she isn't willing to volunteer. It just seems impolitic. Disrespectful."

My mother finally looks up. "But she can ask you anything she wants. Even something disrespectful."

"Well, she's never disrespectful, but . . . yeah. She holds more of the cards." I try to uncrumple and refold the message in my pocket. I need to keep pushing. "Disrespectful to whom?"

"So she's like your boss," Kenny says, cutting me off, still putting the puzzle together.

"Well, no. Not really."

"You're *her* boss?"

"No, no. Of course not." I look again at my mother, who is wondering why it is that I can't disrespect a stranger but she has to endure being disrespected by her son. "Yes. Sort of. She's sort of my boss. It has a similar dynamic."

"But James has the final say, creatively," Daniel points out. "He can veto her edits."

I glower at Daniel—he's not helping—but, still aglow with the idea of Jackie and me discussing him, he doesn't notice. "Only to a point," I respond. "I pick and choose. But I choose most of them! Most of them are spot-on."

"Huh." Kenny huffs.

"The publisher, and thus Jackie, has the *final* say. I mean, they could choose not to accept the manuscript when I'm finished. Refuse to publish it." There are actually *four* empty bottles of wine on the table; I spot another empty over by Ellen, hidden behind the centerpiece. Four bottles between five people—that's a lot, even for us.

"Is that likely?" Naomi asks.

"We'll see. I turned in the latest draft right before coming here. She said she'd look at it over the holiday." I cross my fingers and hold them up for all to see, knowing already my work is not done.

"Wow. You must be on edge."

How much did I *drink?*

"So she's at home reading about us while we're sitting here talking about her! What a weird world we live in," Kenny remarks. I remember all the strange thoughts I too had to come to terms with after I first met Jackie and learned I would be working with her.

"Well, not *us*. It's a novel."

"Yeah, but come on. The sister was a pothead, the brother was kind of absent—which I guess I was, since I was trying to make partner at the time—and the mother started every day by blasting Handel's *Messiah*."

"Oh, Jesus," I whisper, under Naomi's continued protests about being stoned.

Kenny starts singing. "And he shall reign forever and ever, king of kings and lord of lords. Hallelujah. Hallelujah. Hal-lay-ay-lu-jah!"

I bow my head as if in prayer. Shouting and singing continues. I sneak a sideways glance at my mother, who is rearranging the silverware on her plate in conspicuously complicated and noisy ways. She drops her knife between the tines of her fork and it lands with a clang. She repeats this action, and for a moment it is the only noise that pierces Kenny's song. Even the children are silent in the other room, watching a videocassette copy of *Frosty the Snowman*. Then she slides three fingers into a wooden napkin ring and starts drumming with it on the table. Barely, over the racket, I hear Frosty exclaim "Happy Birthday" as he slides on the magic hat and comes to life just as Kenny comes to a close of another chorus. "Hal-lay-ayyyyyyyyyy-lu-jah!"

"KENNY." Ellen glares. "That's enough."

The whole thing is so overwhelming, the sounds of my childhood coming from the other room remixed with Kenny singing and my mother's angry wooden percussion. We are in the dining room of our old house, but everything seems suddenly strange and new. The antique clock that used to hang between the windows is on a different wall. The wallpaper is gone, in favor of mossy green paint. Kenny sits comfortably at the head of the table, as if he has always sat there, but he is a substitute patriarch failing to keep this family in line. As the rapping on the table falls into perfect synchronization with the pounding in my head, I'm finally able to refold the message from Mark in my pocket; in the chaos it feels like solving a Rubik's Cube.

Joe says you didn't do it.

I blurt out the one thing I know will force my mother to engage. "I wonder what Dad would think of all this."

My mother mumbles her response, swallowing the words almost as quickly as they come out of her mouth, and at first I'm the only one to hear them. Kenny and Naomi resume their argument over the whereabouts of the Kennedy letter and Daniel is ready to jump in with a question, probably about defibrillators (if I know him, and, for better or worse, I do), while Ellen has one ear cocked, listening for the kids to see if she needs to rewind *Frosty* and play the tape again. That leaves me as the sole witness to my mother's appalling statement.

"It's probably in the box of his files I have at my house. I swear, one day I'm going to go through everyth—"

Kenny stops mid-sentence when Naomi holds a finger up to pause him. As a mother herself, she's always on high alert for trouble, and something immediately registers to her as not right. "Wait. What did she say?" she asks me. And then, since I am too dumbstruck to answer, she turns to our mother. "What did you just say?"

"Yes, Mother." I glare at her. "What did you say."

For the first time this visit, my mother truly meets my gaze, and we lock eyes in perhaps the most direct staring contest of our lives. She swallows and stutters and then stops before she even starts.

"What. Did. You. Say." I put my napkin on the table like I'm about to rise out of my chair.

My mother clears her throat, shrinking under the weight of everyone's eyes focused squarely on her. "I said, *He wasn't your father.*"

Only once before do I ever remember being on the receiving end of a look like this, and it was when I was maybe six or seven and we were in a store and I wanted something trivial (Silly Putty, perhaps, to reproduce the comics page), and she, defiant, stared at me until I hung it back on the rack. But this time she is willing me to speak, to do something in response. "You're drunk," I whisper.

Daniel stops and looks at me with quizzical concern, but I don't break my death stare. He turns to my mother and sees her glaring back at me; I'm not sure if he heard what she said. Either way, he knows something is wrong.

Kenny stares at Naomi, and from the very edges of my periphery I can see Ellen turn to stare at Daniel; we now have a full Mexican stare-off.

"Aileen, did you just say what I think you said?" Daniel finally manages.

"What did she say?" Kenny thinks he's missed some inconsequential bon mot, at most some insight into the whereabouts of the letter.

"She said he wasn't our father." I make sure she's still looking at me so she can see what those words look like on my face. "I said, 'I wonder what Dad would think of all this,' and she said he 'wasn't our father.'"

"Whaaaaat?" Kenny starts to laugh, but without looking at him I can't tell if it's nervous laughter or because he knows it's absurd.

"No. I said he wasn't *your* father." She holds her stare just long enough to see the dagger go into my heart. I think I recognize a flash of horror across her face, but she looks away at the far wall too quickly before turning her attention to her lap.

"Aileen," Daniel starts.

Naomi jumps in. "Mom, what are you talking about?"

I can feel a hand reach around my heart and squeeze, and the result is not so much pain as it is fear. Because the next thing that happens is I can't fill my lungs, I can't force air into them, I can't get them to expand. My weight grows in my chair, as if suddenly it were rooted to the floor of a house on another planet with a mass infinitely greater than earth's, a planet where my weight would be double or triple what it is. Daniel places his hand on my shoulder without taking his eyes off the unfolding family drama; I resent the weight of it as if it's further anchoring me down. My eyes grow wet, with sadness, with rage.

Naomi is now picking up the empty wine bottles one by one and setting them back down. Kenny looks around the table like a pollster trying to judge the mood of the electorate.

"Mom. Is that true?" he asks.

My mother doesn't speak, so I speak for her. "Is *what* true." The words fall out of my mouth like marbles as I turn to my brother for help. Once in fourth grade, this kid Bruce Snyder—who must have stayed back at least three or four times, because I swear he could shave—threatened to beat the crap out of me after school for telling our teacher that he ate three of my pen caps. Kenny, who was in high school at the time, was waiting for me by the front doors of our school when the final bell rang and escorted me home for a week. I want that big brother now. I want that big brother again.

But it is Ellen who comes to my defense. "James, don't listen to her." She's rewarded with a stern look from her husband, as if she's speaking out of turn.

Kenny is not quite there at the school's main entrance. He's maybe a block away still when the bell rings. He's not prepared to ask the question that demands an answer, so instead he asks, "Are you drunk?"

My mother whispers, "No."

"Of course she's drunk." Naomi pushes an empty bottle of Cabernet away from her in disgust. It tips over in slow motion, and when it lands with a dull thud several drops of red wine hit the salt and pepper pilgrims like blood spatter, for once their permanent surprise faces warranted.

My mother mouths the words *I'm not.*

I wonder for a moment if I'm the only one who sees her do this, but Kenny roars, "Then why would you say such a thing?"

We are frozen in diorama; someone could paint us and we would be exhibited in a museum and studied by future generations. Notice the pained expressions, the stillness of the composition. Everyone has eaten, and yet they are still hungry. Unsatisfied. Look how the figures are all in their own space, separate, even though they look as if they belong together; only the two young men are touching. Take in the heavy brushstrokes, the paint weighing the figures down.

"WHY WOULD YOU SAY SUCH A THING!" Kenny slams his fist on the table and the tableau is broken. We all jump, as do the plates and the silver. Everything hangs frozen in midair, like we've hit zero gravity for a split second, and then comes crashing back down on the table.

"I said it because it's true."

NINETEEN

Y ou've got to be kidding me," my father gripes.

"That's the assignment." The cake pans rattle as she sets them on the counter. My mother is losing her patience.

"He might as well be a Girl Scout."

Three months into Webelos, our den mother announced our December activity would be a father-son cake bake. Based on their reactions, this seemed to many of my packmates at odds with the purpose of Webelos: to transition boys from Cub to Boy Scouts. Peter Headley even pulled out his manual as proof we should be learning about survival, wilderness, and first-aid skills—like we'd been doing. His father had given him a pocketknife, and he was anxious to use it. We had already sat through lessons on building a campfire, finding a good campsite, and identifying edible plants and berries. There was one activity about campsite cooking that involved placing some hamburger meat and a potato in individual tinfoil pouches that we each hand folded; we cooked them on a pile of charcoal briquettes and then ate them in Lance Falchuck's backyard with plastic forks. But baking and cake decorating were not activities you could really do in the wilderness and seemed, to some of the other kids, outside of our stated mission. Which is, of course, why I'm excited.

"Boys should be out collecting rocks, hiking, and staying physically fit. Or put to work picking up trash along Route 89 if they need a project."

My mother doesn't respond—she's used to letting my father talk himself out. I remain silent so as not to give away my position in the hallway around the corner.

"Can't you just do it?" he asks. My heart sinks. Once again, my father pawning me off on my mother.

"What is wrong with you?" she whispers, so that I won't hear. She knows I'm never far. But I always hear.

"It's demeaning. Pamela's working out issues in her own marriage and taking it out on these boys."

"What issues would those be."

"She hates Barry. Probably all men."

"And so she's punishing you with cake. How horrible." My mother slams cabinet doors. I imagine she's assembling ingredients—sugar, flour, baking soda, vanilla extract—for our confection. "If she's so man-hating, why would she volunteer to be on the front lines raising the next generation of them?"

"Maybe it's part of a secret plan to topple us from within. Women like that? They're not to be understood."

More silence from my mother. She can play this game all day.

My father stews before eventually letting out an exaggerated exhale. "What kind of cake does the boy want to make."

"A lighthouse cake," my mother informs him.

"A *what*?"

"A lighthouse."

"I meant what flavor. It has to be a shape too?"

"Yes, it has to be a . . ." My mother stops and I hold my breath. "I will bake you two sheet cakes. Vanilla. I think that's allowed. But you had better get to work figuring out the rest."

"It's Sunday. The game starts at five."

"His meeting is tomorrow night. And it had better shine." More whispering. "Remember the Pinewood Derby."

The Pinewood Derby was the last project my father and I undertook, back in Cub Scouts. Each boy was given a kit with a block of pine, plastic wheels with metal axles, and fathers and sons were tasked with making model cars and racing them together. My father had fun carving and sanding our block into the body of a race car, holding it up for inspection and making small adjustments to the aerodynamics; I took the job of painting it very seriously. I found a corner of his workshop where I finally fit in, and he even helped me look through picture books from the library on fast cars and choose just the right colors—blue with orange stripes. The racetrack itself was assembled in the basement of the Nazarene Church, where we sometimes had our meetings. I overheard my father tell one of the other dads that my paintjob could best be described as "enthusiastic"; I wasn't certain that was an insult, but I also couldn't rule it out. Together we placed fourth. There were only three trophies.

I cried in the car on the way home.

"We don't cry over losing," my father had said, but I wanted a trophy. Yes, they were gold and shiny, mounted to a base that looked like marble, and I had imagined how it would look in my bedroom. But more so, they were a symbol. I would never have one for running or swimming or playing baseball. A trophy would have stated clearly that I could excel at something other boys did. A trophy would have been proof that I was a normal kid.

In the passenger seat I held our race car tightly in my hands and rotated it slowly, as if it were on a barbecue spit. I stopped crying two blocks from our house. In the driveway, after we sat in silence for a moment or two, my father said, "I'll bet some of the other fathers hollowed out their blocks and placed weights inside. I wish I had thought of that." It was only then that I understood that he was disappointed too. "Lou Fletcher even has a drill press. Damn."

"How does making something heavier make it go faster?" I had asked. It seemed antithetical to me.

"I don't know, son," he replied at the time, clearly growing annoyed. "It just does."

"Are you listening to me?" my mother says sharply to my father now, making me jump in my secret spot.

"Yes. Pinewood Derby. I heard you." I hear a kitchen drawer close and my father retreat to his workshop, hopefully to develop a plan.

After I'm sure that he's gone, I slink into the kitchen and stand silently until my mother slips her apron around me, the one that says I'M A PEANUT BUTTER AND JELLY MOM.

"How are we going to make a lighthouse out of two rectangular cakes?" I ask, studying the two cake pans.

"That's your father's department." She opens her cookbook and measures the flour, the whole time my eyes trained on her. "This would go a lot faster, Francis, if you just let me do it."

I blink twice. "That would be against the rules."

"No one would have to know."

I'm already uncomfortable with the amount of help my mother's giving. How do I explain this? "I would know." Scouting, among other things, is about honor.

"Yes," she says, "I suppose you would."

I watch as she combines all the ingredients into a bright melamine mixing bowl. As she puts the paddles into her electric mixer I'm dubious and ask, "Will Dad be able to do this?" Maybe honor is not the most important quality, maybe the goal here is a decent cake.

"That's the great thing about cakes. Grandmothers make them. You don't need the Army Corps of Engineers." The electric mixer whirrs to life.

When the cakes are out of their pans and cooling on wire racks, my father and I stare at them, careful not to look too closely at each other. He'd cut a board in his workshop for us to build the cake on, and he allowed me to cover it in foil. What comes next is anyone's best guess.

"Well," my father says, "we're stuck with each other."

The proclamation lies flat between us. Even I understand it's a mouthful.

"How are we going to make these into a lighthouse?"

My father squats so that his eyes are counter level and he surveys the two cakes. "Do you trust me?"

"Are you going to hollow it out and put weights in it?" This is new, my talking to him in this tone.

My father studies me over the rim of his glasses. "Nobody likes a smartass, James."

I nod, not saying that it was, in part, a serious suggestion.

"What are you wearing?" His eyes land on my apron.

"Do you want one? Mom has one that is blue."

"Take that off. We're men, we're not frightened of a little mess."

I glare at my father and he glares at me, his the more menacing. Without breaking eye contact, I slip the pink apron over my head and drop it on the floor, and only then do I look down, away from him. I'm angry, but I don't entirely understand why. I *am* afraid of a little mess (and deathly afraid of a big one). I wish I could wear an apron all the time in Webelos, especially that day we bent young trees to frame a lean-to—I got sap all over my clothes.

My father pulls a small bowl aside and cracks an egg on the edge using only one hand before tossing the eggshell into the sink.

My eyes grow wide. "Where did you learn to do *that?*" My mother always used two hands.

"The United States Marine Corps."

"Really." I'd heard my father speak of his time in the Marines on many occasions (too many, in fact) and the stories had never once excited me, but any place that could teach you to crack an egg with one hand—with the flick of a wrist and a flourish—could not be all bad.

"After long drives we would cook eggs and Spam on the hood of our Jeeps while they were still warm from the engine."

On second thought, my original assessment was correct.

"What do we need an egg for?"

"For the frosting."

"There's no eggs in frosting." I've helped my mother with enough cakes to know that. "Besides, Mom already made buttercream."

My father looks over at a large bowl of cream-colored frosting as if startled by it. He swipes his finger through it and takes a lick. It's the first time he doesn't seem totally repulsed by the task ahead. "Well, okay. We need to make blue, and we need to make gray."

"Gray?" Gray is the color of seals and manhole covers and stormy skies. Certainly nothing you eat. I try to think of gray lighthouses and can't imagine that either—lighthouses are usually white.

"Blue is easy. There's already food coloring for that." He takes the small blue tube of coloring out of the box and sets it on the table. "But gray . . ." My father scratches the short whiskers under his chin. He didn't shave for church this morning because we were running late. "How are we going to make that?"

Why are we going to make that? is the real question, but I know better than to interrupt my father when he's thinking. "Gray is a mixture of black and white," I offer, hoping that might help.

"That's good." My father rests his hand on my shoulder; it feels heavy and he pushes a little too hard. "The frosting is white, but we don't have black. But I think we could get a gray effect by mixing three primary colors."

I look at the box of food coloring options for primary colors. "Blue, yellow, red!"

"It's your cake. Give it a try."

It's *our* cake. I have the brief, terrifying thought that he's sabotaging this project so as not to appear less than manly. He spoons some of the white frosting into a separate bowl, and even though I hesitate, I eventually add drops of coloring in equal amounts and stir the frosting until a ruddy color appears.

"I think I added too much red," I say; our gray has a brownish hue. I don't know how I could have allowed an extra drop of food coloring pass my careful scrutiny, but the result is hard to argue with.

My father looks over the bowl. "Nah, it's perfect." His graying sideburns are not unlike the color of this frosting: brown with a hint of red, but enough in the way of gray to make it interesting. "We're going to use that for the rocks."

Rectangle pans? Gray frosting? Rocks? Nothing about this says lighthouse to me, and, worse, nothing about it suggests edibility or prizeworthiness. Not only were we doomed not to ribbon, we were likely to be laughed out of the room.

My father must read the expression on my face, because he says, "Boy, what do lighthouses do? What is their primary job?"

If they have a secondary job, I do not know it. Their primary job is to keep ships from crashing into . . . "Oh." I'm almost impressed with his vision; he was giving this real thought.

We frost the first cake blue for the ocean. My father breaks the second cake unevenly (I *gasp*) and places half on top. "Frost that one gray." The cragged edges make the perfect rocky coast. I use a little of the white frosting to make waves and ripples in the water—enough to make the sea look choppy; if we're making a lighthouse cake, it might as well look like the lighthouse was put there for a reason. My father crafts a tower out of the remaining cake, and because it's delicate, he frosts that himself. Together, we use the last of the gray frosting to make a dome on top.

When I stand back to take our creation in, I can't help but be impressed. Perhaps we weren't stuck with each other after all— perhaps we make a pretty decent team.

"You know what this needs?" my father asks, and then he leaves the room. He does that a lot, asks questions and then doesn't wait for the answer. I follow behind him as he treks back to his workshop. I fidget in the doorway as he opens and closes the little drawers that he uses to sort little things like screws. "Aha!" After a few false starts he finds what he's looking for: old parts from a model train set he had as a boy. He plucks out five tiny trees that are the perfect scale for our cake.

"Are we allowed to use those?"

"You bet. I read the official instructions. The cake need only be eighty-five percent edible."

"In that case . . ." I pull one of my father's moves and run inside and up to my room. I return to the kitchen with a little plastic ship that I never play with.

We place the finishing touches on our cake and my eyes brighten. I have visions of the other boys cheering and raising me on their shoulders as I clutch the first-place prize, even though I know deep down I'm the only one who would get that excited about baking.

We win second prize. Lance Davies and his father made a race car cake that noses ahead of us for first. (Foiled by race cars again.)

"Good job," my father says, and he shakes my hand after collecting our red ribbon. I think he's almost relieved we didn't place first.

The cakes are sold in a silent auction to the parents, friends, and judges who were invited to our meeting to raise money for further Webelos activities. I want my father to buy Lance Davies's cake so we can dissect it to see if perhaps it's only eighty-four percent edible and therefore disqualified. My father decides at the last minute to make a play for our cake, but bidding has already closed.

It's not until my mother says good night to some of the other women and makes her way to our car that we learn what she has done. She bought our cake while I was distracted with Lance's. I sit with it in the backseat, and my father even drives extra-slow to keep it from sliding as he goes around corners.

As the bridge that spans the widening gulf that exists between my father and I, my mother sometimes seems feeble. The cables that keep her suspended feel tired and frayed. But tonight, as she turns back to smile at me before patting my father on his leg, she seems fully made of steel.

TWENTY

There used to be this popcorn ceiling in Kenny's room. Stucco ceiling. Whatever people call it. A particular scourge of suburban homes in the 1960s and 1970s. Why bother to fix the cracks when you can slather layer upon layer of ugly crap on top of them and pass it off as style? Look, everyone, what a lovely pastiche of caulk and putty from the local hardware store and diet cottage cheese! Doesn't everything look just as good as new? These treatments are a lie. They don't fix the underlying ceiling, the cracks, the weaknesses, the imperfections. They only serve to cover them up. But now somehow the popcorn is gone and I'm trying to remember when it came down, who did the work and why, in a family that apparently loves to cover up faults and deformities with slop and untruths, someone had the foresight to say: No, here we should make things right.

"You awake?" Daniel asks.

We lie on our backs clutching the blanket up to our necks, our eyes wide open in the darkness, both of us afraid to do much more than breathe. I count to fifteen in my head. "Would you be asleep? If you were me?"

Daniel exhales, carbon dioxide and excess oxygen fluttering his lips.

Naomi volunteered to take my bedroom with my old twin bed since she's alone, and Aaron sleeps in a He-Man sleeping bag on the floor. Kenny and Ellen live close enough to spend the night in their own home, so Daniel and I settled in Kenny's room, which is bigger and more comfortable for guests. Kenny invited us to spend the night at his house, the big brother finally showing up to walk me home— although where and what home is anymore, I'm not sure—but I told him not to be silly. I am an adult; I stand up to my own bullies now.

So they packed up William and Zachary and left, Ellen holding my hand for a few seconds too long, letting go just before it became awkward, and they walked out the door.

The bully is in her own room, just across the hall.

I sat at the dinner table long after everyone left, like I did as a child when I was not dismissed for refusing to eat my peas. My mother retreated to her room; Naomi and Ellen tended to the children. Kenny and Daniel sat with me for a while, but Daniel eventually got up, as someone had to clean up the meal, and Kenny stepped away to gossip with Naomi.

Eventually we all went to bed.

I squint to further study the ceiling, but the only light is from the November moon, whose bluish glow softens the entire room; I can't tell where the walls end and the ceiling begins—it feels like we're in an igloo. Winter is a month away, at least by the calendar, but an icy chill seeps through the windowsill, washing over me like a whisper spilling more gut-wrenching secrets. A swift breeze tickles the maple tree outside, and I can see the shadow of the last of its dying leaves waving at me like hands, large hands, of basketball players or giant, hulking Swedes.

One of the branches raps on the windowpane and Daniel flinches. "What's that noise?"

"The tree," I murmur, as if lulling a twitchy child to sleep.

I planted that tree as a fourth-grader. I remember my father and me extracting it from the neighbor, Miss Egan's, yard. She was a miserable old woman with a crooked back who had never married and owned too many rag dolls that may or may not have been handmade. She always wanted our dandelion leaves, which seemed odd, but I think she used them in soup. She had expressed some rather unkind thoughts about this maple when it was hers, and when those thoughts seemed to percolate into a plan of action we rescued it from a sinister fate by transferring it, roots and all, in a rusty wheelbarrow to its current post outside Kenny's window. We planted it a respectable distance away from the house, imagining its future growth, my father digging a hole for it a few feet closer to the lamppost.

At least he was my father then.

"Night is darker here than in the city, yet the moon and the stars are brighter," I say.

"It's too quiet," Daniel replies. "Too quiet to sleep."

Sure, that's the problem.

I remember noticing when we drove up to the house that the grass, even in November, looked impossibly lush, like Astroturf. I have lived enough time in a glamourous metropolis to understand that what is fake sometimes looks real, and what is real can look impossibly fake. There was nothing fabricated about rural New York, and yet the entirety of it is carefully constructed, perhaps on a cavernous soundstage. The stars are stage lights rigged to camouflaged rafters, the trees made by the world's leading plastic arborist. The house and barn, once so familiar to me, merely false fronts, propped in place by an intricate series of two-by-fours and steel girders. In summer, the sound of crickets is piped in. We saw a production recently of William Inge's *Picnic*, in which a friend of ours played Madge; I remember thinking how much the set looked like home. I'll bet if I saw it again I would be struck by how much the set designer's construct *felt* like home too, now that I was seeing home through more jaundiced eyes.

Daniel takes my hand in his; it feels surprisingly warm around my frozen fingers. My heart weakened, it's unable to pump blood to my extremities. "She didn't know what she was saying." It's the first reference to dinner Daniel's made since we retired to the privacy of Kenny's room.

I chuckle. Not amused—bemused, maybe. Exhausted. Because I know she knew exactly what she was saying. "You wanna bet?"

"Okay, so maybe she knew what she was saying, but you know that doesn't make it true."

I roll over on my side. I'm looking right at his ear, which, in this light, looks like both a grotesque deformity and a painstakingly sculpted work of art. "It doesn't make it not true."

"She was drunk. You said so yourself."

I pause, trying to think exactly what I want to say. How to not only end this conversation but also let it begin. "In vino veritas." My mother is not a heavy drinker. Tonight it was wine that shook the truth free.

Daniel makes a squawk like a Canada goose. His Latin is not very good, but I know he can understand that.

"What is that screech for?"

"Latin? You're quoting me something in Latin? Seriously?" Daniel yanks some of the covers away from me to pile on top of himself. "Sometimes it's hard to know who in your family is the most dramatic."

And now I laugh for real. Because employing a common Latin phrase and lying about your youngest child's paternity are equal crimes. And then Daniel starts laughing, and our laughter twists together like the twin backbones of the double helix of a DNA molecule: It actually feels, in this one moment, like the basis for life. I'm afraid for it to end. Afraid for the hollowness that will open in this room like a sinkhole once our laughter crescendos and starts its slow fade to silence.

I lick Daniel's earlobe, which surprises even me. He swats me away. "The thing of it is, I think she's telling the truth."

"Oh, come on. She couldn't possibly."

"She hardly shares anything about herself; why would she go out of her way to share something made up? It doesn't make any sense."

"She's mad at you still. She's trying to prove something to you, that you don't know her as well as you think you do, that you got it wrong in the book . . ."

"She didn't read the book."

"Doesn't matter. To her, you're publishing a lie. She wants to see you humiliated, to feel shame like she apparently has. And she's using this fabrication to do it."

I shake my head no while taking back my share of the covers. "It's in the book," I say, and then I say it again, as if it's really just sinking in. "It's in the goddamned book. Sometimes he would look at me and wonder how I could be his son."

Daniel doesn't bite. "You should have seen the way my dad looked at me when I told him I wanted to play the French horn."

I smile, mad at Daniel the whole time for making me do so.

"You're just being paranoid," he continues.

"There were times I hated my dad."

"There were times I hated mine."

"I should probably welcome this news."

"It's not news. It's made-up."

"And yet, lying here, I want it not to be true."

"Well, it can't be."

We're almost having parallel conversations. "We baked a cake once. Did I ever tell you? Well, my mother baked the cake. My father and I decorated it. Got second place."

"Second place in what?"

I stuff the pillow farther into its case to prop myself up. "I don't really remember. A competition? It was a lighthouse, the cake. He said . . . He said we were stuck with each other."

"He probably meant in the task."

It's impossible to know what he meant.

I try to focus on ridiculous topics, put my brain to work on other things so maybe I can sleep. What is the object of the sport lacrosse? Do we own a copy of the Periodic Table of elements? How do thumbs work? Yet my stubborn mind always drifts back to Daniel's words. *You're just being paranoid.*

My mother is a woman always in control of who she is and what she says. There's a reason why this came to the surface tonight. Jackie was right: Every mother has a story. And it was time for this story to be told.

⬥ TWENTY-ONE ⬥

I wake up confused and hungover, not from the wine (clearly, I had not done the lion's share of the drinking) but from exhaustion; I have no idea what time it is or how long I've been asleep. The last number I recall seeing on the clock was 3:15 a.m.—a time I remember from reading *The Amityville Horror* as a teenager that particularly haunted George Lutz. He would wake every night with a start to see that time on the clock, and he eventually determined that's when the son of the house's previous owners murdered his family with a shotgun. *Shots fired, shots fired:* my last thoughts before falling asleep. *He was not your father.* Shots fired, indeed.

Darkness hangs over the room, but underneath the shade I can make out the first pink light of dawn—there will be a new day. I look over at Daniel. He's on his back, head facing the wall, and I watch for the familiar rise and fall of his chest. Recently I've watched him sleep a lot, many late nights when I've been wide awake, impossibly caffeinated, trying to work through the frayed edges around the book's central narrative to derive the perfect ending, jealous perhaps that his work, the odd jobs he takes between directing gigs, never seems to keep him from rest. The faintest whiff of brewing coffee wafts under the door; it's not the loud, Handelian wake-up my mother used in the past to rouse us (and for that, hallelujah), but it's effective. I slip out from beneath the covers, careful not to rest my weight on the creaky edge of the bed. Daniel doesn't stir. I'm wearing a surprising amount of clothes; I can't recall if that is by design to stay warm or if I never really bothered to get undressed before going to bed. Perhaps, like a minuteman, I thought I would need to be ready to fight the moment a battle resumed.

I look down the hall and notice my old bedroom door is closed—Naomi and Aaron are still asleep. That leaves one culprit, and when I look across at my mother's door, sure enough, it is cracked open. I stand frozen in the hallway, cold and motionless. Peering halfway down the stairs, something strikes me as different. The wall above the landing is conspicuously empty. There used to hang a framed needlepoint of flowers from A–Z, something my father's mother had made. *A is for amaryllis. B is for buttercup. C is for chrysanthemum.* As a kid I had the whole thing memorized, sitting as I would for long periods on the stairs, not knowing whether to go up them or down, waiting for life to begin. I wait here now, motionless, as if I myself might disappear if I make any sudden moves. I study the stairs, uncertain whether to advance or retreat, and then run my fingers along the wall, looking for the hole where the nail used to hang. When I find it, it anchors me firmly in a past that I remember. It's not all made-up, my childhood, the construct of an imagination gone haywire. I *was* young once, smaller, uncertain, afraid. And now I am grown, bigger, certain, brave.

Slowly, I head down the stairs. The stillness combines with the sound of someone puttering in the kitchen and the rat-a-tat-tat in my eardrums to make it feel like Christmas morning, but there are no gifts waiting for me, no stockings hung with care. To the right of the bottom step is the half-open door to my father's old office. It radiates calm. Although it faces east, and it should be among the first rooms in the house to get light, it seems excruciatingly dark and cold; my mother keeps the shades drawn. I turn the other way, to the dining room. There's light in the kitchen. The coffee smells stronger down here and it pulls me, sings to me, beckoning like a siren toward danger, toward jagged rocks, toward doom. Sure enough, my mother is standing at the kitchen sink, her back to me, looking out the window at the meadow, at the cold frost of a November dawn.

"Coffee's almost ready," she says, but doesn't turn around. I pull a stool up to the counter. The day's newspaper is already thumbed through; it's fat with sales flyers for Black Friday.

We stay silent, waiting for the coffee to finish. When it gurgles the last of its brew and emits a quiet hiss, my mother pours two mugs and slides one my way. I stare at it, like it might be a trap, something explosive, a grenade. But I need the caffeine, I need to feel warmth. I hold the mug for a moment, cupped in my hands, before it gets too hot and I have to set it down. After some silence and some careful study of a Radio Shack flyer, when I think the coffee has cooled, I take a long sip, letting it burn my throat with its bitter heat. I don't usually drink it black, but I don't dare reach for the cream and the sugar. I'm in the presence of a bee; so long as I stay relatively still, there's a good chance I won't get stung.

My mother pulls a loaf of raisin bread out of the bread box and sets it on the counter halfway between us. It just sits there in no-man's-land, in some sort of demilitarized zone.

"His name was Frank," she says.

"Nan's needlepoint at the top of the stairs. The flowers. A amaryllis to Z zinnia. It's missing." It comes out of my mouth somewhere between a statement of fact and the sounding of an alarm. "In fact, a lot of things are missing." This is now verging on accusation. "Photographs. Memorabilia. Books. Have you noticed this?"

My mother looks around the room, confused, from the window, to the hood over the stove, to the door to the mudroom, to the table, to the counter, as if noticing not only this, but the house that she lives in, for the very first time. If we were living inside a movie trailer, this is where the Talking Heads song would fade in.

And you may tell yourself, this is not my beautiful house.

"It's like you've been robbed."

My mother considers this. "I moved some things around."

"You moved some things around?"

"James, please."

I reach for the raisin bread and grab it by the twist tie that holds the bag closed. I twist and I twist and I twist, but its grip on the bag only tightens, so I twist the other way until the paper comes off the tie and I'm left with only the wire and I rip the plastic bag open, exposing the whole loaf of bread to air. "I'm not really hungry."

My mother grabs a cutting board and sets out half the loaf, but it's a new cutting board with indistinguishable characteristics, barely a groove from a serrated knife, and not the deeply notched one from my youth that my father had made. I suddenly have this desire for the house to be a museum dedicated to the way things were. That there be stanchions with a crimson velvet rope blocking off access to the things that were most distinguishably ours as a nuclear unit. We veered off course somewhere, and I suddenly, desperately, want to go back and course correct. To do that, everything must be exactly as it was.

"You need to let me say this."

"Jesus." I mean it to be profane. I also mean it as prayer. *God, help me understand: Why is it we always hold on to an idealized version of the past?*

My mother takes a deep breath, wrapping the torn plastic bag around the other half of the bread loaf like she's diapering an infant for the first time, unsure how to really go about it and aiming instead for maximum coverage. "His name was Frank."

"Stop it." I keep my eyes focused on the bread and make a fist so tight that I can feel my fingernails dig into my palm.

"His name was Frank," she says, now for the third time. "Frank Latimer." As soon as this name sinks in, I recall my lifelong distaste for the guttural sound made by the *n–k* consonant cluster. Bank. Tank. Chunk. Dank. Kerplunk.

Hoodwink.

"Frank was a teacher, you might like to know. High school English."

I scream silently in my head. When I stop, something awful occurs to me. "Oh, God, did we have him?"

"No. No. He taught a few districts over."

There is a long silence, as the engine driving this particular reveal sputters, then dies altogether. When I can hear the house actually settling deeper into the earth, and when my stomach rumbles from hunger but not for food, I turn the engine over until it restarts. "What else?"

"He was older than I was, by several years, not many. A veteran. He fought in World War Two, but only at the end. When he joined the service, the Battle of . . . famous battle . . ."

"Normandy?" Why am I doing any heavy lifting here?

"That sounds right. It was already under way by the time he got there. When he returned, he finished out his service at Fort Drum and then went to the teacher's college over in Herkimer County."

My brain actually hurts. I press on my eyeballs with the palms of my hands. "What else."

It takes her a moment to continue. "He was married. I know that. His wife was . . . religious."

"You're religious."

"Newly religious—some kind of religious that interfered with their . . . marriage. She was younger and naïve, his word, not mine. Their child—their only child—was stillborn."

I press harder on my eyes until I see shooting stars. "I guess that accounted for the religion."

"It was all so long ago. I haven't thought of any of this in years."

"These details are . . ." I start, but I can't think of a single appropriate adjective to assign here. "How did you meet?"

"On a campaign."

Inconsequential is the word I was looking for.

"A campaign for what?"

"On a campaign to elect a Democrat to Congress."

I can't think of anything to ask other than "Why?"

"Why? The man who previously held the seat had been appointed to the New York Supreme Court, so there was an election."

As answers go, it's clear, concise—impenetrable, even. But it makes my head spin more. "You worked on a campaign?"

"Your father said I should get out of the house."

I'll bet he regrets saying that.

"After a month we started skipping the campaign meetings. We would take long drives instead and just talk."

"About what?"

"Nothing. Our daily lives. I liked the way he drove: fast, but not too fast—different from your father. It made me feel like someone else."

"So help me God if this is a euphemism."

"I'm talking about driving a car, that's all."

The next part is a jumbled mess and it's hard to know how much I'll retain. She would tell Frank stories about her daily routine as a stay-at-home mother, careful not to make it sound glamourous (if that were even possible), sensitive the whole time to the hand he was dealt, to his having missed out on his chance at fatherhood. When they would find a scenic overlook he would stop the car; he told her surprising things, stories about the war and the little action he saw, stories that seemed unimaginable. (When the war in Europe had ended he was in a foxhole in Germany in some town with a name like Ulm, and there was an announcement over a loudspeaker—*The war is over, the war is over!*—and he couldn't make out the words over the static and he had to turn to a buddy next to him to ask, "What are they saying? Warm apple turnover?")

"It was at one of these overlooks he told me his wife had been seeing the ghost of their dead child."

"Ghost." I'm certain my ears are deceiving me. "G-h-o-s-t. This story has a ghost." I'm living my own Amityville Horror.

My mother motions for me to keep quiet. "At first it was confined to the crib in the nursery they couldn't bring themselves to take down. And then later it appeared outside the home. On bus benches. The laundromat floor. His wife would stop and talk with the baby that no one else saw, and it scared other people. It was sad, this woman's predicament, but I was excited by it then. These sightings. These stories. It's perverse, I know. That poor woman."

If you are to take my mother at her word, the drives were innocent enough at first—they were, after all, just talking—but eventually the relationship became sexual when they ran out of things to say, when their time together started to resemble the time they spent with their spouses, repeated stories bookended by long silences. When she became pregnant, he asked her to leave my father but she didn't think she could. And when she came around on the idea—when she thought that maybe, perhaps—he wasn't so sure he could leave his wife. What would the town say? They would have to leave their homes, start over someplace new. My mother didn't feel she could do this, not to my father, who hadn't done anything wrong, certainly not to Kenny and Naomi, and not to herself, as it took so much of her being and her soul to establish roots where she was.

"Did you discuss . . . abortion?" I have clear feelings about a woman's right to choose but stumble on the word when the fetus in question was me.

"We discussed it."

"And?" I'm on the edge of my seat, as if I don't know the outcome.

"That wasn't an option for me."

"So you kept it." *Kept me.*

"There was no right answer. We were both sad and felt powerless to stop the sadness. He was trapped, and things with your father . . ."

My stomach flips. *Which one?*

Her eyes fill with water and tears fall down her face, but she continues with her voice barely quivering. "Soon I began to dread our time together more than the thought of staying at home. I rekindled things with your father to explain the pregnancy, and he seemed pleased when I told him about your impending arrival and things got better for a while."

"Did he suspect?"

Silence. I maybe hear someone upstairs, or it could just be the heater. "You came along eight months later. If he questioned the math, he never did so out loud."

We're stuck with each other.

We both stay motionless, unsure of what to do or say next. My coffee's gone cold, but I don't dare reheat it. Eventually I get up, cross to the fridge, and open the door. I stare inside, taking inventory of the contents, pushing aside Thanksgiving leftovers hastily crammed in Tupperware to explore what there is behind them.

"You're out of milk," I say. "The kid will want Corn Flakes."

"There's plenty of fruit and bread for toast."

"He will *want* cereal." I close the door and turn back to my mother. "So, do I get to meet this guy?"

My mother is taken aback. "Frank?" As if I could possibly be talking about anyone else. "You met him once. Or he met you. You were just a baby. He wanted to see you. I didn't know if it was a good idea, but he insisted and I didn't want a scene."

My mother doesn't like a scene.

"Oh."

And then she adds, "You threw up on him."

"Oh," I say again at this new bit of information.

She wipes her eyes with her hands. I could offer her a tissue or a paper towel, but I don't move.

"He would turn up every now and again. That lasted a while. I would see him parked at the grocery store, or across the street at the pharmacy. It always frightened me, seeing him. I thought maybe he was unstable or angry. I was afraid for you. Then, before it got unbearable, it sort of resolved itself."

I huff. "What does that mean?"

"He stopped popping up, and eventually I never saw him again."

Of course he stopped. I was a ghost to him—he would see me places, I would appear, but I was in another dimension, belonged in another world—he couldn't get close enough to touch me. Frank, in a cruel twist of fate, was now the father of two lost children. "For the first time I'll bet he really understood his *wife*." I emphasize *wife* to underscore a moral condemnation, even though I'm not clear in this moment about my level of outrage.

"One other thing."

I wait for a final shoe to drop. My mother doesn't say anything; my head quivers, a sort of physical prompt.

"He wanted to be a . . ." she finally starts.

"A what."

My mother just looks at me until she breaks and whispers, "Like you."

"A homosexual?" I'm thoroughly confused.

"A *writer*."

The room narrows and the silent screaming in my head returns until it bubbles over and out into the kitchen. "No!" I yell, although to what I'm not sure. All of it, I think. "No, no, no, no, no!"

A car pulls in the driveway and the engine stops. I look out the window. Sunlight. Kenny sits behind the wheel but doesn't get out of the car.

"Kenny's here."

My mother bursts into sobs. "*This* is why I didn't want to be written about!"

I don't understand what the *this* is. The affair? The shame? She's fully sobbing now, big heaving jags. Again I make no move to comfort her; instead my throat burns and my body aches with feverish chills and my feet are leaden. I use the last of my strength to remain upright, and just when I feel like I might fall, a question pops into my head. "What is Frank's full name?"

My mother turns away from me, and when I know my own tears are inevitable I take a step back and repeat myself.

"What?" she responds. "Latimer. I told you."

"Is Frank short for something."

No response.

The whole kitchen rumbles like a large truck is driving by, but I know from the heat in my face that the thunder I feel is the manifestation of my growing rage. Through grit teeth: "Was his name Francis? Is that why you . . . Is Frank why you called me Fran?"

She starts to cry even harder as the kitchen walls fully close in around us.

"I told Jackie I was named after . . ." I can't even finish, the humiliation is too much. In my whole life I've never been this angry. "You have no idea what you've done."

◆ TWENTY-TWO ◆

I grab my scarf and my jacket and stuff my feet most of the way into the shoes I kicked off when I arrived (less than eighteen hours ago) and I'm out the door in a blur, closing it quickly behind me before Domino can escape. I lurch toward Kenny's car as I struggle to get my left arm through my jacket sleeve, and when I bang on the passenger-side window it looks like I don't have a hand.

"Christ on the cross," he exclaims. I can read his lips through the window.

"Let me in."

Kenny reaches over to unlock the door and I climb inside; it's warm and Dan Fogelberg is playing on the radio and for half a second I mistake the blast from the heater for a gentle ocean breeze and my body almost relaxes before tensing up again.

"I came by to see how you were doing," he says.

"The leader of the band is tired."

"What?"

I point to the radio. And then I add, "We need milk."

Kenny mutters something in response, but my brain feels like soup and I look around the car as if startled to find myself in it. Fortunately, he repeats himself: "What for?"

This time I understand. "I don't know. For drinking. For Corn Flakes. We're out of it, that's what for."

"You bring your wallet, superstar?"

"Just drive."

Kenny puts the car in reverse, and when we're safely down the street and I can no longer see the house in the side-view mirror, I slap the glove box a good six or seven times.

"Hey, this is a nice car!" Kenny protests.

"It's German. It can take it."

"You okay?"

No, I'm not okay! "Daniel says I say 'melk.' Do I say 'melk'?" Kenny shrugs and flicks his left blinker in preparation to turn.

"Milk," I say, over accentuating the *i*. It sounds completely ridiculous. I turn to Kenny. "Did you know Corn Flakes were invented to cure masturbation?"

He chews on that before answering. "I think I knew. That rings a bell."

"What else do you know?"

"What, you think I knew about *this*? I did not know about this."

My brother's a genius in many things, observant—especially of human behavior. It's what makes him a great attorney. I don't know if I believe him, but I also have no reason not to. "This car smells. Your car smells."

"The kids." Kenny takes a deep whiff. "There may be a McNugget under the seat. I've lost control of my life."

YOU'VE lost control, I want to protest. "McNuggets sound good right now."

Kenny laughs. "It's like seven in the morning."

We drive in silence for another half-mile or so.

"His name was Frank."

"Who?" Kenny asks. I glare at him as he pulls up to a stop sign, then he looks over at me and mouths, *Oh.*

"Yeah, oh."

"You've talked about this already? Like, you just went there?"

"She went there. I didn't want to go there. I wanted raisin toast!" I should have done more to stop my mother from sharing—stuck my fingers in my ears, left the room, blasted a stereo.

"She probably had a lot to say."

"Don't you dare take her side!"

"I'm not!"

"You don't know what it was like for me. He loved *you*."

"Dad? He loved you too."

"He didn't like me all that much. And to think my whole life I thought it was my fault."

"What, you think *he* knew?"

"You think he didn't?"

Kenny stares at me until I focus my attention on the road. "So what did she say. Exactly."

To think back on it exhausts me. "She said his name was Frank."

Kenny exhales his frustration, but seriously, what am I supposed to do, just launch into the entirety of it?

"And . . ."

"And I don't know. There was a whole long spiel that touched on Democratic politics and something that happened in the New York Supreme Court, some other thing that transpired in the European Theater during World War Two. There was a teacher's college in Herkimer County and also a woman who saw ghosts." All of this is now jumbled in some horrific mishmash in my head, and I can feel a tight pain growing at my temples as this is all starting to sound like the plot of some lesser work by Eugene O'Neill. *Did we really talk about ghosts?*

But isn't this entirely about ghosts?

"Why do they call it *theater*, the different fronts of a war?" Kenny asks. "The Pacific Theater. The European Theater. Why *theater*?"

"Seriously?" I ask.

"Seriously."

"I don't give a fuck!"

I press my head against the window and count telephone poles as they go by. When I get to eleven, Kenny says, "That's the kind of thing Dad would have known."

"Whose dad?"

Kenny doesn't respond, he just looks at me with something akin to pity. "There's no chance she's making it up?"

"If she is, she's a better writer than I am."

Kenny nods. He's slept on this. I think in his heart he knows that it's true.

We get to the market, but they don't open until eight. Kenny grabs coffee and donuts from the little bakery on the corner and we sit in the car for twenty-five minutes making small talk, waiting for the store to open its doors. Kenny mostly blathers on about an eminent-domain case he's consumed by and I half listen while refolding a map to restore the integrity of its original pleats.

When the store opens Kenny stays behind to listen to the NPR news update at the top of the hour. I walk inside the sliding double doors and someone says "Good morning" and I almost say "What's good about it," but instead I tighten the muscles around the corners of my mouth and draw them upward as best as I remember how. I grab a basket and locate the dairy coolers at the back of the store. I'm struck by how small it is, the market. Grocery stores in New York are tiny, the carts look as if they were hit by a miniaturizing ray, and the shelves are stocked with itty-bitty cartons of things. If halfway down the aisle you meet someone pushing a cart in the opposite direction, one of you has to back up and retreat. This market is small in other ways. The food looks white and bland, there are no aisles with signs for ethnic selections. No shelves with oyster sauce, or tamarind paste or Mexican prayer candles, and I doubt anything in the store is kosher. I work my way up and down the aisles like my father did on the rare occasions we grocery-shopped together. "You never know what you might need until you see it," he reasoned. My mother, on the other hand, thought it a waste of time to go down an aisle if there was nothing in it you required. But maybe with Frank she opened her eyes to another method: She didn't know what she needed until she saw it. Perhaps that was good for her. I approach the produce, disgusted with myself for trying to draw larger conclusions from food shopping, and then continue my trek up and down each row until I reach the far end of the store—the bakery—not because I want another donut or don't know what I'm shopping for, but to prove to myself that I am indeed my father's son.

I loop all the way back to the dairy coolers before I have to crouch to keep from vomiting. I lean my head over the yogurt and wait for the sensation to pass. When I feel like I can stand up again, I head to the checkout empty-handed. Remembering the milk, I go back and select a half-gallon because the fridge is too full to hold a full one. "Melk," I say out loud again. It just sounds better.

We drive home in silence until Kenny shares a story about Ellen answering a phone call from a marketing survey company asking about lotion.

Q: What do you like about the lotion?

A: Its moisture.

Q: What specifically about its moisture do you like?

A: The moist part.

And then out of the blue he says what I imagine a lot of people think: "What type of person has an affair?" His words drip with judgment, but I don't take the bait. Not when I came this close to kissing Mark mere days ago. Besides, it's not the affair that I'm upset about—at least not yet. That wasn't a violation of her relationship with me. It's not even the lying to cover it up. It was never allowing me to know who I am, all the while knowing my identity was something I struggled with.

When we pull in the driveway, Kenny hesitates. He turns off the engine but leaves his hand on the ignition. "So. You have a father again," he says, all of it still sinking in.

I blow air through my lips. "Appears so." I can tell this is not the reaction he wants. "Jealous?"

"I . . . I don't know. Are you going to contact him?"

I shoot him a look before answering. "Papa Frank? That's . . . something to think about." My leg starts doing this involuntary shaking thing and it rattles the whole car. "Are you coming in?"

Kenny puts his hand on my knee until my leg slows and then stops. "I haven't decided yet," he says.

I sink back in my seat. "She was crying."

"Mom? When."

"When you got here. Sobbing."

"What did you do?"

I look at him incredulously. "What do you mean what did I do? I left to get milk!"

Kenny nods, like he's unsure of what he would have done in the same situation. "You do kind of say 'melk.'"

Silence.

"I can't finish the book now."

"What are you talking about?"

"I don't know."

"You're feeling sorry for her?"

"No! It's just . . . The book doesn't have an end and now my whole life is reset—all the way back to the beginning. I think about what I wrote and now none of it is true."

"Does it matter? I thought it was a novel."

"Yes, it matters!"

"Now I *really* don't know if I'm coming in." I look down, surprised to see Kenny's hand still on my knee. "Can you get out of it?" he asks.

"Out of what?"

"Your book deal."

I didn't even think of the legal ramifications. "I have no idea."

"Do you want me to look at the contract?"

"Jesus, Kenny. Can you not be an attorney for like five seconds?"

With the engine off, the window begins to fog. Kenny just shakes his head; it's clear he wants to say more, but he doesn't. When the silence becomes unbearable he punctuates our conversation with the obvious. "This is so fucked up."

Naomi appears in the doorway, her figure blurred by the window fog. She's waving frantically at us to come inside.

"Look who's up."

"What does she want?" Kenny asks, almost annoyed. He wipes some of the condensation from the windshield with his glove.

"I don't know. The milk?" It's as if there's no real way to figure it out, no action we could take to lower the glass partitions between us. We're in another dimension; there's no way for us to reach her, there's no way for her to reach us. We're so far away, this communication may have been recorded months ago and we're just receiving it now in the way that astronauts in science-fiction movies receive messages previously recorded on Earth.

Disgusted, Naomi sticks out the thumb and the pinky on her right hand and holds it up to her ear. I recognize this sign language: telephone. Someone is on the phone. We step out of the car and she crosses her arms to protect herself from the cold and pulls her sweater tight. "Why couldn't I have had sisters?"

I walk into the kitchen, clutching the milk in the crook of my elbow, tightly to my chest. My mother is holding the telephone out to me, her arm locked, as if the receiver itself might explode.

"*For me?*" I mouth.

She shakes the telephone insistently, like it's growing hotter in her hand by the second. There's a redness and swelling around her eyes; when she catches me looking, she turns away. I take the phone and lift the receiver to my ear.

"Hello?" I can feel the cold of the milk carton through my shirt.

"James, there you are. It's Jacqueline Onassis."

I look up and everyone is staring at me, Naomi, my mother, Daniel—everyone except for Aaron, who runs full speed and headbutts me in the balls. Kenny walks through the kitchen door behind me as I double over in pain and Naomi starts jumping up and down and pointing excitedly at the telephone pressed against my ear.

"It's *her*," she whispers hoarsely, giddily clapping the backs of her hands like a seal. The Presidential Seal.

"Oh. Hello. Hi." I ease my grip on the milk and set it on the counter. I feel my heart beat, as if jumpstarted by one of the defibrillators that earned my father a letter from Jackie's first husband all those years ago.

"I received your message."

"My message?"

"Yes, I came into the office to get some work done and you left a message on the machine."

How could I have forgotten? But honestly, with all that's happened since then, how could I have remembered? I can feel the heat of so much attention on me. I take a few steps away and then stop abruptly; my mother's telephone cord has been replaced since I stretched out the old one in high school, and there's only so far I can roam. "That's right. I wanted to tell you . . . to come clean about something."

"What is it?"

"I didn't do it. What you suggested I do before writing the end."

I can't be certain, but I think I hear Jackie purr. *Mmmmmm.*

I take one last look at everyone gathered around me before I lock my sights on my mother.

I take a deep breath.

"But I've done it now. What we discussed. I want you to know that it's done."

Everything Turned Around

December 1992/1993

Allen is running late for our meeting and my anxiety increases exponentially with each passing minute. This should be done like the ripping of a Band-Aid, and yet here I sit, picking around the edges of a proverbial bandage, just trying to lift a tiny corner, any tiny corner, from my skin. I turn to look at the clock on his office wall for the hundredth time and knock over a stack of magazines with my messenger bag.

"I'm sorry," Donna says, "he should be here any minute."

"You guys need to clean up in here." I kick the last few magazines by my feet to illustrate my point. I'm on edge all the time now, the slightest things set me off. Last night I snapped at Daniel for chewing too loudly, as if this mess were somehow his fault. I catch Donna's reaction to my rude comment, so I quietly apologize by restacking back copies of *Publishers Weekly* along the side of the guest chair. "Who's he with, Reggie?" I ask, wondering if I'm going to be subjected to the sight of my agent limping in with a raw steak over his eye.

"Who?"

"Chinatown Reggie." I look for any glint of recognition but get none; it's obvious I'm letting some cat slip out of the bag.

"Don't worry about those." She points at my effort to make sense of the magazines.

I stack the last few copies on top of the pile before nearly knocking them over again. I set my bag on the floor on the far side of the chair. "Looking forward to Christmas, Donna?" I'm grasping for small talk.

"No."

"No?"

"My son wants a . . . I don't know what you call it . . . some big squirt gun he wants."

"Super Soaker."

"That's the one."

"My nephews want the same thing."

"We took him to see a mall Santa this weekend and when he asked for a Super Soaker, I shot Santa a look, which he picked up on like we were psychically connected. 'Santa doesn't bring guns,' he said, and now my kid has it in for him. I said, Joshie, what are you going to do with a water gun in December? All his friends were getting them, he says. He was afraid he wouldn't be able to protect himself. I said it's New Jersey. Unless they shoot icicles, you're safe until May."

"Did that put him at ease?"

"His birthday's in April so I said we'd revisit it. He's still pissed at Santa though. I swear to God if he had the gun, he'd shoot up the North Pole. What about you? What are your plans?"

"Staying here in the city." Even if I wanted to see my mother right now (I don't), I can't risk any more family secrets gurgling to the surface. On the drive back to the city after Thanksgiving, Daniel and I didn't really speak. Silence felt like a favorite sweater; it wrapped us in just enough comfort to get us home. We watched a little TV and each picked at a slice of pizza and went to bed early but didn't really sleep. It was just easier to say nothing under the cover of darkness. I drifted off for a few hours and had a dream that I don't remember. All day Sunday I vacillated between denial and white-hot rage—it's a miracle Daniel didn't suffer whiplash trying to keep up. First thing this morning I called Allen. "I need to see you as soon as humanly possible," I said, and he told me to come in today.

"How's things with your mom?" Donna asks.

"My mom?"

"Allen said you were having some issues."

"It's tough," I tell her. "Things are tough right now."

"Because of the book?"

"Something like that." I smile, remembering a simpler time—last week, in fact—when that was my biggest problem.

"Can I tell you something?"

"Of course."

Donna pushes back from her desk and scoots her desk chair around to the side so we're sitting face-to-face. "I hate my mother."

"Donna!" I exclaim. I burst out laughing from her unexpected candor; it's the first time I've laughed in three days.

"No, I'm serious. She's a bitch, always has been, always will be. I can't do anything right. She hates my husband; she hates my kid. That may be harsh, but she certainly hates how we're raising him. My hair? It's the wrong color. And do not get her started on my nails or why I won't have them professionally done. She doesn't understand why I would work in the city when I could be a bank teller near my house, or why I ride the train or who makes dinner to feed the kid that I'm raising incorrectly. I wouldn't be surprised if she buys all the Super Soakers in a ten-mile radius so that when I cave and want to give him one I can't, because she thinks he should spend more time with a book. Look where I work! As if I don't know reading is important." Donna exhales deeply.

"That feel good?" I ask.

"You have no idea." She tosses her head back and laughs, released of a burden that somehow feels transplanted in me. "What was my point?"

"It's okay if there isn't one. This can just be cathartic for you."

Donna smiles and I shift in my seat to hear where the rest of this goes.

"If you did everything wrong like I apparently do, your mother would have no problem with you publishing this book. She would just turn the other cheek and quietly disapprove. If she takes real issue with it, it's because she knows deep down that you've done something right."

And if she hasn't read it? I want to ask, but Donna cuts me off.

"And it's clear you love your mother. It comes through on every page of your manuscript."

Allen bursts through the door, a cyclone of dry cleaning and apologies. "James, James, hi. Donna, take this."

Donna leaps up and takes his dry cleaning and his coat and hangs them both on the back of the door.

"Give me one minute, then come on in. Donna, did you get him some coffee?"

"I'm fine, thank you," I say, covering for Donna, who never offered.

"Did she tell you about the fatwah her son put out on Santa?"

"I told him!" They interact like a married couple who spends too much time alone.

Allen steps into his office and I stand to gather my things. I can hear him rummaging through papers as Donna crosses back to her desk.

"I'm serious," she whispers. "If my kid ever wrote something, like you did, about me? I would be thrilled. Because that would mean I was seen." Her eyes get a little misty. "Really seen. As a person. You know? Not his waitress. Not his maid. Not his jailer. A *person*." She nods and I place my hand on her arm and I start nodding too until we're just a couple of bobbing heads. I may have seen my mother as a person, but up until now—I never saw her so human.

"All right, James! Come on in."

Donna pats my hand and I let go, entering Allen's office with caution. Thankfully, he remains fully dressed and exhibits no outward signs of physical distress.

"Sit, sit, sit."

I take a seat opposite him, the same chair where I signed the contracts less than a year ago. My stomach churns thinking of all I've lost between then and now—my identity, for starters.

"What's the emergency?"

No chitchat, I guess.

"The book." I feel like a child in the principal's office, sent here for mistakenly causing a disruption when, in fact, the one who was disrupted is me.

"I figured the book. What about it?"

Somehow it's already my turn to talk again. "It's just. I need more time."

"Why?"

"It's come to my attention that I may have written the wrong one."

"The wrong book?"

"Exactly."

Allen combs his eyebrows upward with his fingers. "How do you mean?"

"I'm wondering if it's possible to write another one."

"I hope you'll write another one."

"A different one, I mean."

"They bought this one."

"Yeah, and maybe they'd buy another one. Instead." How do I explain that I can't publish a book about the search to understand a woman who is clearly not to be understood?

"What's this really about, kid?" Allen picks up his glasses, puts them on like he's about to read something, and then tosses them down on his desk. He probably wants to strangle me, but he remains outwardly calm.

I lie and say, "I don't know." But I do know. I look down at my hands and I don't know whose they are. I mean, obviously mine, but are they also Frank's? I have such long fingers, piano-playing fingers, Daniel once called them, although childhood piano lessons never stuck. Kenny doesn't have fingers like these, my father doesn't. What other qualities do I have that I now don't know their origin? I'm supposed to be writing an ending, but it feels like I'm playing a game—Chutes and Ladders, perhaps, or Sorry!—and just when I'm about to win it all my game piece gets sent back to the start.

"Please tell me you haven't discussed this with Jackie."

"I'm discussing it with you."

Allen scrutinizes me, choosing his next words carefully. "Have you read Pat Conroy?"

"The novelist?" I make a face. What does Pat Conroy have to do with anything? "Yes."

"I met him once at some Houghton Mifflin event a friend bullied me into attending. Usual bullshit chatter, but then later in the evening I overheard him say it was a year or so after he published *The Great Santini* that it dawned on him he'd written exactly the wrong book about his family life."

"A year later?" It had never occurred to me that the particulars of my situation maybe aren't that particular. *Is this what writers endure?*

"So, I'd say by comparison you're early." Allen picks up his glasses again and starts opening the mail with an ivory-handled letter opener, as if my problem is totally solved. He proceeds to read some sort of query letter while I sit there and stew.

I can feel my frustration rising like bile until it gurgles over. "And what on God's green earth did he do about it?" My volume surprises even me.

Allen doesn't look up, despite my raised voice. "Pat?" He pauses while he finishes reading. "He went and wrote the right one. And that was *The Prince of Tides.*" He balls up the letter and tosses it into the garbage before moving on to the next piece of mail. "But he had to write the first one in order to write the second. It's just an ending we're talking about, right? That's what Jackie's been riding you for? You can't come up with an ending?"

"I . . . I . . ."

"Has she been difficult to work with? Has she not given you clear instructions?"

"No, she's been very clear."

"Then just do what she's asking." Allen doesn't wait for me to say what she's asking is impossible. "That reminds me, I got a note from Doubleday. They've locked in a pub date for the book."

"Oh?" Even in my agitated state, this piques my interest.

"Summer. August, I think."

"That's good, right?"

"Is it? It feels like more of a winter book." He shrugs.

"Beach read," I say, and we both chuckle, but me more than him. August. That's eight months away. Do I have it in me to deliver? Jackie's words come roaring through. *Don't tell your story to change the past.* What if I don't want to change it—what if I just want to change it back? *That's still change,* I think, answering my own question.

"Nothing's perfect, kid. You figure that out by now? You wrote a good book. You've done everyone proud."

"Everyone?"

Allen switches his grip on the letter opener so that he's holding it like a knife ready to stab; I really am wearing on his last nerve. "You know how many writers would kill to be in your shoes?"

Immediately I know that he's right. Something awakens in me. I have to make this work; an opportunity like this might not come around again. Like Jackie said, I can't write to change the past. I have to go through the door that's been opened in front of me. Isn't that the way? The world only spins forward, after all. I've been overwhelmed trying to find my right ending. But isn't it just that, if I'm being reductive? Isn't this whole situation simply an ending? An ending to secrecy. An ending to lies. The closing of the space between us that has kept my mother and me apart. An end to this book. If I want to really be a writer, I have to tell the whole story. I have to follow the narrative wherever it may go.

The realization racks through my body, jolting right down to my toes. I don't want to publish the wrong book only to correct it with another, I want to make this one right. It may, after all, be my only one. To find my ending—to find myself—I have to find my father. I have to find Frank Latimer.

Allen snaps his fingers to get my attention. "All we can do is roll with the punches."

I'm going to meet Frank.

"Roll with the punches. You still with me?"

I laugh.

"What?"

"Nothing." And then, my mood suddenly shifted, I tell him, "Says a man who pays to get punched."

Allen makes a playful fist at me, Ralph Kramden–style. "Get out of your head and out of my office. Go find your ending."

Go find Frank.

• TWENTY-FOUR •

I feel hands on my shoulders and jump. It's Daniel.

"What are you doing?" he asks, coming around to my side.

The young woman sitting across the table from me looks up from her work, annoyed. We've shared an unspoken camaraderie over the past few hours, two silent people in the cavernous research room at the New York City Public Library lost in our work; now I'm responsible for breaking our carefully negotiated quietude. The chairs are hard and uncomfortable and the room is cold, but the lighting is soft, both chandeliers and table lamps casting a warming glow, which makes it a good place to concentrate. A casual observer would see the stacks of medical textbooks that dwarf my tablemate and think her work more noble than mine, but I would have to protest; the search for Frank Latimer is about healing too.

"I thought you were coming home. I made popcorn."

"What time is it?" I whisper, hoping to lower Daniel's voice by example. Having spent so much time in this library, I know how bothersome anything but total silence can be. A stray cough can send me spiraling for ten minutes.

Daniel looks at his watch. "Two-forty-five." He says it hoarsely, an approximation of a whisper.

"Shhh." I look up at the mural framed by the ornately carved ceiling for strength; there's just enough pink in the swirling cumulus clouds to imagine they hold the answer to life's questions.

"Do you pay rent here now?"

I offer a silent apology to my table partner. She looks back kindly, as if she too has a boyfriend who doesn't know boundaries and library etiquette. I grab Daniel by his coat and lead him away from the work-tables. "I lost track of time."

Jackie has given me until the end of the month to write an ending; it's clear her patience, like Allen's, is growing thin. I'm doing my best to avoid her until I can deliver, sending just enough notes through Mark to let her know I'm working—like I'm a spy checking in with my handlers while stationed out in the cold. I started spending time at the library in December, convinced that understanding *why* my mother would harbor such a devastating secret was an intrinsic part of my ending. That meant finding Frank Latimer and hearing his side of the story too.

Of course, like any quest, it wasn't as easy as opening a phone directory. In fact, there wasn't a listing for him in any of the phone books in the Ithaca area. That by itself didn't mean much—he could have moved or had an unlisted number—but I had this hunch that he stayed close. That maybe he never stopped shadowing my mother. That he never stopped keeping tabs on me, his second child. I thought about asking the hospital where I was born, but Frank was, of course, never listed on any forms. I found a few teaching commendations and even a picture of him in the *Steuben County Courier*, strapping students into some new contraption called the "seatbelt convincer." (He also, apparently, taught driver's ed.) The photo was grainy and his face in the crowd of students was not much more than a smudge. The father of two ghosts, barely more than an apparition himself.

After admitting to myself one night that I make a lousy detective, I asked my mother for help.

"I can't assist you right now," she said, as if she were in the middle of planning a state dinner. "Please don't ask me again."

So it was back to the books. I researched his name, Latimer, to try to get some fragment or sense of him, of a new familial history, to try and see if I could recognize something about myself. It's of French origin, introduced to the English after the Norman conquest of 1066, deriving from the Old French *latiner*, translated literally as "a speaker of Latin." In the Middle Ages, all important documents were recorded in Latin, making the position of Latiner an important one. Like a teacher today, perhaps. (Although I don't know what's so esteemed about sending a bunch of sophomores careening into a wall to convince them to wear a seatbelt.)

All of this research was getting me nowhere, so I've doubled down, pushing myself around the clock, desperate to find something— anything—more on Frank, to prove that my mother is mistaken, or prove that she's telling the truth. It's the uncertainty of it all that's eating away at me, the circumstantial nature of the evidence that's preventing me from writing a single word. I can't decide if my mother's story would hold up in a court of law, or if the whole thing would fold like a house of cards. In a perfect world, I would just go home and write. Put a pin in this, meet my deadline. But this new obsession is bordering on addiction—I try for a day to stop, to just work on the manuscript, and my hands shake and my brain sputters like I'm going through withdrawal. Am I a fool to think this is all related? Am I just using Frank to procrastinate, afraid of even further rejection if I can't make things just right on the page?

I pull Daniel over to the reference section, alongside a row of fat, forgotten books. "I'm sorry. There was an issue with the microfiche reader and the only woman who could fix it didn't come in until noon."

He pulls a neglected tome from the shelf, confused by our change of venue. He reads the spine and says, "What's a gazetteer?" I want to delight in his not knowing something for once, but I can't really explain what a gazetteer is either. He places the book back on the shelf. "You said you were writing. Why do you need microfiche?"

I don't say anything, which tells Daniel everything.

"You were looking for Frank again."

I was determined to write when I came here today, I was, but then I found myself scouring old newspapers like a junkie looking for a quick hit and found two undiscovered articles on the campaign my mother claimed they volunteered for. And yet, further corroboration of her story—a photograph of my mother with a strange man, perhaps standing behind the candidate at a rally—still eludes me. "I didn't lie. The two things are intertwined."

He looks dejected. "We had plans."

"Is it over?"

"You missed the whole thing."

I rub my hands together in an attempt to warm them. I may have to start bringing gloves; cold air travels in here like whispers. "Is there any leftover?"

"Leftover what?"

"*Popcorn.*"

He takes a few steps away from me before abruptly turning and coming back. "Yeah. It won't be as good though." He shakes his head; I'm a lost cause, it seems. "I popped it on the motherfucking stove." A smile creeps across his face. Daniel's been downright chipper since he received the news a week ago that he was hired to direct a production of Christopher Durang's *Beyond Therapy* at a small theater in the West Village. Rehearsals don't start for a few months, but it's changed his whole outlook on the year, and for our relationship it couldn't be better timed; his good mood balances my dark one.

"How was it?"

"The popcorn? I just told you."

"The inauguration." At noon, Bill Clinton was sworn in as the forty-second president of the United States. I promised we would watch the inaugural address on TV together, which felt like a low-key second chance at New Year's, when I fell asleep well before the ball dropped.

"It was good. There was a poem."

An older gentleman approaches, holding a notecard, and I freeze as if Daniel and I are doing something covert. He consults his card and realizes he's in the wrong spot and moves on. "A poem?"

"Yeah, apparently Kennedy had one." He kicks me playfully.

I run my finger across a collection of atlases and decide I've had enough of the library for one day. It may be the dark corners or the sun setting in the early afternoon or the subject of my research, but I feel depleted. "Walk me home?"

"Sure thing," he says, whispering at last.

Daniel spills more about the inauguration as we step out into the cold, down the steps, and past the stone lions that guard the library. Something about the speech or something about a parade—I'm only half listening as it occurs to me yearbooks might be another place to look for Frank. As we approach Bryant Park I hear Daniel say, "*Saudade* is how my grandmother would describe it." His word catches me by surprise.

"Who?" At first I think he's trying to say Sade, the singer of smooth R&B hits.

"*Saudade*. It's a word my grandmother used to say when she was missing home." Daniel's grandmother was born in Brazil, and so every now and again some Portuguese pops up in conversation.

"What does it mean?"

"Oh. It doesn't have an English translation."

I give Daniel a little shove and he skids on a small patch of ice; I catch him just before he falls. "Easy, fella." I have his arms behind his back like he's under arrest and hold on until I'm sure he has his balance.

"Not a direct translation, anyhow." He turns his head and makes a kissing sound.

"Why don't you just give me the indirect one."

"It's like a nostalgia or melancholy, but more than that. With a recognition that the something we're longing for hasn't happened, or isn't returning. Or maybe never was."

"Why do you say that now?"

"About today? I don't know. All those people in the inauguration crowd. They looked young. They looked hungry."

"They were probably cold." I exhale and my breath forms a tiny cloud before floating away. Daniel casts a sideways glance; this bitchiness is what he's had to put up with of late.

"They want their Camelot. But it's not coming back. It can't come back. The world has moved on in complicated ways. *Saudade.*"

I study Daniel's face. The cold lessens his skin's elasticity, leaving an echo of his solemn look. "Or maybe it never was? Is that the idea?"

"Maybe."

He points to the walk sign across Sixth Avenue and we enter the crosswalk facing west.

"Where are we going?"

"I thought we'd stop for soup at that place."

I don't really want soup, but I keep quiet. The truth of the matter is, it's all too much. Clinton, Kennedy, nostalgia, melancholy. Things that are not coming back. Things that perhaps never were. I feel a deep need to believe there was another time, before, when everything seemed right. Unlike now, when everything feels wrong.

"Tell me something else." I pull Daniel's string to keep him talking so that I don't have to.

"About the inauguration? Clinton was just wearing his suit jacket. No overcoat."

"Idiot. What about Hillary. Hat? No hat."

"*Big* hat."

I think of Jackie on the same dais, how overwhelming it must have felt in person once upon a time. What the view must have been like looking across the National Mall and how small one must feel in the face of such incredible responsibility. Was she watching earlier today, or has she entirely moved on?

The cold whips down Sixth Avenue, but it's invigorating to be outdoors. There are days when I barely get out of my bathrobe, when I manage only a winter coat over pajamas to run to the grocery on a ridiculous errand, to buy pears, for instance, before I remember that pears are out of season.

"What was the poem?"

"Maya Angelou. She has very. Crisp. Diction. It had the word *mastodon.*"

I feel my face contort. "In what context?"

"Who knows. I just remember the word."

The street stretches like taffy; it actually feels like it gets longer, as if we're in some carnival funhouse. When we finally make it to the soup place I stomp my feet to regain sensation in my toes. We read the menu board together before I settle on Thai carrot ginger because they make it with coconut milk and there's something about that that feels lush and warm.

"Eat it here? Or get it to go."

I look around the restaurant and there are plenty of seats. "To go," I say, after some consideration. If we go home we'll turn on the TV to keep us company while we eat. If we stay here, Daniel will drone on about the inauguration, and an inauguration is a beginning—one whose end is unwritten. I need to focus my brain on endings.

As Daniel pays for the soup I turn to the TV mounted in the corner of the restaurant. It plays clips from Washington—the events of the day inescapable. I watch Bill and Hillary wave to the crowds as they walk from the Capitol to the White House, so full of promise and hope. An administration is judged by whether or not it fulfills the promise of its start. *A book should be judged in a similar way*, I think to myself.

I watch as the soup guy tapes lids to our containers, places them in a paper bag, and calls out, "To go!" As Daniel collects our order and I grab two plastic spoons from the counter, inspiration hits: The answers I need are not here, not in the library, not in the city.

I need to take my quest to go.

TWENTY-FIVE

I've spent three nights in as many Super 8 motels, although I hardly notice—they're all the same. The rooms, the sounds (always next to a major road with rumbling trucks at almost evenly timed intervals), the musty smell, the beds, the pillows, the lightbulbs, a maddening hum whose source can never be traced. Even the wall art, which is at least slightly different in each port and designed to make the whole experience more palatable, fails spectacularly in exactly the same way.

I followed the article I found with Frank Latimer's picture to a school in the Hammondsport area, which sits at the tip of Keuka, one of the Finger Lakes. It reminded me of Ithaca that way. The school secretary took pity on me; Frank's tenure lasted for only three years early in the Reagan administration and they've had a lot of turnover so there wasn't much overlap with the current staff. She remembered him fondly enough, said he had an impressive mustache and brought his own lunch and mostly kept to himself. He helped her once with a flat tire, after some students had scattered nails in the parking lot as a prank. He carried pens in his pocket and most of his shirtfronts had ink stains. She didn't remember the seatbelt convincer, but said it's possible the contraption came through on some sort of tour, part of a larger campaign, perhaps, around the time they were debating raising the state speed limit. I tried to absorb her every word, but her neck had this loose skin that jiggled like a turkey's wattle and it was hard not to focus on that. When I asked why Frank left, she had to check her records. Her tall, gray filing cabinet moaned like a yawning tiger when she opened it. She produced a thin manila file that said he took a job in Oneonta. I asked to see the file, but personnel records were private, she said.

Before I even left the school I had already forgotten her name.

I wandered around the town, bundled against the cold and the frigid winds that came whipping down the water. The lakefront had a number of private docks, and I walked out to the end of one and sat to watch the sunset. I could feel the cold boards of the dock through my pants; I should have packed long underwear. I have no ability to change a flat tire, but I do always carry pens. If the goal was to feel a connection with Frank, Hammondsport was kind of a wash. I stayed until my fingers and toes felt like the slushy bits of lake water that lapped at the shore, and the lake reflected the raging fire of a bright orange sky.

Next stop: Oneonta. It's a SUNY town, and that alone made it sparkle with more possibility. I nervously walked the high school hallways looking for the office, peering through the narrow window in each classroom door. There's a sameness to all these mid-century schools. The floors, the lockers, the drab paint colors—the scent alone is instantly transporting. In my high school, I walked the hallways trying my damndest to hide my true identity, head down, hiding behind books; now I wander these halls in search of it, head up, with no props to hide behind. But awkward still. Give me a college campus and I will feel at home. High schools contain haunting memories that jangle my very nerves.

The vice principal in Oneonta, a Mrs. Casky, is less friendly than was the secretary in Hammondsport, but ultimately more helpful. She knew Frank, but she's not sure why I want to. I told her I was a writer from *The New Yorker* (I'm surprised how easy lies come of late—it's as if my mother has opened a floodgate) doing a story on high school English teachers who had writerly ambitions of their own; I was given his name as a lead. It's ridiculous to think this idea would fly at *The New Yorker*, but it seemed to pass muster in Oneonta.

"He was always working on something in the teacher's lounge, that's for certain. Sometimes he was late for class," she said.

"Do you know what it was?" I imagine some brilliant work the world may never know.

"It wasn't a grade book. He was terrible about turning in grades."

"That's interesting," I said. "I can procrastinate too."

She tilted her head and pursed her lips, as if annoyed by my trying to draw a connection. I asked if there was an old yearbook I could see, to make sure it was the same Frank Latimer whose name I'd been given; she walked over to a closet in the back. A minute later she returned with three yearbooks and plunked them down on the counter. "He was definitely here at least one of these years. Faculty's near the back."

I bought myself a moment by studying the book's cover. The school mascot—a not unfriendly-looking yellow jacket—looked straight back at me, as if it were about to buzz my face. *Sting, quickly and with purpose.* I immediately flipped toward the back, but the faculty names jumped from Lancaster to Lester. In the second book I found him on the first page I opened to. It wasn't like looking in a mirror, but I recognized him nonetheless. It was his nose, I think, and something about the eyes. A discomfort of being photographed we shared, as if posing were taking us both away from something more important. I traced his features with my index finger like a blind person feeling a stranger's face, suddenly able to see.

"That him?" Mrs. Casky asked.

"That's him," I said, my voice cracking between the two words.

At the hotel I open a bottle of drugstore cabernet and wallow in feeling lost. The room doesn't have a corkscrew, so I mangle the stopper with a pen that's laid out by the telephone until I can push the remnants into the wine; with each sip I spit out bits of cork. For some unknown reason, Deb from Martha's Vineyard comes to mind. *If you're ever lost, take a right.* I'm not sure this counts as a turn, but I pick up the phone and call my mother.

"I'm in Oneonta," I say, another bid, but not really caring this time if I pique her curiosity. In the brochure left on the table it states Oneonta means *place of open rocks* in the Mohawk language, so I tell her that too.

"I found a letter," my mother blurts out, after we talk about January's snowfall. "It had a return address. In Syracuse."

I drop the phone in annoyance and it lands on the bed with a thud. The Super 8 mattresses could be the open rocks the Mohawk were referring to. I take a big swig of cheap, syrupy wine and can feel the cork bits in my throat when I swallow; I make a sound like a cat trying to cough up hair. Eventually I pick up the receiver. "A letter from *him*."

"Yes," she says, but only after a great pause.

"Well. You're just full of surprises."

"Don't be like that."

"No. You don't get to do this and also tell me how to be." Neither of us says anything for a long time; the room's natural hum mushrooms into a piercing ring. "What does it say?"

"The letter? I never opened it."

"But you never threw it away."

"I guess not."

I rap the phone on my forehead three times before saying, "No time like the present."

"Please don't make me."

I open my mouth, ready to bark at her to open it. But instead I say, "I have his nose." I laugh because I picture myself actually *having* his severed nose and then I think of Isis collecting pieces of Osiris and I stop laughing and actually start to cry.

"Do you," she says, but I don't know if she's questioning this information or if she can't really remember enough about him to know if it's true.

"I think so."

I hang up after she gives me the return address on the envelope.

Outside I take several deep breaths in the cold as I watch the traffic go by; the air is sharp like razor blades. My sweatpants and T-shirt provide little warmth, but I lean on the railing until I spot a car with one headlight out and feel I've seen enough to go back inside. I pour the rest of the wine down the sink and take a hot shower. Afterward, I flop on the bed in only a towel and flip through the TV channels until I've watched every station at least three times. I turn the TV off and study Frank's address. *Milnor Avenue*. Named, perhaps, after the people who make hats? The Latin speaker and the hatmaker. No, wait, that's *milliner*.

In the morning I drive from Oneonta to Syracuse; it takes two hours and thirteen minutes. I stop at a AAA and ask for a map and even though I'm not a member they take pity on me. It doesn't take long to find Frank's house, although I pass it without meaning to and have to throw the car in reverse, parking across Milnor Avenue to get a good, hard look. The house is brick, small, with a red door. The driveway is plowed, and there are burlap bags over what I imagine are rosebushes under the front windows along the walk. Icicles hang over the front door, which seems dangerous; I judge Frank for not taking better care. There's a car in the driveway, some sort of hatchback—it's hard to see exactly what make and model from where I sit. Someone is obviously home—Frank, or maybe a new wife.

I'm drenched in sweat, despite temperatures hovering around freezing. I focused so singularly on getting myself here that only now do I realize how nervous I am. When the windows completely fog, I remove my knit cap to blot the sweat from my forehead; it's as if I'm a burglar afraid of being made. But am I stealing anything so much as reclaiming a part of myself? I wipe a small section of the window so I can continue to study the house. It's as unremarkable as these events are unusual. If Frank is indeed inside, we're only a few hundred feet apart. This is it. The last few steps. The closing of a thirty-year gap I only just discovered.

I don't remember opening the door or getting out of the car, but I'm in the middle of the street anyhow, crossing toward Frank's driveway. My feet move independently of my commanding them to. I'm a marionette; my legs are bowed where they are attached to strings and I do this weird pivot as each leg moves closer to the drive. I place one foot on Frank's property and stop dead like there's one of those electric dog fences keeping me from advancing any farther. It's the mailbox. The source of this current. Across the top is a little sign that says THE DEMBROWSKIS.

Total panic. I pull my cap farther over my brow and look from the house to the mailbox to the car and back to the house again to make sure I have the right number. I even fetch the paper from my pocket with the address my mother gave me; I wrote it down three times, once for each time I made her repeat it. The curtain in the front window flutters, movement in the house. I whip around to cross the street and come this close to getting hit by a Toyota pickup. If my heart had stopped, that started it right up again. Slush from the melting snow is all over the front of my pants, all the way up to my knees.

It's now or never. I turn back to the house, walk up the front steps, and knock on the door three times. I live a lifetime in the thirty seconds it takes for someone to answer—a man, shorter than I imagined Frank to be, and rounder. "Yes?" he says.

My tongue feels heavy, like I'm having an allergic reaction to shellfish, even though I have no such allergy. "I'm looking for Frank Latimer?" My voice doesn't sound like it usually does.

"Who are you looking for?"

"Frank Latimer."

A woman's voice bellows from deeper inside the house. "Who?"

"Frank Somebody," the man calls back. "We are Dembrowski. There's no such person here."

In my heart I knew there wouldn't be.

When I'm safely inside the car, I lock all the doors and turn the air conditioning up to full blast to keep me from overheating and prevent the windows from fogging again. I have only one need: to leave Milnor Avenue as fast as one humanly can.

"They'd never heard of him?"

It's Daniel. After a tuna melt at some ramshackle diner and a couple of hours to collect my nerves while kicking around town, I call him from—wait for it—another Super 8 motel.

"No."

"Did you ask?"

"Not so much."

"Then come home."

"I might still. Ask. I'm staying a little longer."

"You're spiraling."

"I *have* to finish the book." I look over at the manuscript, which I brought with me, looming on the dresser.

"Then finish it! Stop dicking around looking for Frank."

"Wow. I could really use my boyfriend's support right about now."

"I *am* supporting you, and you're being too ridiculous to see it."

"Oh, *I'm* being ridiculous."

"In fact, you are. You think finding Frank is going to be the end of this thing, but it's actually going to be the beginning of a whole other thing. You've jumped in with both feet without really thinking about the consequences. You're conflating a deadline for the book with a deadline for blowing up your whole life!"

I flop back on the bed dramatically like a teenage girl whose parents read her diary. Daniel and I have had some version of this conversation for days. I don't understand his position on this. I don't get why he can't see the two things are related.

"Go ahead. Finish your book. But, please, give yourself breathing room on everything else."

"I don't have time!"

"Yes, you do!"

I can't think straight anymore. "I'm not leaving this motel until I finish."

"You're staying in Syracuse."

"Syracuse is my last stand."

"Then go back and ask, Custer. Go back and knock on the door. Then come home."

Who are you looking for? Mr. Dembrowski's voice echoes in my ear.

Silence.

There are dead flies in the light on the ceiling. I can see them behind the frosted plastic. What a depressing place to meet your end, slowly rotting until some janitor comes to replace the bulb. Is that to be my fate? I never find my way out of this trap and some housekeeper finds my body while restocking miniature bottles of shampoo? Maybe Mr. Dembrowski is right. Who am I looking for? It really isn't Frank, is it?

"Soon. I'll be home soon."

There's one more stop I have to make.

· TWENTY-SIX ·

It's dark when Scott and I turn onto my street, so I'm surprised when I look at my watch and it says only four-thirty. The solstice is still a week away and it feels like each bitter cold day suffers a failure to launch; the sun sets before it reaches its full height in the sky. The days are not different in that regard from things with Scott. Rockets ignite, despite our best efforts not to let them, and each time there is an unspoken dare, fueled by hunger, to go further. But an actual launch is always scuttled—for weather or safety concerns or whatever reasons these things are called off—and we have to disembark before getting anywhere near the stratosphere. As often as I promise myself this is the time we will talk about it, this is the time we will put words to our hungry teenage explorations, we don't. We ride around as we do now, in total silence, two boys without a definition, unsure of what they mean or who they are to each other. Sometimes I ache so much for the sound of his voice, even if it announces nothing of consequence, that I might explode in a ball of fire if I heard it.

Scott pulls his father's sedan to the side of the road in front of my house and says, "Well, shit." My entire body tingles as we roll to a stop and Scott puts the car in park. This is it. This is the conversation. This is when we will say out loud what we are. It's not the most artful preamble, but now is not the time to critique his language skills. It's me who wants to be a writer someday, not him.

I make a noise, I think, not quite a word but a sound. A grunt. I'm embarrassed by this, so I swallow and ask, "What is it?" feigning concern and surprise like there weren't oceans of unspoken things between us.

He nods toward my house.

I turn my head, and in the thick shadows of late December I see my mother step out the front door with a box and drop it on the lawn. It joins several others, making a kind of lopsided barricade. "What the . . ."

"Are those"—Scott does his best to explain what's unfolding in front of our eyes—"decorations?"

I do not answer. When I was younger we had a gaudy plastic crèche. One with hollow characters that lit up from the inside. We would set it on the lawn about now, the week before Christmas, and, like dutiful Catholics, leave it up through the twelfth day of Christmas—nearly a week after our neighbors' reindeer and snowmen came down. It sat in the garage in boxes for most of the year, and my father would set it up under my mother's watchful supervision, usually cursing the cold and his numbing fingers as she took great pains to exhibit the manger just so. We sold it in a yard sale a few years back, the wisemen, the animals, the angel Gabriel. My mother protested, it seemed sacrilegious to mark them with price stickers, but the figures were worn and my father rightly argued discarding Jesus, Mary, and Joseph in the trash would be a worse sin than re-homing them.

"No, seriously, James. What's going on?"

I know exactly what this is, and I seethe with rage. *Now? In this moment? Can't I have anything? Can't I just have this one little moment with a boy?* "It's my father," I quietly admit.

Scott squints and looks again, confused. "In the boxes?" he says, horrified, as if he's discovered my mother's secret identity as an axe murderer.

I close my eyes as tight as I can and wish hard that when I open them, none of this will be happening. I know magical thinking will not make it so, but when I open my eyes the barricade of boxes seems exponentially bigger than it should be—like maybe I drifted off. "I've got to go." I look at Scott and try to say a thousand things with a single look. My right hand on the car door handle, my left giving him a gentle punch on his thigh. Drive, drive away with me, I plead with my vigorous stare. But of course he doesn't. He just looks back at me with his dopey smile; deep down I'm already imagining some future love, another man who loves me enough to clearly receive my telepathy, who would in this moment hear my soundless plea and hit the gas pedal.

"Okay," Scott says, and my grip firms on the handle until the car door opens with a surprising pop. I jump like someone reacting to champagne being uncorked.

I look at Scott in his doofy Luke Skywalker T-shirt and unzipped coat, like this good-bye is good-bye forever, then my weight shifts and the door feels like it opens the rest of the way of its own accord. I tumble out. The cold air is a slap to the face; it actually stings. I stand in the cluster of birch trees, all of us like tall, pale ghouls against the dark winter sky.

I hear the window roll down behind me and Scott shouts, "Call me later," but I'm not sure if it's because he's desperate for the sound of my voice too or if he's into salient gossip or both. Before I can respond, his car tires spin in the salt on the road until they catch traction; in seconds he is gone. I fortify myself for the walk across the lawn just as my mother reappears with another box and tosses it on the pile.

"Mom!" The ferocity of my tone startles us both and she peers in between the trees to make out my approaching form.

"Francis?" She sounds wholly confused.

Ugh.

When she sees me, my mother huffs. I reach her and we stand in silence, like insurance claim adjusters walking through the scene of a fire.

"It's time" is all she says. And then I understand.

We remain still and survey her handiwork. "Does he know?"

My mother shrugs. "He's about to."

I don't understand why today is the day until I do, until it courses through my arteries to the point where even my toes understand and it starts its return trip to my heart. "It's him or me, isn't it? That's the choice he gave you."

"That's between your father and me."

That's a yes. This is a bed my father has made and yet I'm filled with sudden regret that he has to lie in it. Like it's somehow all my fault, and, I guess, on some very real level it is. It's sad. A man's life reduced to possessions, to boxes of things strewn across the front lawn of the house he, until this very moment, called home. If my mother made a different choice, the things in the boxes could just as easily be mine. Either way, our family has already forever changed. Naomi and Kenny have left to start their own lives and my mother and I now face life as a twosome. I'm overcome with desire to know exactly when the last moment was that the five of us were under this roof. Whatever the occasion, it was the finite end to something concrete. Something nuclear, something compound. We are divided, individual atoms now, and while atoms cannot be destroyed, they can certainly be scattered. Just as my father's things are spread out across the ground.

I place my hands on my mother's shoulders; they are bonier than I might have imagined. "Are you sure? Are you sure about"—I don't know what to call the mess around us—"this."

"I'm sure."

There are other ways, I want to tell her. This feels awfully hard to walk back. "I could help you carry everything back into the house. Before he gets home. Scott's parents would let me stay with them. Until this blows over. Or maybe I could crash with Kenny."

"It's already over, Francis."

I shove my hands into my pockets, wondering if my gloves are still sitting on the seat in Scott's car. The crack of a twig makes us both look to the tree line, but not even a raccoon emerges from the darkness. "My name is James."

My mother drops her head. "You're taking his side."

"I'm not."

"James." She looks at the boxes as if she's counting them, as if to double-check that she got them all.

"If you're doing this for me, Mom, I want you to see me. To see who I am. Francis doesn't really exist."

"He does to me."

"Well, maybe you can say hello to him for me." We stand in frosty silence, but I can't let it go. "I'm leaving here too, you know. Kenny's gone, Naomi's gone, it's my turn next. One more year. And you will be here. Alone. Let me go. I'll figure it out." I pick up one of the boxes as if I'm going to bring it back into the house myself. "You shouldn't choose me."

My mother looks up, perhaps to wish on the evening's first star. As if on cue, the clouds part just enough for Orion's belt to shine through. "I already did."

I don't know how to reply, not really, so eventually I just put the box down and say, "It's cold." I feel badly about my outburst, the stark dose of reality. I trace the box tops near me with my fingers and think of how to soften what I've just said. I make a silent vow.

I will always choose you too.

I already know it's one of those promises that sounds easy to keep when you're young and don't yet know how long life can be. My mother has been a constant for just about every day I can think of. The rational part of me knows that it won't always be that way, but there's another not insignificant part that thinks, *How could it not?*

I pull my hand out of my pocket and take hers in it. My entire life my mother has radiated warmth. To the touch, with a smile, with her time and attention, by things she made in the kitchen. But standing here in December among the bulk of my father's things, a perverse Christmas if ever there was, for the first time I can remember her touch feels cold as ice.

TWENTY-SEVEN

I pull the rental car down the driveway and find a spot in the far corner of the parking lot, away from the building that looks like an enormous ranch-style house with oddly placed windows and sliding glass doors that I'm convinced would be welded shut if it weren't for some overriding fire code. In front of my windshield is an ugly, shrinking mountain of slush and grime—a winter's worth of plowed snowfall. The trees are bare, rigid skeletons in formation in front of a soft blue sky. It doesn't look a damn thing like the brochure my siblings and I were shown, which offered lusher, greener photos taken at the height of summer. I don't remember how we found this place. I say "we," but this was, of course, Naomi's work—the only one of us able to function while the rest of us were in denial (or feigning indifference). The cars around me are as nondescript and unremarkable as the building, cars they give away on syndicated game shows, Buick Skylarks and Oldsmobile Cutlass Calais.

Sadly, no one here is winning, on a game show or otherwise.

I always felt it was sexist that it fell on Naomi's shoulders to handle all of this at the time, but, truthfully, Kenny was ill equipped and, on top of everything, had two young kids. Me, I lived in the city. There's no place like this where I lived, at least not one we could afford. And my father would have been unhappy and confused with the noise of New York, plucked from the quiet of upstate only to be confronted with screaming sirens and the endless mental jackhammering; it's enough to drive even those of us in our right minds insane. Besides, I was persona non grata to him. Had been for many years.

I sit in the car, stretching and contorting my legs until I hear a few unsettling pops. It would be more productive to stand and stretch, but

I like the sanctuary, the security, that the car's interior provides. I feel invisible, despite being surrounded by windows, a false confidence that is not uncommon based on the number of nose-pickers I've witnessed on this trip. I rotate my feet in circles, and when I get bored of that I flex my calves. I stretch my neck by looking over at the entrance, only to see someone who looks vaguely like Naomi exit the building, and I slouch in my seat to hide. It hadn't occurred to me that I might run into family while here, and what I would say if I did. Fortunately, it's not Naomi. She would never wear such a hideous coat.

When I enter the building, I'm confronted with a whiff of depression and sadness, and of the meat of bodies stored in heat instead of refrigeration. The smell is poorly masked with some sort of citrus freshener meant to make it all okay, but somehow makes it worse, slapping a happy face on grimaces of tortured pain. It's the smell of animal shelters (although not as pronounced), the faces here, too, hoping to be sprung with each arriving visitor but too broken to yelp and bark.

"James Smale," I say to a woman at the front desk, announcing both my name and the name of my father.

She doesn't even look up. "Room 124," she says, with some sort of French Caribbean accent.

His room number is the same as that of my creative writing classroom in high school. The irony. Room 124. The room that set my brain free is now the very one trapping his. "I can go back?" Surely they don't just let people in off the streets. She finally pays me a glance and holds it a second longer than would be polite before nodding me through. I guess I don't look dangerous, just neglectful. Which is probably true of all visitors here.

I walk down the hall and smile at everyone I pass. A woman sitting in the hall in a wheelchair. She smiles back, all gums and no teeth. An older gentleman with dark lesions on his bald scalp propping himself up with a walker. A man in nurse's scrubs carrying a mop; he nods back at me, both of us unsure who has the sadder task.

I find the number 124 on the wall and trace my fingers over the letters of my name on the nameplate underneath as if I'm blind and reading Braille. I can almost feel Annie Sullivan spelling ASL letters into my hand: F-A-T-H-E-R. But I don't know ASL, so maybe she's spelling something else.

The door is open. I take a deep breath and step inside.

"Hi, Dad," I whisper. I fight with the one annoying Demi Moore–style tear that always forms in the corner of my eye when I visit.

There is, of course, no response.

His eyes are open and he stares vacantly at Oprah on the television set on the dresser. I watch him for a while, before turning my attention to the TV. The episode seems to have something to do with a week in the life of a troubled family. I can't imagine what their troubles are, but I doubt like hell they come close to equaling ours.

Something looks different about my father. Maybe it's just that he's older than he was when I saw him last, two Christmases ago. Before I sold my book. Before I met Jackie. Before Frank Latimer. Back when I was somebody else.

His hair is white where it used to be silver, but it's more than that. Someone's parting it on the other side. His face is sullen, sunken, vacant; I didn't know skin could look gray. I turn away, it's painful to see, and don't look back until the show goes to commercial, then I pull up a chair beside him and sit down.

"It's James, Dad." He doesn't respond to that, so I say "Jimmy," the name he often pushed in my mother's face.

We spoke some on my last visit, but nothing of any consequence; my father seemed to think someone had taken his eyeglasses and replaced them with a pair of identical-looking frames with a slightly different prescription. I told him most likely it was just time for him to see an eye doctor, that perhaps his vision had changed. In fact, I tried to arrange an eye exam with the nurse and Naomi followed up. Several weeks later they found his glasses in a neighboring room—sure enough, another more mischievous resident had switched them.

I'm not sure he had a firm grasp then on who I was, nor am I all that certain now.

"How are your glasses?" I look at them on his face. They're so smudged with fingerprints and grease I can hardly see his eyes. "Here. Let me help you." Carefully I lift them off his face. He flinches, but just a little. I wipe the lenses on the T-shirt under my sweater, but they're so greasy I can't tell if I'm making them better or worse. "Hold on. I'm going to wash them in the sink."

He nods, but I don't think he understands.

In the bathroom I run the water until it's warm, and find liquid soap in a wall-mounted dispenser. I run the glasses under water and lather the lenses with my fingers until they're lost in foam. I look in the mirror and hardly recognize myself—I look older too. When did I become such an adult? When did these lines appear, these dark ones under my eyes? Did I have them a week ago, before I left the city? Is my forehead growing north? Is my face sliding south? When did my pores become so embarrassingly . . . porous? The water runs hot and I can feel my hands burning, but it takes a moment before I register real pain; I rinse the lenses under cooler water.

I wipe the glasses dry and place them back on my father's face. "Here you go. I think you'll be able to see a lot better with these." He flinches again. I sit back down in the chair by his bed. He widens his eyes as if he notices an immediate improvement, and I feel happy that my presence here has accomplished at least one good thing. "So what's new?"

No reply.

"What's new with me? Well, let's see. Still in New York. Daniel's good. He's directing a play, but they're still raising the money. I have a book coming out. In August. A novel about mothers and sons. I guess we haven't spoken about that. It's been a while. Maybe Naomi told you. I'm sure she did. She seems proud of me. I would like to think that you are too."

Silence.

I sound unnatural, like a snare drum, my sentences no more than crisp, staccato notes. I remember being a child, playing with LEGO or some sort of toy. How I would make the people talk, how they would have vivid, colorful conversations on all sorts of topics—movies, car racing, city planning—until a grown-up appeared in the room. And then these toys would revert to the stilted, polite conversation of strangers. It feels like that now. Like I want to have an animated conversation, full of excitement and ideas, except an adult just walked in. But aren't I the adult now?

My father groans and starts banging his hand on the bed.

"Mom's not thrilled, of course, but I'm going ahead with it anyway. We can talk about the why. I just—thought you would get a kick." As much as he hated when I would disobey him, he delighted in the few occasions I would cross my mother. "You're not going to believe who my editor is." *Nope, nope, wrong,* I say silently to myself, as if he had offered actual guesses. "Jackie Kennedy."

I wait for a reaction that doesn't come.

"Well, Jacqueline Onassis now. That's what she prefers to be called. Can you believe it? Not that she prefers to be called that, but that she acquired my book? It took a long time for that to sink in. I'm sure you can imagine."

I'm sure. You imagine. What are these words? I'm not sure of anything when it comes to him. Does he imagine? Can he conjure or visualize or dream?

It was only a few years after my mother kicked him out that he first exhibited signs of his disease. He was still young, so we were slow to catch on; the progression in retrospect was rapid. It was hard to keep on top of reports of his declining health. And, truthfully, I wasn't sure how much I was supposed to care. Naomi stayed involved. Kenny too. But my mother and I were the most aggrieved, and it was hard for us to know just how much concern to muster, although we managed plenty of guilt. It occurred to me much later that perhaps he agreed to leave knowing he was sick. That he was going away to die, the way a dog might crawl under the house, or a wild animal might retreat far into the woods. That I was just a convenient excuse. Though I knew that was a bit of a stretch. To me it was a relief, his illness, even though I know how terrible I am for thinking it. He struggled on his own. It was hard to imagine his starting anew; his best days were seemingly behind him. Wasn't it more merciful this way? To have him succumb to something quickly rather than wither quietly (or loudly) for years?

"I'm still looking for an ending. For my book." I see if that sinks in. "I'm looking for a number of things. I thought maybe you could help." He actually turns in my direction, but stops short of looking me in the eyes. "She really pulled a number on us, didn't she."

I look up just in time to see two terriers trot past his open door. Am I hallucinating? There's an air vent close to the ceiling; maybe they pump in mind-altering drugs, perhaps that's how they keep people here calm.

"Excuse me for a moment." I get up, cross the room, and poke my head into the hall. The dogs greet a woman with an angular haircut angered by severe highlights. She's crouched in the hallway two doors down.

When she sees me she waves. "Hi."

"Are dogs allowed in here?" I say it not as an accusation but as a question of policy. Should I get my father a dog? He's desperate for the company, I think. And maybe it would teach him a good lesson. A dog wouldn't go anywhere. Dogs are loyal, more loyal than families. More loyal than many fathers. Let him sit with that every day.

"These are therapy dogs. Specially trained. We bring them in once a week."

"Ah." One of the dogs sees me and trots languidly in my direction. I reach down and pat the top of her soft head, and then tousle the hair on her skull into some sort of wisp. She's more agreeable than Domino, who, much like my mother, does not seem to like being touched.

"Would Mr. Smale like to visit with her?" It takes me a moment to realize that I'm not the Mr. Smale she's referring to.

"I . . . I don't actually know."

"He knows Buttons. Just lift her onto the bed. They'll be fine."

Buttons raises one eyebrow and looks away, as if she wants it made clear that she didn't name herself. I don't really know the best way to pick up this dog, but after a false start trying to lift her like one might a child, I put my hands underneath her and hoist her into a football carry.

"Look who's here, Dad." I thrust the dog forward before setting her gently on the bed. She intuitively finds an open space between his arm and his body, circles ceremoniously two times, and lies down.

My father peers down his nose, surprised to find a dog curled up in his armpit, but not unpleasantly so. He moves his hand slowly to pet her. He looks right at me for the first time, as if to make sure we're seeing the same thing. I start to pet Buttons too, and our hands touch; it's awkward at first, the accidental grazing of fingers like two teenagers on a first date. How does this escalate? What do we do next? But we find our rhythm and stroke Buttons's back in unison, two parallel pendulums never connecting.

"Casp . . ." he starts, before slurring the rest.

"Casper?" Casper was a dog we had when I was growing up.

My father nods. It's strange to think, with the way his disease works, that all the things I no longer think about are the very things that are readily accessible to him. Memories that are gone or only faint recollections—Casper, for instance—are perhaps as vibrant to him as if he had lived them yesterday. And all the things I'm mad at him for, all the things I obsess over when I'm lying awake at night— his rejection of me, the hateful things he said to my mother—are probably to him long gone.

"So did you know about this?"

My father, of course, says nothing. I'm going to have to do the heavy lifting myself. *About what?*

"About this Frank Latimer character. Name sound familiar?"

Frank What-i-mer?

"Latimer. Frank Latimer. That ring any bells?"

Never heard of him.

"I just don't know if I believe you."

Who is he?

"Well, for starters, it sounds like he fucked your wife."

My father remains focused on the television and I feel immediate disgust with myself for speaking of my mother so crassly. Anger holds a clenched grip.

"Shocking, isn't it. They seem to have had quite the affair."

Oprah cuts to another commercial.

"Maybe if you'd just been a little bit nicer. A little more attentive. A little bit more of a man, maybe that would never have happened." It takes me a full minute to do the math on that. "But then I guess I wouldn't be here." Or I would be fifty percent different. Fifty percent someone else. Fifty percent more him.

It's hard to know what to wish for.

He starts coughing and Buttons and I look at each other, alarmed. I sit him up and administer a few whacks between the shoulder blades in an awkward attempt to get him to stop. A passing orderly sticks his head in the door, but I wave him away. "We're fine. We're fine." I can feel tears forming in my eyes and I don't want anyone to see me cry.

The orderly gives me the thumbs-up and moves on.

I rest my father back down in the bed.

"You did know, didn't you? From the beginning? Is that why you insisted I be called James? To claim some ownership over me? Or was it not until much later. When you wanted me out of the house. Maybe you were done altogether with betrayal."

I'm fully crying now, and it catches me by surprise. I've never done this before, never wanted to give him the satisfaction. He continues to focus on the television, so I find the remote twisted in a blanket and turn it off in a huff before tossing it back down on the bed.

"Doesn't matter. You were a real asshole to me."

The room suddenly silent, my sniveling is amplified. It sounds ridiculous, even to me, so I decide to catalog the items on his nightstand in the hopes that a task will put me at ease. A clock radio, lotion, a lamp, a box of Kleenex, wool socks that seem to have been laundered and folded in two, a photo of the grandkids in a frame, probably from Naomi.

With the television off, he returns his attention to me.

I was the asshole?

"Yeah, you were. I was a kid." I reach for a Kleenex and blow my nose, then return to petting the dog. "And then you got sick, so I was the asshole for not loving you. Real nice."

This is new, this kind of outburst, and to me it's confusing. I don't know what to feel. Is it good? Should I consider it progress? Is this the healing Jackie encouraged me to embrace?

"So about the book. Remember me saying that? I wrote a book. A novel. It's going to be published."

My father thinks on this for a moment. "Casper?" His voice is thin and raspy.

"That's not fucking Casper, Dad. Casper is dead. That dog's name is Buttons." I pause to ascertain if that is even his question. Maybe he's asking something else entirely. I take a breath so deep I could bust ribs. "Is Casper in the book? No. It's a book about Mom. Well, a version of Mom. It's about mothers. And the mysteries surrounding them. You know Mom." I cringe at how awkward I sound.

Buttons starts licking my dad's hand and he looks surprised but not displeased. *Did I know Mom? Did any of us?*

"Well, that's a really good fucking question." I'm surprised by my repeated profanity, my apparent need to appear more masculine.

I watch him spread his fingers so Buttons can lick between them. I'm a little put off by how long this goes on, like maybe I should wash his hands afterward—or should have before, for poor Buttons's sake.

"You're in the book. Not too much." I pause to consider my next words carefully, to evaluate the ability I have (or don't have) to inflict harm, but then I decide what the hell. "At the very beginning you put a gun in your mouth and pull the trigger."

I wait for a reaction, wondering if it's as painful to hear as it was to say. The acknowledgment that for a long period of time he was dead to me. Slowly my father tilts his head to look squarely at me and his eyes water and his forehead crinkles, even more than it's now naturally creased, and he nods.

Wouldn't that have been nice.

"Yeah. Come to think of it. You'd probably prefer it to this." We continue stroking the dog, although our pace slows, the metronome clocking our hands losing its charge.

I remember a time I visited his apartment soon after my parents split. There was only a bed and one chair and a lamp on a cardboard box. All the clocks in the house were turned backward; the one on the stove was covered with tape. "Why are all the clocks facing the wall, Dad?" I had asked. He didn't want to answer me, and so I pressed him on it and he finally said it was because he couldn't stand to watch the time tick by. Only then did it occur to me he might be living with regret.

"The truth is, I didn't think you were an important part of the story. But now . . ." The licking sounds become unbearable. "Now I'm not so sure."

Everything I thought I understood is bathed in new light. Perhaps my father always knew he was raising another man's son, and he stayed and did the hard work of it anyway in the face of such betrayal. Especially then, when it was men who strayed and women who were faithful, a cheating wife a hit to his already toxic masculinity. A gay son? Especially one who wasn't his? Well, that was just the final blow.

"I'm not mad at you." The words feel like a shirt I want to like in the dressing room mirror, even though I know it will be an awkward fit in the light of day. "You know what? That's not true. I *am* mad at you. Nobody in this family ever, ever says that. No one in this family ever says anything. I'm angry, and I have been for a really long time."

Very feebly, as if he's out of the practice of speaking, my father makes a sound with three syllables. Is it a word? There's no real way of telling. I run the sound backward and forward through my head as though I were examining frames from the Zapruder film. Perhaps there is still something there.

Some*thing.*

Some*one.* Perhaps there's still some*one* there and these syllables are important—his *Rosebud*—a memory from a long time ago categorized in the one lobe or the one cortex or the bits of basal ganglia that are still functioning, that are still showing signs of life. He's alive, kicking. Just as my mother was more than a decade ago when she sided with me and threw all of his things out onto the lawn.

Then he slams his fist on the mattress. Once, twice, and a third time for good measure. Then both fists, banging them like a gorilla.

"Good! This is good!" I grab a throw pillow from the chair and start punching that until we are two men expressing primal rage. "You're angry too! It's not fair that you're here! GET IT OUT!"

We punch and we punch and we punch. At another time in my life I wonder if we might have punched each other and my pillow and his mattress are just surrogates absorbing our pain. I can almost feel the sting of a fist connecting with my jaw.

And then, a lightbulb.

"Dad, Dad, Dad . . ." I drop the pillow on the bed and put my hands on his, holding him down until he stops. We sit quietly for a moment as we catch our breath. And then I tell him, "This is what Jackie meant when she told me I was letting my characters off too easily." My father looks at me confused, so I offer, "Jackie, Mrs. Onassis."

This is why my ending feels hollow—it doesn't have the requisite anger! The quarantine lasts only forty days, my characters are not going to solve everything in less than six weeks' time. But they have to at least address the years of resentment they enter the quarantine with in order to position themselves in the right direction moving forward. They have to get really mad. They have to decide they're not going to take it anymore and say so before they can make a change.

And in the tail of that blazing realization, my father's syllables finally connect. At least in my mind they do: *For-give-ness.* We have to get mad, and we have to forgive. *I forgive you,* I say in my head, because I'm not certain yet that I do. But surely I can let my characters forgive. Try it on for size through them. And come back here someday—hopefully soon—and say those words out loud.

I forgive you.

I punch the throw pillow once last time, then reach up and muss his hair, brushing it back in the direction I'm used to seeing it parted, and suddenly, in that one little difference, like a ship approaching the lighthouse cake we made all those years ago, my father appears from the fog.

TWENTY-EIGHT

Spring arrives, and with it an invitation from Jackie to join her for lunch at the Carlyle, which I eagerly accept because this meal is pure reward. I drove straight home after seeing my father, back to the city, back to Daniel. I got in just after midnight and crashed hard. And then I worked for three days and three nights, in our apartment so Daniel could see I was indeed writing; he made pot after pot of coffee and left for long stretches and always came home with food. He hardly said a word, quietly turning on lights for me when it got dark, and turning them off again when it was light, until I wrote the final sentence that I never thought would come. I dropped the manuscript on Mark's desk just before my deadline.

Two agonizing days later Jackie called. The search for my father produced (according to my editor, anyhow) my best work yet and the book is ready for production. I remember Jackie's exact words in telling me the ending was just right: *You built a volcano; how marvelous to have it erupt.* At first it seemed odd, her choice of metaphor, like she was complimenting a child's science project. But what was the quarantine if not extreme heat building inside a confined space, looking for a way to vent? Daniel found me slumped on the floor that afternoon; it's not that I passed out from relief (honestly, it all felt strangely anticlimactic), but now that the book was complete I didn't know what to do with myself next.

In my mind, the lunch marks a transition in our working together—the writing is done and it's now full steam ahead to publication. I perform a little due diligence on the Carlyle to put myself at ease. Allen had some interesting insight; it seems it was John Kennedy who really put the hotel on the map. As a senator in the 1950s he was such a frequent guest they installed a private phone line just for him. After he became president, the press dubbed it the New York White House. When he died, Jackie moved the children into a suite on the thirty-first floor as she hid from the world; the children would play in the lobby. It's odd to me that she would keep this as a haunt, given her history with the place—but who am I to question.

I dress for the occasion in a jacket and tie, and arrive early to experience a drink at Bemelmans Bar, named for its murals by Ludwig Bemelmans, who illustrated the Madeline series of children's books. (I've read he also painted a private mural on Aristotle Onassis's private yacht, the *Christina*, but I know better than to mention that.) I take my Grey Goose on the rocks to a quiet table along the mural where a mustachioed man is handing a pointy-faced child a bouquet of balloons. Surrounding him are whimsically drawn scenes of France with the occasional odd touch like a rabbit in a man's green suit with his arms sternly folded, dogs in their Sunday finest, and a giraffe poking its head through a tall fence. When I take a sip of my drink I notice the ceiling is gold foil. Even the lampshades are illustrated.

I remember the Madeline books; Naomi used to read them to me when we were kids. There was an old house in Paris, covered in vines, and out front stood a dozen little girls in two straight lines. There's something very Jackie about Bemelmans's style, as if maybe she had been one of the twelve girls herself. It's not a stretch of the imagination to picture her as a child in a perfect yellow coat, legs tapered to a fine point like a ballerina's. The murals remind me of something Joseph Kennedy allegedly said to his son, warning him about Jackie's merits as a political spouse: *"Too much status, not enough quo."* My time reading up on Jackie has unearthed a number of delicious remarks.

When twelve-thirty arrives I walk over to the restaurant, the vodka making me a bit punchy. Status, status, too much status.

"Mrs. Onassis's table," I say to the maître d', unsure if the right amount of *s*'s (esses) spills out of my mouth.

"And you are . . ."

"James Smale." He checks the reservation until he seems satisfied.

"Very good. Right this way, sir." He collects a hardbound menu, leads me through the restaurant to a private table near the back (always the back), and motions for me to be seated. "Mrs. Onassis should be here presently."

"Thank you." I accept the menu with both hands, as if it's carved in stone, and give it a quick study. I'm forever afraid of being caught off guard, like in a dream, to have a waiter arrive to take my order only to open the menu and see it's in a language I cannot understand and everything is market price in a currency for which I do not know the exchange rate. I quickly settle on salad as appropriate lunch fare; eating a large sandwich can seem vulgar, and some of the classic dishes (Lobster Thermidor?) I don't understand. I rule out the seafood salad, as I don't like the sound of "lump crab," and narrow in on the *salade niçoise* as the most sensible option.

Just like how the tide rapidly recedes from the shore before a tsunami thunders in, the ambient din of the restaurant drops and a strange quiet falls over the dining room (save for the sound of one falling fork) when Jackie enters. The shoulder pads in her bright-colored jacket along with its narrow waist make her look like the angular shapes in a Kandinsky painting. As she weaves through the restaurant she waves at certain guests with a gentle flutter of her fingers, almost as if she's embarrassed to interrupt, smiling the whole time. She has a large manila envelope tucked under one arm.

I'm standing when she reaches the table.

"James, you look spiffy."

I kiss her on the cheek, inhaling deeply, incarcerating some of her magic and satisfying a room full of prying eyes. "Thank you for the invitation."

"It's my pleasure. Shall we sit?"

A waiter in a white jacket materializes. "Something to drink, madam?"

"Champagne. Two glasses." She turns to me and winks. "We're celebrating."

"Right away."

"What are we celebrating?" I ask, once he is out of earshot.

She says, very plainly, "You."

My face is warm, but not from the vodka.

"Congratulations again on a marvelous ending."

"I just needed to be pushed."

"And I was happy to oblige. You really let her have it!" She seems almost too enthusiastic.

"You're sure it's not too much?" I think about a potential time, years from now, when my mother breaks down and reads the book. How will she take this shellacking?

"I would have reined you in if it was."

I gesture at the package. "Is that what I think it is?"

Jackie opens the envelope on the table and pulls out a galley for the book. "I wanted to place it in your hands myself."

For the first time I am holding an advance copy of my novel. Not a manuscript, not a story, not stacks of loose papers held together by a rubber band. Bound pages. It's weighty and thick, and across the top it reads: ITHACA A Novel. The cover image shows trees at the height of their fall foliage, and yellows and oranges and red pop off the cover like wildfire. At the bottom, in white, is the author's name. My name. James Smale.

"This is . . . something else." You'd think by now I would have learned to conquer speechlessness.

"The cover is luscious. And your name even sounds like an author's."

Have you read the latest James Smale? I imagine readers asking, about some future anticipated work. No, is it good? A whole conversation flashes through my mind. It's sooooo good.

"Remember when we talked about spring?" I ask. We had once imagined a similar cover image with softer colors, yellows and greens under a mellow light. Spring, Jackie had said, suggested growth and renewal. Fall, I countered, represented change, a return (thinking of the Cavafy poem still), but also bounty and a harvest.

"You were right about autumn," she says. I convinced her, I think, with another poem, Keats's ode "To Autumn." "Especially with the fiery new ending. It's a handsome book, James. Your mother will be proud."

Her optimism is almost contagious. "Should I send her a copy?" I chuckle. It's the most I can do to even suggest that our family drama has not resolved itself, and in fact has managed to double.

She picks up on the story I'm not telling her. "Should I?"

I stop laughing.

The waiter arrives with two champagne flutes and sets one down in front of each of us.

Jackie raises her glass and toasts. "To *Ithaca*."

"To *Ithaca*."

"Coming soon to bookstores everywhere."

I rub my temples. "I can't imagine walking into a store and finding it there."

"You won't have to imagine. You're mere months away from living it!"

"That doesn't make it any more tangible."

The waiter returns, and when he asks if we'd like to hear the specials, Jackie affirms that we would; the waiter beams and runs through his prepared list, grinning from ear to ear. I know she doesn't think much of this effect she has on people (after all, she doesn't do a thing to wield it), but it's exciting to watch. When he finishes, she makes a humming sound, as if giving her deliberation the most serious thought.

"I'll have the scallops, *s'il vous plaît*." Jackie doesn't even have a menu, and scallops were not one of the specials. Whether scallops are on the carte du jour, or when you're Jacqueline Kennedy Onassis all dining can be off menu, I do not know.

"*Salade niçoise.*" I hand the waiter my menu. I don't have the nerve to invent my own dish.

I want to tear through the galley, see every typeset page. Instead I arrange my napkin in my lap so as not to appear overeager.

"So how does it feel?" Jackie nods toward the book.

"I'm overwhelmed."

"Is that . . . good?"

"I think so. I'm feeling a rush of things."

She removes the envelope from the table and tucks it under her handbag. "So, now. Tell me how you finally came to your ending."

"Courtesy of an unexpected ally."

"Tell me more."

It's still difficult not to blurt out everything when she gazes so intently at you, but I address the visit to see my father in only the broadest strokes. "Well, the anger we discussed . . . but it took me getting really upset at someone myself before I could accurately let my characters express it. And then it didn't feel right to just leave things there, so I thought a lot about what you said. About healing. I crave it at times in my own life, but I'm guilty of being passive, I think, in my quest to be whole and happy again. So forgiveness was equally important."

Jackie nods. "And forgiving is an act."

"Exactly. I went back to the opening pages and realized both characters had someone to forgive. And in letting them do so, it gave them enough common ground to move beyond their quarantine and start down a path toward forgiving themselves."

"Well, it was superb, moving away from a tidy conclusion. The best endings, I believe, always leave the reader imagining what comes next."

"Which is why, I suppose, I still feel a bit unsettled."

"About the book?"

"About life." And then I come clean. "About the healing in my own life. What comes next, now that the book is done?"

"This is what happens when you write autobiographical fiction. The book ends, but the story continues." Jackie rests her chin on a single finger, like a myna bird on a perch. "Do you remember the riddle of the Sphinx?"

I look at her, confused. "Head of a human, haunches of a lion? That Sphinx?"

"Exactly. In Greek tradition, the Sphinx had a riddle. What walks on four hands in the morning, two at noon, and three at night?"

"Is this like Isis and Osiris? We're going to have to work on getting you more modern references."

She laughs. "I'm curating a book on Egypt."

"I give up," I say, without giving it any real thought.

"So easily? The Sphinx consumed all travelers who failed to answer."

I twirl the stem of my champagne flute between my fingers, slowly rotating the glass on the table while I replay the riddle in my head. I study the bubbles in my glass before it dawns on me that I know this from a Classics course I took in college. "Man. Oedipus gave the correct answer."

Jackie arches one eyebrow as if to say "well done." "Lucky for Oedipus the answer was man."

"Why do you say that?"

"I posit that any riddle whose answer is woman is inherently unsolvable." She laughs and slides her own flute to the side and then places both hands on the table.

"My mother," I say, just to clarify that we're talking about the same thing.

She nods. "It's the fact that you tried. The fact that you wanted to solve your riddle, to stand in front of the Sphinx and not shy away from the question. That is very noble."

"Even if I'm eaten?"

"Even if you're eaten alive." Jackie's eyes glisten.

"What about your own children. Do you mind me asking?" This is the champagne talking.

"Have they solved their riddle?" She considers this. "You'd have to ask them. They'd most likely tell you I like books, and beyond that it's anyone's best guess. They'll probably turn out awful too." Jackie winks, her playful side on full display.

I laugh. "Should they stop trying?"

"Some days I wish they would. But, no. Never." She takes a

pointed sip of champagne before looking at me. "And neither should you."

We hold our focus until I blink and awkwardly reach for the galley. I soak in my name. When I flip the book over, words of praise from other authors (friends of Jackie's, mostly) make my heart skip once again. I'm confronted by my own image when I open the back cover. *What a phony,* I think. I then scan the first few pages until I come across the copyright information and Library of Congress registration. Below that is my name in small print: SMALE, JAMES 1961–. There is no end date. I almost need to double-check that this journey hasn't killed me, but nope—I'm still here. The book may have its ending, but I know that I, as yet, do not. I have to continue to chip away at my riddle, my mother. I have orders not to give up from Jacqueline Onassis herself.

TWENTY-NINE

Two older gentlemen stand outside the theater, outfitted like one imagines people dressed to see plays in an earlier time, the 1950s or 1960s, in tweed or gabardine, ties and pocket squares in colors like salmon and aubergine. They are deep in conversation, each leaning in closely to hear the other. No one notices them, although there's no reason anyone should: They are invisible, at least to the younger crowd that brushes past them to pick up their tickets at will-call. But I can't keep my eyes off them. One has posture like an exclamation point, even in his seventies, and may have once been a dancer. The other is hunched like a question mark, like he's spent a lifetime in the types of folding seats that populate playhouse rows. Question Mark re-dresses Exclamation Point's cravat.

"Stop fussing, it's fine."

"It's not fine. You look like some sort of mercenary."

"And what kind of mercenary would that be?"

"The kind with a crooked cravat." Question Mark stands back to admire his handiwork. "There you go, Fosse."

Exclamation Point immediately loosens the fabric. "I can't breathe. And why do you keep calling me Fosse?"

Question Mark beams. "Because you're a singular sensation."

It's something you rarely see. Older gay men, together, happy. The 1980s took care of that. The Reagan administration took care of that. A cruel twist of fate obliterated an entire generation of homosexual men, save for these two and a few others like them, whom you only occasionally see at delis and museums and theaters fussing over a cravat. I wonder if that will be me and Daniel one day. If forever is an option for us.

"One s-s-singular . . ." Exclamation Point stammers. "That was Michael Bennett."

"Who?" Question Mark asks like he's hard of hearing; it's impossible he doesn't know the name.

"Michael Bennett choreographed *A Chorus Line*. You're thinking of Michael Bennett."

"Oh, yes. Of course." He fiddles with Exclamation Point's cravat one last time. "There you go, Bennett."

The two of them together are a dream in a beautiful sleep. The air is cool, and trees that dot the sidewalk have their full summer leaves. The air smells like Central Park cherry trees mingled with magnolias—although perhaps it's someone's perfume—and slightly of cigarettes, of car exhaust, of the city, but in a distant way that makes the additional layering inoffensive. The only siren I hear is blocks away, gentle, like a mewling kitten. This is the New York I love. This is the city Sinatra sings about. It makes me want to stroll west, to the riverbank, maybe. The very edge of Manhattan might offer the solace I seek. Instead, I'm here to support Daniel in his art, even if his support of mine still feels iffy.

"James?"

I'm awoken from my daze by the sound of my name.

I turn to see Mark standing behind me. "What, what are you doing here?" I stammer.

"It's good to see you too," he says, annoyed.

"Sorry. Surprised to see you is all." We hug, and while I can't help but be excited by his body pressing against mine, I'm careful not to let it linger.

Mark glances over at Question Mark and Exclamation Point and winces. It disappoints me. The dismissal of them, of love. But Mark sent me a supportive note after he read the final manuscript—a gesture that meant a lot to me in the moment—so I also immediately forgive him. "What *are* you doing here?"

"I'm here with friends." He indicates two plastic-looking people behind him; the three of them are awkwardly posed, looking like mannequins in a Macy's window modeling trendy clothes that I would never wear because they'll be out of fashion before fall. "You?"

I clear my throat. "My boyfriend is the director."

Mark looks at me and says, "Ah."

"Ah." We stand in awkward silence.

"Did you invite Jackie?" he asks.

I momentarily brighten. "Would she have come?" The thought that she would even consider it makes me kick myself for not having mentioned it.

Mark shrugs. "Durang isn't really her thing."

He says it like he and Jackie have spent endless hours discussing Theater of the Absurd. As if late at night when they were the only two in the office, when the phones stopped ringing and the photocopier and the fax machines had been lulled into quiet sleep—maybe they had daiquiris and discussed Pinter and Beckett and Pirandello. Maybe she told him a story about lunch ladies and they laughed and toasted the work they would do together.

Maybe I am nobody special.

To her.

To anyone.

I used to like that I had someone to share Jackie with, but now I want it to stop. I want her to be mine and mine alone. I'm annoyed at her for not liking Durang, taking Mark at his word. Is she above him somehow? She prefers Williams and Ibsen and more serious work?

The stage door bursts open and Daniel appears, scanning for me in the crowd. He's holding a program that he's nervously, but expertly, rolled into a tight cigar; he could hold a seminar for factory workers in Havana.

"You coming, babe? I'm holding a seat down front."

"Yeah." I turn back to Mark and motion in the direction of the door to indicate I should go.

"Enjoy the show," Mark says, putting his hand on my shoulder and squeezing. It's not unlike something a friend might do, but he also does it for show, to puff his chest in front of Daniel, to lay some small claim on me. It makes me feel valued, despite myself, but also like the wreck that I am.

"Who was that in front of the theater?"

At the end of the night Daniel and I are lying in bed, exhausted from both the excitement of an opening night and the afterparty for the cast and crew that was held at Marie's Crisis.

In my head I answer him, but out loud apparently not, because he produces a stuffed Snoopy doll and asks his question again, this time through the dog. "Who was that you were talking to in front of the theater? Ruff ruff."

"That was Mark, Jackie's assistant." It's both uncomfortable and titillating to say his name aloud in our bed—even to a stuffed animal.

"Oh."

"Where did you . . . ?" I point to Snoopy.

"The cast gave it to me. It's like Charlotte's."

"No, I gathered that." In the play, the character of Charlotte, a therapist, delivers bad advice, often unfortunately derived from the play *Equus*, through a stuffed Snoopy doll.

"Did you invite him?" And then the real question: "Did you invite Jackie?" Daniel rolls onto his side, eagerly propping himself up on his elbow.

"No. It was coincidence. He was there with friends." I run my fingers through Daniel's chest hair.

"Could you? Invite Jackie? I mean, think of the publicity." Daniel nods enthusiastically.

It's the first time someone has asked me for a favor because of my association with her. "I don't know. I wish I could. I wish she *would* see it. But I don't know." I'd have no idea how to ask her without sounding like I'm using her as bait for the pride of photographers that stalk her. For the mention in Liz Smith's column or a paragraph on Page Six. "Besides. Durang's not really her thing."

Daniel rolls his eyes. There's no way in hell I could know such a thing. "So what did you think of the play?"

"What did I . . . ? Didn't I tell you?" I realize I'm not currently my best self, but am I that self-absorbed that I didn't congratulate my own boyfriend on the premiere of his play?

"Yes, you did. Backstage and at the bar while people were gathered around the piano, singing numbers from *Jesus Christ Superstar*. You had to yell into my ear."

"*Godspell*. 'Day by Day' is from *Godspell*." I smile, thinking how proud Exclamation Point would be of me if he were here to catch this correction.

"Oh, wow, I must be exhausted." Daniel covers his face, feigning embarrassment. "But what did you *really* think? Now that we're alone."

I turn to look him in the eye. "It was great. Really, truly great. I wouldn't bullshit you."

"Thank you."

"I thought the guy who played Bruce was . . . Well, he was good . . ."

"Miscast, right?"

"Just not who I pictured in the role."

Daniel groans. "I know. He's a friend of the producer and put up some of the money."

"It's just he's more of a Bob. You've got two Bobs and a Prudence."

Daniel laughs. "Very different play. I begged him to take the role of Bob. But no dice."

"*You* would be a better Bruce! But listen, no one is going to care. You should be proud." We're naked, inches apart. Telling Daniel he should be proud makes me realize I'm proud of him too. I look at his face, the same face that once made me swoon; I know I've been taking him for granted. He's always around, in the house—like a sleeve of Ritz Crackers, perhaps—but suddenly I have an overwhelming hunger for snacking.

"There were some first-night blips. Some of the pacing. That sound cue. But we'll improve. The show just needs to tighten."

"Just take it day by day." I do a little of the hand choreography that goes with the song, but not too much.

Daniel laughs and he moves his leg and it brushes against my erection. The feeling, electric. He makes a face, surprised—*Where did that come from?*—before rubbing his hand over it again in admiration.

"There was a couple outside the theater tonight. An older gay couple. In their seventies, maybe. One of them had scoliosis. He fussed with the other man's scarf."

Daniel seems confused. "This is . . . dirty talk?"

I push his shoulder, but he grabs my dick to steady himself. "Don't touch me," I say, but when he pulls his hand away I immediately guide it back. We both laugh.

"They were cute. They squabbled, but you could tell they really loved one another."

"Prudence invited them. I guess one of them was a colorful theater reviewer from the early days of *New York* magazine. Something like that." He gesticulates information going in one ear and out the other, but it looks a little like a gesture for blowing his brains out. "What about them?" Daniel asks.

"Do you think that will be us someday?"

"Is your dirty talk going to improve?"

"I'm serious."

Daniel pouts, mimicking my tantrum but not quite mocking it. "I'm serious too."

"My parents aren't together. Your parents are, but they don't really speak. And it's not like there's a lot of role models in the gay community either."

"Why do you worry so much about forever?"

"Why do you not?"

He sighs. "Because there is only here and now."

It's not the time to goad Daniel about his belief that long-term monogamy is a myth, but it's a scab that I can't help picking at. "What am I, a dog? People don't live like that."

"And so they spend all their time worrying about the future. Or chasing the past."

That last bit feels like a dig at me. I lie back and look at the ceiling. Late at night, agitated, unable to fall asleep, I have wondered if something in me is genetically coded. That alongside the DNA for my blue eyes and my big feet is something that is forever going to make me feel restless and unsettled in life. I'm the product of an affair; what if my attraction to Mark—to someone else—was . . . preordained? That maybe because of my questionable past, it's impossible for me to ever be truly present. What if I'm actually attracted to drama and chaos?

The air-conditioning unit in the window makes the thumping noise it does, like a heartbeat, then stops.

"You have a responsibility to share things with me," Daniel says.

"Share what things?"

"Whatever it is that keeps you awake at night." I look at Daniel and he continues, "You think I don't know you're not sleeping?"

The mood ruined, I turn off the light, hoping it will make me invisible. I feel a blast of cool air from the window unit and I keep my eyes open until they adjust and the room turns from black to blue. It's quiet for so long I wonder if Daniel has fallen asleep. When he speaks, my leg flinches in that way it does when sleep comes with the sensation of falling.

"You made your search all about the book."

I make a face so that he knows that I'm offended, even though it's dark. "What is that supposed to mean?"

"You turned in your manuscript and everyone was happy, so you stopped."

"Stopped what."

Daniel hesitates. "Reconciling."

"What are you talking about?"

"This is about Frank, isn't it?"

I push the covers back so that cold air can wash over me. I don't really know how to answer that, other than to say yes, but I'm not in the mood to be agreeable. "No, because that would be the past and there is only here and now." I shouldn't be mocking him, but sometimes I can't help it.

"Forget it."

"Why?"

"Because you're not even listening to me."

"You're not listening to yourself!"

"Good night, James." Daniel rolls over to face the far wall.

This tension is not what I want. I sit, agitated, in the dark until I decide to try another approach. I snuggle in to him and whisper, "Tell me again."

Daniel swats me away like an annoying housefly, so I shake him again and he sighs. "Frank himself is the past, yes, but has a remarkable hold on the present."

"How so?"

"Your mother's in the present. There's an obvious example."

"So?"

"Talk to her. Work this out."

I press my palms against my eyes and grind them until I see vibrant, red static. "I don't know if I'm ready."

"Okay, then." He settles into his pillow.

"C'mon, I'm trying."

"No, you're not!" Daniel bolts upright with surprising force. "You want to find Frank? You've known all along where you can find him." I don't immediately respond, so Daniel grabs my chin and pulls my head toward his. I can just make out the whites of his eyes as they pierce the darkness, and the way he holds my face is surprisingly erotic.

"Yeah, I know." I kick Daniel gently under the sheets, and eventually he lets go of my chin and then envelops me, pinning me to the mattress, and despite the heat and the anger and his body temperature, I don't want him to let go. I get hard again.

"That could be us someday. Those men," he says, kissing my neck; the weight of his body presses mine into the bed, cracking my back in such a perfect way, it should be part of some spa service.

I sputter a last protest. "Yeah, but *will* they, was my original ques—"

"You're ruining my opening night, you know."

"I just . . ." He grinds on my body. "I don't mean to . . ."

"Ruining . . ."

I pull him tightly to me and squeeze my arms around him. "Do you . . ."

He bites my ear. "My opening . . ."

"Ow," I say, even though I don't want him to stop.

· THIRTY ·

I hold the phone receiver up to the light, inspecting it for fingerprints and odd bits of earwax, the unpleasant relics of other, easier conversations, before polishing the phone with my T-shirt because: a) it's disgusting, and b) I'm unable to actually dial. I notice there's a copy of the *Post* on the coffee table, but we don't get the *Post*, so I don't know when or how it got there. I flip through the pages. An elementary school in the Bronx is being closed for asbestos removal. A professor from Hunter College has been charged for possession of child pornography. A man was almost run over by the F train, but some good Brooklynites pulled him to safety just in the nick of time. People can be heroes.

People can also be cowards.

The phone shouts at me the angry signal it makes when left off the hook (GUTLESS! GUTLESS! GUTLESS!), so I place it unsteadily back in the cradle and again wipe it clean of fingerprints, as if I had just committed a crime.

The apartment is hot. I get up and head to the bathroom to splash water on my face. The light is brighter than I remember; did Daniel change a bulb? I look at myself in the mirror, leaning in across the sink to get the most honest view. My eyes are bloodshot from lack of sleep; even my skin looks tired. I turn my face to each side, and then back and forth again. I worry that a lack of symmetry makes me look untrustworthy, duplicitous. One sideburn is fuller than the other. When and why did sideburns come back? I take the scissors from the medicine cabinet and trim a few wayward hairs. When I replace them I see a jar of firming face mask Daniel and I had purchased once at a Duane Reade late at night, thinking it would help wash away the unpleasantness of a friend's painfully dreadful dinner party. I don't even remember if we ever used it. The face mask. The jar is collecting dust.

I wander back to the phone, then back to the bathroom. I forget to turn sideways to pass the bookshelf in the hall and knock a few paperbacks—including Hugo's *Les Misérables*—onto the floor. "Sonofa—" I start, but am cut off by my own laughter that comes from the fleeting (and ridiculous) thought that only France's wretched poor have suffered as much as I have.

In the bathroom I reach for the jar of blue clay and open it. Sure enough, it's untouched. I stare at it. I want to scoop some out, but I also don't want to disturb its unmarred veneer. Eventually I take off my shirt and study my chest in the mirror, the pale skin, the jutting clavicle, the few moles my doctor assures me are nothing. I dip two fingers into the mud; it feels clammy. I take a dollop and swipe it across my forehead, then repeat the motion and smear two lines under my eyes. I make more marks until I look like an overly painted extra from *The Last of the Mohicans*, then wash my hands and return the lid to the jar. I feel empowered. Not only have I decorated my body for battle, I've also taken charge of my skin care.

When I return to the phone it is still judging me, taunting me, daring me. But I am a warrior now, so I pick it out of the cradle, holding it firmly in my hand. I study the buttons momentarily, then quickly press the numbers before it can hurl further insults at me. Jackie's voice in my ear—*You should never stop trying.*

The phone rings four times before my mother answers.

"Hello," I challenge, before she can even say anything. Announcing myself first is a victory; it shows that I am unafraid.

My mother does not say anything. I can hear the faint shuffling of some activity.

"It's been a while." *Am I going to have to do all the talking?*

Pause. "Yes, it has."

"I've been angry," I say, as if admitting defeat. Even though I know that if anger was the right emotion to point my characters in a new direction, it can only serve us too.

"I imagine."

"You do?"

"I do."

"I'm calling to . . ." I stop there to catch my breath and listen for more activity. "What are you doing?"

"Folding towels. Domino is helping."

I don't need to be there to see the dog on the bed, curled up in warm, clean laundry. That's Domino "helping." The folding goes on for another half-minute.

"You sure have a lot of towels." The woman lives alone. How many towels can there be to launder? Or were they not even dirty? Does she just occasionally take them out of the linen closet to wash and refold them to make sure they don't collect dust and that all the seams are even? In either case, she doesn't respond.

"I'm calling with an invitation," I continue. An invitation that's an olive branch of sorts. But of course I don't say that. Daniel's right. The place to find Frank is in the heart of the one person who maybe loved him last. The one place I've avoided looking.

"Oh?"

I have her attention.

"I'm having a party. Or, a party is being had for me."

"What kind of party?" My mother sounds rightfully skeptical. Leaving it at that, it does sound like one of those sitcom devices where a character stages a made-up event to assemble two other characters in desperate need of reconciliation.

I open my mouth to say more, but the mud on my face is drying, tightening, and it becomes harder to move the muscles in my face. I feel like the Tin Man rapidly rusting, desperately calling out to Dorothy "Oil, oy-al, oi-yaa-l."

"A book party. A party for the book. It's being published in a few weeks." I watch as a flake of dried beauty mask falls tenderly into my lap. I stare at it in a state of bafflement at first, like I should lift it with tweezers, a fragile piece of gold foil to be studied under a microscope. How perfect—I'm blathering on so long my face is literally crumbling. "I know the book is a bit of a sore topic, but I'd like for you to be there."

"Do you want Oogle?" For a second I think my mother is having a stroke.

"Do I want . . . *what?*"

"Oogle."

Oogle is the name of an oversized stuffed sewer rat–looking thing—monster, I guess—that my father brought home one Halloween when we were kids. He told us Oogle had magical powers; my siblings were old enough to know better, but I was a believer. I was kind to Oogle, afraid to incur his wrath. He didn't look at all dangerous, perhaps a little misunderstood. But as a kid, you can't leave these things to chance. At the time we acquired him he was as big as I was—bigger, if you counted his yellow hat.

I haven't thought about him in years. "You still have Oogle?"

"In the attic. But I'm not keeping him any longer. Naomi says he probably has mold, and he frightens Kenny's kids."

"I live in a tiny apartment in Hell's Kitchen. I can't take Oogle. That wouldn't make any sense. Can we finish talking about the party?"

My mask is now fully dry. I touch my cheek and my skin feels brittle, the muscles underneath losing their elasticity. This must be what aging feels like. Rapid aging. It's torturous, the idea of Oogle tossed in a trash heap, one more member of our family thoughtlessly discarded. It's not his fault we all grew up; if he were truly magical he would have kept us all young and safe forever.

"Fine, I'll take him."

"When is it?"

My mother and I speak over each other. This is hopelessly awkward.

"The party?"

"Yes."

"It's Friday. In three weeks. Three weeks from Friday. I know you don't like to come into the city. It's a . . ." What is it? "*Ways*. But I thought, maybe . . ." I pause here and take a breath. "I don't know what I thought. I've been angry. I don't want to be. I thought this could be something you could do. For me."

My mother continues to fold towels. Or not. Or maybe she folds and unfolds a single towel and will do so until we hang up.

"I thought it would give us the opportunity to talk. I'd like for us to talk."

"Will she be there?" my mother asks.

"Who?" I'm not being coy. For a split second I actually forget.

"You know who."

"Would that make a difference?"

Silence.

"I imagine she will. I hope so. I would like to introduce you."

"We'll see."

"Okay, then."

"Okay."

"I miss you." I can't stop myself from saying it, but it's the truth, so why should I? I do miss her.

Dead silence. Not even the folding of towels. And then, just before my anger is reborn, screaming into the world anew, she says, "I miss you too."

A sigh of relief; I stand down. "Don't throw Oogle away." I can't help but think that maybe he has powers still. But Jesus Christ. Let's move him way down on our list of priorities.

Again, "We'll see."

"We'll see" is not a no, and I use the last mobility I have in my face to form the tightest smile. I hang up the telephone, proud of myself for calling. It was the right thing to do, even if I'm setting myself up for crushing disappointment.

My expression is completely frozen as I turn on the shower. I wait for the hot water to rise in our pipes and steam to fill the room before

I slip off my underwear and step naked into the tub. My mother will accept my invitation. She has to. Doesn't she? And yet I'm paralyzed with a sinking feeling she won't. Eventually I close my eyes and put my face under the water and streaks of blue run down my body and over my toes, swirling down the drain like Janet Leigh's blood in the movie *Psycho*.

◆ THIRTY-ONE ◆

As the elevator rises inside 1040 Fifth, so does my excitement; my eyelid spasms in the throes of some sort of nervous tic (where did that come from?) and I can feel the floor rattle as the cables pull the small car up toward the sky. I look for some sort of certificate to see when this elevator was last inspected, to vouch for its safety, but when I spot the document in question the date is smudged. *Great.* Even rich people can't be assured of safe carriage. Jackie and I are to go over the final plans for the book launch next week, she's taken personal interest, and everything is suddenly very real. Unless the elevator plummets to the basement, splintering it and me into myriad pieces—in which case things are still real, just no longer for me. My mother will show up for the book party and someone will have to explain that what's left of me is sitting in some decorative urn on the mantel, perhaps a piece of ceramics that Jackie herself acquired while traveling some exotic place with a strange spelling like Marrakech. I hope that, in my mother's shock, as she slowly comes to accept this garish turn of events, someone at least has the decency to offer her a crab puff.

When the elevator doors open, I'm surprised to find I'm inside an apartment. Not in a hallway, not faced with a closed door or with the kind of drab furniture you might find in a vestibule; I am in the foyer of Jackie's home. Did the lobby attendant turn some sort of key when he showed me into the elevator? Did Jackie activate some control from her end? I was too lost in my own thoughts to notice. I jump, startled, when the doors slide closed behind me like I've wandered into a horror film where the audience knows I'm the next victim but I, as yet, do not. The entry is filled with the mild scent of hydrangeas, and just as I convince myself it's some sort of disinfectant to cover the stench of carnage I spot a large vase of the white, puffy flowers on a side table.

"There's my author." Jackie appears, arms outstretched. The light in her apartment is soft and clean; there must be windows in every direction. She looks like she's lit for a film.

"Mrs. Onassis."

"Please, please." Jackie gestures for me to follow her and leads me down one of the halls. This is the first time I've been invited inside her New York apartment and I discreetly peek into each room, marveling at how much square footage some people have on an island with eight million people—the beauty of vertical space. The entry and surrounding hall is easily two of my kitchens, and she probably has, like, five bedrooms to our one.

"It's kind of you to have me over. We could have done this at the office."

"We're moving offices. Didn't Mark tell you?"

"No. He didn't mention. Wait, yes. Maybe." Mark has been our go-between leading up to the book's release; we talk often and have found a comfortable working relationship. At times he seems more excited about the book than Daniel is.

"Well. Everything is chaos."

"Where are you moving?"

"To 1540 Broadway."

I do a quick calculation. "Forty-sixth Street?"

"Forty-fifth."

We step into a library with red-and-gold French wallpaper and matching-patterned draperies. It's decorated with the effortless elegance (a velvet-upholstered chair, a round end table that could have been lifted from Versailles, decorative sculptures on stacks of books) that I have come to know as Jackie's interior style. The only space of hers not to reflect this is her office—the one place I like to imagine she's truly at home.

"How is that going?"

Jackie sighs. "Everyone is fussing over me. 'How will Jackie handle the move? Will she pack her own boxes? Will she wrap her own knickknacks in bubble paper?' After all this time, I'm still the talk of the office."

This is a thorn in her side, that after years of hard work proving herself, people still see her as "other." Mark himself has told me he's seen her elbow-deep in a photocopier one time clearing a paper jam and another time running down the halls in her stocking feet, racing to make a deadline. But even if I can picture her rushing down the hallway, I can't quite conjure an image of her navigating Times Square. Her new commute is troubling to me.

"'How will Jackie handle the move?'" she asks herself. "She's handling it by steering clear of it."

I smile at the thought of Mark having to do manual labor like boxing up his boss's office. He must be cursing his predicament right about now.

"How are you, Mr. Author? Nervous? Excited? Take a seat."

Jackie sits in front of her fireplace and gestures for me to sit on a striped loveseat opposite her. Behind me are floor-to-ceiling built-ins lined with all kinds of books, including an old set of encyclopedias; an oil portrait of a Napoleonic figure on horseback is mounted on the divide. "Excited," I say, before qualifying the sentiment. "I think. Anxious for sure."

"I've had authors tell me they broke down in tears right before their books were released. Be prepared for a rush of emotion."

"I might cry now," I say in a moment of naked honesty. Fortunately, Jackie laughs, so I pass it off as the joke she thinks it is.

"I just came from lunch with my son. He wants to start a magazine. About politics—a fresh, new take, if you can imagine that." Jackie looks heavenward, presumably for strength. "So I might cry too."

"That's wonderful. Isn't it?"

"Is it?" Jackie seems unsure. "You tell me."

"He wants to be an editor. Like his mother." I keep the second half of the sentiment—*instead of a politician, like his father*—to myself.

"That's a lovely way of looking at it, James." She squints as she considers my take. "You have a writer's gift of perception."

I swoon. "I'm sure he'll do very well."

"I wish I had your confidence. I'm not sure it's the smartest investment. Of his time or his money."

On the table next to her chair is a wrapped gift. It sticks out in a room where everything else is curated. It's a book, the gift. I did this a lot as a kid, identify each present under the tree by the mere shape of it; my father would chide me for taking all the fun out of Christmas and shout empty threats about returning all the gifts to the store. My mother always told him to calm down, reminding him that Christmas wasn't about what's under the tree.

Jackie must catch me eyeing the package. "A little something for you. To mark the occasion." She hands me the present.

"May I?" I ask, tearing at the seam of the wrapping before she even gives her permission. I rip open the gift, half adult, half child in the throes of excitement. Jacqueline Onassis bought *me* a present. The book is entitled *Remember the Ladies: Women in America 1750–1815*. I don't know what to say. Like, really. Do not know how to respond.

"It's the first book I worked on at Viking. My first book to mark the occasion of yours. The title comes from Abigail Adams, from a letter she wrote to her husband while he was in Philadelphia in 1776. 'In the new code of laws I suppose it will be necessary for you to make, I desire you would remember the ladies and be more generous and favorable to them than your ancestors.'"

"You have it memorized." I flip the book over to study the back jacket.

"You don't forget a woman like Abigail Adams. I wrote an inscription for you inside. I would hope that after everything dies down, you too would remember the ladies. Your mother, particularly."

"Be generous and favorable to her?"

"Toward her."

I shake my head, more at myself than at her. "Always the editor."

Jackie smiles, pulling her hair back from the side of her face before letting it fall forward again.

"And toward you?"

"Oh, well. You've always been favorable toward me."

She shimmers in that way that she does, and I hug the book close to my chest to express appreciation. I'm dying to read her inscription, but I know better than to do so now. It's enough that I know she wants me to remember her too.

As if I could ever forget.

"Books make the best gifts, don't you agree?" she asks.

"I do indeed."

"President Kennedy and I used to give each other books when we were courting. They were one of the first things we bonded over."

I picture Daniel and myself in bed, me nestled in the crook of his arm, both of us reading, as we do sometimes. I wonder if it was like this for them, the future president and First Lady. "I'm sure he would have very much liked this book," I say, immediately thinking it stupid. Am I trying to come off like I knew her husband? That I had any insight into his taste?

"He would have," she agrees, kicking off her shoes and tucking one leg underneath her. She turns and stares into the empty fireplace. "Although, remembering the ladies was never Jack's problem."

My jaw drops from the unexpected candor.

"Tea?" A stern-looking woman appears in the doorway, startling me. I look up, surprised to see it's not Joan. She's carrying a silver tray with a teapot and plate of sandwiches.

"Right here would be fine, Martha," Jackie says. "Thank you."

The woman sets the tea service on a table next to where Jackie is seated, and the cups and saucers rattle. I glare at her as she pours, willing her to dissipate as quickly as she's appeared; the clock has struck midnight and snuffed out a moment of pure magic. Now everything is awkward, and I can't laugh at Jackie's candor or press her for more. Mrs. Kennedy is Mrs. Onassis again.

"Black is fine, thank you," I say when the woman holds up a small pot of cream. She serves Jackie her tea and exits without saying a word, leaving the tray behind.

I sip from my cup quietly. "I invited her to the book party."

"You invited *Martha*?" Jackie asks, looking over her shoulder after her housemaid.

I laugh. "No. My mother."

"That's wonderful."

"Never stop trying."

"That's right," she says, recalling her advice. She adds lemon to her tea. "Has she accepted the invitation?"

I offer a feeble smile. "Not. Yet." I can feel myself sweating; Jackie, sipping a hot beverage in a sweater, doesn't seem at all bothered. I set my cup back on the saucer and place both on the table in front of me, discreetly fanning my shirt so that it doesn't start to stick.

"It would be so lovely if she came," Jackie says. And then, as if it's just occurred to her, "I'll bet she comes."

"If I were your bookie, I wouldn't know what odds to place on that bet."

"May I say," Jackie begins before pausing. "Without knowing the circumstances. Women like your mother and me, from our generation, we were duty bound. Things were expected of us, marriage and motherhood. But we were girls once, with dreams and aspirations of our own. When we see our children succeed, of course part of their accomplishments are our own. But it also reminds us that life doesn't turn out for everyone the way they dreamed."

I can see a world where my mother could have been happier living another life, with Frank or someone else, or with a career maybe, outside the home, with no man at all. But she chose us, her children. Again and again and again.

"Remember the ladies," I say, breaking the silence, the tea finally welcome to soothe the lump in my throat.

"Remember the ladies," Jackie repeats with just the hint of a smile.

For-give-ness, I hear my father grunt, before shaking it from my mind. "This tea is delicious."

"It's an assam tea. From India. An absolute dream, India. Such splendor. Such color. Have you been?"

"No." I raise my teacup in a little toast. "But you really should reconsider a book. With everything you've seen."

"I've done several books on India. I'll show you," she says, but makes no effort to get up to produce these books.

"No, I mean you should be *writing* a book."

Jackie sets her teacup down on her saucer and studies me, as if considering whether she can trust me, really trust me, for the first time. "James, may I tell you a little secret?"

"Always," I say, desperate to be a confidant.

"Remember when you asked me before? About writing a memoir?"

"On Martha's Vineyard. You said you would not waste your time. So long as there were beaches to be walked."

"That's right, and I meant it. But the truth of the matter is, I have."

A sudden wave comes over me; I'm at ground zero for the biggest breaking news in publishing in years. "You have? That's wonderful!" I have an immediate fantasy of being the first to read it.

"Well, now, not so fast." She can feel my excitement. "My life is my life, and I don't feel any particular need to share it in an obvious or expected way. *However.* If anyone has bothered to pay attention to the work that I've done, they would know that I've been telling pieces of my story all along."

I'm suddenly more in awe of this woman that I ever have been. "Through the books that you've edited."

"Precisely. They all share something about me, express a side of me. Like the books I've done on India."

I'm deeply humbled by the gist of what she's saying, but it leaves me feeling confused. "My book fits into your catalog? Into your life story?"

"I've been a wife. I've been a working woman. A tourist. An ambassador, of sorts, in my thousand days as First Lady. And I will be an historical figure. The answer to some future trivia."

"Maybe. Although who can really name Grover Cleveland's wife?" I look up, expecting a lighthearted laugh.

"Frances Folsom." The name floats between us, slowly wafting my way. Eventually Jackie laughs, but only at the dumbfounded expression on my face. "When you're in a club as elite as that, you tend to know the other members."

I blow on my tea, buying time to process what she's telling me. "But my book isn't about any of those things."

"James, your book says who I am above all."

I'm almost stunned in total bafflement, even though the answer is right in front of me. "A mother."

She nods.

I sit back in my seat, understanding our relationship, perhaps for the first time. "Well, that's just"—I think about what it is, exactly, that I want to say—"a whole other level of responsibility."

"It's not meant to be."

"How can it not be? You're one of the—you know—women of the twentieth century." I try not to use any of the words I know she detests: Famous. Iconic. Paragon.

Jackie looks deep in her cup as if reading the tea leaves.

"But to tell your story—"

She cuts me off. "You already told my story."

"That's a lot to digest."

"Have a sandwich, then, to wash it down." She smiles and holds out a plate of small sandwiches and I take two and eat one over my saucer; I struggle to chew through the cold cucumber.

"I'm hopeful. That she will come to the party," I say after swallowing, sensing Jackie would like to move off the subject. "My mother. It's difficult to imagine it without her. But I don't know. There is still so much hurt. The past is a funny thing."

"It has such power over us. Such sway."

"It's wily. The past morphs and changes even though, in theory, it should be set in stone."

"The past is all perspective," Jackie says, not at all thrown by my rambling thoughts.

"I suppose. I long for it, though. The past. Even though I wouldn't trade a moment of this. And even though I know in my head the past wasn't as good as I remember it. I ache for it still."

"I think we ache for the certainty of our past, perhaps, more so than the goodness of it. Writers open themselves to many perspectives, they put themselves in their characters' shoes. It muddies your image of things. Much easier to see the past through a single lens, but it's never the whole story, is it."

"This makes sense to you."

Jackie looks down and crosses her hands in her lap. "I know it sounds a bit bizarre, but in Camelot, Camelot, that's how conditions are."

I've felt so flummoxed by this thought in my little world, and Jackie has lived most of her adult life in the long romantic shadow cast by history. What must it be like to have a whole nation idealize a past that you know firsthand was painfully imperfect? "Do *you* long for it ever? The past?" It may very well be the most personal question I've ever asked her.

Jackie looks again at the fireplace, as if there were roaring flames that only she could see. "I long for a past that maybe never was."

"*Saudade*, the Portuguese call it," I say, and then, "Daniel's mother is Brazilian." I can't be sure she's listening but I add "My Daniel" anyway, and then don't say anything more. I'm struck with profound gratitude that our paths have magically crossed for this brief moment of existence; she is, I see now, the only logical editor this book could have had. My book, my valiant quest to understand my own Arthurian legend with Igraine at the heart, to define my own Camelot, in the tender hands of Guinevere herself. My eyes well with tears even though knights are not supposed to cry.

"I'm scared," I say, wiping my eyes with the backs of my hands.

"Of what?" she asks gently.

I reach for the second sandwich on my plate before deciding I can't eat it. "I'm not sure." But I do know. I'm scared of not knowing how to make things right.

"You have wells of strength inside you, James."

I nod, but I can't look at her—*compliments*—and I rub my hands together like I myself might be starting a fire. "I want to thank you. For this adventure. I'm not certain what comes next, but I want you to know how grateful I am that you saw something in my writing that made you want to take a chance on me. I can't tell you how good it feels to finally be . . ."

"Celebrated?" Jackie asks.

I reach for just the right word. "Noticed."

"You're going to be a lot more than noticed at the party." Jackie leans forward, like she might pat my leg. "I don't worry about you, James. Some of my authors, I don't know if they have another book in them, let alone a career. Not you. You are interested in the truth, and that search will always give you things to write about."

"Thank you. That means . . . everything to me."

In one fluid motion she rises from her chair, standing like a flamingo on one leg before placing the other on the ground. "I have a copy of your book somewhere." She crosses over to a mahogany secretaire; I follow and she moves some papers around, exposing the desk's gold foil inlay. "Ah, here." She holds up the book. "I was hoping you would sign my copy." She picks a pen out of a desktop pen stand and offers it to me.

"May I sit?"

"Of course," she replies, and pulls back the chair.

I trace the desk's gold inlay with my fingers, around the table to the corners, where the leg posts bulge like the corner pockets on a pool table. Like everything else of Jackie's, it's flawlessly made. I open the book to the title page and stare at the blank space between *ITHACA* and my name. Absentmindedly I almost put the pen in my mouth to chew on it while I think, but stop myself just in time.

Jackie senses my hesitation. "President Kennedy signed the Limited Nuclear Test Ban Treaty at this desk. So no pressure on you to come up with something momentous."

I look up at Jackie with my best *You've got to be kidding me* expression. She laughs and places her hand warmly on my shoulder. "It's true!"

I'm acutely aware of her touch.

"Why don't I give you some room," she says, and squeezes my shoulder twice. I hear her refilling her tea before retreating from the study; I look over my shoulder and she hesitates for just a second in the doorway and we share a bashful smile. "Don't ever stop trying," she offers again. "Do that for me."

My hand starts to shake and I mouth the word *promise*.

When I'm certain she's gone, I put pen to paper, but nothing comes. Complete and total writer's block. I'd be lying if I said I hadn't thought about this moment, signing a book for Jackie. But nothing ever seemed right. Everything sounded too gimmicky, or trite, and did not encapsulate all that she has meant to me. I glance over at her bookshelf for inspiration and my eyes land on a collected work of poems. The Cavafy poem springs to mind, and I know instantly that it's perfect. Fortunately, I have the final stanza memorized.

> *For Jackie, who gave me the marvelous journey and*
> *taught me to understand what Ithakas mean.*
> *With gratitude, always. James.*

I set the pen down and turn around to survey the room. The books, the wallpaper, the fireplace, the bouquet of fresh red roses on the table beside her chair, the very place she was sitting just moments before, her shoes still on the oriental rug. Of course, she's just a woman walking around her house in her stocking feet, the way my mother often does. But the sight of her shoes in front of the chair makes it appear that she's been Raptured. There's a small moment of dread when my heart feels like a lump—the fear, I suppose, that she's somehow, at least temporarily, leaving my life.

Later, when we've gone over the publicity plans and she imparts some insight on how to speak to the press and handle any potentially negative reviews, we say our good-byes. Once I'm back in the elevator that will (or will not) return me safely to the ground from my afternoon in the clouds, I crack my gift to read Jackie's inscription.

I remember a story Mark once told me where Jackie was feeling obligated or pressured by a business acquaintance to give her autograph. She relented, but signed only Jacqueline Onassis, denying them what they wanted most from her: the allure of Jackie and prestige of Kennedy. But here she has written:

> *For James, a son who would make any mother proud.*
> *With great affection, Jackie Kennedy Onassis.*

As the elevator descends, I jump, knowing full well that the force of my landing may compromise the elevator's already questionable integrity. But I don't care. With the floor dropping beneath me, I stay airborne for fractions of seconds longer and it is there that I feel truly alive.

· THIRTY-TWO ·

I'm standing in the middle of the room and people are buzzing about and my tie is too tight, the room is too loud (how can sixty people make the noise of a jet engine picking up speed down a runway?), and this jacket makes it hard to lift my arms quickly enough to snag a glass of champagne from the passing waiter's tray. I curse my jacket. Tweed. Obvious. I'm playing the role of writer as relic, just as I have to imagine these parties in dark-paneled rooms with brightly dressed literati will soon be a part of a publishing museum; the publishing world, it seems, is changing.

I maneuvered out of a rambling conversation with a forward-thinking lunatic who congratulated me on the book and then rejoiced in telling me that in ten years there will be no more bookstores. Or there will be bookstores, he said, but they won't have any books. They will just have a computer and a giant printer, and everything will be print-on-demand and you will choose your own cover and binding, depending on how much you want to spend. Want a leather-bound copy of Dumas's *The Three Musketeers*? Fork over your wallet and take a seat. Booksellers like LensCrafters—your chosen title in under an hour. The thought of it is bleak. I mean, I can live without book parties. I can't live without bookstores. I look across the room, and someone who looks a bit like Gay Talese (but who is not Gay Talese) has witnessed my champagne fiasco, so I playfully wobble my empty champagne flute between my fingers while raising my shoulders and making a face.

Can't get a drink at his own party, the man seems to say.

What are you going to do? I shrug in return.

Upon our brief introduction, Doubleday's editor-in-chief told me

they used to keep a suite on Fifth Avenue for book parties and random entertaining back in the halcyon days of publishing, when authors were stars and editors were names and books were events. My
editor is still a name (and a star and an event, for that matter), and the
publisher has high hopes that my book could do well, based on its
association with that name, and a party is just the way to announce
that this is a capital *N* (ENNN) Novel even if I'm a capital *N*
(ENNN) Nobody. But these parties are growing increasingly rare and
publishing houses no longer keep suites, so we're in a large reception
area on one of the floors in the Broadway building Doubleday is in
the midst of moving into. Because of this, people don't really know
how to act. Guests smile and nod and we make polite conversation
about the state of the business or about my chances of making "the
list," which is for most people the *New York Times* Best Sellers list, but
for one gentleman, a writer himself, it was eventually revealed to be
the long list for the National Book Award, which I can't imagine is
on anyone's radar but I suppose is what passes for cocktail chatter at
these things.

Making me feel even more like a nobody is the fact that I barely
know anyone here. Daniel is not even by my side. His show was extended, but the actor who played the lead dropped out.

"Guess who they want to replace him?" he asked. He was eating a
banana in our kitchen and you could tell he was suppressing a smile.

"You?" I must have said it with some degree of judgment, because
he tossed the banana peel in the sink instead of in the trash.

"You don't think I can do it?"

"Obviously I think you can do it," I told him. "I said as much on
opening night. Remember? You would be a better Bruce. I said that!"

"I sense a *but*," he said.

"Of course there's a but!" If he was now going to be onstage,
how was he also going to be at my book party? "You can't be in two
places at once," I told him. That seemed like a simple statement of
scientific fact.

"Congratulations." A woman in funereal black interrupts my

thoughts by resting her hand on mine. The veins on her hand are alarming.

"Thank you."

She looks around the room for Jackie (it's always for Jackie), and when she doesn't see her she carefully but swiftly removes her blue hand and moves on.

The waiter passes with more champagne, and this time I'm able to swap my empty glass for a full one by keeping my elbow close to my side (it's best not to fight the jacket) and reaching out with just my forearms, looking tragically like a Tyrannosaurus rex. I take a full, long sip and let bubbles explode in my mouth like Pop Rocks.

Perhaps because we're similar in age and most everyone else is at least twenty years older, the waiter feels comfortable leaning in. "I heard Jackie Kennedy is going to be here," he whispers, like an old-timey gossip. *Swirling headlines, swirling headlines.*

"Oh, you heard that too?"

Of course Jackie Kennedy is *not* here; her absence is dubious, and the party feels disquieted and unresolved. A bunch of worker bees and drones, waiting for their queen, standing in this newly constructed hive.

"Congratulations." It's the publisher. Or CEO. We've met once before. He's the only other gentleman here wearing tweed; we're both hanging on tightly, he to the past, me to a future I'm not sure I'll even like.

"Thank you. Very kind." I offer my champagne flute and we clink glasses.

"She's very proud of you, you know that."

"I was hoping she would be here."

He puts his hand on my shoulder. "She does this. She wants the spotlight to be . . ."

"On the author. I know. I get it." It's exactly her modus operandi. But in this case her fame wouldn't detract from me, it would draw attention to the book. Moreover, I could use a friendly face.

"Working on anything new?"

"One wasn't enough?" We both laugh. "I may have something up my sleeve," I say.

"Good. We like our writers writing!" He smiles and squeezes my shoulder before letting go. "Oh, there's . . ."

He looks at me apologetically before slipping away.

"It's okay. Go." I give my permission to the empty space where he just stood and am left once again without even the waiter to talk to. I flash back to my argument with Daniel.

"Your book party isn't going to be over before I get there," he promised at the time. "I will let you be the toast of the evening, then I will race across town and I will be there to celebrate you too. I may be wearing some makeup still, but I will make an entrance, and I will be there."

Toast of the evening. Ha. Most people don't seem to know who I am. I take a few steps and set my drink down on a counter that I think is some sort of reception desk. I look around to see if I should grab a napkin to use as a coaster but quickly decide not to bother. I mean, the veneer is nice, but let's be honest—it's not like any nuclear test ban treaties were signed on its surface.

"Having fun?"

I spin around to see Mark.

"Oh, thank God." This time I hug him and don't feel like letting go. Since I can't raise my arms in this jacket, my hands meet around his waist in a way that feels even more intimate. I inhale deeply and his skin smells like wet soil after the rain, but in a really high-end way; it's clear he paid a lot for a fragrance expertly designed and tested to make the wearer seem like he is not trying very hard. Of course this wearer is, trying hard, but it smells so good and I am so desperate it's all I can do not to lick him. "Thank you."

"For what?" he asks.

I realize I don't know. It just kind of slipped out of my mouth. "For believing in me."

"Are you kidding? Your book is maybe my favorite of ours."

I squeeze him again before letting go. "I'm being weird. I'm just so glad to see someone I know."

"You know people." Mark leaves his arm around my shoulders and starts discreetly pointing around the room. "That's Liz, your publicist. You know her. And that's the features editor from the *Times*. He's good friends with Jackie. I can introduce you. Over there is the team from marketing, and Peter did your book cover, and Janet did the story on you for *Kirkus*."

As Mark talks, all I can hear is an electric hum, the buzzing of telephone wires hot with voices. It takes some time for the sounds he makes to form words and another moment still for me to remember their meaning. "Oh, right. I know Janet."

"Where's your agent?"

"I'm right here," Allen says, materializing from behind a cluster of other guests.

"I thought you'd left."

"No, duty called. I was pitching an editor on another client."

"Allen, this is Mark, Jackie's . . ." I struggle in this moment not to embarrass him.

"Assistant. I'm Mrs. Onassis's assistant."

They shake hands. "It's a pleasure to meet you, Mark."

"Did Donna come?"

"No, no. She was going to but then got in some fight with her mother over childcare. Listen, this time I really am leaving."

"Allen," I object.

"I know, and I love you, kid. But I'm going to catch the second act of *Shakespeare for My Father*."

"Nothing happens in the first act," Mark offers.

"That's what I heard," Allen confirms.

"*Something* happens in the first act," I protest, in defense of play-wrights. Still, I shake Allen's hand and we agree to have lunch and as fast as he appeared he is gone.

"So that's your agent," Mark says.

"Yup."

"He seems—"

I honestly don't know how Mark is going to finish that sentence, but I cut him off anyway. "You have no idea."

"What about your boyfriend? Where's he?"

"Not here." I raise both eyebrows suspiciously.

"I see," he says. Is that glee he's trying to mask? "Another drink?"

"Sure." I say it with just the amount of disinterest I know he responds to, and he scuttles into the crowd. I survey the room because now we're playing a game, or, more accurately, now I am playing a game. (Mark, it seems, is always playing.) I spot someone else not involved in conversation—young, handsome—and I hurry over, hoping for some common ground.

"Hi. James. The author here tonight." I smirk, but not in a smarmy way, just enough to let him know I'm in on how ridiculous all of this is.

"David." He reaches out to shake my hand. "Congratulations."

"Thank you, thank you very much." It comes across as a second-rate Elvis impression and I wince. "What are you doing here?" A poor rebound.

David laughs. "Are you this accusatory with all of your guests?"

"You know what? I think I am. I'm having a hard time believing that anyone is here for me."

He laughs. "It's okay. I was the same way at my book party. Couldn't believe any of it either."

"Oh, you're a writer! Thank God."

"I am. I wrote a book for Jackie, in fact. And we're doing another one together. A biography on Jean Harlow. Comes out this fall."

"Jackie," I say, as if trying to place the name. I take a quick scan around the room to see if she has arrived fashionably late. Fashionably *very* late. European fashionably late.

David can tell what I'm doing and he puts his hand on my arm. I squeeze my bicep, reflexively. "She doesn't like these things."

"I . . . sort of figured that."

"She wants the emphasis to be on you. On the book."

"She didn't come to yours either?"

David tosses back the last of his drink. "Ah, no."

I see Mark approaching with two glasses of champagne.

"Say something quick about Jean Harlow. Died young, right?"

"Twenty-six," David says, caught off guard by my breakneck change in direction.

Mark is upon us, so I laugh like something is funny, even though it's horribly timed: There's nothing funny about dying at twenty-six. "David, do you know Matt?"

Mark hands me a glass of champagne, annoyed. *"Mark."*

"Mark. Right." I feign horror. "This night." I make a gesture like this is all so wild and I couldn't possibly be expected to keep anything straight.

"I know Mark," David says, and they shake hands.

"Jean Harlow died at twenty-six," I tell Mark, employing this new information.

Mark nods.

"So young," David says.

I turn to Mark. "Jeez, if you were Jean Harlow you'd only have five or six years left." I grimace, punctuating the thought with a silent *yikes*.

David, catching on, leans in and adds, "Harlow was an American film actress from the 1930s."

"Yes, yes, I get it. I'm young," Mark says, already tired of the whole routine. "In many circles that would be considered an asset."

"Huh," I utter, as if the thought of youth being desirable had never occurred to me. A woman who is the spitting image of Alexis Carrington saunters by. It's only after she passes that I turn to catch a good look at her. "Was that Joan Collins?"

Mark and David shrug in unison.

"If you'll excuse me, I need to say hi to someone." David shakes my hand and heads for the makeshift bar.

When we're alone, Mark says, "'Matt'? Very funny."

"I thought so."

Mark studies me in a way he hasn't since our first night having drinks at the Royalton. "Who *are* you tonight?"

I take a long, slow sip of champagne and give the only answer I have. "Who am I on any night?"

Mark squints with something adjacent to admiration. Respect, maybe. "I don't know. But not this."

He takes my hand and we weave through the crowd, and as he pulls me forward the room spins and I realize I may be a little bit drunk. Faces pass in a blur, but we are invisible to most of them, the Friends of Jackie. Laughter crescendos and there's a bizarrely timed cackle. I hear the toasting of glasses, the rustling of uncomfortable clothes, the buzz of gossip, the tap of dress shoes, which may be my own.

"Where are we going?"

"Bathroom. You like bathrooms."

"I like hotels," I clarify, worried Mark may have drawn the wrong conclusion from our previous encounter.

Without looking back, he says, "This is a hotel."

I crane my neck to remember where I am. "This is an office build-ing." Moving forward, looking backward, the champagne further weakens my resolve. *Is this an office building?* "It's *your* office build-ing," I say, mustering the last bit of certainty I have.

We reach the men's room and Mark kicks open the door and gives a final yank that all but twirls me inside like we're doing some unre-hearsed Viennese waltz. I think of the painting of ballerinas in Jack-ie's old office and how ungraceful I am in comparison: I almost slam into a sink. The door closes slowly behind us and the party becomes little more than a muffled din. Mark pushes the three stall doors open to make sure we're alone.

"Shut up," he says.

"I didn't say anything."

"You were about to."

He's got me there. All the glorious confidence I'd displayed out there dissipates when we are alone.

"You like this. Attention," he continues.

"From you?"

"From everyone."

I bite my lip and then slowly nod. How do I explain that the people here mean nothing to me? That everyone I want to be here isn't? I can't. Not without some sort of dithering reply. He's standing very close and my heart beats faster and it may be the champagne, or it may be the twenty-five sad push-ups I did before the party, but my chest feels tight and I think of my mother and how she felt on those drives with Frank Latimer, when everything was charged and dynamic, and how easy it is in any given moment to be weak.

And how much I want to be strong.

Mark presses against me and it becomes clear the dizziness I feel is from the blood draining from my head and flooding to my groin.

"This is"—I pause, letting that hang as the most existential of statements before adding—"wrong."

"I know. That's what makes it so fun."

Mark kisses my neck and I grab his hair—not mashing him closer, not pulling him away. His lips are soft and his stubble the perfect rough and my dick is now completely hard and I stumble against the sink and when I reach out to brace myself I must hit something because water comes flowing out of the faucet.

"Oh, God," I whisper.

I wrap my arms around his waist and pull him in toward me until we are pressed so tightly together there isn't even room for air between us. I can feel the stiffness in his pants with my own and I press myself even harder against him and the world is spinning with possibility and I kiss him full on the mouth. For no real reason other than I'm drunk and he's there. He showed up. He expressed interest.

The kiss isn't even that good. His tongue does this overeager lizard thing; I try to kiss by example, but it's futile to get him to stop. I'm already bored of it when the door opens. Startled, I try to pull back, away from Mark, but I can't really and I dip the elbow of my sleeve under the water and instead push him forward. I glance at my sopping-wet elbow patch before we both look up, busted.

It's Daniel.

FUCK.

Mark pulls back and does his best to hide behind the door. But it's no use.

"Hi." My voice drips with guilt.

"There you are." Daniel is still trying to register what he's seen.

"You made it!" I try to sound both casual and like I'm excited to see him. I hold out my elbow. "I spilled." As if that lie is any sort of explanation.

"I'll come back," Daniel says, and retreats out the door.

"No! There's no . . . Stay!" I'm fumbling with myself, attempting to diminish the obvious bulge in my pants. What fresh hell. I glare at Mark. "Goddammit, *Matt.*"

I burst through the door and reenter the party. I can see Daniel across the room, headed for the exit. This time, for whatever reason, I am not invisible. As I race after him, three people stop me to offer congratulations.

"You're wonderful."

"You must feel so proud."

"Tonight is your crowning achievement!"

Thank you, thank you, thank you; I make gestures promising I'll return. I literally peel one woman's hand off my arm as I try to barrel through.

When I reach the hall, I see the farthest bank of elevator doors start to close. I shove my arm inside the car just as the doors close on my wet elbow before a bell rings indignantly and they are triggered to reopen. Daniel is facing the back of the elevator, but there's a mirror so I can read the anger on his face.

"Don't go. Not like this."

"Why should I stay?"

I furiously backpedal. "It was nothing. A stupid slipup. It's not a big deal."

"Oh, it's not?"

"You don't even believe in monogamy."

"That doesn't mean I believe in being lied to!"

"You know what? This is partially on you. You never gave a damn about this book. Him? At least he's interested in my work!" For a hot second I actually think I can get away with blaming this on Daniel.

He meets my gaze in the mirror. "Your work, your work. Always so consumed with fixing your book."

"That's right! What's wrong with that?"

Daniel spins around. "Why don't you fix your life!"

"What?"

"I know you're going through some shit, and I'm sorry about that, I really am. I have given you a wide berth to process it. But really. Who the fuck do you think you are?"

"Daniel . . ."

"Not the man I fell in love with, that's for sure."

"Daniel, please."

"YOU'RE NOT!" Daniel yells, and it catches the attention of several partygoers who have spilled out into the hall. I want to protest, to try to explain. I look over at the other guests. *I deserve that.* I almost say it out loud, but they pretend not to notice me. One man goes as far as to check a pager that hasn't beeped.

"Okay."

"So why don't you figure that out."

The elevator alarm sounds, I've held it open too long. Several other guests appear in the entry to see what all the commotion is about. Daniel spins around to push my hand away from the doors and they start to close. I see him point angrily at me and he looks like Uncle Sam. "Don't come home tonight."

An Uncle Sam who doesn't want me.

"Daniel!"

I leap to press the down button, but it's too late; Daniel is gone.

I press the button a dozen more times, hoping it has magical powers to erase the last three minutes, hoping that the doors will reopen and Daniel will arrive fresh from his play and he will be so excited to see me there waiting for him. That what just happened was a cautionary vision, a glimpse from some future party that hasn't actually been written.

Of course it isn't and none of this happens. Pushing an elevator button dozens of times in rapid succession only serves to make you feel like an asshole. I am an asshole. My elbow is wet. I hate my fucking jacket. I hate what I've done to Daniel. I hate that no one I care about is here. I hate the excuses I make. I hate that I feel like a prisoner at my own party. Can I leave? Are there rules? Will I be blacklisted? Will I ever publish another book? Do I want to publish another book?

Ding.

It's the elevator behind me. As the doors start to part, before they can fully slide open, I desperately say, "Daniel," and imagine how happy I would be to see him even if he only came back to yell at me more and tell me what a horrible person I've become. I could tell him how much I really do love him, that I realize that now, that these past few months I've been an insufferable jerk. That it's not genetic, that I am responsible for my own choices, that I am deeply, deeply sorry. I spin around, hoping to see his face. But it's not Daniel who emerges.

I stand perfectly still, frozen in shock, and everything melts away. I look at the woman standing in front of me, clothes not fresh off the runways of Paris but decidedly off the rack, hair not in a flawless helmet but mussed as if she were lost or confused. She looks just as petrified as I must, and it's all I can do to whisper.

"Mom."

THIRTY-THREE

We walk down the long, empty corridor of my mother's Midtown hotel in total silence; all I can hear is her dress, the amplified rustling of coarse, synthetic fabric. A lightbulb is out or I'm seeing a dark orbital spot and an imminent migraine will be the price I pay for three hours of nervously pounding champagne and holding in tears. The longer we walk, the lengthier the hallway seems to get and the more I expect to run into the twins from *The Shining*. "Come play with us, Danny," they'll say, and it will make me long for Daniel even more.

"Where is your room?"

My mother points to the very end of the hall.

The walls are beige, the carpet is a darker beige, everything is some sort of beige except for the discarded room service trays placed just outside people's doors. But even the half-eaten meals are largely in bread bowls or burger buns, or the remnants of some unfortunate chowder, so count them as beige too. It's not like the party was the height of glamour, but this is some kind of opposite bookend. My mother's room is the very farthest from the elevator, and when we get to her door she fishes endlessly in her purse for the key. She pulls out everything from a grocery list to a plastic rain bonnet before I intercede.

"Do you want me to go down to the front desk and ask for another one?"

"No. I have it here somewhere." She abandons the purse and nervously pats down her light raincoat and finds it in a pocket. "Here it is."

The icemaker in the closet behind us drops a fresh batch of ice with a sound like shattering glass. We both jump. "That's a nice sound," I say, already imagining my being jolted awake every ten minutes—if I ever get to sleep at all.

Inside, the room is dark. My mother hesitates before entering, so I push ahead, saying, "Here, let me." I fumble for the light switch on the wall. The fluorescent overheads hum and sputter before finally bathing the nondescript room in ugly light. I usher my mother inside and she drops her purse on the desk. I close the door behind her, take a few steps into the room, and then we both shove our hands into our pockets.

"Well. You sure made a mess of this night," she says.

The charge hangs in the air for an awkward moment and then we both bust out laughing. It's bold for my mother to strike such a tone, but I like this punchy new side of her.

The moment she stepped off the elevator at the party, I enveloped her in a tight hug—too tight, per our established rules of engagement; she knew immediately something was wrong. I came clean with a litany of wrongdoings, as there was no point in hiding my misdeeds. It was a lot for her to take in, and as soon as she acclimated, she assigned degrees of urgency like we were in triage.

"Are you going to be okay?" she asked, and I said I thought I would be.

"Do you need to go back to the party?" she asked, and I said yes I did.

"Do you need a moment?" she asked, and I said that it was best to just get it over with before the shock wore off.

So we reentered the party. Several people asked if everything was all right and I assured them it was (a lie) and introduced them to my mother before they could slip in any follow-up questions.

"You must be proud of your son," they would say, and oddly, I think enough people telling her so did make her feel something akin to pride. She smiled and laughed politely and even had a glass of champagne. It had been a long time since I had seen her smile, and even if it was just for show, it was a show I enjoyed watching. It was nice to see my mother out in the world, among other people; she's lived too much of it cooped up.

Afterward, our walk through Times Square was mostly quiet, except when I grabbed her arm and asked if she remembered when she and Dad walked me through Manhattan when I was young, her holding on to me tight.

"We did that?"

"Dad did that. I'm not sure you were so thrilled. But you did tell me New York is where writers live."

"Huh."

"It made an impression."

She looked up at the neon billboard for Coca-Cola and said, "I guess so."

It was clear her recollection wasn't as sharp as mine, which angered me at first, but then I tried to walk it back by finding something nice to say. "Is that a new dress?" She hates shopping, being fawned over by department-store saleswomen whose makeup and hairstyles might as well make them alien creatures; a new dress would be a big deal.

My mother looked down at the black dress under her raincoat. "Yes. I didn't have anything to wear."

"It's pretty," I said, and we moved on.

I catch my reflection now in the mirror over the dresser. The fluorescent light is not doing my skin any favors; is it really possible for a person to look *green*? Is this how I looked all night? "Thanks for letting me stay."

The room has double beds, a dresser, a desk, and a television. By the door, an alcove serves as a closet and an ironing board with a frayed fabric cover pokes out. The one piece of art, a watercolor of daisies in a vase in a field, somehow makes the room sadder. But it's a step up from my tour through a string of Super 8s earlier this year.

"This will all be fine," my mother finally says. "Daniel loves you."

"I haven't been very loveable of late."

"He's a good man."

"No one is arguing that."

"I watch him play with your nephews until *they're* tired. No one would do that if they didn't care."

I think about this and even though I know that it's true I still protest. "They're less complicated than I am."

"You should spend more time with them, if that's what you think."

My mother removes her coat and I reach to take it from her. "I just wish he cared more about the book. I could have used his support." I wrestle with a hanger from the closet before realizing it's attached to the bar and my hand slips and I knock all the other hangers about, turning them into the world's worst chime. I look back at my mother, who opens a nightstand drawer and places her hand on the Bible as if she were about to swear an oath.

"It's not that he doesn't care about your book, it's just that he cares more about you."

I manage to attach her coat even though the hanger itself is alarmingly small; my blazer with its wide shoulders would slip right off. I count one bathrobe. Then it sinks in what my mother is saying and I grab on to the closet bar for support. I have everything in Daniel and haven't cherished it.

"Which bed do you prefer?" I ask, when I can finally stand on my own.

"I think the one by the bathroom is best."

I cross and sit on the bed by the window. It feels remarkably intimate, sharing a room. We somehow went from barely speaking to sleeping side by side, a remarkable jump in just a few hours.

"I'm sorry Jackie wasn't there," I offer.

"I'm not."

"No?"

"I didn't come to meet her; I came to see you."

This lands like a sucker punch. "Still, I would have liked to introduce you. You have a lot in common."

Silence.

"Oh?"

The fluorescent lights start to hum, or they have been humming and it finally reaches my ears. Outside, someone lays on their horn and another kind soul honks in return. I can't be sure of it, but I think I hear shouting. We're only blocks away from my apartment, but the ambient sounds are jarringly different and they rattle my already addled brain. "You're both my editor, cutting scenes from my story, sending the narrative in different directions." I smile, thinking this quite clever, not immediately aware how it lands. When I look at my mother, I can read the distress on her face. "I'm sorry."

"You don't have to be."

"It's just . . . you let me stay here tonight. I shouldn't come out on the attack." My fingers feel numb and I make two fists but immediately unclench them when I realize it's not the visual to accompany an apology. My mother is frozen, uncertain what to say or do next. "I'm not mad about Frank," I continue. "I need you to know that. These things . . . happen." Mark's face with its stupid grin flashes in front of me. "But I struggled my whole life with identity. To know who I really was. Why I didn't feel connected. Why I never truly fit in. And all this time you had the answer! You could have saved me when I was spiraling and you didn't."

My mother nods, and it's a long time before she speaks. "It breaks my heart to hear you say that. From the day you were born, you've always been more yourself than anyone I've ever met. I guess I felt deep down you didn't need to know anyone else in order to know who you are."

I look at my shoes until the icemaker across the hall drops more ice, shattering the silence. It's as disruptive as I had feared. "Can I interest you in some ice?" I ask. Jackie was right, I do have trouble hearing compliments.

My mother circles her bed to take a seat across from me, smoothing out the bedspread with her hands. "It's okay to be angry."

"I'm not angry." I even think that's partly true. "I'm actually grateful."

"I wasn't going to leave you on the street."

I take a sharp breath. I can picture myself wandering all night through the city, seeking a twenty-four-hour McDonald's or some other relatively safe refuge. "Not for that. Although I am grateful for that too." The floating dark spot returns in my eye like a cloud threatening rain. I rub my eyelid in a vain attempt to get rid of it. "You chose me. Again and again, you chose me."

She picks at a thread on the duvet, a perfect metaphor; I wait for everything to unravel.

"I just wish I knew something about him. Not about him, I guess you told me that. About what he was like. I think that's the piece that's missing." I look right at her so she knows that I still want to know this, even if she doesn't think I need to.

"How do you mean?"

"I don't know. Was he funny?" I flop back on the bed and stare up at the ceiling, wondering if I need to tick off a list of characteristics. "Never mind. You probably don't remember."

My mother turns on the table lamp with a loud *click* before turning it off again.

Click.

"I don't have to remember. You're just like him."

I take a breath so sharp it's almost a gasp. I'm awash in my own foolishness; everywhere I looked, and it never occurred to me to look within.

Eventually, I sit up and untie my shoes and kick them off my feet, then place them neatly at the end of the bed. I walk in across the room in my socks and secure the chain lock across the door and adjust the thermostat to cool. It takes thirty seconds or so for the fan to kick on.

"Kind of funny, this," I say.

"How so?"

"You and I. Locking ourselves away."

My mother looks at me, not getting it.

"It's like the quarantine. From the book." A siren speeds by and then fades. "The book is coming to life." I can only imagine this is my mother's worst nightmare.

"Maybe I should read it again."

My ear immediately dissects that sentence.

"Wait. *Again?* I thought you didn't read it."

"Of course I read it. Are you insane? I read it the moment you first gave it to me."

"Then why would you say that you didn't!"

My mother shrugs. *Why do we do anything.*

I don't know whether to be annoyed that I've been lied to again or to be ecstatic that she's read the book I wrote for her or to feel dumb for believing her in the first place. "Well, a lot has changed, if you wanted to"—I can't believe I'm saying this—"read it again."

"You're an excellent writer."

I'm too stunned to say anything other than "Thank you."

She gets up to retrieve a bag of toiletries from her suitcase and walks into the bathroom. I hear the faucet and I head over to the window to give her the maximum amount of privacy the small room affords. The city's heart pulses and I watch brake lights head toward the Battery and oncoming headlights shine like spotlights.

"So, remind me, in this quarantine."

"Yeah?" The fan cuts out just as I speak, making it seem like I'm shouting.

Silence from my mother as she rummages through her lotions and makeup. Then, after a beat, "How long did that take?"

"Forty days," I reply. I study my reflection as I look out at Midtown. Lights from the building across the way sear onto my face. "Do you want me to call the front desk and inquire about a weekly rate?"

My mother sticks her head out of the bathroom, a terry-cloth headband pulling her hair back as she wipes away her makeup. "Pass."

Maybe I'm just completely drained, but her flat delivery strikes me as our funniest exchange yet. I laugh until she can't help but laugh too. And then the ice machine does its thing and we laugh again until we can't remember whatever was funny in the first place.

Then someone in the next room bangs on the wall to silence us.

I place my blazer over the desk chair and pull back the covers on my bed. "Don't worry. The quarantine is fiction. Besides, I'm leaving on tour in a few days."

"Just as well. We can't really fix our problems by hiding from them."

I guess that's the difference between a novel and real life. "No. I don't suppose we can."

I lie back against the headboard, too tired to undress any further, and think about Daniel and what he is doing right this very minute. I hope nothing stupid. I hope not kissing someone else just to get back at me, even if I would deserve it. I hope he is lying in bed, missing me just as much as I'm missing him. I turn my head toward the phone on the table between the two beds and think about calling him, letting him know I'm okay, but worry about making things worse. I have to let us both sleep it off.

"You don't have a toothbrush," my mother calls from the bathroom.

"I don't have anything," I reply, the reality of my predicament sinking in.

"What do we do?"

"I think we both get a good night's rest."

"Yes, but what do we do about your teeth?"

They'll still be there in the morning. "Do you have toothpaste? I'll use my finger." An old trick from dating before I met Daniel.

"That's disgusting."

Her revulsion makes me smile. Maybe the book is coming true for us. Not the actual quarantine part, but the healing that was the result.

What Tomorrow Will Do

May 1994

✦ THIRTY-FOUR ✦

It's dark and I barely hear the tapping on the door. I was dreaming, I think, of Jackie's empty shoes sitting there in her apartment by the fireplace. There was more to the dream, but alas: Everything minus the shoes is a hazy, half-formed hallucination. I recognize the feel of my pillow underneath my head; I am definitely in my own bed. Was I really asleep? Was I drifting in that mysterious place between sleep and awake, where real-world sounds commingle with fantasy? I've been exhausted, I know that. *Ithaca* was well received. Strong reviews (each as surprising to me as the last), and while the sales were modest, my book sold enough copies to garner a second contract. I've been working late, night after night, fueled by caffeine and panic, obsessing over getting my new manuscript just right and wondering—in my darkest thoughts—why I signed up for this agony all over again. Jackie has called twice in the past few months to make sure that I've been writing, and I assured her I was. This seemed to please her and, wanting to please her, I left it at that. She called a third time, more recently, during a few-days' stretch when I felt helplessly blocked, when I wasn't writing. I didn't return the call. I was hoping she would think I was busy.

The tapping comes again. Three soft knocks. Tentative. Halting. "James."

The door opens and a sliver of the softest light creeps in, casting a golden isosceles triangle on the floor, connecting the doorway to the far corner of the bed. Daniel enters, closing the door most of the way behind him, narrowing the triangle into a dagger. He sits on the edge of the bed, and I can feel the mattress sink under his weight. He waits for his eyes to adjust, and then places his hand on my forehead, like my mother used to when she felt I might be ill. I lie perfectly still, wondering what this is all about, afraid that words can only ruin this beautiful tableau.

I break the silence first.

"I think my wrist is giving out. It might be tendonitis." I roll completely on my back and make a fist and twist it around several times on the end of my right forearm.

For several weeks after the book party I wasn't sure our relationship would survive. My mother returned home and I slept on the couch before leaving on a small book tour, mostly the Northeastern Corridor between Washington, D.C., and Maine, with Chicago and San Francisco tacked on like incongruous additions on an otherwise sturdy house. Daniel and I agreed on a break for those two weeks; as I checked in to each new hotel, I would ask the desk clerk for messages, hoping for a kind note from Daniel—but there were never any messages, except once from my publicist, who had booked a local radio interview. When I returned, I wasn't sure that I still had a home. I braced myself for the sight of my things in boxes, crowding the landing outside our door, just as my father's possessions were once stacked unceremoniously on the frozen lawn.

I remember I knocked, even though I had a key.

"Hi," I said, when Daniel came to the door. I leaned in the doorway, hoping somehow it would make me seem cool and irresistible in a slouchy, James Dean kind of way.

"You're such a loser."

My backpack slipped off my shoulder, hitting the ground with a thud, followed immediately by my heart. I slowly pointed at his face. He was wearing eyeglasses, something that was new. "Nerd." I wasn't prepared to engage in name-calling; it was the best I could come up with.

"Are you going to stay out there, or are you actually coming in."

"In, I think." I lifted my backpack a few inches off the ground. "I hope."

It took him a few seconds, but he stepped aside and I came home.

As he sits with me now on the bed, Daniel's face is backlit, expressionless, blank. "I'm sure it's not tendonitis," he says.

In October we went to Paris, just the two of us; we strolled the Champs-Élysées and laughed about the time I asked Jackie about Charles de Gaulle. Slowly things resumed there, better than they were before. We bickered plenty over stupid things, like if we wanted to order crepes that were savory or sweet. Daniel's residual frustration with me sometimes gurgled to the surface in unexpected ways, like when we were pushed around a bit in the Louvre by crowds waiting to see the *Mona Lisa*. I wanted to see her, knowing she too had a special history with Jackie, but Daniel got fed up and left to wait outside. I absorbed all the hits I had coming, and sometimes I looked at him like we didn't know each other at all. When he wore his glasses they became like a simple disguise that made it look like he was masking a secret identity. But he had never been more of a Superman to me.

I roll my wrist again and again. "Are you sure? Do we not have tendons in our wrists? Because it really might be tendonitis." I think of the typing and the book signings, and the long-form writing for when I can't type and the thank-you notes and the masturbation as procrastination and banging my fists in frustration and everything the last ten months have brought. I start rotating my left fist and I swear I notice a difference. I feel Daniel's touch leave my forehead, and seconds later he clasps my hands in his and forces me to stop.

Although things are good again, there is always part of me that fears he will awaken to the realization that he can do better. That, while he gave us a second chance, my selfishness is just too much. Conversely, the whole close call with Mark made me realize that I cannot. Do better.

And then Daniel leans in and whispers in my ear, his warm breath shattering my world. I look up at the ceiling expecting to see stars where there are none, then close my eyelids and mash them tightly together hoping to see stars there.

Instead, there's just angry static—a satellite signal lost.

Daniel takes my hand and tugs. "Come."

He pulls me into an uncomfortable sitting position like I'm some sort of monster come to life, stitched together from the awkward-fitting parts of other ill-matched bodies.

He pulls again, but this time I pull back. I pull away. I know where he wants to take me. Through the crack in the door I can hear the muffled trombone voice of Ted Koppel or Sam Donaldson. I fall back against the pillow. As long as I lay here I don't have to hear what they are saying. As long as I can't hear what they're saying, I can deny that what Daniel told me is true. Even if I knew this day was coming ever since Mark called the house a few months back.

"I thought we agreed it would be best if you didn't call here." I had instructed Mark after the book party that if he needed to reach me, it was best to get me a message through my agent. I couldn't risk Daniel answering the phone.

"She's sick," he said. She wasn't telling people yet, but she was sick and he wanted me to know.

"That's not possible," I said, knowing of course that it was. I held on to the phone long after Mark had to go; I remember wanting to cry, but no tears came, and the feeling was worse because there was no release.

"Come," Daniel says again. He tugs, putting his arm around me this time and suddenly I am on my feet. *Rise.* I think about Jackie's response to my question about de Gaulle in our first meeting, now more than two years ago. *Like the Frankenstein monster,* she had said as we sat in a conference room and just talked and everything about it was magic.

Jackie.

"I need to call her. She called here for me and I didn't call her back."

"Shhhh," Daniel hushes, and he rubs his hands through my hair.

"No, no. She left a message. I wasn't writing then so I didn't call her back. I am writing now, so everything is fine. I'm going to call her and tell her that I'm okay."

Daniel hugs me tighter, but that's the extent of his compassion. "You can't call her. You can't call her anymore."

The flash. Apparently official now. I don't need to see the news. When he opens the bedroom door, the light shining across his face confirms everything. Daniel is Walter Cronkite. He even removes his glasses and pinches his nose to hold back tears.

"When." I don't have the strength to make it sound like a question.

"Earlier this evening. They just broke in with it now."

And thus the ordinary end to an extraordinary story. In many ways the opposite of Dallas. This is the way the world ends. *T. S. Eliot*. Not with a bang, but with a whimper.

We sit together on the couch, holding hands. Reporters are standing outside her apartment at 1040 Fifth, crowded by well-wishers. The images are searing, and it takes my brain time to attend to them. I'm already misunderstanding things. Not well-wishers.

Mourners.

I've been there, is all I can think. I've been to that building. I took the shaky elevator. I've been inside her home. There's a copy of my book in there; I wrote a special note for her inside it.

The reporter and Ted Koppel do a back-and-forth, but I can only hear the stifled voices of adults in a Charlie Brown cartoon, their words muffled trumpets, nonsense.

"Did you know she was sick?"

"Of course." A few weeks after the call from Mark, Jackie released a statement to the press, that was February or March. The announcement was upbeat and her prognosis seemed good. So much so that I couldn't bring myself to raise it as a topic of discussion the last time we spoke. I knew the statement couldn't have been her idea; if she had her way, she would suffer the whole ordeal in private—she certainly didn't want to discuss it with me. Besides, she had access to the very best, cutting-edge healthcare available, treatments out of our reach. So it didn't occur to me to worry. Not really, anyway. She was still young, and very much alive.

Forever young.

"Yeah?" Daniel asks.

"Everyone knew." There was a story, after all, in *People* magazine.

"Did you know she was *this* sick, I'm asking."

I think I shake my head no, but I'm not even sure I do that. I had reasoned the hospital wouldn't let her make it seem like all would be fine if it wasn't going to be; if something dramatic happened, the hospital would appear liable. But how could they have stopped her? No one dared tell her no.

There's a spring in this couch cushion, a coil. A sproil? It makes sitting here uncomfortable. Why have I not felt it before? I look up at Daniel; we are huddled together in the center of the sofa like two people who had just escaped a house fire and are sitting on a curb across the street watching our lives go up in flames. I guess lately I've been too happy and distracted to notice this spring, this coil, snuggling with Daniel as I have. Passions reignited. That much is good.

Everything else, however, is sproiled.

The reporter's words settle in focus. "Mrs. Onassis's longtime spokesperson and longtime friend Nancy Tuckerman confirmed that she died at ten-fifteen this evening, about an hour and twenty minutes ago in her Fifth Avenue apartment, just across the street from Central Park, where she was photographed only Sunday with her longtime companion Maurice Tempelsman."

Longtime, longtime, longtime. I mentally mark up the reporter's speech the way Jackie took to a manuscript. LAZY! FIND BETTER LANGUAGE! REDUNDANT! An hour and twenty minutes ago. I was walking up the steps, coming home from the library. The library where I was surrounded by books.

She loved books.

"Tempelsman was at her bedside along with thirty-six-year-old Caroline, the mother of her three grandchildren, and her son, John. Other people were there, including her former brother-in-law Senator Ted Kennedy and the actress Daryl Hannah, a friend of her son's. She had lapsed in and out of a coma today, and was in fact in a coma when she passed away this evening. Her sister-in-law Ethel Kennedy, the widow of Robert Kennedy, also a close friend, said the apartment was filled with love. Again, Jacqueline Kennedy Onassis passed away earlier this evening at the age of sixty-four."

Daryl Hannah from *Splash*?

"There was a mermaid there?" I don't mean it as a joke—it's the only takeaway my brain can register—but Daniel snickers anyway, wiping away a tear. He squeezes my hand and it feels good, like maybe I'm no longer in danger of falling.

The reporter throws it back to Ted Koppel, who brings in a medical expert to talk about non-Hodgkin's lymphoma. The expert says that fifty percent of people diagnosed are still alive five years later, and that the way Jackie succumbed to the disease only a few months after diagnosis was unusually fast. I want to scream. A few months since *announcement* of the diagnosis. There's no doubt Jackie tried to keep her health private for as long as possible before that. All of this feels like sloppy reporting, but in truth I don't know anything different— I just don't like what's being reported. I don't like any of it at all.

I'm not ready for this news. I didn't call her back. Was she sick when we worked together? When she sat next to a fireplace in summer? Did I somehow know this? Is that why I dreamt of her shoes? Now she is gone and I'm panicked I never said thank you. Did I say thank you? Perhaps I did. But I never said *good-bye.*

There was a mermaid there.

The broadcast cuts to black-and-white photos of Jackie on Air Force One, standing by LBJ as he is sworn in. Then her climbing the steps to the Capitol Rotunda. Her kissing the coffin. John-John saluting his father. She looks little more than a girl herself, so poised, statuesque, yet she is probably my age in these moments. And I am but a child, still.

"Remember the ladies," I say, recalling one of the many gifts she gave me. That women of her generation had obligations, duties. But they were girls once, with dreams and hopes of their own. And then I remember what she said next: *especially your mother.*

I can't help but wallow in the fragility of life. What if my mother were taken now? What if there was still so much left unspoken? In the hotel room the night after the book party she held my hand and told me she had fun. That she was proud of me, even—just as Jackie said she would. But did I tell her anything? Seize that opening? Did I apologize for my own behavior? Did I truly forgive her for hers? What kind of son am I?

"The ordinariness of it all is oddly comforting," Daniel says, interrupting my thoughts. Ordinariness doesn't seem like a word. If we were playing Scrabble I might challenge him on it based on its number of syllables—it's much too much a mouthful for its meaning. But if I'm going to throw around words like sproil, I don't know that I have the moral high ground.

"How do you mean?" But I already know exactly what he means. There was no Dallas. There was no Ambassador Hotel. There was no gunshot. There was no actual Walter Cronkite trying to hold back tears on TV. There was only Daniel waking me from my own slumber.

"She was human."

"Turn it off," I tell him. Daniel looks at me. I can feel my eyes sting, and I resist the urge to cry because I don't know what else to do but to fight. I'm not going to be able to hold back tears for long and I don't want to see pictures of Jackie as everyone knew her. I don't want to see the woman who belonged to everyone. "Please."

I want only to remember my friend. I want only the version of her who belonged to me. A woman with her hands in her hair, legs tucked beside her, asking me always to try.

For James, a son who would make any mother proud.

Daniel gets up, and I sink farther into the couch, as if he'd dismounted the opposite end of a seesaw. He snaps off the television set and the room is deafeningly silent.

THIRTY-FIVE

On Tuesday Daniel and I both dress in black suits, he exceedingly handsome in his, mine feeling alarmingly small—like I grew four inches overnight. He assures me I look fine, then reassures me when I threaten to change, and when he finally gets me out of the apartment we walk over to Eighth Avenue to hail a cab. I fidget with my father's cuff links as we wait. My mother gave them to me years ago, after he left, because she remembered I had admired them as a child; I debated not wearing them, but they remind me of the journey I've been on. Without Jackie, it seems like I'm going to be in charge of reminding myself to never stop trying. We ride in silence to St. Ignatius Loyola Roman Catholic Church, although Daniel turns once and offers a feeble smile and in that one expression a whole conversation is had. We've been good at this of late: talking less, communicating more. Traffic slows and then grinds to a halt; there is very little honking, as if the whole city is paying respect. We get out of the cab at Eightieth and Park and walk the final four blocks—it's impossible to get any closer by car.

The church is a hundred years old maybe, a neoclassic structure built of what I'm guessing is limestone. It looks not unlike a government building, more courthouse, perhaps, than church, or maybe a building for customs. It's not showy like Manhattan's neo-gothic cathedrals like St. Patrick's or St. John the Divine. For Jackie, it seems just right. The announcement in the *Times* said that she was baptized here; when I read that I got very emotional—this solemn occasion a homecoming, of sorts. The night after she died I made Daniel go with me for daiquiris (although we could find only the sweet kind that sorority girls drink on spring break) and we toasted a remarkable woman who lived many lifetimes, and yet still died impossibly young. The drinks proved excellent lunch ladies again; the more we consumed, the more we were able to laugh and reminisce and rejoice. (Until we were drunk, and then we were sad again.)

As we make our way up Park Avenue, the crowd becomes thick and suddenly we are in a throng of spectators and police have the street cordoned off. I grab Daniel's arm to keep him from plowing too far ahead.

"I don't . . ." I start, but I'm not sure what it is I'm hesitant to say.

"You don't what?"

"I don't want to push." But what is it I do want? "Can we just stand here and watch?"

Daniel reaches for my hand and quietly squeezes. There is some police activity, talking on walkie-talkies and waving and making signals. I look east where two officers are pointing.

"She lived just two blocks over."

Daniel points in the direction of Fifth Avenue.

"And a few blocks up."

We maneuver a bit closer without being aggressive; the crowds are held back by metal barriers. I motion for Daniel to follow me up Park in the wake of two photographers who are not as concerned with being respectful, but stop short of the bank of television cameras set up across the street from the church. We are two of the only people wearing suits; the rest of the crowd is dressed more comfortably for the eighty degrees predicted.

After we stand there a good, long while, a hearse appears on Eighty-Fourth Street and rounds the corner onto Park. A hush falls over the crowd. A number of black sedans follow until the hearse glides to a gentle stop. Family members step out of the cars and I'm relieved to be in the company of others dressed in black; it makes me feel less out of place. I forget for a moment and look for Jackie's face among the mourners, her familiar sunglasses, her ramrod posture, her perfect lampshade of hair.

Of course she's not among them.

The pallbearers assemble. They are nephews mostly, there's a family resemblance, although one man is older and clearly has white hair. They huddle together, going over their instructions one last time before pulling the casket out of the back of the hearse and then, in unison, hoisting it onto their shoulders; the flowers draped over the coffin flounce gently. John and Caroline appear and follow their mother up the steps. I move to wave my arm, like they might know me, just as I feel that I have come to know them.

"Do you want to try to get in?" Daniel asks.

"No," I tell him. And after another moment, "I can't."

I expect Daniel to protest, but he doesn't.

I spot a black woman with graying hair a few people over and nod toward her. She's dressed in her finest too, as if for church, and is holding a transistor radio and fidgeting with the antennae.

"Try to listen?" Daniel asks. I nod and we move subtly toward her, careful not to bear down.

She adjusts the radio until she picks up a weak signal and we hear Bryant Gumbel speaking and then, a moment later, Katie Couric chime in—she's picked up an NBC broadcast before losing it again. The woman looks up at us and shakes her head. "I just put new batteries in this thing."

"May I help?" I ask, and she hands me the radio. I fidget with the dial until Bryant and Katie return. I hand the radio back.

She studies our suits as if she's found compatriots in a foreign land. "Did you know her?"

"Pardon?" I say, buying time to formulate an answer.

"Did you know Mrs. Kennedy?" she asks again, pointing to our suits.

I can feel Daniel staring at me, curious to see how I'll respond. I look down at our clothes and offer what is now so apparently true. "Mrs. Onassis?" On more than a few occasions I have exaggerated our acquaintance, a ridiculous attempt at posturing. But today I only have the truth. "I knew her only a little."

The woman is satisfied with that response. People aren't here to

pry or to gawk, everyone is so well behaved and you can tell they
genuinely want to feel part of something that now feels forever gone.
There's no pushing, there's no yelling—in fact there's an almost unsettling quiet throughout crowd.

"Here," the woman says, handing me her radio. "You boys hold it
for me and we can all listen in."

I hesitate to take the radio, and when I do I hold it with both
hands like I'm the gentle custodian of someone's most prized possession. Together we listen to Bryant and Katie and a third voice I don't
recognize, they mention the notable guests, the current First Lady,
Hillary Clinton, and a former in Lady Bird Johnson, Senators Edward Kennedy, John Kerry, and John Glenn, her sister Lee Radziwill,
the director Mike Nichols, and Jackie's children. They reference the
crowd, and it's weird to think they are talking about us. That we are
indeed part of this—something bigger than ourselves. Katie speaks
of the opera singer Jessye Norman, here in attendance, and Bryant
mentions something about Franz Schubert before they cut away to
listen.

There are no cameras inside, at least that I'm aware of, only micro-
phones to broadcast the service. Outside many people stare at the
church façade with no real way to listen, and there are others, like us,
huddled around battery-operated radios sharing information as best
we can. The faint whisper of "Ave Maria" drifts through the air, muffled by the church walls, amplified only slightly by the scattered radios. But the crowd, previously swaying and fidgeting uncomfortably
in the midmorning heat, stands still in awe, as if one of the world's
great voices was on the steps of St. Ignatius singing only for them,
only for us. The woman next to me links her arm with mine in fel-
lowship as we listen to this hymn.

When Ted Kennedy gives the eulogy, the crowd remains equally
still, even though only those of us with radios can hear him speak.
"She made a rare and noble contribution to the American spirit," he
says. "I often think of what she said about Jack in December after he
died: 'They made him a legend, when he would have preferred to be a

man.' Jackie would have preferred to be just herself, but the world insisted that she be a legend too. She never wanted public notice—in part, I think, because it brought back painful memories of an unbearable sorrow, endured in the glare of a million lights."

I look up the avenue and down; there are several thousand people spanning multiple city blocks. If we were just a few of those million lights, the bright, prying whites of our eyes ever focused on her every move, we are dimmed today in her honor.

We listen to every word, Daniel, this woman, and I. And there are many. Mike Nichols offers a scriptural passage. John reads from Isaiah, and Caroline reads "Memory of Cape Cod" by Edna St. Vincent Millay. When they take the microphone I can feel others around us lean in, but I don't mind. In the end, six simple words offered by the officiating priest stand out above all the others: *So dearly beloved, so sorely missed.*

I hold it together and keep my composure the entire time, stoic like Jackie always was, until Maurice Tempelsman, her Belgian, addresses the mourners. He reads from "Ithaka" by Constantine Cavafy.

"Ithaka gave you the marvelous journey; without her you would not have set out. She has nothing left to give you now."

My shoulders slump and I start to weep, Daniel rubs my back and the woman with the radio looks up at me with a kind smile. She doesn't say anything, but rubs my back too, and I nod and then wipe my eyes and whisper, "I may have known her more than I thought."

After the service, we watch as the doors open, and the first mourners exit somberly onto the street. Limos line up in front of the church and I study faces that I imagine belong to members of the Kennedy and the Radziwill and the Bouvier families. Daniel squeezes my hand with excitement when we catch a glimpse of Mike Nichols; a director himself, that's a sighting that's extra-meaningful to him. He's been so good to me these last days and weeks, I'm happy there's a small piece of this grandeur that feels like his. Eventually the coffin is brought out and as it's carried down the stairs I can clearly see the flower arrangements adorning it are in the shape of a cross. People twitter with insight, things they've read, things they've heard; the hearse is headed to the airport, President Clinton himself will meet the casket at Washington National, she will be buried in Arlington National Cemetery next to her husband—her first husband—one final act to discharge her obligations to history.

As the hearse pulls away and the crowds start to thin, Daniel asks if I'd like to go somewhere, perhaps to get something to eat. I ask if we can stay a little longer. We say good-bye to the woman with the radio and she hugs us both and tells us to be "good boys." When she embraces me, she whispers, "I admired her husband. How lucky you are to have known her in any way at all."

We stay until even the cameramen lining the sidewalk start to pack it in. Eventually Daniel puts his arm around me; I nod and we turn to head down Park Avenue toward home.

"Could we walk in the park instead?" I ask.

"Of course," Daniel says, and we cut over on Seventy-Ninth Street.

We find shade under the trees and relief from the heat and we both loosen our ties and remove our jackets. I remove my father's cuff links and put them in my pocket before rolling up my shirtsleeves.

"It was really lovely," Daniel says.

"It was."

As we walk in Central Park, Daniel starts talking about things he saw in the crowd, people he made out, details that moved him. I do my best to listen, but there's a woman ahead in a yellow cap—I can just make out the top of her head as she weaves through a sea of people. I remember Jackie in her bathing cap on a similarly warm day, bobbing in the waters of Squibnocket Pond like an angel gliding through the heavens. Daniel's voice fades and I stop to recall something Ted Kennedy had said:

She graced history. And for those of us who knew and loved her—she graced our lives.

• THIRTY-SIX •

When I wake and whisper to Daniel that I need to go away for a few days, he nods, tousles my bed head, and smiles; I worry this may trigger memories of the last time I ducked town, but he seems to know where I'm going and why. The morning light streams through our narrow window that opens to the top of the air shaft. From my side of the bed I can just make out the faintest sliver of blue sky. When I think of the to-do list that comes with this decision and compare it with my day if I were to tackle some writing (maybe stepping out only for a pizza, or pint of ice cream to bring home), it's tempting not to get out of bed at all.

"I'll miss you," Daniel says.

"I'll miss you too." And when I feel I don't have Daniel's full attention, I grab his chin and turn his head so that he's looking at me.

He smiles while scratching his bare chest before enveloping me in a big hug. "I know you will."

I'm able to rent a car at the second Enterprise location I find (the first only has luxury sedans available, which I know will be a point of contention) and I make it through the Lincoln Tunnel with little effort; the traffic gods are with me. Maybe they know I have a hard day ahead, or maybe they think I've been through enough. As I drive north through New Jersey I flip through radio stations to find something, anything, to keep me distracted, calm. The Carpenters are on a seventies station and I somehow take that as a good omen. Even though the song is "Rainy Days and Mondays," I sing a full verse of "Ticket to Ride" before realizing my mistake.

I stop only once, for coffee.

My mother called when she heard the news that Jackie had died.

We talked and she did motherly things like ask if I was okay and listened to me when I answered. She told me about the day when Bobby was assassinated. To her it was like she tucked her children safely in bed in one world, a world she understood if not entirely admired, and we all woke up in another world that didn't have any rules at all. It was nice to hear her memories and be able to pair them with faint ones of my own.

We talk, not often, but regularly now. She's even softening on the book, or so I hear from Naomi. Apparently my mother calls her local library to put the book on hold; when her number comes up, she removes her name from the list then calls to add it again—just to make the book seem in demand. It's her little game and she seems to enjoy it.

"If you tell her I told you, you're dead," Naomi threatened. But still it was information she thought I needed to hear. Naomi even admitted she goes "undercover" to her local bookstore to face copies on bookshelves out and exclaim emphatically how good the book is when anyone is in earshot.

The last time my mother and I spoke, she asked about my search for Frank. This didn't seem like prurient curiosity, but an understanding that I was going through something traumatic and could use, at the very least, a friend. When I said I had instead gone to see my father at the nursing home, she asked how he was and offered to go with me if I wanted to go again. It was a good reminder that when it came to my father, she too was nursing a broken heart.

None of this makes me certain that she will actually get in my car today, and when I pull in her driveway I realize how nervous I really am. How essential I have come to see this trip as part of our healing. How easy it would be for her to say no. Despite our renewed relationship, despite her trip into the city on her own, my mother is still a woman most comfortable within a close radius of home. I fidget in the car like a young man picking up a prom date, sweating even in the car's AC, wondering where to pin the corsage. Only after I see her appear in the bay window do I get out and walk up the drive.

"Hi," I say when she answers the door.

"Hi," she says in return while looking down the driveway to see if anyone else is with me, or if there is otherwise cause for alarm.

"I was wondering . . ." I start. "I was thinking . . ." That's no better. I hate that this is so hard.

"What were you thinking?" She says it without any trace of the accusatory tone that would have previously poisoned a question like that.

"Do you have any interest . . ." *Good Christ, spit it out.* "Do you want to go for a ride?"

My mother looks back at the house, at all the reasons to say no, the cleaning, the dishes, the ironing, the safety of her own bed, years of patterns and habits and fears, and then at me, and finally over my shoulder at the world beyond, at the future that beckons gently to us both.

"What do I need to bring?"

When I share our destination, she suggests I stay the night and we start fresh on the road in the morning. The drive, after all, will take us five hours due south. I agree, and we get take-out sandwiches and head for an evening walk in Stewart Park along the shores of Cayuga Lake—something we did a lot when I was young. We find just the right bench looking out over the water under the shade of a large willow tree.

"How is your writing?"

"It's good," I say, as I peel back the wax paper around my sandwich. "Maybe a little chaotic." I laugh gently, since I'm writing next about my father. "My subject has doubled in scope." I want to tell her there are days when I wonder why I'm doing this to the family again, but she seems to understand this time that it's my story to write. "In truth, I haven't written much since Jackie died."

"I suppose it's not a race, what you do." My mother takes a bite of her sandwich before lifting the bread to see what's inside. "Did you find anything more on Frank?"

"I think after seeing Dad I kind of stopped looking. He was my father, for better or worse." I open a bag of barbecue potato chips and offer her one, before correcting myself. *"Is."*

She takes a chip and says, "Thank you."

"Maybe one day I'll start the search again. Maybe this new book will prompt me to. But right now I don't feel pressure."

"I know you wonder what happened. To us."

"To you and Frank? Or to you and Dad."

"To you and me."

I listen for a moment as the water laps the shore. "Right." It's part of the mystery I still haven't solved.

"When you settled on writing, you started questioning. You wanted an answer to everything, even the questions you didn't yet know to ask."

I remember how relentless I was at first, like a reporter on a new beat wanting to prove his worth.

"I was afraid you would find out about Frank before I had the courage to tell you. And if that happened, I would lose you forever."

The sun is setting and house lights start to dot the far shores of the lake like shimmering fireflies.

"It must have been lonely. Keeping that inside all this time."

She considers this. "The days were long, but the years piled up very quickly."

I'm suddenly overcome with a longing to see Jackie, to tell her I did it—that I was not consumed by the Sphinx. In this moment I solved my riddle, here, at dusk, as the lake and the sky become one color. Jackie pushed me so hard on the book's ending, but it was really another ending she had in mind all along. This one, right here, right now, my mother and I together.

We finish our sandwiches and my mother offers me her pickle like she used to do when I was a kid. It's something, because I know that she really loves pickles. The air is cool and it's a nice change from the stickiness of this warm early summer, and we sit together until the mosquitos get the best of us.

In the very last of the day's light, with only a tiny orange ribbon above the hills on the horizon, she asks, "How about some ice cream? My treat."

On the way home, we stop to get cones at a place with a walk-up window. "On our next trip I'll treat for ice cream," I tell her. "I know just where to go."

"Oh, yeah? Where's that."

"Mad Martha's on Martha's Vineyard. They serve something called the Pig's Delight."

My mother makes a sour face as she holds her single scoop. "That sounds awful. *Let's do it.*"

In the morning we surprise Kenny at his house by leaving him with Domino and a bag of dry food. Ellen, seeing my mother and me together, immediately intervenes and says she's happy to dog-sit; we hit the road just after dawn. We ride for the first few hours mostly in pleasant silence, stopping for coffee and plain donuts crisp with the flavor of nutmeg. At one point my mother slips off her sandals, sets her bare feet on the dash, cracks the window, and lets the morning air rake over her like she's performing some sort of cleansing ritual. It's cleansing for me too.

Despite heavy traffic around Washington, we arrive at Arlington National Cemetery by early afternoon. It feels good to stretch our legs. We meander through the visitors' center, collecting a map and several brochures. Buses of boisterous kids fill the entrance, and because of the time of year I can't tell if they are here on the rowdy last days of school or the excited first days of summer camp. JFK's grave is only a short walk from the entrance, but we take a circuitous route, almost as if to prolong the errand and ditch the organized tour groups.

"Did you know Taft is the only other president buried here?" I ask while skimming through a list of notable graves.

"Maybe we should drop in on him," my mother says, as if he were an old family friend.

But instead of stopping we pass by Taft and continue along Sherman Drive to Arlington House, before cutting in along a walkway to our destination.

"Have you ever been here?" I ask, wondering, as much as the Kennedys meant to her, if she has somehow made this pilgrimage before.

"No. You?"

"No."

The entrance to President Kennedy's grave consists of an elliptical plaza featuring a low wall of granite stones etched with quotations from his inaugural address. We stop and read them, and my mother circles back to read them again. I step away to take in the Washington Monument, which towers in the distance—we're both stalling for time. I watch as my mother waits for a group of kids to move on so she can run her fingers across the lettering on the first stone: LET THE WORD GO FORTH FROM THIS TIME AND PLACE TO FRIEND AND FOE ALIKE THAT THE TORCH HAS BEEN PASSED TO A NEW GENERATION OF AMERICANS. I know she remembers watching this address as she has told the story many times; I was in her arms, less than three months old. I take a few steps back to give her even more privacy and wonder what the words meant to her then, when she was part of that next generation, and what they mean to her now that there is a new generation behind her. When she completes her second pass, she takes her cross necklace and holds it tightly in her hand before kissing it.

She finds me in the plaza and I offer my hand and she takes it. Together we step forward to the actual graves and wait behind several people for our turn. My heart pounds in my chest. I've imagined this moment many times—introducing my mother to Jackie. Never once like this, but still. I'm finally bringing these women together.

John Kennedy's grave marker lies flush with the ground, JOHN FITZGERALD KENNEDY 1917–1963, surrounded by smaller stones set in the grass. All three are simple and unceremonious, without any elaborate adornment. Behind him, the Eternal Flame, dancing on the breeze. To the right, a fresh burial, a mound of earth.

Jackie.

"There's no stone," I say, poorly masking my disappointment. How can I pay my respects to a fresh mound of dirt?

My mother nods. "There will be."

All of it, so new. It's hard to remember just a few weeks ago I was working on a book, hoping to impress my editor again. It seems so long ago, and yet it is so recent they haven't even placed a marker.

"The children," my mother whispers, her voice quivering. She indicates two smaller gravestones. One says simply DAUGHTER AU-GUST 23, 1956. Stillborn. The other PATRICK BOUVIER KENNEDY AUGUST 7, 1963–AUGUST 9, 1963. It's such a stark reminder of the lives Jackie lived before we ever met, of the sadness that seemed to encircle her.

"He predeceased his father by only ten weeks." I point to Patrick's grave. How is this not something we remember more clearly? It's almost unthinkable, a sitting president losing a child. How is this not one of the first things that springs to mind when remembering him?

Because history tragically intervened.

My mother produces a travel packet of Kleenex and gently wipes her eyes, before offering a tissue to me. I take one, but I'm not feeling imminent tears. "I wish there was a stone for Jackie." The trip isn't even over and already it feels incomplete.

"I'm sorry it's not how you wanted this to be."

"None of this is how I wanted it to be." I summon my dormant Catholicism and say a silent prayer.

. . . we therefore commit her body to the ground, earth to earth, ashes to ashes, dust to dust . . .

And then, when finished, I whisper, "Good-bye, Mrs. Onassis."

We step to the left to make room for other visitors waiting their turn and then out of the way completely. We find a quiet spot down the walk.

"I thought we were . . . *close*. She never even told me she was sick. I had to read the details in *People* magazine like everyone else."

"Well."

"Well, what?"

"You weren't close."

I turn and give my mother a look like she just slapped me across the face. Why would she say such a thing?

"You *weren't*," she says, doubling down.

We stare intently at each other, neither of us blinking or backing away. I want to yell and scream and stomp my feet in childish tantrum, but of course she's right. I would like to think that I was as unique to Jackie as she was to me. But who am I to think that? Of course I wasn't. I was but one in a long line of people who entered her life, who fussed and fawned and invented a relationship that wasn't entirely there.

"You weren't." My mother takes my arm and tucks hers around it and pulls me tight to her and I realize her telling me this is not hateful, it's not even mean-spirited, it's just the level truth. She's telling me this in part to keep me from spiraling over this loss, to keep me moving forward, and maybe, in part, to tell me that she and I in fact are the ones who are.

Close.

"I'm beginning to see that now." My face grows red at the harsh candor of it all and from no small amount of embarrassment for my behavior over the last two years.

"But she was very fond of you."

I feel my cheeks with the backs of my hands and they feel warm, almost sunburned. "Oh, how do you know," I say, as if she's a bother.

"She told me."

My head turns at lightning speed. *"What?"*

My mother freezes, like a child caught with a hand in the cookie jar. "She called me and told me so."

I'm not sure whether to ask how or why or when.

"Well, she had my number, thanks to you. From Thanksgiving."

"What did she say?"

"We just talked, mother to mother."

I'm losing my patience. "What. Did. She. Say."

I think of all the things Jackie and I discussed in private, how I felt these conversations belonged to me and me alone. There are still things I haven't told even Daniel. They were special treasures I had, and they are to this day among my most prized. There's a good chance my mother feels that way about their conversation, but I don't care. I have to know what was said.

"We talked about motherhood. About you, and our children. She invited me personally to the book party, so I came. You don't say no to the First Lady."

"Did she say anything else?"

My mother looks up at the sky as if she's trying hard to remember. "Oh, yes. In the end she said, 'If they grow up to be all right, that is our vengeance on the world.'"

I nod as this sinks in. "And did they?" I ask. "Turn out all right?"

My mother brings her gaze down from the clouds. We both turn back and look at the graves one last time, watch as the Eternal Flame, lit by Jackie herself, dances in the gentle wind. "You bet your ass they did."

It's unlike my mother to cuss, and it's always the most emphatic punctuation when she does.

We continue along the path toward Bobby's grave, and we when we reach it, another flat stone, this time in front of a white cross, we stand quietly and take it in. People have thrown coins, pennies mostly, on the grave.

"Francis"—my mother says, and I don't know if she's addressing me, reading the grave, or remembering another time with Frank—"why me? Of everyone. I think about that. Why did you write about me?"

I look at her in wonder. How in the world could she not know this? "You're the most extraordinary woman I've ever met."

My mother winces. (So this is where I get my difficulty hearing compliments.) "Well," she says, unsure how respond. "Until recently." She nods back up the walkway toward Jackie.

I sit on my reply until my mother turns her head back and is looking me square in the eye. "That I've *ever* met."

We stand there, panicked in the face of such honesty, each unsure what to do next. There's a sting in my eyes and I can see it in hers too before it grows too strong and I almost can't see. "Oh, Francis." The way she says it lifts a burdensome weight off of me, one I've worn so long it had become like a second skin, and I know in that moment that I am her boy again.

Acknowledgments

The Editor is a work of fiction. This novel is not intended to be a definitive portrait of Jacqueline Onassis's time in publishing, but rather my interpretation of a woman at the height of a remarkable career. There are two nonfiction books that I highly recommend if you are curious to know more about her professional life: *Reading Jackie: Her Autobiography in Books* by William Kuhn and *Jackie as Editor: The Literary Life of Jacqueline Kennedy Onassis* by Greg Lawrence, as well as countless other biographies that touch on her extraordinary third act. Nevertheless, I would like to thank Mrs. Onassis for her intelligence, her strength, her grace, her style, her leadership, and for being a continuing inspiration to many, including me.

Thanking one's agent has become de rigueur; instead I will thank my *friend* Rob Weisbach. Your contributions to this book are many, and they won't ever be forgotten. You challenge me, you inspire me, you cheer me on—there are days I don't even want to order lunch without running it by you first. (How do you feel about the chopped salad for me?) Every writer should be lucky enough to have such a fierce advocate and generous teammate.

I owe an enormous debt to my editor, Sally Kim. Your clear and vibrant editorial vision made you a true partner in this endeavor; your fingerprints are on every page. From our meet-cute at a bookstore (shout-out to Pages: A Bookstore in Manhattan Beach, California) to the first time we knocked back a daiquiri, you led me down a path of discovery, just as Jackie did for James. Thank you for the marvelous journey.

I couldn't have found a better home than I have at Putnam. I'm grateful for their energetic team, especially Ivan Held, Alexis Welby,

Katie McKee, Ashley McClay, Christine Ball, Emily Mlynek, Jordan Aaronson, and Gaby Mongelli.

A book has many friends; I'm even fortunate enough to call a few of them my friends too. They include: Molly Lindley Pisani, Bethany Strout, Matthew Allard, Julia Claiborne Johnson, Michael Peters, Ryan Quinn, Trent Vernon, Barry Babok, Laura Rowley, Samuel Rowley, Susan Wiernusz, and Evie, Emmett, Harper, Eli, and Graham.

Thank you to my parents, Norman Rowley and Barbara Sonia, for their lifelong love, enthusiasm, acceptance of and belief in me.

Writing is a solitary endeavor; it helps to have a loyal dog for company. Thank you, Tilda, for your companionship and for dragging me out of my chair every few hours. And to Lily, who continues to make all things possible.

Finally, my undying gratitude to Byron Lane. My first reader and my last, my love, my everything.

Star-Crossed Lovers

LOVESWEPT®

Kay Hooper
Star-Crossed Lovers

Doubleday

NEW YORK · LONDON · TORONTO · SYDNEY · AUCKLAND

LoveswepT*

PUBLISHED BY DOUBLEDAY
a division of Bantam Doubleday Dell Publishing Group, Inc.
666 Fifth Avenue, New York, New York 10103

Doubleday and the portrayal of an anchor with a dolphin
and the word Lloveswept and the portrayal of the wave device
are trademarks of
Bantam Doubleday Dell Publishing Group, Inc.

Library of Congress Cataloging-in-Publication Data
Hooper, Kay.
Star-crossed lovers / by Kay Hooper.—1st hardcover ed.
p.   cm.
"Loveswept."
I. Title.
PS3558.0587S7   1990
813'.54—dc20   90-33461
                                                          CIP

ISBN 0-385-41389-0

RDH

I will not let thee go.
The stars that crowd the summer skies
Have watched us so below
With all their million eyes,
I dare not let thee go.

I will not let thee go.
I hold thee by too many bands:
Thou sayest farewell, and lo!
I have thee by the hands,
And will not let thee go.

—ROBERT BRIDGES

Star-Crossed Lovers

Preface

No one knew how it had all started, or even when. A fascinated historian approached each family just after the turn of this century with the idea of researching and writing the story; each family shot at him. Aggrieved, he talked to the press instead, and a publisher had become interested enough to offer an advance.

With interest and support backing him up, the historian did a thorough job of research, and came up with a story colorful enough to satisfy all but himself. To the end of his days, he complained that he had never been able to find the source of the feud; he had traced a long and violent sequence of events all the way back to the fifteenth century, but even that didn't answer the basic question of when and how things went wrong.

Upon publication of his book, the historian was hardly surprised to learn that Cameron Stuart had promptly taken out an ad in a national newspaper proclaiming the feud had started, of course, with Tavis Logan throwing in with the house of York during the Wars of the Roses and then sealing his treachery with a marriage to a "weakly French slut."

Grady Logan, not to be outdone, had taken out a larger ad insisting it had been Wingate Stuart who had supported the York claim to the throne and then had stolen Tavis's French wife— unpardonable villainy. Which meant, Grady pointed out triumphantly, that Cameron was descended from that French slut.

And the feud went on.

The historian shook his head and sighed while newspapers and magazines ran bits of his book to feed curious readers.

It had been a Logan, said the Stuarts, who had whispered gently but forcefully into Henry VIII's ear to rid himself of his Spanish queen, thus helping to oust Catherine of Aragon. A Stuart, cried the Logans, had rigged the evidence that had lost Anne Boleyn her head.

Jane Seymour, having died in childbirth, apparently escaped the effects of the Stuart-Logan feud, but popular belief held that Anne of Cleves was accepted by Henry only because of the flattering portrait a Logan had put before him; a Stuart had gleefully helped Henry out of that marriage.

Logan retaliated by subtly pointing out the prettiness of Catherine Howard at court, and Stuart caused her downfall— and the loss of her head—by guiding the king's council to find strong evidence of her infidelity. Both sides claimed the happy marriage Henry enjoyed with Catherine Parr.

It seemed there was much fodder for the feud during Henry's reign, between the king's marriages and his strong mistrust of the Plantagenets, to say nothing of his break with Rome. Since both Logan and Stuart were of the old nobility, it seemed to have been the height of insanity to cut at each other by using a suspicious king as a tool— but both, somehow, survived.

They survived also the short reign of the last Tudor

king, Edward VI, the nine-days' "reign" of Lady Jane Grey, and the few years of "Bloody" Mary I. Both Logan and Stuart were somewhat foolhardy when it came to their feud, but neither was fool enough to use Elizabeth I as they had her father, Henry; nor were they reckless enough to encourage handsome sons to chase after the Virgin Queen.

Both Stuart and Logan had eyed askance Elizabeth's successor James I, winced when James's son Charles I declared war on Spain, and shook their heads when he lost his. They had kept quiet and still while Cromwell "reigned" and were relieved when Charles II was crowned.

By the time George III began having his troubles with madness, both Logan and Stuart, separately, of course, had decided to try their luck with America. And both were incredibly lucky in their adopted land; but the family feud went on.

Too late to choose opposite sides in the Revolution, they lost no opportunity in later years and generations to keep feeding the fire. (They had a fine time during the Civil War, for example, though hampered a mite by the fact that both families lived in the Deep South.) What one supported, the other attempted to destroy; what one had, the other had to better.

At times the feud was ridiculous, such as when Jeb Logan painted his privy red to match Cal Stuart's house. Cal had retaliated by creeping over one night to move the privy behind its pit; when Jeb came out for his before-bed visit and walked into the pit, his enraged screams could be heard for miles.

And, inevitably, the feud was sometimes tragic. Stuarts and Logans had been killing each other, for good and bad reasons—or no reason at all—for generations, and the move to America did not stop that. Theirs was a long list of duels, brawls, and deaths. They stole property from one another, destroyed property, sabotaged each other's reputations and business dealings. They imbued their children with their hatred, encouraging more destruction and revenge for destruction.

The historian had discovered a single pattern in the feud which he found fascinating, but no one else seemed to grasp its significance. As nearly as he could determine from the historical evidence, it appeared that in each generation events conspired to produce a critical moment during which the feud could have been stopped.

It seemed to happen in the youth of each generation, when they themselves had no personal grievance against each other and might have risen above the hatred of their elders. But, inevitably, the critical moment was overlooked, or discounted, or those involved simply failed to pass the test. They were drawn into the feud and found their own reasons for continuing it. None had been able to find within themselves whatever was needed to stop the hate.

On it went, a circle with no beginning and no foreseeable ending. In sheer pigheaded spite they chose similar homes, similar businesses, and similar lives. Flying in the face of all logic, they chose to live near one another, so that children brought up to hate were pointed at specific targets.

Long after other well-known family feuds had ended, wounds healed and forgotten, the Stuarts and Logans continued to hate and plot, until the situation was ripe for a shocking conclusion.

It was a pity the historian couldn't have lived to see the finale. He would have loved it.

Prologue

"Damn him!" Charles Logan looked at his son with bitter gray eyes. "I don't suppose we can prove it?"

Jonathan Logan shook his head, the same hard emotion reflected in his blue eyes. "Not a chance, Dad. The inspector was smart enough not to put the money in his own bank account, and my source at city hall won't go on the record with what he knows."

"But he's sure it was Stuart?"

"Who else?" Jonathan laughed shortly. "The inspector was paid to keep us tied up for weeks while he looks at every piece of wire in the building; he's not about to accept our word that the electrical work is up to code. And you can bet Stuart's building has already been approved. Unless we do something to slow Stuart down, we don't have a hope in hell."

The elder Logan turned to stare out the window of his tenth-floor office. In the distance, between two other buildings, he could see his own latest effort rearing skyward. From the outside it looked complete, but even now his

7

crews were at work doing what they could inside it. Until the inspector passed all the wiring in the massive building, most of the work couldn't be finished.

Though always fiercely competitive with his nemesis, Charles Logan never permitted slipshod work due to haste. But on this job, he had pushed his crews to do it right and *fast*, because there was so much at stake.

And now . . .

"Dad? We aren't going to take this lying down?" Jonathan's voice was incredulous. "If Stuart finishes his building first, he'll get the Techtron contract and it's worth millions. He'll crow all over Atlanta that he beat us—"

"He's not going to beat us." Charles's voice was deadly quiet. "No matter what we have to do, he's not going to beat us."

Frowning, Brandon Stuart gazed out his office window as he listened to one of his foremen. He said nothing until the man finished his report, then turned to stare at the man.

"We've dealt with these suppliers for years, Carl. What the hell's going on?"

The foreman shrugged helplessly. "Beats me, boss. To hear them tell it, half the material we order is out of stock, and the other half turns out to be not what we ordered. I've had to send four trucks back just this morning. It feels to me like we're being stonewalled."

"Logan," Brandon Stuart said, making the name a curse.

The foreman blinked. "I don't see how, boss. Unless— well, I suppose they could be favoring his orders over ours. All the places we're having trouble with supply him too."

"I want it stopped," Stuart said in a voice that grated. "I don't care what it takes, or what it costs, I want it stopped. I won't let that bastard beat me!"

• • •

"They don't know about it?"

"No, my love, they don't. They don't know how strongly the seeds of hate took root."

Troubled, she said, "Dangerous."

Cyrus Fortune smiled at his lady, but though the smile glowed with the love he always showed her, there was little reassurance in it. "The wild card, I'm afraid. I can't be sure how the others will react to it. But a festering wound must be opened to let the poison out."

"She'll be hurt."

Cyrus sighed heavily, his benign dark eyes fully expressing his sorrow. "I don't see how it can be avoided. That wasn't a part of my plan. But I should have anticipated what he would do."

"Nonsense." Her tone was bracing, but she softened it with a smile. "At any rate, I feel sure you'll do what you can to lessen any unanticipated blows."

"What I can." Cyrus glanced out the small window at the thick white clouds beneath them and sighed again. "But where there is love—real or manufactured—there must be pain as well. Some blows can't be softened."

There was nothing she could say to that, and she knew him too well to pretend answers she didn't have. Instead, her small hand slipped into his, and she remained silent while the sleek jet cut downward through the clouds toward its landing on the island of Martinique.

One

"You need help?"

They faced each other, surprise in both their expressions instantly supplanted by mistrust and wariness. He stopped dead in his tracks as though he'd run into a wall, and she felt a sudden compulsion to pick up something heavy.

Michele Logan recovered first, throwing off impulses that were ridiculous, she told herself. "Damn thing died on me," she said, waving a hand at the rental compact parked off the side of the road. She looked at her would-be rescuer and swallowed a giggle—surprising herself at the burst of humor and wondering if chivalry was dead, choked to death long ago by the Logans and the Stuarts.

"I'll look at it," he offered, proving that Stuarts could overcome destructive impulses just as well as Logans.

At least when the familiar battleground was more than two thousand miles away.

Michele stood back, still conscious of her own wary tension, and watched Ian Stuart bend down to peer beneath the car's raised hood. She caught herself glancing up and down the deserted road, and felt like laughing aloud to discover she was fearful of even being seen with a Stuart.

Her father, an otherwise reasonable man, would have been tempted to disinherit her after one glance at her companion . . . or thunder about doing so.

But her father was back in Atlanta, not here on the island paradise of Martinique. In fact, there was no one here who could possibly know or care that representatives from both sides of a very old feud had unexpectedly encountered each other on the road to Fort-de-France.

She studied the enemy, trying to be as objective as possible. He was a big man, with powerful shoulders setting off an obviously athletic body of unusual strength. He was the kind of man who looked sexy in jeans and formal clothing alike, drawing feminine stares wherever he went. At the present, he was wearing jeans and a pullover shirt. He had wheat-gold hair worn thick and just shaggy enough to make a woman want to run her fingers through the shining strands.

Most women, Michele reminded herself, surprised that she had to. *But not me.*

She also reminded herself that she had never been attracted to fair men, but then had to admit silently that blond hair went awfully well with a tanned, handsome face and ice-blue eyes. Still, Ian Stuart was the last man in the world she could ever be drawn to.

In a peculiar way, they knew each other well. Ian Stuart and Michele's brother, Jonathan, were the same age, and the families both owned houses and businesses in Atlanta, Georgia. As children, Michele and Jon had competed against Ian in horse shows and rodeos, and the boys had brawled on and off their different schools' football fields.

Michele knew for a fact that Jon had lost at least one

high-school girlfriend to Ian Stuart, and that Ian had lost two desired horses at auction to Jon's determined bidding.

Michele was twenty-six, Ian was thirty-one, and this was the first time in their adult lives that they had met face to face and alone.

She didn't know how to react to the unexpected situation. All her life she had listened to invectives directed at the Stuarts in general and their neighbors in particular; she'd even spat a few curses of her own. She could have listed their treacheries going all the way back to the fifteenth century. Instinct told her she should be raining invectives of her own now, but common sense questioned the need for it.

Ian looked up and saw her watching him, his pale blue eyes as wary as her own probably were. He straightened slowly and looked at her for a moment in silence, then glanced at the compact. "This needs a mechanic, which I'm not," he said in a neutral tone. "I'm going into Fort-de France; I can send a tow truck back. Or," he added after a moment, "I can give you a lift."

Michele found herself wondering if the earth would open up and swallow them both at this heresy, and laughed as she realized her muscles were braced for a thunderclap. It was ridiculous! "Thanks, I'd appreciate a lift," she said. "I can call the rental company from the hotel and have them deal with it."

"Where are you staying?"

"The Arcadia."

"So am I."

Moments later, sitting comfortably beside Ian in his own rental car, she dismissed the fleeting guilt at her traitorous behavior. Because it *wasn't* traitorous, not really. She was a sensible woman and saw no reason why she should prefer to roast in the hot sun rather than accept a brief ride from a man who had never done her an injury.

"Lucky you came along," she ventured casually. "I might

have been stuck out here all day." There had been a few passing cars, but none had stopped.

"I half expected you to throw the offer of a ride back in my face," he murmured.

"At home, I might have," she admitted, turning her head to gaze at the colorful tropical landscape all around them. "But who can fight in paradise?"

Ian sent her a glance, taking the opportunity of her distraction to study her unobtrusively. It had been years since he'd been this close to Michele Logan. On that last memorable occasion, she'd been thrown by her horse during warm-ups for a Grand Prix jumping event, and he had offered her a hand up. Sixteen-year-old Michele had rewarded him for his pains by roundly cursing him, and had regained her feet under her own power.

She had also beaten him in the event.

Ten years had changed her . . . a lot. Then she'd been thin as a rail and all legs; she was slender now, but no one would ever compare her to a rail. The faded jeans and pale blue T-shirt she wore clung to every curve, and those curves were voluptuous enough to inspire erotic fantasies. Her legs were still long, but they, too, were the stuff of men's dreams. Her waist-length black hair, wild as a colt's mane for most of her childhood, was confined neatly in a French braid now, and the severe style emphasized the delicate bone structure of her lovely face. Those bones had seemed awkwardly arranged during her childhood and adolescence, but maturity had smoothed sharp planes and angles into striking beauty.

On the rare occasions in the past when Ian had seen her—at a distance, naturally, and usually across crowded rooms—he had always been conscious of faint surprise. From tall, robust parents of average looks had come this slight, smoke-eyed, raven-haired woman of unusual and distinctive beauty; she was a throwback to the Celtic ancestors she and Ian could both claim, as physically unlike her present-day family as he was unlike his own.

Ian wondered if the differences were only physical; her brother Jon would have chosen a ride with the devil over one with a Stuart.

Feeling her attention shift back to him, he said, "What are you doing in paradise?"

"Vacationing," she answered in the same pleasant tone she'd been using, her low voice rather husky. "November in Atlanta was unbearable. All that cold rain. I had vacation time coming to me, and the company wasn't willing to let me take it next year. So, Martinique."

She had chosen not to enter the family construction business, he knew. He thought it odd, but interesting that she was employed by a large insurance company as an investigator.

"I'd planned to come with a friend," Michele said, "but she got held up by her job and won't be arriving for a few more days. How about you?"

"Business," he answered. "I'm supposed to be meeting a potential client here, but he's been delayed."

"You're an architect, aren't you?"

He nodded, very conscious that she was looking intently at him. His awareness of her surprised him more than a little. "Like your brother," he said, and from the corner of his eye saw her grimace slightly.

"I wonder if, pardon the pun, that was by design."

Smiling faintly, he said, "Jon and I both being architects? I don't know about your father, but mine wasn't happy with my career choice. He felt growing up around the construction business provided all the knowledge I'd need to take over the company one day. I was born to follow plans, he said, not draw them."

She laughed softly, and he was astonished to realize how focused his senses were on her. It was just like the first instant he'd recognized her there by the car, when he had felt the shocked wariness of encountering not an enemy, but something totally unexpected.

"Not by design then," she said dryly. "Dad hit the roof

when Jon announced his career plans. He complained that all those summers working for the firm had been wasted. He's come around in the last few years, though, especially after Jon convinced him that an architect would be an asset to the family business."

"Mine still has reservations," Ian said. "We argue about once a month, regular as clockwork."

"Who wins?" she asked, amused.

"Me. Dad says he takes consolation in the knowledge that strong-minded men breed strong-minded sons."

"And daughters," Michele commented somewhat dryly.

"Your father didn't like your being an investigator?"

If she was surprised by his knowledge, it didn't show on her face. "Are you kidding? Whenever he catches my eye, Dad looks wistfully at some of the old paintings hanging on the walls of our house. All done by our ancestral Southern belles, of course. He didn't mind my showing horses or running barrels in the rodeo, but he winces whenever he has to face the fact that his gently nurtured daughter is a licensed investigator."

"Were you never tempted to get into the family business?"

Michele was silent for a moment, her gaze directed at the windshield but unfocused. Then she looked at Ian. "The business end of it interested me, but some of Dad's goals weren't mine. I couldn't see expending so much energy in a rivalry that was so . . . bitter."

It was the first time either of them had mentioned the feud. Ian wanted to probe her feelings on the matter, especially since her statements indicated she was far less rabid about it than her father and brother. But they reached the hotel just then, and as he pulled the car into the circular entrance drive, he felt a definite reluctance to part company with Michele Logan.

A parking valet came out to take the car, and they walked into the cool lobby together, both silent. Neither spoke until they were in the elevator. Michele pushed the button for her floor, watched him follow suit, and realized absently that his room was three floors above hers. Then Ian broke the silence in a mild tone.

"We're both alone here for the time being. Have dinner with me tonight."

Michele was conscious of shock, but it took her several seconds to realize why.

Because he was a Stuart.

All her life, she had been told repeatedly and with passionate insistence that there was nothing on earth worse than a Stuart—except two of them. Told, moreover, by the father she had always adored. And no matter what logical protests her rational mind could counter with, it was impossible for her to discount what had been drummed into her since childhood.

As the elevator doors opened onto her floor, Ian pressed a button on the control panel to hold them open. He looked at her steadily. "Here at the hotel, of course. The food's great."

She drew a short breath, freed at last from a cold place she was horrified to find inside her. A place that had been sown with dark seeds. She felt shaken and was aware of an almost overpowering relief; the seeds might have been sown, but there was nothing dark and twisted growing there. Only an echo of what might have been.

Or what might yet be.

That flashing insight reminded her that she was far more than a mere continuation of a story that had been written in stone five hundred years ago. She was an individual with her own thoughts and beliefs, and it was entirely up to her whether she *chose* to hate another person—with or without sufficient cause.

And neither this man nor his family had given her any cause to hate.

"Michele?"

Had he ever said her name? She didn't think so. It felt unfamiliar coming from him, a roughly beautiful sound like nothing she'd ever heard before. She looked up at him, uncertain and more than a little wary, but the cool hint of challenge in his eyes made her decide. "Sure." Her voice was unsteady, and she concentrated on firming it up. "I'd be glad of the company."

Ian smiled. "Good. I'll meet you in the lobby, then. Around seven?"

Michele nodded. "I'll be there. And thanks for the rescue, Ian."

"Anytime."

She got off the elevator, almost immediately turning right to head down the hallway to her room. It wasn't until she was inside that a shaken laugh escaped her. She felt strange, as if all her emotions had been tumbled about and left in a heap.

She dropped her purse on the big bed and kicked off her sandals, then went to adjust the temperature of the air conditioning. It was unsettling to discover the room was actually cool according to the thermostat; it seemed hot to her. Deciding firmly that the time spent in the sun after her car broke down had given her a very mild case of heat exhaustion, she called room service for a pitcher of iced tea. She spent the next few minutes on the phone with the car rental company, then changed into shorts and went to let the waiter in with her order.

After he'd gone, she banked the pillows on her bed and curled up with a glass of cold tea. She'd turned the television on to a news channel, but didn't pay much attention even though she stared at the screen.

Ian Stuart. A peripheral part of her life for nearly as long as she could remember, he had suddenly appeared center stage with no warning. And she didn't know how she felt about that.

A scene from ten years before sprang vividly into her mind, surprising her with its clarity. A show ring during warm-ups for a Grand Prix event. She'd been riding a young horse, expecting nothing from him and intending only to school him over moderate jumps so he could become accustomed to shows. He had balked at the third jump and shied violently, throwing her.

Ian had been there, riding an experienced jumper, and he had been the first to offer her a hand up. Mortified at having been dumped like a Sunday rider practically at his feet, she had spat a few biting comments on his ancestry and had picked herself up without his help. The sting to her pride had been painful, and it was lucky her young horse wasn't a timid one who would have been easily ruined by being pushed too hard too soon; when she rode him into the ring later, she was riding fiercely to win.

She had held her mount with iron control, refusing to let him run out at the jumps, driving him over them with sheer determination, riding him harder than ever before. The result had been a spectacular victory, and her horse had become the best jumper she'd ever owned.

All because of embarrassment.

The memory gave her pause. Was it only the ten years between sixteen and twenty-six that made her feel differently about Ian Stuart now? Or *did* she feel differently? She hadn't ridden to beat him that day because of family rivalry; the feud between their fathers hadn't even entered her head. She had done it because the toss had made her feel like a fool, and she'd wanted to show Ian that she was a first-rate rider and could handle any horse.

Childish pride, she decided. That was all. She hadn't even thought about Ian during the years after that occasion. Oh, she'd seen him from time to time at a distance at social or charity events, and both her father and Jon had offered frequent scathing remarks about the doings of Ian and his father. But she hadn't thought about him consciously, hadn't considered his unique and disturbing place in her life. She'd been busy finishing school, going to college, getting a job. She had dated regularly, but hadn't become deeply involved with any of the men she saw.

The phone on the nightstand rang, and Michele nearly jumped out of her skin. Grimacing, she picked up the receiver. "Hello?"

"They've done it to us again," Jon announced without preamble.

She didn't have to ask who "they" were, or why her brother had called to tell her about it; Jon tended to keep in touch with her almost daily if she was away from home, and was always quick to report the latest underhanded dealings by the Stuarts.

"What now?" she asked, suppressing the knowledge that her brother would demand her immediate return if she told him that Ian was in Martinique and in the same hotel.

"They've bribed half the inspectors, that's what." As always, when he spoke of the Stuarts his normally pleasant voice was hard. "Our crews are sitting on their duffs waiting for the final inspections of the electrical and plumbing work, and the inspectors are staring at every piece of wire and pipe in the damned building."

"Jon, you don't really believe they've bribed city officials?" She made the attempt even though she knew it would be fruitless.

"Payoffs and kickbacks. Hell, you know how it works."

"I don't suppose you have any proof?"

"Michele, what's wrong with you? Since when have the Stuarts been stupid enough to leave fingerprints?" Even that backhanded compliment was grudging.

She leaned back against the headboard of the bed and sighed softly. She loved her brother, but, like their father, he had a wide blind spot when it came to the Stuarts. "Sorry," she said in a light tone. "I guess it's just hard to hate in paradise."

Jon grunted a response that could have meant anything, then asked, "Is Jackie with you?"

"No, she was delayed. She'll be here in a few days."

"What're you going to do?"

19

Michele could hardly help but laugh. "Brother dear, I believe I can entertain myself for a few days alone. I've been pretty good at that since I left the crib."

"Well, be careful." He sounded amused by her tart reply, but also a bit restless. "Big girls have more to worry about than little ones, and you're a long way from home."

"I'll be fine, Jon. You just promise me that you and Dad won't try some harebrained stunt to get even with the Stuarts for what you *think* they're doing."

He laughed. "I'll probably talk to you tomorrow, Misha."

His childhood nickname for her reassured her only a little, because he hadn't promised. "Jon—"

"Don't fall for some tall, dark stranger. Bye."

Michele cradled the receiver, troubled. She got up to refill her glass, then settled back on the bed. She didn't feel guilty at not having told Jon about Ian's presence. Her brother had always been overly protective of her when it came to men, and he would have reacted violently to the knowledge.

But she was disturbed, both by what could be happening in Atlanta and by her own actions here. Her rational mind told her that having dinner with a man in the hotel was nothing to be worried about, but the fact that the man was Ian Stuart troubled her a great deal.

She glanced at the clock on the nightstand. Five. In two hours, she was supposed to sit down to a civilized meal with the sworn enemy of her father and brother. The very thought seemed melodramatic, but Michele wasn't tempted to laugh, or even to mock it. She was only too aware that the simple act of having dinner with Ian Stuart was enough to tear violently the fabric of her family.

If they ever found out.

He was standing near the desk in the lobby when Michele came out of the elevator, and she walked toward him steadily with the unnerved feeling of having burned her bridges. She had dressed to give herself courage; the midnight-blue linen dress she wore was full-skirted and high-necked, but left her back and arms bare, and she knew the style suited her.

He must have thought so, too, for she could see the appreciation in his striking pale blue eyes as he looked at her. He, too, was dressed informally in a light-brown jacket and dark slacks, with his white shirt open at the throat.

"I thought you might stand me up," he murmured as she reached him.

"I almost did," she admitted honestly.

"What made you change your mind?"

Michele drew a short breath. "Sheer cussedness, I guess. I like to make up my own mind about things."

"And people?"

"And people." She managed a smile.

Ian smiled slightly as well, but his eyes were very intent. "Of course, the fact that no one's going to know about this didn't influence you at all."

"Of course not. Besides, you could have hired a photographer to take pictures to send to my father." She blinked, conscious of shock at her own words.

Ian took her arm lightly and began leading her across the lobby toward the dining room. "I didn't."

"I'm sorry. I don't know why I said that."

"Because you've been taught to suspect the motives of anyone named Stuart."

"Do you suspect my motives?"

"No."

Michele looked up at him as they walked, a little surprised to find that her head barely topped his shoulder even though she was wearing heels. "Why not?" She was honestly curious, wondering if their upbringings had been so different or if Ian had simply risen above his.

Ian didn't answer until they'd been shown to their

table in the quiet restaurant. When they were supplied with menus and left alone again, he looked across the table at her. "Because I think you're honest, Michele. If you wanted to fight me, you'd do it openly."

"With all my motives flying like flags?"

"Yes. I wish you could believe the same about me."

She hesitated, but couldn't lie. "I want to. The rational part of me does."

"But," he murmured.

Michele nodded. "But. I was thinking about it up in my room. Do you suppose that after five hundred years it's become imbedded in the genes?"

"I'd hate to believe that."

"So would I." She bent her head and began studying the menu, adding lightly, "I'm starved. I skipped lunch so I could explore the island."

The soft lighting in the dining room combined with her black hair and gleaming blue dress to lend her a curiously insubstantial air. And her manner toward him intensified the impression, because she was troubled and wary. Ian couldn't stop looking at her, even as he told himself this was worse than reckless, it was insane.

He wasn't worried about sitting across a dinner table from Michele Logan; that was certainly harmless and even his father—after an initial explosion—would be able to make little of it. What bothered him was his reaction to her. Every fleeting expression in her smoke-gray eyes fascinated him, and her delicate face held his gaze as if she were his lodestar.

When he had taken her arm and walked beside her through the lobby, he had been vividly aware of her warmth, of the faintly spicy scent of her perfume. He had wanted to put his hand on her bare back, to touch the pale gold skin that looked so soft and silky. Then she had glanced up at him with those haunting eyes, and he'd felt a jolt to some part of him. He didn't know what it meant, but he knew instinctively that something had been forever changed by it.

"I think I'll have the chicken." She looked at him, faint color rising in her cheeks. "How about you?"

He realized that she had felt him staring at her, that she was disturbed by the steady gaze. "The same," he said, without the faintest idea of what he was agreeing to.

Michele folded her hands over the menu and fixed her eyes on them. In a conversational tone, she said, "What we were talking about before is something neither of us can forget, you know. Suspicions. Whether they're imbedded in the genes or the mind, they're still there."

"I don't have any reason to hate you, Michele. And you have no reason to hate me."

She nodded. "I know. But not hating is one thing; becoming friends is something else. Even if we could, I mean. Even if we wanted to. Because it isn't just us."

"Why?" He leaned toward her unconsciously, wanting her to look at him so he could see what she was thinking and feeling. He didn't think about what he was saying, he simply felt compelled to make her understand something that was very clear to him. "It's just us here, Michele. No fathers or brothers looking over our shoulders. Nobody around who gives a damn if we're enemies, friends . . . or lovers."

She felt a strange flare of heat at the last word and didn't know if it was the word itself or the husky way he said it that caused her reaction. She didn't dare meet his eyes because she was half afraid of what she might find in his gaze. Tension wound tightly inside her, like a spring coiling, and she couldn't seem to hold her breathing steady.

"Michele?"

Softly, still without looking at him, she said, "When I was a little girl, I didn't know that Stuart was a name. I'd heard my father say it many times, but all I knew from his tone of voice was that a 'Stuart' was something bad."

Very deliberately, he reached across the table and covered her folded hands with one of his own. "I thought Logan was a curse until I was seven. But I'm not seven anymore. And you're not a little girl. We have to start with just us, Michele. Or else blindly follow twenty generations of tradition in our families."

She stared at the big hand covering hers, feeling the warmth and heavy strength of it. Finally, she raised her eyes to his, seeing in them some of the intensity that she had felt earlier. "I don't think I'd be a very good trailblazer," she said unsteadily. "There's so much I'd be risking. So much I could lose. Would lose." Her father's love. Her brother's.

For a brief moment, Ian's hand tightened over hers, then he leaned back and withdrew from her. "All right," he said quietly. "I suppose that not hating is something."

Ian signaled the waiter, going on in the same mild tone. "We can at least have dinner in peace; the families don't have to know we're even on the same island."

Michele gave her order and listened as he gave his. She felt a strong sense of loss and also a bitter feeling of failure. She had never really failed in her life, not at anything that mattered to her—and somehow Ian mattered to her very much. She wasn't sure why, perhaps simply because it *was* her nature to make up her own mind about things. Sometimes, there was no choice to make. If she could have believed that the feud could be stopped because she and Ian made peace between them, she would have risked it, she told herself fiercely. But she knew both her father and brother too well to think that was possible.

"Don't look so troubled," Ian said softly. "Maybe when it's our turn to carry the torch, we can do a better job with it."

"No," she said. "Maybe you don't want to hate, but Jon

does. Dad's poisoned him. He's heard so much more than I have. I don't know, maybe he got the brunt of it because he was older. Or maybe because he'd always keep the Logan name. Dad isn't rational where you're concerned. And no matter how good your intentions are, Ian, if somebody hates you long enough and tries to hurt you often enough, you'll hate too."

Ian frowned slightly. "It sounds as if your father is more bitter than mine. Do you know why?"

She shook her head. "No. But Jon knows something. When we were younger he said that your father had done something terrible to ours a long time ago. He wouldn't tell me what it was."

"It must have had something to do with a woman."

She was surprised. "Why do you say that?"

"Otherwise, Jon would have told you."

Michele thought about that, and somewhere deep inside she felt a little chill. Had some unknown woman intensified an already bitter rivalry? What had happened? Women were vulnerable when men feuded; they could be hurt in so many ways. They could be used as weapon or as victim. As soon as that thought occurred to her, she felt another chill and then anger hard on the heels of it. These damned *suspicions*! Ian had merely suggested that the two of them make peace, not crawl into bed together.

Into bed . . . together . . .

Her breathing seemed to stop for an instant, and a wave of dizziness swept over her. Images flashed in her mind, images that were raw and powerful—and undeniably exciting. For the first time in her life, she felt the shocked awareness of her own sexuality, and the images were so strong they were almost overpowering. The thought of being in bed with Ian Stuart triggered a surge of emotions as confused as they were complex.

"What are you thinking?" he asked suddenly.

Michele felt heat rise in her face. She wasn't about to confess the erotic images still playing through her mind, not the least because they shocked her to her bones. "I was . . . wishing that it was simple. Wishing it was just us." She heard the husky words emerge, and felt another jolt because she knew it was true.

"Would you trust me then?"

"I don't know. But I'd only be risking myself if I took the chance."

The waiter arrived and began to serve their food just then, and Ian didn't respond to what she'd said. Michele was grateful for the reprieve, using it to try desperately to cope with these stunning, unexpected, and wholly unfamiliar feelings. She ate food she didn't taste, bewildered by what had happened to her—and why it had happened.

Why *had* it happened? Why had her chance encounter with Ian and the reckless act of having dinner with him sparked these wild surges of desire? How could she possibly feel such things for this man of all men? She had never felt desire until now, not at all; her strongest interest in a man had been mild and detached compared to this.

But now . . .

Tension coiled in her as her emotions churned chaotically. Make peace with Ian? No, that would never be possible now. Even if it were just the two of them, she knew that what she wanted of him had little to do with peace. It was as if some barrier inside her had collapsed into rubble at the slightest touch, and what she saw beyond that shattered wall terrified her.

"Michele?"

She looked up at him, seeing a lean, handsome face that was all too dreadfully familiar now, because something, some deeply buried instinct, told her it had always been behind that wall. Waiting.

It was too much to accept, to think about; she had to get away from it. She set her fork aside automatically and pushed her chair back. "Excuse me," she murmured, rising jerkily to her feet.

"Michele, what's wrong?" He was on his feet as well, staring at her with concern and something else in his eyes.

She couldn't answer him, because all the answers were so terribly dangerous. Without another word, she hurried away from their table. She heard him call after her, but the sound of her name only made her move faster. She was almost running by the time she reached the lobby, and barely noticed a few startled faces as she raced across and fled out into the night.

The hotel boasted a strip of private beach, deserted this late, and it was there Michele ran. She kicked off her heels almost as soon as she left the hotel, leaving them where they fell. She passed the blue-lit pool and blindly followed the path through the lush garden until she felt sand under her feet and saw the moonlit darkness of the ocean.

When she reached the water she turned, racing on the wet sand. For years she'd made a habit of morning runs to keep in shape. She ran fast now, the wind tearing her hair free of its braid and whipping her skirt out behind her. She ran because she had to escape.

Two

"Michele!"

He caught up with her at the northwest end of the beach as she approached a ridge of volcanic rock jutting up from the sand that marked the boundary of the hotel's private beach.

When he grabbed her hand and forced her to stop, pulling her around to face him, she felt an instant of anger and half raised her free hand as if she would have pounded on his broad chest.

She stared up at him, her clenched hand motionless now. She could see him clearly in the moonlight, and she wished it was dark because she knew he could see her just as clearly.

"What are you running from?" he demanded.

Almost idly, she noted that he was in excellent shape since he wasn't even breathing hard from the race. Her own heart was pounding, and she couldn't seem to draw enough air into her lungs. "Let me go," she demanded.

He released her hand but only so that he could grasp

both her shoulders firmly. "I want to know why you're running, Michele."

She felt smothered by him, trapped, despite the open space all around them. He was so big, and he'd caught her all too easily and quickly in spite of her head start. She couldn't escape him. But she had to stop this before something irrevocable happened, before it was too late. Panic rose in her, and this time her fists did pound against his chest.

"Let me go! I won't let you do this to me, I won't!"

Ian barely felt the blows. He had run after her instinctively, thinking only of stopping her because there had been something wild and frightened in her eyes. It was in her voice now, in the supple strength of her slender body as she fought desperately to get away from him. Her words made no sense to him, but the thin sound of her voice did. She was afraid of him somehow, almost terrified, and the realization was like a knife in his chest.

He should have released her simply to reassure her that he wouldn't hurt her, but he didn't want to see her run away from him again. Without stopping to think, he pulled her into his arms, trapping her hands between them and holding her firmly.

"Michele, stop it. Be still. I'm not going to hurt you." He forced himself to speak quietly. She went on struggling for a moment, but then her breath caught as her movements made her lower body press against his, and she seemed to freeze.

A small wave lapped over their feet gently. His hands were on her bare back now, and her skin was every bit as soft and smooth as it looked. Her hair had come loose, tumbling down her back and over his hands like warm, heavy silk. She was utterly still, hardly seeming to breathe, but her delicate body was pressed against his and he could feel every curve, feel the warmth of her.

"No," she said in a very soft but distinct voice. Her head tilted back slowly as she looked up at him, and moonlight shimmered darkly in her eyes. Against his chest, her fingers uncurled and spread, but she didn't try to push him away.

His own fingers were moving, lightly probing the straightness of her spine as one hand slid up toward her nape and the other found the small of her back. She felt so fragile against him, so feminine, and his entire body was reacting wildly, all his senses so sharpened it was almost painful. His heart hammered against his ribs, and a jolt of pure, raw desire settled in his loins with a throbbing ache.

"No?" he murmured, knowing that they weren't talking about fear now. Her eyes were wide, fixed on his face, her lips slightly parted and trembling.

"Don't do this. Don't let this happen." Her voice was little more than a whisper.

His arms tightened around her. "You knew it would happen, didn't you? That's why you ran."

The admission she had made horrified her, leaving her painfully vulnerable. "That's insane! How could I possibly even think— Let me go, Ian!"

"You knew," he repeated, his voice deepening and going rough. "You felt it too."

Michele shook her head, but it was a helpless not a negative gesture. If she had felt trapped before, it was nothing compared to this feeling. The very suddenness and stark force of the attraction had granted her no time to find a defense, and her effort to escape had been useless. And somewhere inside her, deeper than thought, was an acknowledgment of inevitability.

Being in his arms felt so *right*. Her body had known that the instant it had touched his, and she couldn't deny the sharp excitement surging through her.

Michele felt him move, a subtle shifting that brought her more intimately against him. She gasped at the sensation and managed a single, strangled protest. "Don't."

Ian bent his head slowly, blocking out the moonlight

until all she could see was the glimmer of his eyes. Her own eyes closed slowly as his lips touched hers. For an instant she sensed that she was poised on the brink, as if she still had a choice. But then the choice was made, and there was no going back. She felt herself melt even closer against him, her arms lifting to his neck, her mouth opening wildly beneath the increasing pressure of his.

As easily and simply as that, something detonated between them, and the shock waves of it made them both shudder. Ian gathered her even closer, lifting her up against him so that she was nearly off her feet. Her breasts were pressed to his chest, burning him even through their clothing, and her yielding loins fit his as if their bodies had been made for each other.

Michele was drowning in waves of heat, totally helpless against what was happening. She had been kissed before, but the experience had always left her unmoved. Apparently she wasn't a sensual woman; she had never felt the slightest urge to go beyond kisses. In Ian's arms, though, no simple urge drove her; the need to be closer, to have more of him, was a compulsion stronger than anything she'd ever felt before.

His mouth was hard and hungry, the deep exploration of his tongue making her entire body quiver. She responded without thought or hesitation, the urgency inside her sweeping all else before it in a tide of need. Every stark, new sensation was somehow familiar, as if she had always known how it would be with him. The hard strength of his chest compressing her aching breasts, his taut belly against hers, the throbbing fullness of his loins nestled intimately in her yielding softness—it was all familiar and what her body craved.

His hand tangled in her hair, and his legs widened as his other hand slid below the small of her back to hold her harder against him. Pleasure exploded inside her, hot and dizzying, and a moan of desire caught raggedly in her throat. Then he lifted his head abruptly, and the sound she made in response was a murmur of disappointment.

"Michele." His voice was dark, liquid, the heavy need in it a sound that was almost pain. His entire body was taut, and his chest rose and fell as if he had run some desperate race.

"Don't stop," she whispered, tightening her arms around his neck as she tried to pull his head back down.

For an instant, Ian almost gave in. The slender body in his arms was warm and willing, moving against him even now with a need that matched his own. And her breathy plea snatched at his control, the implicit surrender filling his mind until he could hardly think of anything but drawing her down to the wet sand and fusing their bodies together in a heated mating. Only the sure knowledge that she would hate him afterward gave him the will to stop.

Both his hands found her hips, and he gently forced her lower body away from his. She squirmed in his hold, trying to move closer again, and Ian bit back a groan. Harshly, he demanded, "Who am I, Michele?"

She blinked up at him, bewildered. "Ian," she murmured.

His hands tightened, and he made himself go on, hating this. "Ian what? Finish it."

Her lips, pouty from his kisses, quivered suddenly, and she went still in his grasp. "Stuart," she whispered.

"Is that who you want in your bed?"

The stark question went through Michele like a cold knife, bringing sanity at last. Her arms were still around his neck. She removed them slowly, then stepped jerkily back until his hands dropped from her. Her legs were shaking, her body was shaking, and it hurt to breathe. Part of her wanted to cry out to him in anguish, demanding to know why he had spoiled it, why he'd had to remind her of what they were; another part of her was trying to cope with the enormity of what she'd almost done.

"Thanks . . . for reminding me," she forced herself to say as steadily as possible.

"I want you, Michele," he said in a low voice that was almost guttural. "Right now, right here in the sand, I want you."

She was dimly aware of understanding that he had stopped because the choice she would have made in the heat of desire was a blind one.

Michele knew it too. Her mind had been programmed implacably against him for twenty years, yet her body craved his desperately at the first touch. There was no way to reconcile that conflict. No way at all.

She drew herself up stiffly. "You shouldn't have come out here after me," she murmured. "You should have let me run."

He shook his head slowly. "You can't run from this."

"I have to."

"Michele—"

"I have to. I won't destroy my family, Ian. That price is too high; I can't pay it. There can't be anything between us. Not even peace."

"There *is* something between us. It isn't hate, and God knows it isn't peace, but it's real, Michele. You can't ignore it. And you can't run away from it."

"Watch me."

He swore under his breath, then said roughly, "And if I pulled you down in the sand right now? If I kissed you and touched you until you were holding on to me just the way you were a few minutes ago? Could you run then?"

With naked, simple honesty, she answered, "No."

He took half a step toward her, almost as if her admission had yanked at him, then stopped and held himself as stiffly as she. "But you'd hate me, wouldn't you?"

"I think I would." She felt tears sting her eyes and blinked them back. Her hands spread unconsciously in a gesture of helplessness, then fell. "Stay away from me, Ian. For both our sakes. For the sake of that torch we might be able to carry better than our fathers have."

"And that's it?"

Michele felt impossibly tired; her entire body ached dully with the throbbing echoes of what he had awakened in her. She nodded and turned away from him.

"Wait." He hesitated, then muttered an oath and shook his head as if he were at a loss. He reached into the pocket of his jacket and withdrew her small clutch bag. Holding it out to her, he said, "You left this at the table."

She accepted the purse automatically, and then kept walking back up the beach toward the hotel.

He didn't follow her.

She found her shoes near the door she'd run out earlier and picked them up without bothering to put them on. Her hose were ruined, she knew, and both sand and the residue of salt water clung to her feet and ankles. She didn't care. Ignoring the few curious stares she garnered in the lobby, she crossed to the elevators and rode up to her floor.

She felt immeasurably changed and numbly bewildered by the suddenness of it. Yesterday she had been confident and secure, her emotions on an even keel, virtually detached from the feud that had altered and ruined so many lives. But in only a few short hours, her detachment had been stripped away from her.

Her father had often been annoyed by her disinclination to join him in cursing the Stuarts, but he had shrugged away her lack of venom because he loved his daughter. Perhaps he even knew on some level that hate was a particularly ugly thing on the face of a woman. Still, it had never occurred to him that at the core of herself she didn't hate as strongly as he did. He simply expected it of her.

And she knew without a shadow of a doubt that if he

discovered how close she had come to lying in the arms of his enemy, it would devastate him.

Michele had once thought the feud rather melodramatic, but her wry amusement had died on the day she'd first seen—really seen and understood—the depth of her father's hatred. She'd been no more than thirteen, becoming a woman with all the reluctance of a tomboy, and she'd fought her father fiercely when he had decided it was time for her to wear a dress and play hostess for some of his business dinners. Since her mother had died years before, he had been without a hostess, and Michele unwillingly had accepted that role.

Michele leaned against her door for a moment, then fumbled in her purse for the key and let herself into the room. She closed and locked the door and tossed her purse onto the bed, dropping her shoes on the floor.

It was during that first business dinner that a chance remark by one of the guests showed her the feud in a new and far more serious light. She had left the room for some reason, returning moments later and reaching the doorway just in time to hear the remark. She couldn't remember, now, the exact words, but one of the men had said something about how beautiful Charles Logan's daughter was going to be one day. She had paused, unexpectedly pleased. But then another man laughed and said something that had driven the pleasure away.

"Stuart has a son just about the right age. That young man has a roving eye; take care it doesn't light on Michele. What perfect revenge that would be!"

She had felt shock, and then she had seen her father's face and had understood what hate really was. His stony expression and the cold glitter in his eyes had been so dreadful that she had felt sickened by it. And even though his response had been uttered lightly, she had heard the implacable truth in it.

"The day a Stuart lays a hand on my little girl is the last day he'll ever see. They won't even have to waste

money burying him because I'll blow the bastard into a million pieces."

She wasn't a little girl now, but she was still her father's daughter, and though the appalling truth that she had virtually invited seduction might possibly stop her father from getting his gun and going after Ian, nothing would prevent him from disowning her.

Ian was far less concerned by what a relationship between them would do to his father, she knew. Perhaps his father *was* less bitter. Or perhaps it was just that Ian knew what was, to Michele, a painful truth; a man could sleep with the daughter of an enemy and call it revenge. Or he could simply confess to a sexual attraction and shrug off who she was.

But a woman . . . no, it was different for a woman. To sleep with the son of her father's enemy would be the worst possible blow she could deal her father, and one from which he would never recover.

She was on the point of collapsing onto the bed when there was a sudden hammering on the connecting door to the next room, and a lively voice called out.

"Michele! Hey, open up—I made it!"

Jackie. Her best friend since childhood, and the one outsider who understood all too well the hatred between the Logans and the Stuarts. Orphaned and living with an aunt and uncle, Jackie had spent more time in Michele's home than in her own while they were growing up, and as a result, she had heard the Stuarts cursed for most of her life.

Michele glanced down at herself and then stepped to the mirror over the dresser. The reflection she saw made her wince. Her hair was tumbled wildly around a pale face, her lips swollen and reddened, her eyes holding a strained, darkened expression. But there was little she could do about her appearance; another bang on the door indicated that Jackie was waiting impatiently.

Opening her side of the connecting door, Michele deliberately spoke first. "When did you get here? I've been walking out on the beach."

Jackie looked her up and down, and then laughed. "No kidding. You look like hell, friend."

"Thanks a lot." Michele kept her voice light.

"As a matter of fact, the desk clerk told me he thought you'd gone out. I just got here a few minutes ago. Keep me company while I unpack, will you?"

"Let me take a shower first. I've got sand practically up to my knees."

"Okay," Jackie said amiably, turning back toward the open suitcases on the bed. "I guess you've eaten?"

"Uh huh." Had she? She couldn't remember. But she wasn't hungry.

"Well, I'm going to call down for something. The airplane food was the usual cooked cardboard. Want anything?"

"Not to eat. Some iced tea."

"I'll order it."

Michele retreated from the doorway. She got a sleep shirt from one of the dresser drawers and went into the bathroom. The bright light in that tiny room, unlike the shaded lamps of the bedroom, showed her even more clearly how she looked. Jackie had noticed nothing unusual, but Michele knew her friend too well to expect her to go on missing the obvious.

She stripped out of her clothing and took a long shower. When she got out, she dried off and wrapped her thick hair in a towel, then pulled the sleep shirt over her head. She was trying not to think, to keep her mind blank, but another glance in the mirror brought back vivid memories of Ian's kisses.

She *looked* kissed, thoroughly kissed, her lips faintly swollen and their color deeper than usual. She held a washcloth under cold water and then pressed the cloth to her mouth in an effort to erase the signs.

What she was doing sent a pang of bitterness through

37

her. How dreadful to feel the need to wipe all evidence of a man's kisses from her face! Especially when she had invited those kisses and had responded wildly to them. Michele fiercely pushed the thoughts away.

Room service had come and gone, leaving a tray on the small table by Jackie's balcony doors. Michele took one of the chairs—the one out of direct light of the lamps—and poured herself a glass of tea, while Jackie took the other and began eating the club sandwich she'd ordered.

"So how's Martinique?" she asked cheerfully. "I know you've already explored since you got here yesterday."

"It's just what the travel brochures promised. The scenery is gorgeous; wait until you see Mont Pelee. Fort-de-France has colorful houses and palms lining the streets. It's really beautiful."

"Well, since you were walking on the beach tonight, I gather the hotel has a respectable one?"

"So-so. It's only about half a mile long, and we're so close to the harbor that there's a lot of water traffic. But the hotel grounds have a lovely garden, and there's a big pool." She conjured a smile. "The service is good, the food's fine, the bed's comfortable, and rum is cheap."

Jackie giggled. "Neither of us likes rum."

"Well, it's cheap if we want any. In the meantime, we can lie on the beach or by the pool, and when we get tired of being lazy we can explore the island. I only got a quick look at it today, so there's plenty left to see."

"It sounds wonderful," Jackie said with a luxurious sigh. She was a redhead with bright green eyes and a vivid face. Full of life she seemed like a sister to Michele, who had loved her since they were children.

"A nice vacation. Speaking of which, I thought you were going to be held up a few days?"

"The crisis was resolved sooner than expected." Jackie grimaced. She was employed by one of the television stations in Atlanta, where crises occurred on a regular basis, especially in the news division where she worked as an assistant to a producer. "As soon as the dust settled, I told Doug I was gone and vanished before anything else could happen."

"He didn't waylay you at the airport?"

She grinned. "Obviously not. I'm here. I could have sworn I heard somebody calling my name in a pitiful voice as I escaped into the wild blue yonder."

"Leaving a note for Cole?"

Jackie's piquant face softened instantly at the name of the man in her life, but then her mouth twisted. "A message on his answering machine, dammit. He was out of town."

Michele hadn't yet met the paragon who had stolen her friend's heart, but she'd heard his name often enough during the past weeks.

"Where is he this time?"

"Lord knows. You'd think even a sales representative would know where he was going, but Cole never seems to. He barely had time to send me a dozen roses with a note. He said this trip would last only a couple of days, so I'll try calling him tomorrow. I wish he had been able to get time off. It would have been great."

"Thanks," Michele murmured.

Jackie cocked an eyebrow at her. "Not that you aren't loads of fun, but boasting a gorgeous man on my arm is definitely preferable to my childhood friend and roommate from college. Besides, I want to find out if he snores."

"You haven't yet?"

"Who's had time to sleep?" Jackie managed to look both deliriously happy and slightly self-conscious.

Michele felt a pang of envy, and instantly smothered it. Smiling, she said, "Then why on earth are you taking your vacation with your old college roommate? I know we planned this trip ages before you met Cole, but I would have understood—"

"I know, but he said he was going to be working long hours for a while, and I needed a break. Besides, Cole and I are too new to be making demands on each other. I don't want him to get the idea that I can't move a step without him."

"Just don't feel obligated to stay here with me."

"I won't." Jackie finished her sandwich and rose to resume her unpacking, adding in a calm tone, "By the way, what's happened to you?"

Michele sipped her tea to give herself a moment. "What do you mean?"

"Look in a mirror. I'd guess you've had some kind of shock. Obviously you're not going to volunteer any information, so I suppose I'm going to have to pull it out of you."

Michele had always confided in her friend. But this was something she couldn't confide to Jackie, who would never understand; she might not have Logan blood, but she had adopted the family and seemed to be convinced that a Stuart was the lowest animal on earth.

Michele felt very alone, trying to think of something that wouldn't be a lie—and wouldn't be the truth.

Jackie continued to unpack, but darted inquisitive glances at her oldest and closest friend. At last she said softly, "It must have been pretty bad."

Drawing a deep breath, Michele said, "I need to wrestle with it by myself for a while. Do you mind?"

"Your father and Jon are all right?"

"They're fine."

Jackie nodded. "Okay. Just don't forget I'm here when you're ready to talk about it."

"I won't."

After a long, thoughtful look at her friend, Jackie announced she was going to take a shower, and Michele returned to her own room and moved around restlessly.

The ringing of the phone startled her. She frowned as she went to the bed and sat down, glancing at the clock on the nightstand before answering. Jon wouldn't call twice in one day unless . . .

"Hello?"

"Michele, don't hang up."

She felt her heart begin to pound, and swallowed hard. It was the first time she'd heard his voice over the phone, but she had no trouble recognizing it. "I wasn't going to," she said steadily. "I wanted to tell you something. Jackie got here a little while ago, so I'm not alone now."

"And you want me to stay away," Ian said flatly.

"I told you that on the beach."

He was silent for a moment, then sighed. "That isn't going to be easy, Michele. I meant what I said out there. I want you." His voice was low, and the last three words were a husky demand rather than a mere statement.

Michele leaned her head back against the headboard of the bed and closed her eyes. Why didn't she just hang up? She *should* hang up. Her pulse was racing and she felt hot. "Even if I knew I could trust you, it wouldn't be possible. Don't you understand?" Her breath caught as the haunting suspicions flooded up from the depths of her mind. "Or maybe you understand all too well."

"What's that supposed to mean?"

"Do you want to destroy my family, Ian, is that it? Is that what you're trying to do?"

"This isn't about our families, dammit, it's about us." His voice had sharpened and gone hard. "You and me, and what's between us. It doesn't have a thing to do with anyone else."

"You're wrong."

"No, I'm not. Twenty generations, Michele. Twenty generations of people living with hate and suspicion. Maybe you want to be part of that, but I don't. Your brother can hate me to hell and back, and I won't fight him. Do you understand that? I won't fight him. If I have to, I'll leave Atlanta, but the feud stops with me."

"Why?" She cleared her throat and steadied her voice. "Why are you so determined?"

His voice went low and rough again. "I held a Logan in

my arms tonight. Maybe it never would have happened if we hadn't met in paradise, but it did happen. I can't be certain about much, Michele, but I know I could never hate you. So how could I hate your brother?"

Tears stung her eyes, but still she was remembering Jon's evasiveness earlier. What if something was happening, or about to happen, in Atlanta that would force Ian to hate? What if her father and Jon gave him no choice?

"Michele, please trust me. I won't do anything to hurt you, but I can't stay away."

She drew a shaky breath, fighting an intense longing. But clashing with that were suspicions and fears and the overwhelming knowledge that it just wasn't *possible*. "If you don't want to hurt me, you have to stay away. Goodbye, Ian." She cradled the receiver gently.

For three days, Ian stayed away. He made certain Jackie never caught a glimpse of him. He recognized the redhead as the one who, on the rare occasions he had been anywhere near her, had looked at him as if he were a leper. He had always felt more hostility coming from her than from Michele.

Still, he managed to watch Michele from time to time as she and her friend came and went. She was clearly bent on spending as little time at the hotel as possible, probably to keep away from him. But on the third day Jackie dragged her out to the pool, and Ian overheard the redhead laughingly say that she'd had enough sightseeing for a while and wanted to be lazy.

A slow anger built inside Ian when he saw Michele glance uneasily around. The hellish feud between their families had done this to her—and to him. A grown man and woman, attracted to each other yet fighting to ignore their feelings because they were supposed to be enemies.

Attracted? Lord, the word was useless to describe what he felt when he looked at her.

It had hit him only the night she'd hung up the telephone on him that he had wanted Michele Logan for a very long time. He had vivid memories of her at varying ages . . . and of his admiration for her talents and determination, as well as her beauty. He had known it somewhere deep inside him for years, but it wasn't something he had allowed himself to dwell on because the very idea had been unthinkable.

Until now. They were thousands of miles from home and the battleground both recognized; perhaps that had made it easier to consider the unthinkable. And after he'd held her in his arms, had been burned by the fire between them, the unthinkable had become the necessary.

Watching her during those three days, Ian went over and over it in his mind. He listed all the arguments against them, tried to see and understand that her risks would be greater than his, asked himself why he couldn't just forget this insanity.

But when he saw her just after dawn on the fourth day, he knew that he couldn't forget her, he couldn't let her run away, and he couldn't stay away.

The sun was barely up, hanging low and brilliantly orange over the island when he came out of the garden and caught sight of her on the strip of sand. The beach was deserted except for them. She was walking slowly along the waterline toward the place they'd stood when they'd kissed. And just as it had been before, he followed her without thought.

She reached the low ridge of volcanic rock, and this time climbed up a couple of feet and sat staring out at the sea. Her shining raven hair was hanging down her back in a simple braid, the end tied with a bit of lace. She was barefoot and wearing a white dress that made her look even more delicate and feminine than usual. The dress had a full skirt and thin straps tied on each of her shoulders.

She was unaware of his approach, and Ian reached her before she saw him. He felt his stomach tighten as he stepped up to her. He was standing literally between her legs; she had her feet braced apart on the rock, her skirt bunched up carelessly and draped between her thighs. They were nearly at eye level since he was still on the sand.

Michele's eyes widened, but she didn't say a word.

He didn't dare move closer; even without touching, their proximity and provocative positions charged the air between them. But he couldn't help lifting his hands and resting them lightly on her thighs, just above the knees and below the bunched folds of her white skirt.

"Where's your friend?" he murmured.

"She's sleeping in. She isn't a morning person."

"Have you been out here every morning? If so, I wish I'd known."

Michele cleared her throat softly. "I usually run in the mornings. I didn't feel like it today." She was trying not to shiver in pleasure as his thumbs rhythmically brushed the sensitive flesh of her inner thighs.

"I tried to stay away," Ian said roughly. "But I can't, Michele."

She started to push his hands off her but somehow couldn't complete the motion; the moment she touched him, it was as if her own strength drained away. She was throbbing for his touch.

He wanted to move fully into the cradle of her legs, to kiss her moist lips, to feel her in his arms again. The driving urge to lose himself in her until there was nothing on earth but the two of them and the fiery heat of mating was so powerful it filled his mind and sent a shudder through his body.

Her eyes closed suddenly and her slim hands gripped his wrists almost frantically. "I don't even trust you," she said in a voice that was nearly a moan. "Don't do this to me!"

Ian drew a deep breath and grimly hung on to his control. How could they sort through the tangle of thoughts and emotions when their physical response to each other was this explosive? It was almost impossible to think at all. He'd never wanted a woman so badly in his life, and it was clear that her need was just as great.

"Look at me, Michele," he ordered tautly.

She caught her breath, her lids lifting slowly to reveal shadowed, haunted eyes the color of a mountain fog.

"Let me teach you to trust me. Give me a chance. Give us a chance."

"Even if—" She broke off as he shook his head briefly.

"One step at a time," he urged, his voice still rough and strained. "We have to be sure. If you can't trust me, we'll never know how it could be between us. It'll end right here." He wondered if he had a hope in hell of keeping that promise when he could barely hold his own desire in check. "Please, Michele," he added softly.

She felt something inside her give way, deeper than the first wall that had crumbled the other night. And quite suddenly her mind was clear and quiet, the pain of indecision gone. As if she'd been straining against some irresistible pull and had finally let go and accepted the inevitable.

She gazed into those striking pale blue eyes, and her hands slowly relaxed their grip on his wrists. "All right," she said unsteadily. "Now what?"

Ian turned his hands to catch hers and stepped back, gently drawing her down to stand with him on the sand. "Now we try to get to know each other," he said.

Michele looked up at him, her fingers unconsciously clasping his. "I'll have to tell Jackie."

"How will she react?"

"Not well. She practically grew up in my house, so she's heard the Stuart name cursed most of her life. I'm not even sure she'll keep the confidence."

"She could call your father or brother?"

Michele shrugged. "I'll try to talk her out of that. I don't want them to know, Ian. I don't want to hurt either one of them if—if it isn't necessary."

He nodded, accepting that. "Why don't you both have breakfast with me? On that little terrace by the garden."

Not sure Jackie would even consent to sit at the same table with a Stuart, Michele managed an uncertain smile. "I'll ask her."

Ian held her hand as they began walking back toward the hotel. Striving for lightness, he said, "Tell her she can be watchdog, and protect you from the dragon."

Three

Jackie Flynn leaned over the balcony railing and breathed in the morning air happily. She wasn't, by nature, a morning person, but this island life agreed with her, and she was finding it no hardship to rise earlier than usual. She was beginning to understand why Michele loved mornings. She was already up and about, probably running on the beach since that was her habit. Even on vacation, Michele wasn't the type to laze away her days.

Jackie leaned farther outward, peering to the left to try and catch a glimpse of the garden path to the beach, which was obscured by a wing of the building. She spotted Michele.

With a man.

A big blond man, Jackie noted with interest, and he was holding Michele's hand in a way that was possessive rather than casual. She watched them emerge from the garden and walk past the pool, every step bringing them closer. Her smile faded, a niggling uneasiness growing inside her. From her position she could see Michele's face well, but only the man's profile as he talked earnestly with her.

There was something about him. . . .

The conversation several floors below was finally finished, and the man half turned to watch Michele walk on alone. Jackie could see his face now, all too clearly. She jerked back away from the railing, feeling sick.

"Oh, my God," she muttered.

Jackie was standing in the doorway to her room.

She looked pale, Michele thought, and her eyes held a queer, stunned expression. "Jackie? Are you all right?"

"I saw you." Jackie swallowed hard. "I saw you with him."

Michele slowly crossed the room to the table by the balcony doors and sat down in one of the chairs. Her friend's extreme reaction didn't surprise her, but it saddened her and made her think bitter thoughts. Twenty years of poison had made Jackie hate someone she didn't even know, someone who had never lifted a hand against her, and that was a terrible testament to the power of brainwashing.

"Tell me I didn't see that," Jackie begged, coming into the room and sinking down on the corner of Michele's bed. "Tell me it wasn't Ian Stuart."

"It was."

"Michele . . ."

"I had car trouble the day after I got here," Michele said steadily. "He stopped to help me." Then a touch of painful mockery entered her voice. "The sky didn't fall, Jackie. I wasn't hit by a bolt of lightning. He didn't turn into a Medusa or a gorgon or Jack the Ripper. He just offered me a ride back here, and that night we had dinner together."

Jackie's piquant face was marred by her anguished

expression. "Michele, he's a *Stuart*! He and his father have done their best to ruin your family for years—"

"No. Not Ian."

"Oh, and I suppose he told you that?"

Had he? He'd said that he wouldn't fight her brother, Michele remembered. That the feud would stop with him. But he hadn't actually denied any involvement in the past. She felt pricking little doubts creeping nearer and fiercely pushed them away.

"Jackie, try to understand. I didn't go looking for this; I didn't know he'd be here on the island. And the last thing I want to do is hurt Dad and Jon."

"But?" Jackie demanded sharply.

"Something happened that first night—"

"Did he hurt you?"

Michele shook her head, sighing. "No, nothing like that. It happened inside *me*, not because of anything he did. For the first time in my life, I—I felt like a woman. Everything came crashing in on me, so many emotions and needs and fears. It scared the hell out of me; I ran like a thief."

Jackie was staring at her, frowning. "Actually ran? Where?"

"Out on the beach."

"He followed you."

"Yes. And he knew why I was running, what I was running from. When he kissed me—"

"I knew it!" Jackie exclaimed, her normally pleasant voice hard. "The bastard's trying to seduce you!"

Michele felt a flash of sheer rage. "Is he?" she snapped back. "Then he missed a great opportunity that night, because I couldn't say no. I asked him *not* to stop!"

Jackie drew back a little and they stared at each other, shock on one face and anger on the other. It wasn't the first time they'd quarreled, but it was by far the most serious disagreement they had ever had.

"He's up to something," Jackie finally said, her tone unsteady. "He wants to hurt you, Michele."

"Why are you so sure of that? Because he's a Stuart? Does his name make him incapable of anything but hurt when it comes to me? Can it possibly be that he's just a man who happens to find me attractive?"

"Is that how it is with you?" Jackie asked. "Do you find him—attractive—because he's just a man? Do you feel that way in spite of his name, Michele? Or because of it?"

"What do you mean?"

"Forbidden fruit. It's supposed to taste sweeter."

Michele felt a jolt, the ugly little doubts creeping nearer again. Then she shook her head and muttered, "Nothing's that simple."

"Isn't it? Ian Stuart is the last man in the *world* you should get involved with. Your father would disown you in every sense of the word. So would Jon."

"I know that."

Jackie looked shocked again, and uneasy, as if she'd expected the reminder to cure her friend instantly of this madness. She stared for a moment, then said in a thin voice, "It would be a feather in his cap, wouldn't it? He could destroy your family and enjoy himself doing it. Make you care about him until nothing else mattered, until you broke your father's heart and—"

"That's enough." Michele tried to stifle her anger as she got to her feet and squared her shoulders. "You're my closest friend, Jackie, and I know you want what's best for me. So let me find out for myself what that is. Maybe it won't be Ian, but I have to make up my own mind. I can't hate him just because I've been told I should."

Jackie was silent for a moment, then asked stiffly, "I guess you expect me to keep my mouth shut about this?"

"To Dad and Jon? I hope you will." Michele slipped her feet into sandals and made sure her room key was still in the pocket of her skirt. "Maybe there won't be anything to tell them, in the end. But if there is, it should come from me."

Staring at the floor, Jackie said, "All right. I'll keep quiet. Maybe you'll come to your senses before they're hurt by this."

Michele went toward the door, then stopped and looked at her friend. "Ian's invited us for breakfast. Do you want to come?"

"I'm not hungry."

Not that she'd expected any other response. "We'll be at a table on the terrace if you change your mind." She was almost at the door when Jackie's quiet voice stopped her.

"Michele?"

"Yes?"

"He can hurt you so badly. He can hurt you more than any other man ever could."

There was nothing Michele could say to that, because it was the truth. Silently, she left the room and went to join Ian for breakfast.

"She didn't take it well," Ian noted a few minutes later.

Settled in her chair across from him in the morning sunshine, Michele conjured a faint smile. "Afraid not. I can't even blame her for it, really. She's a wonderful person, but she isn't any more rational about you Stuarts than anyone in my family is."

"I suppose she pointed out all the reasons you shouldn't see me again?"

"Oh, yes." Michele sighed. "All the reasons I'd thought about and a few I hadn't." Then she shook her head. "No, that isn't true. Jackie didn't say anything I hadn't already said to myself. It just sounded . . . worse coming from her."

Ian's jaw tightened. "I can imagine."

Michele glanced past him, then stiffened a bit. "You won't have to. I guess she changed her mind." Ian rose as Jackie moved toward them, and Michele added in a low voice, "I hope you have a thick skin."

He certainly needed one, Ian decided during the next hour or so. Jackie didn't hide her hostility one bit, and if she could get a barbed comment in, she didn't hesitate. Ian didn't mind for himself; it would take more than the venom of this antagonistic redhead to make him lose his own temper. But he minded for Michele, because he knew it bothered her. She didn't say very much, hardly touched her breakfast, and more than once angry color rose in her cheeks.

The last thing Ian wanted to do was come between Michele and her friend; the cost of this relationship would likely be high enough without that loss. But he couldn't bear to sit by and allow this hate-filled young woman to tear their relationship to pieces before it had a chance.

He signed the check, rose, then gently pulled Michele to her feet. "If you'll excuse us?" he said pleasantly to Jackie.

She ignored him, looking at her friend instead. "Jon'll probably call, Michele. Want me to tell him you're slumming?"

Evenly, Michele replied, "I never knew you were cruel, Jackie. Until now. Tell him any damn thing you want to." She turned away abruptly.

Ian saw Jackie's face whiten, but whether with anger or shame he couldn't say. He caught up with Michele in a few steps, and took her arm, guiding her back through the lobby and toward the front doors.

"Well, that little experiment was a mistake," he said wryly. "She hates my guts. And it isn't even her fight."

"I'm sorry." Michele's voice was low, her head bent.

He didn't reply until they were in his car and heading away from the hotel. "You don't have any reason to be sorry. Jackie's as much a victim of five hundred years as we are."

Michele half turned on the seat to look at him. "But we aren't reacting the same way. Why not? What makes you and me different?"

"Something stronger than both of us. Something that might even be stronger than the feud. That's what we have to find out, Michele."

The barbs Jackie had planted stung Michele's flesh . . . and she wondered what influence they would ultimately have on her relationship with Ian. All through breakfast, she'd been conscious of the aches of longing inside her, and every jab from Jackie had only made her more aware of it.

Gazing steadily at Ian now, she felt the longing intensify, numbing her doubts and suspicions. She wanted his arms wrapped around her, his mouth on hers, his hard body pressed against her. She wanted to forget that they were anything but a man and woman. Her wishes were so simple, so clear, so untroubled by any doubt, fear, distrust.

"Where are we going?" she asked huskily.

Ian sent her a quick glance, and a muscle leaped in his jaw as his hands tightened on the wheel. "Dammit, don't look at me like that," he warned in a taut voice.

It should have embarrassed her that her feelings showed so plainly on her face, but somehow it didn't. She was aware only of a tingling satisfaction that his response was so instant. "I can't help it," she murmured.

He drew a short breath, and the telltale muscle in his jaw flexed again as he stared straight ahead. "You'd better try, because it makes me want to drag you into the backseat like some horny teenager."

Michele tried to look away from him, but she couldn't. His blunt statement sent a stab of excitement through her, and the recklessness of that feeling pushed everything else out of her mind. She had to press her lips tightly together to keep herself from saying there was nothing she'd like more than to take him up on that rough promise.

Ian glanced at her again and instantly forced his attention back on the road. His brief look was enough to jerk the threads of his control painfully tight. He was going to plow the car into one of the palms lining the street if he wasn't careful, or else just pull over in front of someone's house and make love to her no matter who happened to stroll by. She was sitting there beside him in her prim white dress—except that it wasn't prim at all. The bodice had some kind of fishnet panels down both her sides and another in front, between her breasts; golden flesh was clearly visible through the net all the way to her slender waist. She wasn't wearing a bra; all he had to untie were the flimsy straps at her shoulders and smooth the sheer linen away to feel her naked breasts in his hands. The way she was looking at him only made matters worse. Her haunting gray eyes were soft and unfocused with the desire of a woman.

Ian cleared his throat harshly and held on to control with an iron grip. "Michele, for both our sakes, we have to be careful. If we become lovers before you trust me. . . ."

Lovers. The word made a wave of heat wash over her. To be Ian's lover, to lie in his arms, to feel his weight on her, to know his possession. That was what this was all about, she knew, what both of them had hesitated to name aloud. It was the connection that drew them together even though they were supposed to be on different sides of a war. Not rational or even sane, the compelling attraction existed, and they had to decide how best to deal with it.

She turned her head away finally, staring through the windshield, trying to gather her scattered wits. "Where are we going?" she repeated in a steadier voice.

"The waterfront park," he answered, his voice still a little strained. "I thought we could walk for a while. Talk."

"With lots of people around," she murmured.

"Lord knows I'd rather be alone with you. But I think we should avoid that."

Michele didn't protest his decision, even though a part

of her wanted to. Ian was right. It was too dangerous for them to be alone, too tempting. She remained silent until they were walking slowly along one of the paths of the waterfront park. The place was busy with tourists, mostly American, but nonetheless it was a quiet and peaceful place.

"You said I was too honest to have hidden motives," she said, glancing up at him. "How can you be so sure? I mean, you must have listened to as many attacks on Logans as I have on Stuarts over the years."

"Attacks on Logans, yes," he admitted. "But always against your father and Jon. I don't believe my father ever said a thing against you personally. The closest he ever came was when he raked me over the coals when you beat me in that Grand Prix event ten years ago. He said I ought to be ashamed of myself for letting a Logan brat on a green horse beat me."

Michele couldn't help but smile. "I was determined to win that day—but not because you were a Stuart."

Rather dryly, Ian said, "I know. You were mad as hell at being dumped at my feet."

Startled, she said, "Yes, but how did you know that?"

He walked a few more steps in silence, then drew her hand through the crook of his arm. "It was in your eyes. Not hate, but something fierce and obstinate. As I remember, you had a few nasty things to say about my ancestors when I offered you a hand up, but that seemed more or less automatic."

She looked at her hand resting easily on his arm, with his hand lightly covering it. The offering of help she had furiously scorned at sixteen she had accepted the other day. And she wondered suddenly if anything would have been different had she accepted the first time.

"What are you thinking?" he asked.

Michele sighed. "What else?"

"It's never far away, is it?"

"It's not something either of us can forget. Ian, you

said you wouldn't fight Jon. But have you? In the past, I mean?"

In a deliberate tone, Ian said, "I've never done anything against your father, your brother, or their company, Michele. I've never used an unfair business tactic to gain an advantage over them. Never."

"I had to ask," she said quietly.

"I know." His hand tightened over hers. "Let's make a bargain. No more talk about the feud, or our families for a while. We're two people getting to know each other, and that's all that matters now."

"I'll try."

"Good enough," he murmured.

They spent the entire day exploring the island. With all the caution of people walking a tightrope, they steered a careful course between the attraction they felt and the conflict of who they were. In getting to know each other, they discovered a surprising amount of common ground as well as a peculiar bond of understanding.

The latter, Michele thought, was certainly due to who they were. It was ironic, but the very threat to their relationship was also what enabled them to so quickly gain a sense of each other. They shared a unique background, a history linking their families for five centuries, and no matter how negative that link was, it was a powerful bond.

Michele was thinking of that as she unlocked her door early that evening. She and Ian had eaten lunch and dinner away from the hotel, not returning until late, and she wondered what Jackie had made of their extended absence.

The worst, no doubt.

The connecting door was closed on Jackie's side. Michele sighed but made no attempt to open it. Given her friend's present state of mind, there was really very little for them to say to each other. She went to take a shower, emerging a few minutes later dressed for bed in a sleep shirt.

"Michele?" Jackie was standing in the doorway to her room, wearing short pajamas and looking as if she'd been crying. "Can—can we talk? I have some iced tea in here."

Silently, Michele followed her friend into the other room, sitting down by the balcony doors and accepting a cold glass. "Did Jon call?" she asked.

"No."

Conscious of a niggling worry, Michele frowned at her glass. It wasn't that Jon called every single day, it was just that during his last few calls he'd been unusually silent about what was going on with the company—and the feud. He knew his sister had never approved of the "eye-for-an-eye" concept, and though he was quick to report some foul deed of the Stuarts, he was generally silent about what he and their father did in retaliation.

That was what had Michele concerned. Though Ian had denied any involvement in the troubles between their families, he had said nothing about his father, and Jon had seemed certain that a Stuart had been behind the company's recent problems—though that was, of course, his inevitable reaction to difficulties with the business. She couldn't help but feel uneasy about what might be happening in Atlanta, especially since she and Ian were trying to build a bridge instead of a fence.

"I'm sorry," Jackie blurted as she sank down on the bed and drew her legs up. "Sorry for the things I said, the way I acted this morning."

Michele was more than a little surprised. "That's quite a change of heart," she noted slowly. "Quite a *sudden* change of heart."

Jackie looked miserable. "I've been thinking about it all day. I'm your friend, Michele. I should be on your side no matter what. Lord knows nobody else is going to be."

"How can you be on my side? You hate Ian."

"No matter how I feel about him, I know how hard this has to be on you. I could see it on your face the other night. And you were right, it's your decision. It has to be. You aren't a child or an idiot. If your feelings for Ian are strong enough to overcome the fact that he's a Stuart, then—well, who am I to tell you it's wrong?"

Michele nodded, still surprised. "I'm glad you've changed your mind."

With a rather uncertain smile, Jackie said, "Hey, I know how tough a relationship can be with the normal number of strikes against it. You don't need me pointing out the obvious."

Michele sipped her tea, then said quietly, "You aren't giving us a snowball's chance in hell, are you?"

As quietly, Jackie said, "I can't lie to you, friend. I can't see a happy ending for this. We're thousands of miles from home, and maybe you *can* see Ian differently here. But back in Atlanta, he's a Stuart and you're a Logan. In Atlanta you're on opposite sides of a war. And sooner or later, you have to go back to your real world."

"Maybe we can go back together."

Jackie stared for a long moment, then leaned back on the bed. Her lips twitched in a sudden, rueful smile. "Well, if that happens, I want to watch. It ought to have about the same affect as Sherman's march through Atlanta."

In spite of her change of heart, Jackie turned down Ian's occasional invitations during the next two days. She was civil enough when she found herself in his presence but took care to avoid him. Michele accepted Jackie's limited support, then firmly closed her mind to all the problems that lay ahead. She also accepted Ian's determination to avoid the temptations of being alone together, and though it cost her sleepless nights she was even grateful for his resolution.

They explored the island, swam in the hotel's pool and walked on the beach—always with other people around. They shared meals and thoughts and opinions. They became familiar with each other's expressions and moods. Their closeness grew, and with it an ever-heightening sense of where their relationship was leading.

She had realized only in her early twenties that she had been ridiculously overprotected when it came to men. Since she'd been something of a tomboy, it hadn't disturbed her that her father had refused to allow her to date until her eighteenth birthday, or that her brother had found fault with every boy who'd expressed an interest in her. And she hadn't protested the situation simply because she hadn't been much interested in the dating scene.

It was only when she finished college and found a job that the reins had begun to feel uncomfortably tight. She continued to live at home because it *was* home, but also to avoid a fight with both her father and brother, and there definitely would have been a fight. Living under her father's roof, Michele felt she owed him the respect of conducting herself according to his rules. Perhaps because he felt the lack of a strong feminine influence in his daughter's life, Charles Logan had always been fierce about conventions—and his were decidedly old-fashioned.

The Logans were a family shaped by a Southern heritage, and Charles wasn't the only father of such a family who still harbored visions of Southern belles and gentility despite the realities of life in the final quarter of the twentieth century. He would have been shocked and deeply mortified if Michele had chosen to live openly with a man outside marriage. Though his remarks on the subject had been clumsily delivered during her early adolescence, his meaning had been clear; nice girls were virgins on their wedding nights.

And Michele Logan was a nice girl.

"You're very quiet."

They had spread beach towels on the sand just outside the garden and in the shade, away from the path of traffic to and from the beach. There were other hotel guests on the beach, but they were some distance away—visible, but not intrusive.

Michele set her book aside and rolled over on her stomach. She gazed toward the ocean rather than at Ian, wishing she had the nerve to dive into his arms and abandon everything else. Her doubts were growing rather than disappearing. She felt a sense of desperation, a painful feeling that she was going to lose something infinitely precious if she didn't act—and act quickly.

"*Can* I trust you?" she asked abruptly.

"I hope so."

She sat up and looked at him. They were both wearing bathing suits; he also wore a light windbreaker, and she a sheer linen caftan over her two-piece suit.

"After these past few days . . . I just don't know." Michele shook her head. "Does trust come in a blinding flash? Am I supposed to wake up one morning and say, 'Yes, today I trust Ian'? Or look at you and somehow know?"

"Michele—"

She felt tense, quivering on the edge of a chasm. "It isn't going to happen, Ian. You can't overcome twenty years in a week. That's all we have left, a week. Not even that, because your client is due here day after tomorrow. And I go home in seven days."

"What are you saying?" His voice was rough.

Michele struggled to find the words. "What happens when I go home? I'm no more certain of anything than I was the first day. I don't know if I can trust you. I don't even know if I trust myself to—to understand what I'm feeling. All I do know is that what we don't find here, we won't find in Atlanta."

Ian took a deep breath, aware that they had reached some kind of turning point. Michele had weighed it all in her mind, he knew, had wrestled with it in silence even while she'd walked beside him and smiled up at him and talked of other things. She had struggled against a life-time of conditioning and had ended up, now, certain of nothing except her uncertainties.

And it was an impasse; Ian didn't know what he could do to win her trust. Frustration gnawed at him, because he wanted Michele to the point of madness and she was held tauntingly out of his reach by a feud neither of them wanted any part of. He had pushed himself to the scream-ing limits of restraint when he wanted nothing more than to lock both of them in his room and shut out the world, and the waiting had him tied in knots.

"Ian?" She was gazing at him and felt a flutter as if something caged deep inside her sought escape. She'd never seen him look like this, his lean, handsome face hardening, his eyes containing a glitter that was hot and bright with a promise she instinctively understood. For an instant she was conscious of panic, but then heat rushed in to overwhelm her doubts and fears.

He leaned toward her, and Michele found herself being eased back onto the blanket. She felt the hardness of his thigh against hers, the strength of his arm under her. His head lowered, his mouth brushing hers very lightly, and his breath was warm.

"Maybe we haven't been looking in the right place," he muttered huskily.

Michele gazed up into those vivid eyes, smothered by the pounding of her heart, his first touch sending a dam-burst of sensations flooding through her body. The strength of her own feelings made her hands shake as

KAY HOOPER

they lifted to touch his face. "Maybe we haven't," she agreed in a whisper.

Ian made a low, rough sound and buried his face between her breasts. She caught her breath raggedly, her fingers sliding into his thick hair as she felt his mouth moving on her. The sheer material of her caftan was a frail barrier, but even that was too much, and he impatiently sought the warm flesh beneath. The first three big buttons down the front of the garment yielded, and he nuzzled between the lapels to find the curves of her breasts.

Michele's skimpy bathing suit was the final barrier, but Ian didn't try to remove it. His mouth slid along the cup of her bra, his tongue darting out to taste her silky skin. He felt her shudder, felt her fingers tighten in his hair as a smothered moan escaped her, and that soft, uncontrolled sound sent a jolt of frantic need through him.

"Yes?" he demanded thickly against her.

She moaned again, and her voice was so low it was hardly more than a whisper. "Yes . . . yes."

Ian raised his head and then kissed her deeply, molding his mouth to hers hungrily. Her response was instant, heated, her body arching against him wildly. He forced himself to remember where they were, and it was like fighting his way through a red-hot haze of necessity. Muttering a curse, he caught her hands and got to his feet, pulling her up.

"Ian?" Her voice was unsteady, bewildered.

"We're going up to my room," he said roughly. "Now."

Michele didn't protest. She couldn't have. She held on to Ian's hand like a lifeline, and even if her father and brother had been standing in the lobby, she wouldn't have paused or even hesitated. The need inside her was so strong it was like something with a life of its own, filling her until it could hardly be contained, until the pressure of it was almost unbearable. Was unbearable.

She didn't care what this cost her, what she lost because of it. Whatever price was demanded of her, she'd pay it.

In the elevator alone, Ian pulled her into his arms. "I'm not going to give you a chance to change your mind," he murmured, staring down at her with blazing eyes.

The fierce jolt of pleasure when Michele was pressed against his hard body made her catch her breath and close her eyes. Her arms slid up around his neck, and she stood on tiptoe to fit herself more intimately against him. "I don't want to change my mind," she whispered, all her emotions and senses fixed on him and nothing else.

Ian made a rough sound and lifted her into his arms as the elevator doors opened. He carried her down the hallway to his room. The maid was just coming out, and he brushed past the startled woman with an impatient, "Excuse us," kicking the door shut behind them.

A nervous giggle died in Michele's throat when he slowly lowered her to her feet beside the bed that lay in a bright spill of sunlight streaming in the balcony door. Her arms lowered, her hands trailing down between the edges of his partially unzipped windbreaker. His chest was hard, covered with a mat of thick golden hair that felt wonderfully sensual against her palms. She curled her fingers to probe the solid muscles beneath springy hair, aching to touch him all over. In the back of her mind was the vague thought that she really should tell him she'd never been with a man before, but the confession couldn't escape the tightness of her throat. She wanted this, wanted him, and nothing else seemed to matter.

"Michele . . ." He surrounded her upturned face in his hands and kissed her, his mouth warm and hard. She shivered as she felt the gliding touch of his tongue teasing the sensitive inner flesh of her lips, and opened her mouth wider under his in a mute plea for a deeper caress. Instantly he responded, his mouth slanting across hers, his tongue stroking hungrily against hers.

Dizziness washed over Michele in a hot wave. Desperate to touch him, she pulled at the windbreaker, hardly feeling the steel teeth of the zipper bite into her hands as she jerked the edges apart. He shrugged out of the garment and tossed it aside, then got rid of her caftan by simply yanking it open and pushing it off her shoulders. Without even thinking about it, she stepped out of her sandals and the pool of material at her feet, kicking them aside.

Gasping as his lips left hers, Michele felt his hands on her, moving over her back, unfastening the flimsy string ties of her top. She bit back a moan as the scrap of material was pulled off her and her naked breasts rubbed against his chest as she pressed herself closer. The fire inside her was burning out of control, her need so urgent she had to clench her teeth to hold back the wild, primitive cries she could feel rising in her throat.

Ian held her hard against him, his mouth buried in the warm flesh of her throat. She was so alive in his arms, so utterly responsive that he had no more control than a teenager. He wanted her with a burning fever that was worse than hunger, worse than thirst. Groaning harshly, he slid one arm down until it clamped below the swell of her bottom, then lifted her against him so that his face was buried between her breasts.

He could feel her heart thudding wildly, feel the sting of her nails digging into his shoulders. He explored the valley between her breasts, then slid his mouth hotly over a swelling curve and captured a tight nipple. She jerked, a whimpering sound escaping her as he sucked strongly.

Michele couldn't believe what she was feeling. His mouth on her breast sent pleasure stabbing along her nerve endings, and deep in her belly an awful ache throbbed emptily. She clung to him, almost sobbing at the shocks battering her senses.

"Ian . . ." Her voice was thin, shaking, her eyes closed tightly. "Ian, please . . ."

He shifted his hold on her slightly and bent forward to lay her on the bed, then straightened briefly to get rid of his shoes and trunks. Before Michele was fully aware of his absence, he was with her again. She felt his hands on her hips and lifted them instinctively as he stripped off what remained of her bathing suit and threw it aside.

Michele opened her eyes slowly, realizing that she was naked only when she saw him looking at her. A fleeting shyness vanished before it could take hold, because he was looking at her with such hunger it almost stopped her heart. She wouldn't have believed she could lie naked on a bed in a pool of bright sunlight while a man looked at her and feel only sharp excitement, but that was what she was feeling.

"Michele," he said tautly, kissing her deeply again and again before trailing his lips over her warm throat. His hand stroked her breasts, her quivering belly, then slid lower to gently probe the dark curls between her tense thighs.

She felt him touch her, and an explosion of pleasure forced a gasp from her throat. Tension wound inside her with an almost brutal intensity, her control over her own body totally gone as it responded blindly, instinctively to the ancient mating drives. Her legs opened for him and she clutched at his shoulders desperately as his caress sent shockwaves of heat through her.

"Make it stop," she whispered raggedly, almost afraid of these wild feelings. "Ian, please . . ."

He drew a shuddering breath, fighting for a last remnant of control as he spread her legs wider and slipped between them. She was ready for him, her body warm and moist, her smoky eyes darkened and sleepy with desire. His own need was so wildly urgent he thought he'd explode, but he held himself back fiercely for the searing pleasure of entering her slowly.

It had never occurred to him that she might be a virgin; he'd seen men looking at her since she was sixteen, and given her sensual response to him, it seemed obvious that desire was something she had felt before. Even when her body resisted his slow entrance, the truth didn't hit him at once.

"Easy," he murmured, feeling a new tension tremble in her and seeing her eyes widen. He kissed her, holding her mouth with his hungrily as he bore down. He felt as well as heard the soft sound she made, and that was when he understood.

Four

"Michele? Baby?" Ian felt as if he'd been kicked in the stomach, shock and something else jolting through him. And with that came a rush of hunger so intense he groaned aloud with it, shuddering as he fought to leash the wild urges of his body. He knew he'd never forgive himself if he hurt or frightened her, and it was only that knowledge that enabled him to find a measure of control.

She was looking up at him, her haunting eyes glimmering with wetness, her lips trembling. Slowly, the hands clutching his shoulders slid up around his neck, and her body moved tentatively beneath him. Her breath caught. "Ian?" she whispered.

He lowered his head and kissed her deeply, again and again until a kittenlike sound escaped her and she moved restlessly under him. Slowly, with exquisite care, he pressed deeper into her trembling body.

Michele was astonished at the sensations, dimly shocked at the stark intimacy. She could feel her flesh stretching to admit him, and then an increasing pressure that

67

brought a flash of pain. Even with that, she didn't want him to stop, because deeper than the pain was an intolerable burning that cried out for his complete possession. She hadn't realized a man could be so strong, the male force of him compelling her to accept whatever was necessary because satisfying the need he had aroused in her was all that mattered.

He was murmuring to her huskily, tender words of comfort, kissing away the tears that trickled down over her temples. Then she felt a sharper pain as something gave way inside her, and even as she cried out, she was conscious of nothing but a fierce satisfaction. His heavy weight settled slowly, fully on her, and the last whisper of pain ebbed as she felt him throbbing inside her. It was an utterly alien sensation, and yet she had never felt anything more right.

"Michele?" He was braced on his forearms, his eyes darkened to sapphire as they searched her face, and his breathing was harsh and strained.

The hovering tension began spreading through her again, and her arms tightened around his neck. All the unfamiliar feelings tugged at her senses, and she made an unconscious sound of pleasure. "Don't stop," she whispered.

A hoarse groan rattled in Ian's chest as he briefly considered the sheer impossibility of that. It would kill him to stop now, to withdraw from the hot velvety clasp of her body. Electric tremors shook his muscles, and the ache in his loins was a pounding torment. The strain of holding himself rigidly back for so long was like floodwaters battering a dam, and he knew he was a whisper away from going absolutely berserk.

He clamped his teeth together and began moving slowly inside her, aware on some dim level of his mind that he had never felt anything like this. The pleasure was unbelievable; his desire had reached a peak of sweet torment. His need for the woman whose slender body cradled his had gone beyond the point of madness; he felt consumed by it—and by her.

The soft sounds she made roused an almost primitive savagery in him, a fierce possessiveness as unfamiliar as it was powerful. She was *his*, he felt it with every fiber of his being. He wanted to bury himself in her, to fuse their bodies until nothing this side of death could ever separate them.

Michele felt that wild need take hold of her again, gripping her mind and senses so tightly that she could only give in to instinct. Her body knew how to match his rhythm, how to give itself totally to him and the fiery desire between them. The feelings rose in her like a tide, a force of nature she had no hope of fighting or controlling. She said his name over and over, barely aware that she was crying again, that she was straining to reach some unimaginable place. And then she was there with a suddenness that stole what was left of her breath, violent waves of shattering pleasure thundering over her as a soundless wail tore free inside her.

Ian held her strongly as she writhed under him, the internal shudders of her ecstasy caressing him with a stark pleasure that was agony. The final fragile thread of his control snapped, and he drove into her wildly, blind and deaf to everything except the woman in his arms and the exploding force of his release.

Michele felt herself floating for what seemed like a long time, her body limp and sated. She was gradually aware of her surroundings, of his heavy weight, of dim aftershocks somewhere deep inside her. He was still with her, and she loved the stark intimacy of that sensation. She loved the feeling of his hard body covering hers, the smooth strength of his hips against the insides of her thighs, the mat of hair on his chest sensual against her breasts. She loved the way the muscles of his back and shoulders felt under her probing touch.

She loved him.

It should have come as a shock, that realization, but instead it crept gently into her mind and settled there as if a place had been made for it long ago. She understood, now, why her need for him had been so great, why she had taken fire at his simplest touch and offered herself to him without hesitation. She loved him. He was the last man in the world she should have loved, and the odds against them were so great it was terrifying, but none of that mattered right now.

She loved him. And she let herself luxuriate in that strange and wonderful new feeling without counting the cost of it.

Ian pushed himself up on his elbows, his eyes still darkened as they gazed down at her. "I'm sorry I hurt you, baby," he murmured huskily.

Michele had a vague memory of pain, but it didn't seem important; like all pain, once gone it became only a word. She lifted her head to kiss him, then smiled.

He felt his heart lurch, the curve of her lips and the misty depths of her eyes getting to him in some mysterious way he couldn't even name. "You should have told me," he said, hearing the rasp of his voice.

"Why?" she asked softly. "Would you have stopped?"

He half closed his eyes. "I couldn't have stopped if the roof had caved in on us," he told her. "Lord, Michele, you had me so crazy I hardly knew what I was doing."

"You did just fine," she assured him solemnly.

He couldn't help but smile, his worry about having hurt her fading in the knowledge of her obvious pleasure and contentment. He kissed her gently, then began to ease away.

Her legs tightened. "Don't go. I like you there."

"I like me here too. But I'm too heavy for you."

She shook her head slightly, her arms remaining securely around his neck. "No, you aren't." Her eyes were closing, and her voice was fading a bit. "Stay with me."

Ian knew she was drifting off to sleep, the culmination

of days of tension and their fierce lovemaking having the inevitable effect on her. He was exhausted himself, but had no intention of giving way to sleep while she bore his weight. Despite her assurances, he knew he was too heavy to lie for long on her petite body.

So he kept his upper body braced on his arms and waited for sleep to envelop her completely. During those moments, he gazed down at her, very conscious of the fact that his desire had been merely blunted. Even now, as physically weary as he was, he could feel faint stirrings, tremors in his flesh, that told him another wave of need was not far off.

She seemed almost fragile as she cradled him in sleep, her slender, small-boned frame an exquisite but delicate vessel for the fiery passions that had blazed inside her with such unexpected and mesmerizing force. In her innocence, she'd been obviously surprised at the sensations of joining, yet totally involved in what was happening between them. Her capacity to give and receive pleasure was heart-stopping in its uninhibited simplicity.

Ian brushed a strand of silky black hair away from her temple, feeling his pulse quicken and the stirrings in his loins intensify. She was so beautiful, so wildly exciting.

The enormity of what they'd done swept over him, even though he tried to push the realization out of his mind. Carefully, he eased away from her, and when she murmured in sleepy protest gathered her into his arms. She immediately cuddled closer to his side, her peaceful sigh warm against his skin.

His own longing for sleep had vanished, chased away by the renewal of desire or by his disquieting thoughts. From the beginning, he had refused to look further than the present, intent on exploring what lay between them, defining it, forcing her to accept the reality of it. He had called it passion, but he knew it was more.

He also knew, only too well, that what could flourish in paradise would be brutally attacked in the real world.

And the men who would attack it, his father and Michele's especially, were experts in the destructive art of warfare. They'd give no quarter, either of them, no mercy even to their children.

Ian's arms tightened around Michele as, finally and completely, he faced the truth of what they were up against. It wasn't words now; it wasn't some far off "what if," an abstract battle that would be fought only if their rational minds weighed the risks and counted the struggle worthwhile. The time for deciding had long passed—if it had existed at all.

Maybe they'd never had a choice.

Michele was only vaguely aware of discomfort at first. She felt hot and sticky, and the brightness seeping behind her closed eyelids was annoying. Her internal clock told her it was the middle of the afternoon, and she wondered dimly why she was trying to sleep at such a ridiculous time of day. She shifted restlessly and abruptly felt trapped by something hard.

Her first impulse was to escape, but even as she lifted her head, she remembered where she was. And whom she was with. She opened her eyes, blinking at the brightness; the sunlight was really pouring in now, and no breeze found its way through the open balcony door to disturb the hot stillness.

Ian was looking at her gravely, both his arms holding her securely. "Hi."

I am lying naked, she thought, wondering if she was supposed to feel shocked by that. *I am lying naked on a fully made bed in the sunlight with a naked man.*

She felt her lips twitch and smothered an absurd impulse to giggle. "Hi. Is it my imagination, or is it awfully hot in here?"

"It's awfully hot. The air conditioner isn't on." His arms tightened briefly around her, and then he slid from the bed, totally unconcerned by his nudity, and picked her up.

"I can walk," she noted idly, wondering if she could.

He kissed her, then turned toward the bathroom, ignoring her mild objection. He carried her into the small room, opened the shower stall and set her on her feet inside, then joined her and closed the door behind them.

Michele was feeling a bit unnerved by the sheer size of him in the small cubicle, and she was completely unprepared for the sudden blast of cool water over her heated skin. "Damn!" she gasped, pushing soaked hair out of her face and wondering when her braid had come undone.

Ian chuckled and kissed her briefly. "We need to cool off," he said blandly.

"You could have warned me before you turned on the water," she said, but it was only a murmur. Too overwhelmed by desire before, she hadn't really looked at his body; she couldn't help but look now, and what she saw fascinated her. She'd known he was big, but naked and enclosed with her in the shower stall his size and raw strength were compelling. He had the hard muscles of a construction worker rather than an architect, rippling under taut bronze skin. The thick mat of blond hair on his broad chest arrowed downward over his flat stomach, and as her gaze followed that path her mouth went dry.

"I think you had your eyes closed before," he said, the words light, his voice deep.

She felt heat from a new source rise in her cheeks, but there was also a sharp stab of excitement at the knowledge that he was becoming aroused by her scrutiny. "I must have," she admitted, meeting his darkened eyes a little shyly.

He smiled, then pulled her toward him a step, gently turned her so that her back was to him, and reached for a small bottle of shampoo to begin washing her hair.

Michele purred with pleasure. His long fingers felt wonderful moving over her scalp; at first the touch was soothing, but slowly tension spread through her. She could feel her heart thudding hard, her breathing grow shallow. Obeying his touch, she turned again as he rinsed the lather from her hair.

His face was still, eyes very intent on her. He reached up to angle the stream of water slightly away from them, then picked up a bar of soap from the corner ledge of the stall and very slowly began washing her body.

Michele was still surprised that she felt no self-consciousness or embarrassment. It had to be due to Ian— the way he looked at her body, the way he touched her, made her feel beautiful and desired, made her feel proud that he found such pleasure in her. His hands stroked over her breasts gently, tracing their shape, brushing lightly over the tight nipples in a touch that brought fire to her sensitive skin. Then, with agonizing slowness, he slid a soapy hand down over her belly and between her thighs.

She gasped and reached for his shoulders to steady herself as her legs went weak and shaky, all her consciousness focused totally on what he was doing. The faint soreness she'd hardly been aware of became a different kind of ache, one she could barely endure. Hunger filled her; throbbing heat radiated outward from the core of her. His fingers probed gently, sending hot shivers of desire singing through her veins until she whimpered with the force of it.

Ian made a rough sound and then slowly withdrew his hand, sliding it over her hip and around to shape the curve of her buttock. "Easy," he muttered, his face taut, and seemed to be telling himself that as well as her.

"Why?"

His eyes flared at the urgent protest of her voice, and he swallowed hard. "I don't want to hurt you again. You'll be sore, baby, you need time."

The only pain Michele was aware of was the burning ache she knew he could satisfy. Consumed by the sudden need to touch him, she took the soap and began sliding it over his hairy chest until she worked up a lather, then dropped the bar back onto the ledge. She explored slowly, touching him the way she wanted to, delighting in the feel of him. Her fingers brushed the hard nubs of his nipples, and when he shuddered she felt her own excitement spiral wildly.

"Michele . . ."

The taut warning had no power to stop her, and even the unexpected sensuality of her own nature was little more than a dim and unimportant shock. His stomach was flat and hard, his hips smooth, his thighs powerful. She could see the effect her touch was having on him, and it was both reassuring and unbelievably thrilling to know that he could no more resist her than she could resist him.

With curiosity as well as need driving her, she felt compelled to learn every part of his body. She had taken him inside her, and yet she hadn't touched him, not like this, and the urge to go on touching him was overpowering. Barely aware of his harsh breathing, she moved her slippery hands back up his thighs and very gently closed her fingers around him. She felt him jerk slightly and heard the rough groan that rumbled in his chest, and his response only spurred her on. His flesh was hard in her hand, pulsing with living need, and everything inside her seemed to dissolve into a hot liquid pool of desire as she touched him.

"Lord," Ian muttered hoarsely, pulling her into his arms. The force of his sudden movement put them under the shower spray, and the water streamed over them as he covered her wet mouth hungrily with his. He wanted her so desperately that he didn't have the will to get them out of the stall; even the few steps necessary were totally beyond him. Touching her had strained his control to the limits; her delicate hands on him were more than he could stand.

Her arms went up around his neck and she pressed her wet body to him, whimpers of intolerable desire tangling in her throat. She was on the raw edge of tension, so ready for him that waiting even a moment was impossible. She felt the cool tile of the wall at her back, and her legs parted as his hands slid down to her bottom.

She felt herself being lifted, felt a blunt pressure against her aching flesh, and then the burning sweetness of his invasion. Her legs locked around him strongly as she drew him even deeper into her softness, and the tension inside her snapped with a violence that made her moan into his mouth. His deep thrusts held her at the searing peak of pleasure, her body shuddering under the assault on her senses.

Ian was hardly aware of the sounds escaping his tight throat or of anything except the shattering sensations. She was writhing against him, her silky flesh so tight and hot around him, the waves of her pleasure caressing him with a sweet agony that pushed him wildly over the brink into a heart-stopping release.

Michele felt so utterly drained that she could only bury her face against his throat as her legs finally slid down his. She could feel his heart thudding against her, and when their bodies slowly disengaged she sighed with a mixture of satisfaction and regret.

"Lord, Michele," Ian said huskily, tangling his fingers in her wet hair and pulling her head back gently so he could kiss her. His lips brushed hers warmly.

She smiled at him, then said idly, "We're in the shower."

"And we could have broken our necks."

"Maybe we'd better get out, then."

The reasonable comment struck him as amusing. After the acrobatics of moments ago, he doubted they were in danger by just standing in the stall. But he obediently turned off the water and opened the door.

A few moments later, wrapped in one towel and drying her hair with another, Michele sat on the edge of the bed and gazed down at their clothing scattered on the floor. "I don't have anything to wear," she said, "except for a bathing suit and a caftan without any buttons. Did you do that?"

"Don't you remember?" he asked, pulling on a pair of jeans.

"Well, no. Not that it matters. I can always hold the edges together."

Ian came to the bed and sat down beside her. "You don't need anything to wear. Stay with me."

She finger-combed her damp hair and looked at him uncertainly. "Tonight?"

"And tomorrow night. And as many nights as we can manage." He kept his voice light.

"All right," she said simply.

"We have to talk."

A shadow crossed her eyes. "I don't want to talk."

He eased her back onto the bed and kissed her gently. "Baby, we have to. You know we do."

The faintly swollen curve of her lips was unsteady for a moment, then firmed. In her eyes was anxiety and reluctance and regret. "Yes. I know."

"We'll work it out," he promised, pushing from his mind the certain knowledge that there was no painless solution. "Why don't you call room service and order some food. I'll be right back."

"Where are you going?"

His smile went a little crooked. "Unless you're on the pill, I'm going to that shop in the lobby."

Michele felt herself blushing, which was, she told herself, fiercely ridiculous. "Oh."

He kissed her again. "I've been so wild for you I didn't even think about protection. I'm sorry."

"I didn't think about it either," she reminded him.

His eyes burned down at her, and one hand rested possessively over her stomach. "We may be too late," he said gruffly.

The possibility of carrying his child sent a surge of warmth spreading through her. But she wasn't certain of his feelings even now; as wild as their desire for each other was, he'd said nothing about their future. And the odds were so strong against them. . . .

Conjuring a smile, she said ruefully, "Stuart seed taking root in a Logan? Our ancestors would be spinning in their graves."

"And our fathers foaming at the mouth," Ian added. "Still, unlikelier things have happened."

"I know."

He hesitated, then kissed her lightly. "Whatever happens, we'll face it together."

After he'd finished dressing and gone, Michele rose and found a shirt in his closet. She put it on and borrowed his comb to untangle her damp hair, then called room service and ordered food to be sent up. She picked their scattered clothing up off the floor. Then, after a slight hesitation, she called down to Jackie's room. Her friend answered on the first ring.

"Hi, it's me," Michele said.

"Hello, stranger," Jackie replied dryly.

"I just wanted you to know that I—I'm going to be with Ian for a while. Didn't want you to worry."

There was a long pause, and then Jackie said, "So. You're lovers." Her voice was flat.

"Does that surprise you?"

"No. No, it doesn't surprise me. Jon called a little while ago. I told him you were fine, and out on the beach. I don't like lying, Michele."

"You weren't lying. I am fine."

"If you say so." Jackie's voice was still flat and polite.

Michele sighed and gave up. "I'll talk to you later, all right?"

"Sure."

After hanging up the phone, Michele continued to sit on the bed, gazing at nothing. Jackie's reaction had been only a sample, a mild sample at that, of what awaited her in Atlanta. She hadn't wanted to think about that; in Ian's arms, she'd been able to forget.

But she couldn't forget for long. She loved Ian—but did she trust him? Even now, even after all they'd shared, she didn't have that answer. Alone in his room without the sight and touch of him to send every rational thought spinning into oblivion, she felt wary, uncertain, painfully vulnerable. And in the back of her mind were dark stirrings she couldn't seem to banish. Jackie had been right; Ian could hurt her more dreadfully than any other man.

For herself, she had no choice but to accept that possibility. The greatest shock of her love for Ian wasn't that he was her family's enemy, or that she went wild in his arms with a passion she hadn't known herself capable of. The greatest shock was the complete disappearance of her pride. She'd been raised to be proud, that being the single surviving trait of a Southern heritage; raised by a man whose pride in his name and in his person was immense.

But her love for Ian put such arrogance in perspective. Because she loved, she was achingly vulnerable, and that lowering of all barriers left her with the knowledge that pride didn't matter. As long as he wanted her, she belonged to him. For the rest of her life, she belonged to him.

For herself, it didn't matter who he was. But her father and brother would never see it that way. And along with her own natural uncertainties and doubts at accepting a man as her lover, she had to cope with the terrible knowledge that her relationship with Ian could be the spark that would ignite violence between their families.

"Are you decent?"

Startled, she looked up and saw Ian peering at her around the partially opened door. She hadn't even heard his key in the lock. "Of course I'm decent," she said, pushing her anxiety back into its dark corner.

He looked at her thoughtfully, then said, "No," and disappeared. Moments later, he opened the door all the way and pushed a room service cart in ahead of him. "Decent enough for me," he said calmly, "but not the waiter."

"I'm wearing clothes."

"You're wearing my shirt—and you look sexy as hell in it. Have I told you you're beautiful?"

"Umm . . . I don't remember."

"I must have been saying it inside my head, then. You are beautiful." Ian was concentrating on shifting the food from the cart onto the table by his balcony door. "I thought so when you were sixteen."

"What?" That really did surprise her.

He pushed the emptied cart back out into the hall and then came back and shut the door. He came to the bed and drew her to her feet, enfolding her in his arms. "Now why does that surprise you so much?"

Michele blinked up into his smiling face. "Well, I was gawky. All bones."

"All lovely bones. And wild hair and haunting eyes. You've been in my head ever since, like a song I couldn't forget. I used to catch a glimpse of you across some huge, crowded room, a theater lobby, or restaurant, and I'd wonder what would happen if I went up to you, considering the curses you'd spit at me when you were sixteen—"

"I wouldn't have," she murmured, realizing that it was true.

Ian kissed her, holding her hard for a moment. Then he guided her to the table and put her in one of the chairs while he took the other. "We better eat to keep up our strength," he said in a slightly rough voice. He looked at her, his eyes burning.

Reading the heated expression correctly, Michele felt a jolt of desire. Lord, just a look from him and she went weak. She fixed her gaze on her plate, concentrating on eating even though she'd forgotten what she'd ordered.

Ian ate automatically, hardly able to keep his eyes off her. She looked so delicate enveloped in his shirt, the dark cloud of her hair making her appear almost sixteen again. He knew she was troubled, knew that during his absence she had begun to confront what lay ahead of them. And he also knew that if he took her in his arms, she'd forget the problems. For a while.

The desire between them pushed everything else away, leaving only them and what they felt. But with the sharp edge of that blunted, however momentarily, the world and the problems outside crept closer.

In a low voice, without looking up, she said, "Do you think we can stop the feud?"

"I don't know." He wished he had a better answer.

She looked up then, gray eyes clouded. "Between our fathers, it's always stopped short of violence. Have you realized that—our relationship could change that?"

"We won't let it happen, Michele."

"How will we stop it? By telling them it's just us, that they aren't involved? They won't see it that way. By telling them we didn't plan this? That won't matter. They won't understand, Ian. They'll never understand."

He was silent for a moment, then pushed his plate away and sat back. Reluctantly, he said, "It'll be worse on you, even assuming we can keep them from striking out at each other. No matter how furious my father is, he won't disown me. I'm his only son, the last of the line."

Michele shivered almost unconsciously. "Dad . . . won't be that rational. I'd be lucky if he gave me time to pack. Years ago, I heard him say what he'd do if a Stuart ever touched me. I saw the look in his eyes. I'm afraid of what he might do to you and your father."

"Michele . . ." He reached across the small table and covered one of her hands with his.

"I don't even know how to tell him. Or Jon." Her hand turned under his, holding on as if to a lifeline. "I think

I'm more afraid of what Jon will do. He's always been very protective of me—and he hates you."

"But he loves you," Ian said quietly. "So does your father. I can't believe either of them would hurt you." Even though part of his mind was telling him she was right, that her family could very well react with a violence that would catch her in its storm, another part of him found it impossible that any man could look into her eyes and say or do anything to hurt her.

Michele pulled her hand away and met his gaze very steadily. "Can't you? Do you want me to tell you how they'll look at this, what they'll say? They'll say that you set out to make a fool of me, that you cold-bloodedly seduced me with the intention of tearing our family apart. They'll say you used me as a tool or a weapon to further delay the completion of Dad's building, that you wanted to—to disrupt our family any and every way you could, put us at each other's throats—"

"Michele—"

She rose jerkily and stepped away from the table, away from the sudden dark realization in his eyes. She leaned against the open balcony door and stared out on paradise. "That's what they'll say," she whispered.

"And that's what you think, isn't it?" Ian rose as well, going to her and turning her around roughly to face him. "My Lord, you still don't trust me."

She stared at the pulse beating in his neck, unable to meet his eyes. "I can't get it out of my head," she said unsteadily. "The words. All the awful things I've heard for twenty years. I try not to—but I keep hearing them. And I know what it'll do to Dad and Jon, I *know*. I'm the best weapon you could use to destroy them."

"Even now?" His voice was tight. "Even now, you think I'm using you?"

Feeling the hot sting of tears, she looked up finally into his hard face. "I don't want to. Don't you see, Ian? When you hold me, it doesn't matter because it's just us and I know I have to take the chance. I can't fight what you make me feel."

"But you can't trust me not to destroy your family."

She saw her hands go up, saw them touch his face in some aching effort to soften him. But the touch seemed to go unfelt, his expression remaining hard and his eyes flinty. Despair swept over her as she tried to make him see and understand the pain tearing at her.

"Please . . . You made me face this. You said we had to talk about it. I'm trying to tell you that no matter how strongly you make me feel, and even though I could never hate you, I still can't forget what I've been taught. And if I can't forget that, if I can't trust you with all that I feel, after everything that's happened between us, then how could my family ever survive this? Ian . . . what we *are* will destroy them."

He pulled her suddenly into his arms, holding her as if something had tried to snatch her away from him. He hadn't wanted to face the fact that it could never, ever, be just them, that what they felt for each other couldn't be held separate and apart from the feud between their families. But he had to accept it now. They were each bound by ties of blood and love to opposite sides of a battle that had raged for centuries, and no bond between them, by the simple fact of its existence, could end that war.

His father wouldn't disown him, but the bitterness and sense of betrayal would always be between them. And her father and brother would never be able to accept him in Michele's life. Not with the feud raging stronger than ever between the families.

"We'll find a way to stop it," he muttered into the dark silk of her hair. His arms tightened around her, and he lifted his head to stare down at her. "Somehow. We won't let it destroy them—or us."

Michele let herself be comforted by his certainty, because the alternative was simply too painful. In any case, there was no going back. She pushed all the horrible words back into their darkness, and with their banishment came the sharp awakening of everything else she felt for him. The desire rising in her with such abruptness held more than a little desperation and she knew it, but she didn't care. These feelings were honest and untainted by dark things; these feelings were all she could really be sure of between them.

"I want you," she whispered.

His breath caught as she pressed closer, and his eyes flared with instant heat as his head bent to hers. "Michele," he murmured against her lips. "Michele . . ."

Late the following morning, Ian swore creatively as he dressed, his feelings obvious. "It isn't enough that the client has to arrive a day early," he said irritably, "but then he has the nerve to ask me to meet him on the other end of the island and spend the day walking over the job site."

"It can't be helped," Michele said, lying on her side in bed as she watched him.

"Come with me."

"Do you really think that would be wise?" she murmured.

Ian looked at her, lying in his bed naked except for the sheet draped over her, and he knew exactly what she was thinking. They had decided to eat dinner downstairs in the restaurant the night before. They'd stopped by her room so that Michele could put on something besides a caftan with no buttons, and then had gone on to the restaurant.

They hadn't made it to dessert.

Smiling just a little with a smile that was pleased and secret and so intimate it nearly made his heart stop, she said, "Your client probably wouldn't be thrilled to watch us vanish into the bushes."

He leaned over the bed, placing a hand on either side of her. "Do you think that would happen?"

"You tell me."

Ian knew damned well it would; in the last twenty-four hours, touching her had become as necessary as breathing, and since her desire was as strong as his, those touches just couldn't be casual ones. "You make me feel eighteen and at the mercy of my hormones," he told her.

"Good." Smiling, she lifted her face for his kiss.

"Dammit. I hate to leave you," he murmured against her mouth, thinking that if he ever saw her smile like that at another man, he'd kill the bastard. The primitive impulses and urges he felt around her no longer surprised him, for he'd learned the simple truth about himself: He was a man deeply, possessively, and irrevocably in love.

She sighed regretfully as he straightened, then said, "Just for a few hours. I should spend some time with Jackie anyway. Call home. Things like that."

"I'll be back before six. No matter what the client says."

"All right. I'll be here or in my room."

After he'd gone, Michele stretched like a lazy cat and reluctantly got up. She wanted to hold on to the peaceful feeling of well-being as long as possible, and determinedly kept her mind sedate as she dressed in the clothing that had been very hastily abandoned the night before.

The memory brought a smile to her lips as she left his room and slipped downstairs to her own to shower and change, but the smile left her as Jackie's closed door reminded Michele of things she wanted to forget. After the brief but painful discussion between her and Ian yesterday, neither of them had wanted to return to the subject of their future, and so it had been left hanging.

Michele still didn't want to think about it. She knew the problems wouldn't vanish by being ignored, but the wonderful hours with Ian and the delight she had found in his arms was an interlude she wasn't yet ready to jeopardize in any way.

She was dressed and brushing her drying hair when Jackie suddenly appeared in the connecting doorway.

"Hi. Abandoned so soon?"

Looking at her friend, Michele wished she could say something to ease Jackie's worry; her studied unconcern and flippant tone didn't hide her anxiety. "Ian had to meet a client on the other side of the island."

Jackie came far enough into the room to lean a hip on the low dresser. "Oh. So you're at loose ends?"

"For a few hours anyway."

"Then let's go have our fortunes read."

Michele wasn't surprised by the suggestion. Jackie's interest in fortune telling was a long-standing one; since her early teens she'd been dragging various of her friends to palmists, tarot card readers, and psychics. She had collected her share of futures, most of them containing the invariable promise of a tall, dark, and handsome man—and the fact that the man she had recently become involved with could easily fit that description had only deepened her faith in destiny.

It wasn't a belief Michele ever shared. Humoring Jackie, she'd gone along and had her fortune read a number of times. She, too, had been promised a tall, dark stranger in her future. One enthusiastic palmist had even told her flatly that her first lover would be a dark man with burning eyes.

Well, Michele thought now with a flash of amusement, she'd gotten it half right.

Mildly, she said, "I'm game. Have you already found a fortune teller on the island?"

Jackie drew a card from the back pocket of her jeans and looked at it. "This was pushed under my door this morning. There's some kind of small carnival out by the harbor, just for the day. And a Mrs. Fortune offers tarot readings."

Wondering idly why there had been no card under her own door or Ian's, Michele came to the conclusion that

Mrs. Fortune no doubt had a limited supply of cards; most of her breed made a marginal living at best. Luckily she had shoved one under the door of a true believer in fortune telling.

"Okay," she agreed. "Are you hoping you'll get a prediction of when Cole will propose?"

"This time," Jackie said lightly, "I'm not so much interested in my future. It's yours I'm wondering about."

Five

The carnival was like most that Michele had seen in the States. There were a few rides for children, a number of exhibits and games, and the place was packed. The only obvious difference was that the carnies here called out to customers in three languages. Most of the patrons were tourists, a large majority American, all clearly willing to accept the games as honest, the exhibits as containing at least a reasonable facsimile of what was so luridly painted on the outside of the tents, and the rides as safe.

Mrs. Fortune's tent was surprisingly subdued, given its atmospheric background. It was a soft violet in color, and boasted only a sign in Old English script above the tent flap promising that tarot readings were conducted inside. Outside and to the right of the opening stood a man, and he made no effort to try and entice the milling tourists to enter the tent. He merely studied the crowd, occasionally smiling or nodding if someone looked his way.

Jackie, who had no interest in anything other than a

possible glimpse into her friend's future, had Michele by the arm and was leading her inexorably to the tent.

Michele had accepted her fate, but as they drew near the man outside the tent, she found her whole attention focused on him. He was certainly a fascinating-looking man. He was extremely large, for one thing, his formal white suit tailored exquisitely on a frame that didn't seem to hold a bit of fat. And he was, Michele thought, very old, even though his erect posture held the years at bay. He had a healthy thatch of snow-white hair, a full white beard, and dark eyes that shone benignly and contained a friendly, tolerant wisdom. Elegant hands were folded casually over the top of a gold-headed cane, which he used to lift aside the flap of the tent.

"Ladies." His deep voice was rich in tone and incongruously gentle for so large a man.

"How much?" Jackie demanded without preamble.

"You have a card?" he murmured. When she produced it, he added softly, "One free reading, then."

"Yours," Jackie told Michele, and pulled her friend inside.

Experienced in the various trappings of the fortune teller, Michele was surprised by the interior of the tent. There were no velvet hangings, no burning candles or incense, and no peculiar statuettes or symbols lying about. There was only a comfortable couch on one side of a low, plain, glass-topped table, with a chair on the other side. And bare tent walls.

The woman who rose from the chair at their entrance was also something of a surprise to Michele. She was petite and delicate. Instead of the usual gypsy-type draperies she wore a very modern and tasteful ruby red dress that enormously flattered her snowy hair and milky complexion—to say nothing of a still-splendid figure.

"Welcome," she said softly, her voice low and sweet.

Jackie shoved Michele forward and waved her card. "My friend's come for her reading."

"Please sit down," Mrs. Fortune invited, seating herself gracefully in the chair.

Michele sat, with Jackie beside her, and watched as Mrs. Fortune leaned forward to open a carved wooden box at the side of the table. The woman seemed to hesitate only an instant, then drew out a deck of tarot cards wrapped in cloth. She unwrapped the cards and set the cloth aside, then held the deck out to Michele. "Cut the cards, please."

Obeying, Michele studied the woman curiously. She was absolutely lovely, her face totally unlined even though Michele felt she was very old. Her eyes were a vibrant green, so unusual a shade that they seemed iridescent, their depth and clarity curiously compelling.

Michele had a sudden and rather unnerving impression that if any mortal human had been granted the ability to open a door into the future, this woman had. She had remained purposefully silent and sat very still, all too aware that many so-called clairvoyants were adept at reading body language and listening to subtle changes in voice as they skillfully guided their "clients" through the practiced fakery of what was called in the craft of a professional seer a "cold reading."

But the beautiful old lady didn't even glance up, and she never once asked Michele anything. She laid the tarot cards out on the table slowly in a complicated pattern, studying each one in silence for an instant before placing the next. When the pattern lay complete, she began speaking in her soft, clear voice, her tone holding no drama or mystical theatrics. One delicate finger lightly touched each card as she interpreted it.

"Your past. You are descended from a very old line, their roots in the dark Celtic moors. In your veins runs the hot blood of a warrior strain, and in your soul is the knowledge of a terrible conflict you were born to resolve. An unexpected meeting cast all that you feel into chaos. There is a man you cannot trust, yet cannot turn away from."

Michele didn't stiffen, but only because she was concentrating fiercely on remaining motionless. Still, she could feel her pulse quicken, and the hands clasped together in her lap were cold.

The old lady went on without looking up. "Your present. You stand between enemies. Old, old enemies. All around you are the shifting patterns of things seen—and unseen. Events set in motion by your blood, but not by your hand. Old hurts must be avenged; the need for revenge is a terrible hunger, a dreadful thirst, and it must be satisfied. Danger is everywhere, a trusted voice, a strange but familiar face, eyes veiled against you. You feel great doubts and fears, but great passions as well. You risk much. Star-crossed lovers."

Michele heard Jackie gasp, but she herself remained utterly silent. She had a peculiarly detached feeling, staring at that delicate hand as it moved lightly from card to card, and listening to the soft, relentless voice.

"Your future. You will feel torn between what was and what must be. Two paths lay before you, one leading to the destruction of all you hold dear, the other leading to a triumph of the heart and the spirit. Neither way is without pain. Neither way is without tragedy. Even now, the events set in motion entangle you and all you care about; even now, the seeds sown decades ago grow twisted to bear a dark and bitter fruit. You cannot change what must be, but only preserve with your own will a hopeful future. The confusion of heart against mind is a battle you must fight and win if you are to find contentment. You must abandon much to win all. You must find courage in the truth you feel, for that alone will show you the way."

The old lady looked up then, her vibrant eyes darkened with compassion. Gently, she said, "It was always intended, child. Always meant to be. You were destined to love the enemy of your family."

Michele gazed into those sympathetic eyes, and she

could almost feel them looking into her soul. "I don't believe in fate," she whispered.

"Yes, you do," Mrs. Fortune said quietly. "You've always known what he could be to you."

Michele didn't remember rising or turning away. She didn't remember walking from the tent. She just found herself outside, walking steadily beside a very silent Jackie, and when she heard her own voice shake she wasn't surprised. "Did you arrange that? Pay her to say that?"

"No." Jackie was too subdued to take offense. "If I had—she wouldn't have said what she did. The last thing I wanted to hear was that you were fated to love Ian Stuart."

"I don't believe in fate," Michele repeated.

"Are you in love with him? Michele? Are you?"

"Yes."

"That appears to have gone rather well," he said, coming into the tent.

She looked up from the cards still lying in their pattern on the table and stared at him. Her vibrant eyes held a speculative gleam. "Cy, what happened to the stacked deck?"

Mildly surprised, he said, "Wasn't it in the box?"

"No."

"Well, no matter, sweet. You were able to follow the script, after all."

"I wasn't following a script."

"No?"

"No. I read the cards just the way they fell. Each had only one possible interpretation."

He looked down at the pattern on the table, then back at her. In the depths of his benign eyes was a tiny smile. "Now, fancy that," he said placidly.

She shook her head slightly and leaned forward to gather up the cards. Conversationally, and as if to herself, she said, "I don't know why I'm surprised. After all these years, you'd think I would have become accustomed to it."

"To what, love?"

"Your witchery."

Cyrus Fortune folded both elegant hands on his cane and looked at her with a tender smile playing about his firm lips. In a sedate tone, he said, "She cut the deck. You dealt the cards and read them. How could I have possibly controlled that?"

A soft laugh escaped her, the sound tinged with love and wonder. "You didn't control it. You simply knew it would happen just that way." Then she sobered and looked up at him gravely. "Cy, if you had arrived on time thirty-five years ago . . ."

"Those two people would not now exist."

"Could you have ended it then?"

He hesitated. "There was a chance."

"I think you were right when you told me everything happens in its own time," she said. "And this is the time. They *were* meant to love."

"Yes."

"It isn't over, is it?"

"No," he said gently. "It's just beginning."

"Have you told him?" Jackie asked in a strained voice.

They were on the terrace of the hotel having a late lunch—or were supposed to be. Neither had done more than pick at her food, and both had been virtually silent until now.

Michele shook her head. "I want to. I've wanted to a dozen times. I just . . . somehow, I haven't been able to say the words."

"It was bad enough thinking you just had to have some insane fling. But this . . ."

"Don't you think I know?" Michele's voice was unsteady despite all her attempts at control. She looked at her friend, her emotions confused and uncertain. "Jackie, I didn't go looking for this. It scares the hell out of me, what Dad and Jon are going to do when they find out."

"Do they have to find out?"

"It isn't just an affair!"

Jackie looked away, finally, from her friend's glittering eyes. "All right. What does Ian say?"

"We've tried to talk about it. But there aren't any answers. No matter what we do, this is going to have a terrible effect on our families. The tension between them has never been stronger. Our fathers are competing for that big contract, both of them pushing to get their current projects finished. I don't know what's going on in Atlanta now, but Jon was convinced the Stuarts had paid off some of the inspectors, bribed them to stall the project."

"They've done it before," Jackie said flatly.

"Have they? That's the worst part of this feud, Jackie, and you're blind if you can't see it."

"What are you talking about?"

"Nothing's ever proven. Accusations on one side, denials on the other, over and over. But it's a *private* battle. Oh, half the South knows about it, but it's still private. We don't go to court, don't gather evidence to present to a jury. That isn't the way it's done. We just sling mud back and forth, and go on hating because it doesn't *end*."

Jackie was silent for a moment, then shook her head and met Michele's gaze with a stubborn glint in her own. "All I know is that you can't stop it. You heard what Mrs. Fortune said. Choose the wrong path, and you'll destroy everything you care about. And it doesn't take a clairvoyant to tell either of us that the wrong path is any kind of relationship with Ian Stuart."

Michele drew a short breath. "She also said I was destined to love him."

"She didn't say he was destined to love you."

That hurt, all the more because Michele felt so vulnerable and because the horrible, dark suspicions just wouldn't go away. There was a part of her that believed Ian cared about her, that it wasn't just passion, but so much had happened between them so quickly that she felt raw and unsure.

"Forbidden fruit," Jackie said in a taut voice. "Maybe he wanted a taste too."

"He wouldn't risk so much for that," Michele whispered. "Not simply that."

"What's he risking? His father wouldn't disown him," Jackie said, unknowingly echoing Ian's own words. "He's an only child, an only son. Besides that—maybe his father thinks that's all a Logan woman's good for. He might not give a damn that Ian's slept with you; it'd only give him something new to taunt your father with."

"Don't."

Jackie looked down, knowing Michele was on the ragged edge and hurting. "I don't want to keep saying such things. But you've got to face the fact that you're risking everything. Your father and Jon could never accept Ian as your lover. Never. Michele, they'd rather see you dead."

Michele got up from the table and walked away. She was moving blindly, hardly aware that she was retreating to her room like a wounded animal seeking its burrow. She desperately wanted Ian, wanted his arms around her and his body hard against hers. She wanted him to push away the darkness that seemed to be closing in on her, the confusion and pain.

Her friend's statement that both her father and brother would choose to see her dead rather than in the arms of the man she loved was a terrible thing to hear. But worse than hearing it was the devastation of believing it was true.

"Michele?"

"Leave me alone, Jackie." She was standing by her balcony doors, staring out.

"We can go home," Jackie's voice was pleading. "Today. Nobody has to know. Things can be the way they were—"

"Nothing can ever be the way it was." That was the only truth she was utterly certain of. Nothing in her life would ever again be as it had been.

"Look at what he's done to you already. You're so brittle, a touch would shatter you into a million pieces. This is tearing you apart. No matter what you do now it's only going to hurt you. Michele—"

Michele jerked around, but whatever she would have said was lost as the phone rang loudly. She drew a breath to steady herself, then went to the bed and sat down as she lifted the receiver. "Hello?"

"Michele."

She felt suddenly cold, a tremor of fear chasing down her spine. Her father never called her like this, not unless something had happened. "Dad? What's wrong?"

"Jon's been hurt." His voice was flat. "Early this morning at the building."

"How bad is it?" She was terrified of hearing the answer, more terrified of not hearing it.

"I don't know. They haven't been able to tell me anything definitive yet. He was barely conscious when they brought him in, but he managed to say who was responsible."

"Responsible?" The coldness spread through her body. "It wasn't an accident?"

"No, it damned well wasn't," her father said, his control slipping and allowing the harsh and malignant feelings he was experiencing to sound in his voice. "Jon caught a saboteur, Michele, red-handed. He managed to choke the truth out of him before the bastard's handiwork brought a wall down almost on top of him."

Michele couldn't have asked; she didn't want to hear. But her father was going on in a voice vibrating with hatred and filled with utter certainty.

"The son of a bitch thought he'd keep suspicion off

himself by being out of the city when it happened, but his hired gun couldn't talk fast enough. Ian Stuart planned it all weeks ago, then called yesterday and set his man to work. If Jon hadn't gotten a tip and gone out there, the damage would have been ten times as bad."

"No." She thought she said it aloud, but her father apparently heard nothing.

"Come home, Michele."

"I'll be on the next plane," she murmured.

"The car will meet you."

Michele hung up the phone, vaguely surprised to see that her hand was steady. She felt hollow inside, all her emotions numbed and still.

"What's happened?" Jackie demanded anxiously. "You're white as a ghost."

Tonelessly, Michele repeated the conversation. "I have to go home," she finished.

"Start packing. I'll call the airline. And I'll pack too. I'm going back with you."

Michele didn't try to dissuade her friend. The next two hours passed in a blur, and it wasn't until they were on a plane bound for Atlanta that the numbness retreated and left her feeling emotionally battered and so confused she could barely think.

Ian? No! It couldn't have been him. It was all some horrible mistake; it had to be. There *had* to be another explanation for what had happened. He'd said he wouldn't fight her brother, that Jon could hate him to hell and back and he wouldn't fight him. Could he have lied about that and made her believe him? Could he have held her in his arms with a desire she knew was real while plotting coldly against her family?

She didn't want to believe it, *couldn't* believe it despite her father's certainty and her own agonizing doubts. How could she love a man capable of such treachery? There had to be another answer . . .

"Michele?" Jackie's voice was tentative. "You couldn't have known Ian would—"

"I don't know that he did."

"But your father said that man named Ian as his employer."

"Then it's his word against Ian's, isn't it?"

There was a moment of silence, and then Jackie said, "You must believe it. You didn't leave a message for Ian."

Michele kept her head turned away, directing her gaze out the window even though she saw nothing. "No, I didn't leave a message. I just ran like a coward. Afraid to face him."

"What could he have said if you had stayed to face him? That he didn't do it? Of course he'd say that. Michele, this time somebody got hurt. Jon got hurt. And Lord help the Stuarts if he was hurt badly."

"I know." Oh, yes, she knew. The fuse had been lit now, and it was only a matter of time before hate exploded. What had the fortune teller said? That the desire for revenge was a terrible hunger and thirst? Michele knew only too well that her father was hungering now, that whatever restraints had held the feud away from the brink of violence had been snapped. Her father wouldn't wait for proof; he had all he needed.

Michele stared out the plane window at the blanket of clouds below, fear for her brother and the painful uncertainties about Ian tearing at her, and filled with the knowledge that any hope of peacefully stopping the feud was gone now.

"You cannot change what must be . . ."

Was there nothing she could do except endure, stand by helplessly and watch while everyone she loved was torn apart by this?

The company limo was waiting when she and Jackie emerged from the frenetically busy terminal at the airport. Their luggage was quickly stowed, and they were driven directly to the hospital. It was still November in Atlanta, and far from paradise a cold rain was still falling. The city looked bleak and dreary, especially at night.

At the hospital, they were directed to the right floor, and as soon as they stepped out of the elevator Charles Logan strode toward them. He was still upright and vigorous in his sixties, conceding nothing to age except the gray streaking his brown hair and the lined, weathered face of a man who had worked much of his life outside. His gray eyes were the only similarity between him and his daughter; he was a tall man and powerfully built, his rugged features holding none of the delicacy Michele had inherited from their Celtic ancestors.

"Dad? Is Jon—?" She hurried toward him with Jackie at her heels.

"It's all right," he said, hugging her briefly. "A mild concussion and broken wrist, but he'll be able to go home tomorrow."

The relief was overwhelming, but Michele was still very aware of the tautness in her father's expression and the cold gray gleam in his eyes. "Can I see him?"

"Room 484. He's awake."

"I'll wait out here," Jackie said, obviously as relieved as her friend to hear the news.

With the somewhat courtly air he inevitably adopted whenever he was around young women —especially pretty ones—Charles Logan offered his arm to Jackie. "Why don't I buy you a cup of coffee?"

"Sounds good to me. Michele, tell Jon I said hi."

Nodding, Michele left her father and Jackie and made her way down the hall to Jon's room. She opened the door cautiously, but he was sitting up and looked around quickly, his frown smoothing away. There was a strip of bandage over his right eye, and his left arm was held in a cast from fingers to elbow.

"Michele! Sorry to drag you back from your vacation. Dad shouldn't have called you."

She crossed the room and bent over the bed to kiss him lightly. "Don't be stupid." She kept her voice easy with an effort as he smiled at her.

Jonathan Logan was a tall and physically powerful man like his father, and he shared the slightly rough-hewn features that made both men ruggedly good-looking. He had medium brown hair and had inherited blue eyes from both parental sides. But his father's genes were clearly strongest in him. Like the elder Logan, Jon was stubborn, a bit arrogant, and easy to anger. He was close to his sister despite a five-year difference in age, and his protectiveness of her stemmed both from his affection and from an extremely strong sense of family responsibility.

Michele had always adored her big brother, but love had never blinded her to his faults. He had never quite accepted the fact that she was a grown woman perfectly capable of taking care of herself; to Jon, she was still the little sister with a troublesome streak of rebelliousness.

"You don't have much of a tan," he noted critically.

"I have enough. Haven't you been listening to the surgeon general?"

Jon grunted. "I've been listening to too damn many doctors in the last few hours. Pull that chair over and have a seat."

She obeyed, trying to keep her expression calm under his searching scrutiny. Apparently without success.

"You look worried to death," her brother said softly. "Cut it out. I'm fine."

Michele linked her fingers together in her lap and looked at them for a moment, then raised her gaze to his. "Jon, what happened?"

"I'm sure Dad told you."

"Yes. But I want to hear it from you."

He shrugged. "I got a tip yesterday afternoon—"

"From whom?"

"Beats me. A man, or sounded like it. Maybe one of Stuart's people turned traitor. He called the office and said if we didn't want anything to happen to the building we'd better keep an eye on it during the night."

Michele felt a helpless sense of anger sweep over her.

"And, of course, you didn't even consider increasing security or calling the police."

Jon avoided her eyes. "I knew who it was, and I wanted to catch them at it. Hell, I'd been waiting for a chance like that for years."

"You could have been killed!"

"I wasn't." His mouth firmed stubbornly. "I decided not to tell Dad, to go myself. It seemed to me the only kind of sabotage the bastards could hope to get away with would have to be pretty subtle, but I knew they'd want it to be crippling as well. I rigged a couple of booby traps in the control room for the electrical system, figuring that was most likely. Then I decided to check the elevator banks, and that was where I caught him. He'd already planted explosive charges to snap the cables."

"What happened?" Michele asked, dry-mouthed.

"Well, I didn't know he'd set a timer that was busy ticking away. Once I got my hands on him, he was only too happy to talk. He said he'd been paid in cash—half up front a couple of weeks ago—and been told in detail what he was supposed to do. He'd gotten the call yesterday telling him to get busy. Ian Stuart hired him."

"He was sure of that?"

"Of course he was sure. For God's sake, Michele, he called him by name!"

Something was nagging at the back of Michele's mind, a lesson learned in her own investigative training. Slowly, she said, "Did he say how he was hired? I mean, had he met Ian Stuart in person, or was it some other arrangement?"

Jon was frowning at her. "I didn't have time to ask. The explosives went off, and instead of just snapping the cables, part of the blast went outward. Half a wall came down on top of me. I didn't know anything else until our security guys dug me out of there. Unfortunately, the saboteur was long gone by then, and we aren't likely to find him."

Michele looked at her brother searchingly. "But, don't you see, Jon? That man could have been hired to say anything. Maybe his job wasn't so much to cripple the building as it was to have the Logans and Stuarts at each other's throats. Maybe that's why you were tipped. Just so that you could be pointed at a specific target."

"What'd be the point?" But even as he asked, Jon was scowling.

"You know as well as I do. That Techtron contract is worth millions; the Logans and Stuarts are the top commercial builders in Atlanta, but not the only ones. If we eliminate each other, somebody else is going to come out on top. Look, everybody knows that Dad and Brandon Stuart are in a race to finish their current projects. Their bids on the Techtron contract were so close that the decisive question is: Who can start first? If both companies get bogged down in fighting each other, Techtron won't be able to start their project when they want—unless they hire someone else."

Jon shook his head. "The Stuarts are behind this, I know they are."

"Jon—"

"Dammit, Michele, they've already tried to sabotage us! They've bribed the inspectors to slow us down."

"How do you know that?"

"I told you. I have a source at city hall."

"How good a source?"

"He's never been wrong. And I pay him a fortune to make sure he never is."

"Maybe somebody else is paying him more."

Jon moved restlessly on the bed. "Will you listen to yourself for a minute? You've dreamed up this whole conspiracy theory just because you don't want to admit the Stuarts are out to get us. You've always given them the benefit of the doubt."

"What's wrong with that? Jon, you don't have any proof. You've never had any proof—just reports from elusive sources that you pay to feed you information. Sources who could be taking somebody else's money to tell you what you want to hear. And I didn't *dream up* the fact that everyone in Atlanta knows the Logans and Stuarts would rather fight each other than anything else. You don't have to tell me the explosion wasn't reported to the police, or even to the insurance company; the feud doesn't work that way and everyone knows that too."

"So?"

"So, a third party could easily decide they could do what they liked without any threat of being caught or prosecuted. They could know that the Logans and Stuarts would never look further than each other for a villain. Just point us at each other and keep applying pressure until we destroy ourselves."

"That's ridiculous, Michele."

"Is it? Is it any more ridiculous than—than carrying on a battle that started with some petty grievance nobody can even remember more than five centuries ago? Any more ridiculous than hating because we're *supposed* to hate, because we've been told we should?"

"They're our enemies," Jon said, staring down at his immobilized wrist.

"Are they? Are you sure?"

"Yes. After—" He broke off abruptly.

"After what?" A memory surfaced, and she went on evenly. "Jon, you said something once about Brandon Stuart and Dad years ago. What happened then?"

"Never mind."

A wave of absolute fury swept over Michele, and her voice shook with it. "Never mind? That's a hell of a thing to say to me, Jon. You and Dad can't wait to launch an all-out war with the Stuarts, and you tell me to never mind? Don't you think it's my business? Damn you, it's my family too! I think I deserve to know why my father and brother hate so deeply they can't even be rational about it. Tell me!"

"All right," Jon snapped. He drew a breath, then said, "Thirty-five years ago, Dad and Stuart fell in love with the same woman."

Despite Ian's remark that the bitterness between their fathers must have been deepened by a woman, the information still came as a shock to Michele. "What?"

He laughed shortly. "Pretty, isn't it? Dad wouldn't say much, but she must have played them off against each other. Dad fell hard, would have done anything for her. And he thought she loved him when—well, when they slept together."

"What happened?"

Jon shrugged. "A few weeks later, she broke down and told Dad she'd made a mistake, that she had realized she loved Brandon Stuart. She and Stuart announced their engagement, and he was strutting like a rooster for having beaten Dad. I'm not sure what happened then, except that there was some kind of confrontation between them and the woman left. Just walked out on both of them, apparently."

Michele could see how her father would have been enraged at losing to a rival—pratically a Stuart—but the story seemed incomplete to her. There had to have been more to it than what Jon knew. "And that's why Dad hates Brandon Stuart so bitterly?"

"Isn't it enough? Dad loved that woman, Michele, and Stuart took her away from him."

Slowly, Michele said, "It sounds to me as if she made up her own mind, and probably with a lot of pain. But she ended up without either of them."

"Maybe she found out she didn't love Stuart as much as she thought. Dad sure as hell wouldn't have taken her back after that."

"Right." She stared at her brother. "Even though he loved her so much."

Jon's eyes narrowed at the sarcasm. "Obviously, you don't understand how Dad felt."

"Obviously. Has it occurred to you that Dad and Mom were married a little more than thirty-four years ago? His heart must not have been too broken. Or maybe Mom caught him on the rebound. Is that his story?"

"I didn't ask," Jon said tightly.

"Maybe you should. Maybe we should both ask." Michele wondered if she looked as shaken as she felt. How odd, to find that so many certainties in her life had been built on shifting sand. Her father had always talked as if his children's mother was the one great love of his life; now it seemed that he had loved once before, and that the emotion had been great enough to spawn an equally powerful hatred.

Holding her voice steady, she said, "That may or may not give Dad a good enough reason to hate. But what about us, Jon? Where is it written that we have to hate because of something that happened before we were born?"

"Michele, they're trying to ruin us!"

"And if they aren't?" Everything inside her seemed to be focused on her brother, all her will bent on finding a chink somewhere in the wall of hate. "If someone else is using the Stuarts—and us—for their own gain? Can you at least consider the possibility?"

"Give me some real proof," he returned flatly. "Something more than theory."

She rose to her feet and stood gazing down at him for a moment. "Isn't that funny," she murmured. "You didn't need any real proof to believe it was the Stuarts."

Jon didn't react or speak again until she reached the door. Then his question dropped quietly into the silence. "What's happened to you, Michele?"

She half turned to look back at him. "Maybe I don't want to be a lemming."

"A what?"

"A lemming. It's a little animal. Every so often, the lemmings crowd together and rush toward a cliff. They commit mass suicide. Maybe a few centuries ago, someone told them it was the right thing to do."

After a moment, Jon shifted his gaze back to his broken wrist. "See you at home tomorrow, Michele."

She left the room, feeling tired and angry. The anger was new, and she welcomed it, because it was better than pain and hopelessness. She was angry at the stubborn blindness of her father's and Jon's hatred, angry at whatever long-ago ancestor had started this mess, and angry at herself for not having the courage to tell Jon what had really happened to her.

As for the latter, she realized it was less a matter of courage than a desire to cause the least amount of pain by her confession. God knew this was the worst possible time to break the news to her family, though there would never be a "good" time. Still, if she could somehow stop the feud, or at least defuse it before something horrible happened, before someone else got hurt because of it . . .

She didn't get the chance to offer her theory to her father until late the following morning as he was preparing to go to the hospital and get Jon. The brunch they had shared had been silent, with Michele trying to think of the best way to bring up the subject and her father preoccupied with thoughts of his own. In the end, she blurted it out, and like Jon, her father didn't believe it for a moment.

"Don't be absurd, Michele. Jon choked a confession out of that saboteur."

"Maybe he was paid to lie."

"No, it was the Stuarts all right. And this time they've gone too far. Jon could have been killed, to say nothing of the time and cost to repair the damage to the building."

She felt cold as she looked into the hardness of her father's eyes. "What are you going to do?"

"Nothing for you to worry about," he said calmly.

"Not worry? Dad—"

The phone on the hall table rang just then, and her father grasped the interruption. "Get the phone, honey," he said, laying aside his newspaper and rising from the table. "If it's for me, tell them I'll be back in a couple of hours."

He went out into the hall with her to get his coat, and Michele answered the phone with half her mind still occupied with the possibilities her father was considering for revenge. None she could think of was at all comforting.

"Hello?"

"Michele."

Her heart seemed to stop and then begin pounding against her ribs. Nobody said her name the way he did, and just the sound of it made her ache with longing. But she couldn't talk to him, not now when everything was so confused, and not with her father three feet away shrugging into his coat.

In a polite voice, she said, "I'm sorry, you have the wrong number." And hung up the phone.

It was a pity, she thought vaguely, that phone manners didn't extend to the rest of life. If everyone apologized for the mistakes others made, the world might be a kinder place.

"Are you coming to the hospital with me?" her father asked briskly.

Michele stood in the entrance hall of their stately old home and looked at her father. "No. I haven't even unpacked yet. I'll see Jon later."

Looking at her narrowly, he said, "You're too pale. Did you sleep well?"

"Not very. Jet lag, I expect."

"Good thing you're still on vacation for the rest of the week. You should get some rest, honey."

"I will."

When she was alone, Michele admitted to herself that rest was the last thing she could afford. Unless she could somehow prove that neither Ian nor his father was working against her family—and prove it quickly—then violence from both sides wasn't just probable, it was inevitable.

As so often in the past, the calm but tense status quo between the families had been disturbed yet again. A rivalry that was equally matched and that employed the same tactics could hold steady for years with neither side gaining the upper hand; in world politics, it was called the balance of power, and though it was a brutally delicate highwire act, at least it preserved both sides. But it required no more than a single nudge to upset the balance.

And someone was supplying that push.

Michele wasn't even sure that her theory was correct. It was still possible that Ian's father was bent on delaying his rival's building. It was even possible that Ian himself had planned the sabotage. But she couldn't believe that. Despite all the doubts and dark suspicions, the almost instinctive compulsion to believe the worst of a Stuart, she simply could not accept that the man she loved was capable of such treachery.

She wanted desperately to see him, talk to him, but dared not risk that. Too many people knew of the feud, and both she and Ian were familiar faces in the Atlanta social and business worlds. If just one whisper reached her father's ears before she could defuse the situation between the families . . .

Michele squared her shoulders and went to get her purse and car keys. She was a trained investigator, and all her experience told her to start with the simplest question and work toward an answer. And she had her question.

Who would have the most to gain by setting the Logans and Stuarts at each other's throats?

Six

Ian cradled the phone and sat gazing across his office. She couldn't believe he'd done it, he told himself, feeling the cold fear of his own answer. Not after all they'd shared. Even with twenty years of programming against anyone named Stuart, she couldn't really believe he was the kind of treacherous bastard someone had made him out to be.

Could she?

He wanted to call her back, to demand that she talk to him, see him. But he hesitated, because he knew what she was going through now, her brother injured in an "accident" that had Stuart written all over it and her father no doubt plotting to get even. And there had been no time for her to learn to trust him, no time for them to reach a real understanding of each other.

He had returned to the hotel, discovered she had left, and had nearly gone crazy in the hours it had taken him to get home and find out what had happened. His only consolation in those endless hours had been the certain knowledge that something *had* happened, that she wouldn't have run from him without a word otherwise. Even then, he had hoped it was something simple, something not touching on the feud.

A lost hope. It hadn't taken him long to find out what had happened, and he couldn't bring himself to blame Michele for refusing to talk to him; even if she wasn't sure he had caused her brother's injuries, the doubts had to be tearing her apart. Still, he had no intention of giving up. He didn't want to do anything to make the situation more difficult for her, and he was all too aware that this was not the moment to seek her out; one more spark between the families and Atlanta just might go up in flames for a second time.

"When did you get back?" his father asked, coming into the office.

"Late last night." Ian looked at him thoughtfully, unconsciously searching.

Brandon Stuart was so different physically from his son that he might have been forgiven a tinge of doubt concerning Ian's paternity, except for the fact that Ian was the image of a Stuart ancestor a few generations back. The elder Stuart had black hair distinguished by silver wings at his temples, dark blue eyes, and patrician features so fine they just missed being delicate. He was a couple of inches under six feet tall and slender.

A man who moved somewhat lazily, he tended to be calm, not given to outbursts of temper, his occasional anger usually taking the form of an icy rage as quiet as it was deadly. A reasonable man in most things, he'd been shaped by his heritage and his own experiences to regard the Logans with bitter loathing, but he hadn't gone overboard in his efforts to instill the same feelings in his son; though he had made his own feelings very clear without mincing words, the wife he had lost only a few years before had persuaded him that it would be wrong to teach Ian to hate.

He and his son shared a suite of offices on the top floor

of a downtown building, a convenience since Ian was very much a part of the family business despite a growing list of clients he worked for independently. After his mother's death, the stately old home he shared with his father had proved to hold too many memories for them both, and they had decided to sell it. Ian had chosen an apartment near the office, while his father had moved into a condo farther out.

Close in many ways—and sharing similiar temperaments—their differing personal interests and frequent disputes virtually demanded that they lead separate personal lives. If too much of their time had been spent together, they doubtless would have been at loggerheads more often than not; living apart they managed a solid relationship built on mutual respect and an often rueful understanding of each other.

As Ian had told Michele, they continued to argue from time to time, and hotly, but since neither was willing to either force the issue or back down, their relationship was never pushed beyond the breaking point.

"Did you get the project?" Brandon Stuart asked now, making himself comfortable in the visitor's chair in front of the massive old pine desk.

"I got it. Howard wants the preliminary designs by the first of the year. He wants to start construction by spring."

Brandon nodded, then said, "You don't look too happy for a man who just acquired a lucrative client."

Flatly, Ian said, "Jon Logan was injured early yesterday morning at their building." He knew damned well that his father was aware of what had happened, and wasn't surprised by his mild reaction.

"Well, building sites are dangerous places. You'd think he'd know that at his age."

"It wasn't an accident."

Calmly, Brandon said, "Naturally, they blame it on us. Not surprising, really, since they haven't a hope in hell of completing their building on time now."

Ian drew in a sharp breath and released it angrily. "Just tell me one thing. Did you arrange it?"

"Of course not. Explosives? I hope I have better sense than to resort to that kind of violence."

"I hope so too."

Brandon studied his son and frowned. "You believe I'm capable of setting an explosion?"

"Where the Logans are concerned, I believe you're capable of almost anything. You didn't arrange it? You knew nothing about it?"

"I've answered both those questions." A shade of responsive anger colored Brandon's voice. "I certainly won't say I'm sorry for the Logans' misfortune, but I had nothing to do with it. What the hell are you so angry about, Ian?"

Until that moment, Ian had been half certain that his father had stepped over the line and resorted to violence. But he believed the denial—and it opened up a new and unsettling possibility. If not his father, then who?

After a moment, he said, "I managed to get hold of one of their security people early this morning. He didn't want to talk to me, but I finally convinced him there was no harm in just telling me what had happened. He was one of the men who helped dig Jon out after the explosion."

"So? What did he have to say?"

"Jon caught the saboteur red-handed. And the man told him that *I* had hired him to do the job."

"That's ridiculous," Brandon scoffed. "You weren't even in the country."

Ian shook his head. "You're missing the point, Dad. If that's what the man said, then the chances are good it's what he honestly believed. My guess is that he was paid to say I was responsible. Somebody set me up."

"For God's sake, Ian, all you know is what Jon said. Of course he'd pin the blame on you. It's just the excuse they've been looking for to turn this into a war."

Trying to hold on to his patience, Ian said, "Has it occurred to you that someone else could be taking advantage of the suspicion between the two families? That the objective wasn't to slow the Logans down but to start us fighting each other so that neither building is finished on time?"

"That's insane."

"And a five-hundred-year-old feud isn't?"

Brandon was silent for a moment, then shrugged. "Even supposing there's something in this idea of yours, what the hell do you want me to do about it?"

Ian knew the question was rhetorical, but he chose to take it literally. "I want you to do nothing to aggravate the situation until I can find out what's going on."

"If you think Charles and Jon Logan are going to sit still after this, you're mistaken. They'll strike out at us, Ian, and *I* won't sit still for that."

For the first time, Ian began to understand how a feud could continue for centuries. It was a blind, automatic response: you hit me and I hit back. Toss hate and suspicion into the equation and it became a never-ending circle.

"Dad, somebody has to stop this insanity."

"You think you can?" his father asked dryly.

"I'm damned well going to try. I'm sick and tired of the whole mess. But it won't do me much good to try and find answers unless you agree to back off."

Brandon studied him for a moment, then shrugged. "I'll increase security around the building so they can't get near it, and I'll keep my mouth shut for the time being. But that's all I can promise, Ian. If this thing gets even uglier, I'm not about to sit still for it."

Ian knew his father too well to ask for more. He was reasonably sure the Logans wouldn't move immediately to exact revenge, since plans take time. At best, he'd have a little breathing space, but not much. A few days, maybe a couple of weeks.

The first thing he had to do was reach Michele. He wanted to see her so badly that it was a constant, dull ache inside him, and the possibility that she could believe he had arranged the sabotage tore at him. Intellectually, he knew that things had happened too fast between them, that with the best will in the world Michele couldn't overcome twenty years of brainwashing in only a few short days; emotionally, he wanted her to believe in him, to trust him no matter what her family said.

Another impossible hope.

He had known that what he felt for Michele was more than passion, more than desire, but some barrier in his mind had refused to let him see the truth of his own feelings. Whether, as Michele had lightly said, it was stamped in the genes or merely in the mind, a tradition of hatred and mistrust spanning centuries was a difficult thing to surmount. Desire he could admit, but love had quite literally been unthinkable.

Until it had happened.

Michele came into the house a bit warily. She'd been gone all day, first to the building site where Jon had been hurt and then to her office. The company she worked for had always been tolerant of their investigative staff's erratic work hours, and no one had been much surprised to see her appear with days still left of her vacation. She had shut herself in her office and spent hours working by phone and by computer, trying to find some proof that a third party was intent on causing friction between her family and Ian's.

The results had been nebulous, leaving her feeling frustrated and worried.

"Michele."

She looked up to see Jon coming down the stairs toward her, his broken wrist in a sling. He was frowning, and she felt sorry the moment she realized her extended absence had worried him. She put her purse and car keys on the hall table and waited for him.

"Shouldn't you be in bed?" she asked lightly. "Where's Dad?"

"No, I'm fine. And Dad's in his study working on the books. Where've you been?"

She managed a smile. "Jon, when are you going to realize that I'm not a kid anymore?"

He reached the bottom of the stairs and stood looking at her, his eyes narrowed. "I asked a simple question, Michele. Would it hurt you to answer?"

Well, she'd expected it. "I suppose not. I went down to the building. I wanted to get a look at the damage and see if I could find any part of the timer left intact."

"You shouldn't have gone down there." His frown deepened, and he added unwillingly, "Find anything?"

"Bits and pieces." She knew that Jon respected her training and abilities as an investigator, even though he had never agreed with her choice of career. He didn't like the idea of his sister poking around the burned-out remains of buildings in cases where her employers suspected arson, or dealing with people unscrupulous enough to try other ways of bilking insurance companies.

"You can't do much with that."

"I've worked with less."

"Okay, I'll bite. What did you figure out from the bits and pieces?"

His mocking tone sparked Michele's temper. She crossed her arms over her breasts and spoke deliberately. "Well, I figured out that the device our saboteur used didn't come from around here. It's state of the art, and right now you can only find it on the West Coast—if your connections are good enough, and you're prepared to pay through the nose."

"So? It's the jet age."

"True, and therefore I did some checking. The Stuarts haven't had anything shipped in from the West Coast for more than three years, their jet hasn't been west of the

Rockies in nine months, and no employee has been out of Georgia at all this year."

Jon was honestly startled. "How in God's name did you find all that out?"

"It's what I'm trained to do. I piece together puzzles, Jon, and since insurance companies work with the police sometimes, I have access to a lot of computer data banks."

He scowled. "Then you missed something. One of them called and ordered the device, or went after it and used a commercial flight."

"No calls to the West Coast, on their business or private lines, in the last year. And neither of them has been out there on any commercial flight this year."

"Then they hired somebody to get it!"

Michele drew a breath. "Why would they? Why be devious on that end and then hire an explosives man who knew exactly who he was working for? It doesn't make any sense. And another thing, Jon, who tipped you?"

"What?"

"Somebody called and told you to keep an eye on the building; who was it?"

"How the hell should I know?"

"Didn't you even stop to wonder? Didn't it bother you just a little bit that for the first time in my knowledge you were tipped hours ahead of time that something was likely to happen?"

"Maybe one of their employees got cold feet."

"Know your enemies; after five centuries, we certainly do. We don't involve employees in the feud; neither do they. In fact, it's strangely out of character for them to hire an explosives man."

After a moment, Jon turned and went into the living room. Michele, feeling the first glimmer of hope that she was getting through to him, followed and sat on the arm of an overstuffed chair near the door. She watched as he went behind the bar in one corner, waited patiently while he fixed himself a soft drink.

"I could use something stronger," he muttered, "but the doctor said not to for a few days."

"Jon, don't you see that the sabotage at the building just doesn't fit the Stuarts'—or our—way of fighting? Sure, our families killed each other right and left at first, but there hasn't been a death or serious injury caused by the feud on either side for more than a hundred years. And no open destruction, not like that, not something that could easily get the police involved. There aren't any duels anymore, or outright murders. We fight in other ways now. Subtle, sneaky ways, unethical certainly, and sometimes illegal, but not violent."

He was staring down at his drink and looked up only after a long silence. His gaze was searching, his expression seemed troubled and faintly anxious, maybe even wary. When he spoke his voice was matter-of-fact. "All right. I'll do some checking myself. If there's somebody else in this, they have to be after the Techtron project, like you said. The number of builders who could handle the work is limited; I should know something within a few days."

Michele almost held her breath. "And Dad? Can you keep him from doing something crazy?"

"I'll try."

She nodded, weak with relief. "Good. Maybe one of us can find some proof."

"Misha?" Jon was looking at his glass again. "What did happen to you?"

Not for the first time, Michele acknowledged that her brother read her face and her moods too well; he knew that this intense and stubborn defense of the Stuarts was new, that it had to have been caused by powerful events or feelings. Maybe he even felt the change in her, or saw some sign of it. She wondered if she looked different but didn't ask him that. And she didn't tell him the truth, because he was still unconvinced and she dared not risk an admission that would both shock and enrage him.

"I told you," she said finally, steadily. "I don't want to be a lemming. Five hundred years is five centuries too long to hate."

Jon might have probed deeper, but the phone out in the hall rang just then and Michele welcomed the interruption. "I'll get it," she told him.

He nodded, still looking at his glass.

She went out into the hall and picked up the receiver. "Hello?"

"Michele. Don't hang up."

Driven by urgent necessity, she had managed to keep her thoughts off Ian, but now the sound of his voice, the way he said her name, was like the shattering of a dam holding back floodwaters. The feelings swept over her so powerfully that she could only endure them in silence, her eyes closing as she fought the urge to blurt out her love and pain and fear.

"Michele? Dammit, talk to me!"

She opened her eyes and glanced toward the living room, very aware of the quietness in the house and her brother's keen hearing. In a voice that was little more than a whisper, she said, "I can't. Not now."

"Baby, I didn't do it. I swear to God I didn't."

She swallowed hard. "I know."

"I have to see you," Ian said intensely.

"It isn't possible."

"We can meet somewhere. Now, tonight."

"I can't."

He hesitated, then said in a flat tone, "Then I'll walk up to your front door and ring the bell."

It might have been an empty threat; Michele thought it probably was, because he knew the risks as well as she did. But the fact that he made it at all told her something of Ian's state of mind. She tried to weigh the risks in her own mind, but all she could think of was how badly she wanted to see him. Needed to see him.

"All right," she murmured. "Where?"

"Three-twenty-four South Highland. I'll meet you in the lobby." He hung up.

Michele cradled the receiver and stared down at it for a moment. After checking Ian's phone bills, she knew that address; it was his apartment building. She took a deep breath, then went to the living room doorway and spoke casually to her brother.

"I have to go out for a while. Tell Dad and Leona I probably won't be back for supper." Leona was their housekeeper.

"Where are you going?" he asked immediately.

"You worry too much, Jon. See you later." Before he could demand an answer, she quickly retreated to gather her purse and keys, then left the house. She wasted no time in driving her Cougar away from the neighborhood; it was doubtful her brother would resort to following her, but she was already taking one chance too many.

The evening traffic was fairly light, and she pulled into the parking lot at the apartment building just over half an hour later. Since it was well past dark, the building showed few features except for lighted windows stretching upward, seemingly into infinity. Michele parked her car and made her way to the entrance; it was a security building, so the bright lobby boasted a guard at a high desk who looked up as she came in.

Then she saw Ian walking toward her. She hadn't seen him in more than twenty-four hours, and it felt like forever. He was wearing dark slacks and a white shirt open at the throat with the sleeves rolled up over his forearms, and she wondered vaguely how she could have seen him across crowded rooms for years without realizing that he moved like a big cat, with riveting grace and power.

Or maybe she had realized. Maybe she had known it for

all those years, without being able to admit it to herself. Maybe that was why no other man had ever stirred her blood.

His eyes were darkened, his face very still. He took her hand without a word and led her toward the elevators. The guard, unsurprised and uninterested, went back to his magazine.

Neither of them spoke in the elevator. Michele looked down at their entwined hands, and for the first time a sense of peace and certainty stole over her. The fortune teller's warning flitted through her mind, and she knew that, right or wrong, she had chosen the path she had to follow.

The elevator opened onto the top floor of the building, and Ian led her down the hall to his door. The moment they were inside, he pulled her into his arms and held her tightly.

"You didn't believe it," he said huskily. "Thank God you didn't believe it."

"When I left Martinique, I wasn't sure," she admitted, holding on to him fiercely. "Dad was so certain. But all the way back here I kept thinking that you *couldn't* have, that it simply wasn't possible."

Ian drew back just far enough to kiss her. "After you hung up on me this morning, I was afraid you believed it," he murmured against her mouth.

Michele smiled up at him as he lifted his head. "Dad was in the room," she said simply.

His eyes burned down at her. "I know we need to talk," he said in a hoarse, thickened voice, "but right now all I want to do is carry you to bed."

The rough statement made Michele's legs go weak, and her heart begin to pound erratically. Heat blossomed inside her. She shrugged off her shoulder bag, letting it drop carelessly to the floor, and lifted her arms to encircle his neck. "Please," she whispered.

Ian groaned as he gathered her up into his arms and strode through the apartment to his bedroom. What she did to him! From the first time they'd made love Michele had been completely uninhibited, so utterly honest and natural in her desire that it had stolen his breath. It was nothing short of miraculous that she could feel so strongly for him of all men; and the knowledge that she had never felt it for another man made it even more astonishing. It was as if all the fiery passion inside her had lain dormant waiting for him.

He set her on her feet beside his bed and turned on the lamp on the nightstand before sweeping the covers impatiently away. Then his fingers went to her neat braid and unclipped the narrow barrette; her thick hair freed itself instantly, unwinding from the severe style until it tumbled about her shoulders in a dark, shining cloud. He loved the look and feel of her hair loose, loved to run his fingers through the long, silky curls.

She was coping familiarly with the buttons of his shirt, pulling the tail free of his pants, and as she pushed the material off his shoulders he shrugged free of it.

"Wait," he murmured, catching her hands as she reached for the buckle of his belt.

Michele was no longer even mildly shocked at her own fervent eagerness. "Why?" she whispered.

Ian kissed her hungrily, then eased down on the edge of the bed and drew her forward to stand between his thighs. "Let me," he said huskily, slowly unbuttoning her silk blouse.

She caught her breath and went still, watching his absorbed expression. She understood dimly that Ian wanted to make it last, and fought to control her own wild need. His deliberation fed the exquisite tension spreading all through her body, and she could feel her heart thudding unevenly.

He reached the final button and slowly pushed the blouse off her shoulders, his hands lingering to stroke her arms lightly. Michele shivered and forced herself to remain still, even though every instinct urged her to move. He unfastened her slacks and pushed them down, and this time she moved only to step out of her shoes and nudge them and the pants aside.

Ian found the front clasp of her bra and opened it, but instead of stripping the flimsy cups of lace and satin away he bent his head forward to nuzzle between them. Michele felt his warm lips, the gliding touch of his tongue between her breasts, and her hands lifted to stroke his thick hair unsteadily as all her senses responded wildly to the caress. She could hardly breathe, and bit her bottom lip to hold back the sounds rising inside her.

He held both his hands at her narrow waist and used his lips and tongue to push aside very slowly the material hiding her breasts from him. When the straps slipped off her shoulders, she shrugged the bra to the floor, her fingers returning immediately to twine in his hair. For long moments he concentrated on the flushed and swollen curves, his mouth tasting her firm flesh with scalding hunger. Michele couldn't be still now, because her breasts were full and hot, the nipples so tight they were actually painful. Her fingers dug into his thick hair, and a moan escaped her throat.

"Ian, please," she whispered, sure she wouldn't be able to bear the sweet torture a second longer. The tension inside her was so great it was as if she hung suspended, anticipation coiling like agony. And then his mouth closed over a taut nipple, and she jerked at the instant, fiery pleasure, crying out because there was no room inside her to contain the incredible sensation. All the remaining strength flowed out of her legs, and she almost collapsed against him.

His hands slid over her bottom and lifted her, and she instinctively parted her legs as he settled her onto his lap. Only his pants and her silken panties separated them, and she was desperate to feel his flesh against her, and inside her. His mouth on her felt wonderful, but she wanted more. When his lips finally trailed up her throat to find hers, she kissed him wildly, demanding that he stop the torment.

A chuckle or a growl rumbled in Ian's chest, and he rose still holding her tightly against him. He turned and bent forward to lay her on the bed, then straightened and swiftly got rid of his remaining clothing. He couldn't take his eyes off her as she lay waiting for him. He had never really noticed what desire looked like on a woman's face, but on Michele's it was something he couldn't get enough of. Her delicate beauty altered with passion, grew somehow more intense, and he thought he had never seen anything more lovely. Her haunting eyes were pools of smoky gray, infinitely deep, a siren's eyes filled with eons of secret female wisdom, and in her husky voice was the ancient enchantment that could steal a man's soul and make it her own.

He came down on the bed beside her and covered her mouth with his, as frantic with need as she was. He hadn't wanted to hurry, very conscious of the fact that it could well be some time before they would be able to meet again, but both his urgent desire and her inflaming response were snapping the threads of his control. He was past the point of being able to move slowly; his craving for her was a compulsion that couldn't be mastered.

He stripped off her panties roughly and then spread her legs and moved between them. The need to bury himself in her, to sheathe his aching flesh in her welcoming heat was overwhelming, but a deeper, more powerful need kept him braced above her just on the point of entry.

"Michele," he said in a voice he hardly recognized, a voice that was strained and guttural because it came from a place inside him almost too profound for words. "Michele, I love you."

She was utterly still for an instant, staring up at him

with wide, bottomless eyes. Then those eyes were filled with emotions so stark he almost wanted to hide his own eyes from them, almost wanted to look away and tell her not to feel that much for him because he couldn't bear it. But he had to bear it; he had no choice. What he felt for her was just as primitive, every bit as complex and wonderful and terrifying as what he could see shining in her eyes.

She lifted her head to kiss him, and a smile of wonder curved her lips as her arms tightened around his neck. "I love you," she whispered. "I think I've loved you all my life. Ian . . ."

He groaned, a wild tangle of love and desire coiling inside him until he thought he'd burst with it. Slowly, he bore down until the tight heat of her body enclosed him. He wanted to fill her with himself, to fuse them together in flesh just as this essential love was fusing them in spirit.

Michele had thought she could never feel more than she had on Martinique, but she was wrong. With love acknowledged on both sides, it seemed that some final, dimly perceived barrier between them had shattered. Every physical sensation was more intense, the intimacy more stark, the joining more complete. The emotions inside her surged until they couldn't be contained, until they escaped in tears and broken murmurs of love.

Passion had formed the first tenuous bond between them, but it was love that anchored and strengthened it, love that reached across a chasm left by five centuries of hate. A strong, solid bridge was built out of the most fragile and powerful emotion of the human heart, an emotion that was all the more remarkable because it existed between two people who were born and bred to be enemies.

In the lamplight quiet of the bedroom they lay close together, both still caught up in the wonder of their own feelings. Ian was the first to speak, his voice low and husky.

"No going back."

Michele lifted her head from its resting place on his shoulder and looked at him gravely. "Was there ever a point when we could have?"

He brushed a strand of her silky black hair away from her cheek, his hand lingering to stroke her soft skin. "I don't think so, baby. Even with everything against us, we fell in love. Maybe we never had a choice."

After a moment, Michele told him about her visit with Jackie to the fortune teller, repeating as much of the prediction as she could remember. "I've never believed in that," she finished. "Fate. But now I can't help wondering. She couldn't have *known*, Ian, not so . . . so completely. She said I was born to resolve an old conflict, and destined to love the enemy of my family."

Ian didn't scoff, even though he was a man with little faith in so-called psychic abilities. With a slightly twisted smile, he said, "I'd like to believe it was just a fluke, but if I were truly master of my own fate, I would have kept driving when I saw you by the roadside."

"You didn't know it was me," she objected.

His smile deepened. "Oh, yes, I did."

"But you looked surprised when I turned around."

Ian raised his head and kissed her, then admitted, "I was surprised. Shocked, really. I didn't understand what I was feeling until later; all I knew was that I took one look at you and knew you could never be an enemy."

Her smile faded. "I'm sorry I left the island without a word. I was just so confused."

"I know. And worried about Jon. The hospital said he had a slight concussion and a broken wrist. How is he?"

"He's up and around." Michele frowned. "I think. . . . He acts as if he believes I'm different somehow. I've been trying to make him at least accept the possibility that somebody else is behind the sabotage, and he's suspicious of my motives."

"You think he might guess about us?"

"I just don't know. And I don't know how he'll react if he does guess. A week ago I would have said he'd go after you with a gun, but . . ."

"But?"

"It's a feeling more than anything I can put my finger on. He seems. . . . It's as if he's fighting to hold on to the hate even though the emotion's just half there."

"Habit, maybe." Ian looked thoughtful.

Michele wished she could focus on whatever it was she sensed about Jon, but shrugged it away for the moment. "Anyway, I spent the day trying to get some evidence he'd accept, and I finally convinced him to at least check a few things himself."

After a moment, Ian said, "We really do have to talk about this." Even as he said it, he was stroking her slender body gently, unable to stop touching her. "Why don't we have a shower and then go rustle something up in the kitchen?"

"Can you cook?"

"Yes. Can you?"

She smiled gently. "No."

"Trouble boiling water?"

"Oh, I can do that."

"Then you can make the coffee."

Michele did make the coffee, but only after a prolonged interval in Ian's shower. And it was while they were digging into the excellent omelettes he had prepared that she made a somewhat rueful statement.

"I think I'd better get a prescription for the pill."

With an answering smile, Ian said, "Maybe you'd better. I can't seem to be practical when I get near you."

Michele had done a bit of calculating after coming home from Martinique, and she had a strong feeling that unless either she or Ian were infertile she had very likely already conceived. Her cycle was extremely regular, never influenced by stress or emotion, and her next period was due in less than two weeks. Her doctor would doubtless want to make certain before putting her on any form of birth control.

The timing, of course, was hardly perfect, but Michele couldn't find it in herself to be disturbed. If she was carrying Ian's child it would delight her; even now, just the possibility sent a surge of utter contentment through her. She wanted a baby, their baby, and no doubts or shadows over the future could dispel that longing.

"What are you thinking?" he asked suddenly, huskily. "Your face is so soft." It was more than that, but he couldn't find the words to explain what he saw. Just as passion made her fiercely beautiful, this mood now made her lovely in a new and strangely moving way. She looked serene, mysterious, the little smile curving her lips both tremulous and pleased.

Meeting his intent gaze, she said softly, "I'm thinking that I might be pregnant. There's a good chance."

Ian felt his throat tighten as he reached across the small table and took her hand. The thought of his child growing inside her delicate body made him realize just how badly he wanted it to happen. For the first time, he wondered if his carelessness had been, on some deep level, deliberate. "I know we haven't found all the answers yet, but no matter what happens I'm not going to lose you. Marry me."

Michele didn't think about how their families would react or about anything else except the happiness filling her. Nothing in her life had felt as certain as this. "Yes," she whispered.

Some time later, with no clear idea of how she'd gotten there, Michele sat up to find herself on Ian's lap; they were in the living room, and he was sitting on the couch. She had no fault to find with the arrangement, but a glance at his watch made her say in surprise, "I've been here for hours."

Ian looked at the watch as well and sighed. "Dammit, I don't want you to leave."

In spite of her happiness, the reminder made her aware of all the problems lying ahead of them. "I don't want to go. But we have to be careful, Ian. You know that."

"I wish it were a joke," he said broodingly. "The Hatfields and the McCoys. A comic strip in the Sunday paper. But even when our feud was comical, it wasn't very funny. And it isn't funny now. We're forced to act like teenagers with disapproving parents, as if we aren't mature enough to make up our own minds. I don't want stolen meetings and phone calls on the sly, Michele."

"Neither do I." She swallowed hard, then added steadily, "We have to stop the feud—or at least prove somebody else is involved it in."

"And if we can't?"

She drew a deep breath and met his eyes gravely. "Ian, I'll marry you tomorrow if you want me to. I'll live with you here or anywhere. No matter what happens between our families, I want to spend the rest of my life with you. But I'd always blame myself if I didn't at least *try* not to hurt Dad and Jon."

"I know." He kissed her gently, then forced himself to concentrate. "You said you'd spent the day trying to find evidence. Any luck?"

Michele told him what she'd found out about the explosive device the saboteur had used. "It isn't much, but it is something. That timer came from the West Coast, probably from California. And it wasn't cheap."

Ian was frowning. "Odd. If somebody's trying to push the feud toward violence, why use a device that neither side could easily acquire? A bundle of dynamite or a lump of plastique would have done the job just as well, and both are easily available in construction work."

"I know, that's bothering me, too. If the purpose was to

cover his—or her, I suppose—tracks, it would have been smarter to go with the ordinary. Something as uncommon as that device could be traced back to a buyer."

"Do you think you can do that? Trace it back?"

Michele hesitated. "Maybe. Given enough time. And the odds are better if it was purchased legitimately. The company I work for has a West Coast office, and I have a contact there who owes me a favor. He might be able to find something."

Ian nodded slowly. "You work on that end, and I'll see what I can find out here in Atlanta. If one of our rivals is behind this, somebody knows about it; you can't keep such an elaborate plan completely quiet."

"It's going to take time," Michele reminded him. "And that's something we don't have a lot of. Jon promised to try and keep Dad from retaliating, but I don't know how long he'll be able to." She paused, then said quietly, "We can't do anything that might strike a spark. In the state he's in, it won't take much to push Dad over the edge."

Seven

Ian was silent for a long moment, then sighed roughly. "I know what you're saying. As much as I hate to admit it, I even agree. But I don't know how long I can stand not seeing you, Michele."

She felt the same; the thought of not seeing him, possibly for weeks, made her ache inside, but she concentrated on the belief that maybe— just maybe—they could find a way to keep from building their future on the ruins of their families.

"It won't be easy," she admitted. "And even if we do find proof that someone else is involved, we might not be able to stop the feud. But we have to try, Ian. I don't think either of us could be happy if we didn't at least try. If just one person—the wrong person—sees us together. . . . Too many people know about the feud. Too many people who don't understand how serious it is. The whole thing could blow up in our faces. We can't take the chance."

He pulled her against his chest and just held her for a

long moment, his cheek pressed to her silky black hair. "All right," he said quietly.

Michele wanted to stay in his arms forever, and even though she knew she should leave she couldn't make herself go. "What will your father do when he finds out about us?"

"I honestly don't know. He won't like it, but whether he'll accept it is something else. He's willing to concede the possibility of a third party being involved in the feud— especially now that he knows neither of us caused that explosion. And he doesn't like being used; that's to our benefit. I'll keep trying to convince him."

She half nodded. "If I can get Jon on our side, maybe he can help me convince Dad." Then she sighed and gently pushed herself upright again. "I'd better go; it's almost midnight."

Ian didn't protest again, even though he wanted to. She certainly knew her father better than he did, and if she believed he was so close to the edge, then they had to avoid calling attention to their relationship, at least until they could somehow manage to defuse the tension.

He walked her down to her car, reluctant to let her go until he absolutely had to. Standing by her Cougar in the brightly lit parking lot, he pulled her into his arms and kissed her, wishing they had another hour, another night. It was so bitterly unfair that the woman he loved, the woman who might well be carrying his child even now, couldn't walk beside him in public for fear of violence exploding between their families.

"I love you," he murmured against her lips, holding her tightly. "No matter what happens, don't forget that."

"I won't forget. I love you, too. And I'll fight for us, Ian, I promise you. I don't want to destroy my family, but if I have to make a choice—"

"You won't," he interrupted firmly, even though he knew it could easily come to that.

Insistently, she said, "If I do, I'll walk away from *them*— not you."

He held her for a moment longer, then reluctantly let her go. "I hope you don't have to." He reached into his pocket and withdrew a key, pressing it into her hand. "A key to the apartment, just in case. I'll tell the security guard he's to let you pass at any time."

"For when Dad throws me out?" she asked in a light voice that didn't quite mask the pain.

Ian touched her cheek gently. "Any time. We don't know what could happen, baby. If you need to come to me, for any reason, then I want you to."

"All right."

Another worry was nagging at him, and as she got into the car, he added, "Michele, . . . be careful. Both our families have an enemy now, and he doesn't seem to care who gets hurt."

The caution sent a chill through her. She hadn't thought about it that way, but the ruthlessness of an enemy who could plant explosives and then lure a potential victim to the site—even if the intention was merely to point suspicion at someone else—was only too obvious.

Neither way is without tragedy. The fortune teller's warning crept into her mind, and she shivered. "If I find out anything, I'll call you."

"Call me anyway," he said. "If I don't at least hear your voice, I think I'll go out of my mind." He made no pretense of keeping the statement light; his voice was low and rough with unhidden feeling.

Michele nodded, her throat too tight to speak, and when he closed the car door she started the engine and backed out of the parking space. He remained there, gazing after her, and her last glimpse of him in the rearview mirror showed her only a big, shadowy figure with gleaming hair under the stark lights.

She drove home slowly, trying to think, to plan. Even with the damage to her father's building, he was only weeks away from completing the project, just as Brandon Stuart was weeks away from finishing his building; both had been originally scheduled to be completed by the first of the year, and that deadline was a critical one if either company hoped to win the Techtron project. The race was still on, more intense than before, and if the saboteur meant to cause more trouble, he was likely to find plenty of opportunity. He would probably wait at least a while, hoping that he had done enough to start the centuries-old hatred boiling, but if neither side reacted, he'd have to throw more wood on the fire. Logically, he would strike at the Stuarts next, a seeming retaliation from the Logans, assuming that Michele's father didn't strike first.

How much time did they have? Very little, she knew. And unless she could convince Jon the Stuarts weren't behind the sabotage, there was no hope at all of controlling their father. He might listen to Jon, even if he didn't like what he heard, but he wouldn't listen to her.

She parked her car in the curving drive of their big, old house and let herself in quietly. There was a lamp burning in the entrance hall, but the rest of the house appeared dark. Leaving her purse and keys on the hall table, Michele started up the stairs. She was on the third step when Jon's voice came quietly from the dark living room.

"A little late, aren't you?"

Michele waited there as he slowly crossed the hall to the bottom of the stairs and stood looking up at her. She felt a flash of resentment, but it quickly vanished; she couldn't afford the emotion, couldn't take the chance of alienating Jon over his usual protectiveness.

Dryly, she said, "I talked Dad out of the curfew when I was twenty, remember? This isn't the first time I've come in after midnight."

"No," he agreed. "It's usually your job, at least according to you. But you're on vacation this week, Michele." His gaze was very intent, searching; she had the feeling that he wanted to ask her outright where she'd been, but that for some reason he didn't want to hear the answer.

Because he thought he knew the answer.

Michele wondered if it showed on her face. Keeping her voice calm, she said, "Yes, I'm on vacation. I'm also trying very hard to find out who ordered the sabotage. Your source at city hall, Jon—I want to talk to him."

The distraction worked, at least for the moment.

"He's on vacation," Jon said. "Up north somewhere."

"Now, isn't that . . . convenient," she mused, more to herself than to Jon.

"For God's sake, Michele, he takes a vacation every year!"

She looked at her brother. "In November?"

Jon hesitated, then swore softly. "No. Usually in August. And, before you ask, I don't know if he took his regular vacation this year; I had no reason to be in touch with him that month."

"Did he tell you he was going on vacation?"

Again, Jon hesitated. "No. I have his home number, and I called his house tonight. His wife answered and said she was packing to join him."

"For how long?"

"Couple of weeks, maybe more."

Even granting her suspicions where Jon's informant was concerned, it still sounded to her as if the man had left Atlanta in something of a hurry. She didn't like it. She didn't like it at all.

"Misha, . . ."

"Maybe I can track him down," she said, saying the first thing that came into her head. Because Jon had been about to ask her a question she wasn't yet ready to answer; she'd heard it in his voice.

"He could lose his job if you start asking questions about him."

She wasn't at all sure she cared; paid informers weren't her favorite people. "I'll be discreet. But I'm going to find out who's behind this, Jon. You could have been killed, and Lord only knows what could happen next." The very thought of what could happen next, all the myriad possibilities woven like a net around the people she loved, made her feel cold and afraid.

After a long moment, Jon said, "You're very sure someone else is involved."

Michele drew a deep breath. "Positive. I'll need your source's name and anything else you know about him. We'll talk in the morning."

"All right. Good night, Michele."

"Good night." She went on up the stairs to her bedroom on the second floor. And it wasn't until she was changing for bed that a glimpse in the bathroom mirror told her what Jon had seen. It wasn't in her face or eyes; the light in the hall downstairs hadn't been good enough for that. But it had been good enough for him to see a definite change. When she'd left the house hours before, her hair had been neatly braided in its accustomed style. She had forgotten to put it back up before leaving Ian's apartment; it now hung loosely around her shoulders, the curls a little wilder than usual because she'd gotten her hair wet in the shower.

Michele couldn't think of a single good reason why she would have taken her hair down—except the truth. And she didn't think Jon had been able to think of one either. Sooner or later, he'd ask the question, and she'd have to answer.

Sooner or later.

The following days passed slowly. Michele got in touch with her counterpart on the West Coast and persuaded him to try and find out who had acquired the state-of-the-art timer.

"Legally, or under the table?" he asked, frankly curious since she'd told him the matter was personal rather than business.

"Both, if you can manage it; I have no way of knowing

if he had a legitimate reason for buying the thing. I can't even tell you how far back to look, Steve. At a guess, a few months. There are only three legitimate sources on the West Coast, and the thing's so new there *can't* be many illegitimate ones. But this guy may have really covered his tracks."

"So you want a list of every buyer for, say, the last six months? That's a tall order, Michele."

"I know. But if you come through for me, I'll owe you a dozen favors."

"Um. And I suppose you need to know yesterday?"

"Yesterday wouldn't have been soon enough."

"Gotcha. Okay, I'll see what I can do. I know of a few shady dealers in explosives, so I'll try them too. I'll let you know as soon as I find out anything."

"Thanks, Steve."

"No problem. By the way, are you as gorgeous as you sound?" He always asked that, and Michele always gave him the same calm answer.

"No. I have crossed eyes and buck teeth. If you can't reach me at the office, call me at home." She recited the number.

"One of these days," he said pleasantly, "I'm going to fly east and find out for myself."

"Don't bother."

"Ah—she has a man in her life."

Michele could hardly help but laugh. "Yes. And, believe me, that's a story in itself." The thought of Ian made her recall the saboteur's apparent motives, and she added more soberly, "Steve, along with that list of names—see if you can get descriptions of the buyers, okay?"

"Descriptions? Why?"

"He might be using an alias. I'm groping in the dark; he's nameless and faceless."

"Michele, you want to tell me what's going on?"

She had never met Steve Ashe, but over the past couple of years they had talked frequently, and phone relationships between strangers were sometimes close simply because they were unlikely to meet face to face. The normal guards of people came down somehow, until a name and a familiar voice became a friend.

". . . a trusted voice, a strange but familiar face, eyes veiled against you."

She shivered unconsciously as the fortune teller's warning flitted through her mind. Stupid to bank too much on that, she told herself. There was no way to look at cards on a table and see into the future, just no way. But her uneasiness grew. So much of the reading had been uncannily on target.

"Michele?"

"Sorry. My mind wandered for a minute."

"Are you going to tell me?"

"There isn't much to tell. A project of my father's was sabotaged, and I need to find out who's responsible."

"The police can't help?"

"No." She didn't elaborate.

Steve sighed. "When I call in my favors, one of them's going to be a request to hear the whole story."

"Find out who bought that timer and I'll tell you gladly."

"Do my best. I'll be in touch, Michele."

After she'd hung up, Michele sat at the desk in her office for a long time thinking. There were innumerable details she could check, nebulous though they were. The rival companies here in Atlanta that could handle a project the size of the Techtron contract numbered only a half dozen or so; she could begin looking into them, searching for the signs of equipment, supplies, and manpower being readied for a big project and, conversely, those same resources being already committed to an ongoing project and unavailable for anything new. She could piece together the recent histories of the owners of those companies and look for ambition and/or a driving need for a lucrative contract.

Jon had promised to do some checking on his own,

but Michele had no intention of leaving it entirely up to him. He knew the construction business better than she did, but she had the training and experience in gathering evidence piece by piece and putting it together.

Assuming she was given the time.

She was grateful to have the work to do, not because it took her mind off all the problems—it could hardly do that—but because she felt less helpless with a definite plan of action, however sketchy. And if she was never distracted from her longing to be with Ian, at least working herself to the point of exhaustion allowed her to sleep at night.

Two weeks passed, with no results on either her end or his and no chance for them to safely meet, and Michele was very conscious of the growing tension in them both. She could hear it in Ian's voice when they talked briefly on the phone, and she felt it in herself. And it wasn't just one kind of tension, because they couldn't be together; they were edgy waiting for their saboteur to make his next move, frustrated by their inability to find answers, and very conscious that time was running out.

The only bright spot during those weeks was Michele's inner certainty that she was indeed pregnant. She almost held her breath when her period was late, but by the fourth day she was sure. She called her doctor—from the office, of course—and made an appointment after briefly discussing the matter with him and settling on a date that would ensure the test was accurate. She decided not to mention it to Ian until it was confirmed, but she was certain.

It was a bittersweet joy. She felt all the wonder and happiness of a woman who wanted her baby with all her heart, and yet she couldn't forget the presence of a nameless, faceless enemy who could destroy everyone she loved—possibly even her unborn child. Ian had promised to be careful, and so had Jon, but Michele's anxiety wasn't eased.

And when the answers finally did begin falling into place, they brought only a new set of questions.

Steve came through with flying colors, even though it took him nearly three weeks to cover the necessary area on the West Coast. He sent the list directly to Michele's computer, and it was obvious he'd done a thorough job. As soon as she looked over the information, she called him.

"I owe you a dozen favors," she said.

"And I'll make you pay through the nose." Then he sobered. "Any help at all?"

She studied the list on her computer screen. "I'm not sure yet. You've got about thirty names here, and all but three of them are located on the West Coast *and* legitimately involved with demolitions work. No addresses on these three?"

"No, sorry. The names are probably aliases; all three bought a timer from a man who had no business selling them, and all three paid in cash; it's a miracle he got names from them. I got descriptions of two: George Norris is a blonde in his twenties and looked mad as hell at somebody, and Robert Andrews is dark, slick, and probably a thief of some kind. The opinions are those of the man who sold the timer."

Michele looked at the third name on the list. "And Nicholas South?"

"Now, there," Steve said with satisfaction, "we hit a wall. Our shady dealer in rare explosives just couldn't seem to recall what Mr. South looked like. In fact, he had all the signs of having been paid to keep his mouth shut. Would your man be cagey enough to buy a little silence?"

"He might," Michele said slowly, feeling the first flicker of real hope. "Steve, do you think that dealer would be willing to talk if the price were right?"

"I think he'd sell his soul for the right price. How high do you want to go?"

"As high as it takes. Just get the information and I'll wire you the money."

"It may take a few days or more," Steve warned. "The guy operates out of a van, and he doesn't park in one place for very long."

"Let me know as soon as you find out something."

"Right."

Michele didn't know if a description of the elusive Mr. South would do her any good at all, but, like Steve, she was doubly suspicious of anyone who paid to cover his tracks. As for the companies and men she was checking here in Atlanta, four rival construction firms had been eliminated with fair certainty; all four were currently involved in lengthy projects demanding all their resources and couldn't possibly have taken on the Techtron contract. She had two companies left to check; if those proved doubtful as well, then she'd have to try and discover another motive for the sabotage.

As the days turned into weeks, his simmering rage began to boil. All the careful planning, the moves timed and executed with the precision of chess pieces on a board, had not produced the results he'd expected.

Something was wrong. They weren't reacting as they should have done. By now, the fight should have been fully begun. They should have been tearing each other to shreds while he enjoyed the sight from the sidelines. Instead, the tense balance had somehow been maintained, with both families quiet.

He thought about it for a long time, struggling to contain his rage so that he could consider. He knew, of course, about the curious twist of fate that had entered his game; that knowledge was certainly a weapon he could use to his advantage. But he had decided to time that perfectly, to choose just the right moment to strike the final destructive blow.

Still, he had the uneasy feeling that someone else was using the very knowledge he meant as a weapon somehow to heal the damage he had already inflicted. Not them, no. They couldn't possibly have overcome what he'd done to them; there was no way she'd trust him after he had hurt her brother. And they hadn't seen each other, he knew that.

But he was disturbed. His plan had been meticulously arranged, yet now he could feel an alien touch, a ghostly hand deflecting or softening his blows. The conduits through which he had so carefully fed information were being severed before they could be used to further antagonize, the buffers between himself and his enemies moved silently out of the way. He was less protected now.

He looked down at the devices on the table, and his control over rage slipped another notch. So be it, then, he decided angrily. He would have to be bolder, strike with less concern of protecting himself. Another push, and if they failed to react, follow that with a deadly shove.

It occurred to him that deaths would bring the police into the situation, but he was beyond caring. No one would look further than the feud for suspects. There had been no fatalities in more than a hundred years; perhaps it was time to teach them a forgotten lesson about the power of hate.

Like the month before, December bowed with a cold rain designed to make warm-blooded Southerners shiver miserably. With the Christmas shopping season in full swing, the city was gaily decorated, but the bright splashes of color, vibrant lights, and glittering tinsel did little to cheer gloomy skies.

Michele, who usually scorned anything but a light jacket in winter, dug her fur coat out of the closet whenever she left for work each morning. Her workload was unusually light for this time of year, so she was able to devote most of her time to the painfully slow search for an enemy.

She had done her best to track down Jon's informant,

but that gentleman had either hidden —or been hidden— very thoroughly, and she had no luck. As for the rest, she spent long hours sifting through information, frustrated by the elusive feeling that she was looking in the wrong place entirely, that there was something she was missing.

"Michele?"

She looked up from the papers spread out on her desk to find her brother standing in the doorway. It was late Friday afternoon, the leaden skies and bitter cold outside promising sleet or freezing rain within hours.

"Has something happened?" she asked instantly, her heart leaping into her throat.

"No, not that I know of." He came into the office and sat down in the chair in front of her desk, looking as tired and tense as she felt. He'd been unusually quiet these last weeks, almost subdued, watching her from time to time with an expression she couldn't define. He had managed to keep their father from retaliating against the Stuarts, though not without a struggle; Michele had overheard at least one bitter exchange between them and knew that the two of them were at odds for the first time she could remember.

Jon was becoming convinced despite himself. He had quietly agreed with Michele when she eliminated four of their rivals, and had offered the reluctant opinion that the remaining two firms were already stretched too thin to be able to take on the Techtron project.

"What are you doing here?" she asked finally, gathering the papers into a neat stack and tucking them into a folder.

"I came to take you home."

"Jon—"

"Look, you've barely come up for air in weeks. You drag home at eight or nine o'clock at night, and you head back here before this place is even open for business. The security guard downstairs told me they've been letting you in and out because you're the first one here and the last to leave. You can't keep up this pace, Michele. You've lost weight, and you look so brittle I'd be afraid to touch you."

Jon wasn't the first to scold her, although her doctor had been even more blunt about the matter. She'd lost eight pounds he didn't think she could spare, and even though that happened sometimes early in a pregnancy, he told her she had to start taking better care of herself. Especially now.

Michele had made an effort after the doctor's warning, forcing herself to eat and to get enough sleep, but she hadn't been able to slow down because what she was doing was so terribly important to her. With every day that passed, she was more and more conscious of time ticking away. Something was going to happen; she could feel it like a cold, dank fog, like something that could be seen and felt but not captured.

She set the file aside and shrugged as she gave in to her brother, feeling the tension in her shoulders and neck. "All right, all right. I'll go home."

"Good," he said. "You can get some rest before the party."

Blinking, she said, "What party?"

Patiently, he said, "Look at your calender. It's that annual charity do to raise money for the disadvantaged kids in the city. Christmas, remember? It's just around the corner. You go with me every year, and I bought our tickets a couple of months ago."

"I really don't think—"

"It'll do you good to get out. Jackie'll be there. Come on, Michele."

It was a black-tie event, the first of the glittering social functions scheduled between now and New Year's, and Michele had attended most of them in the past. On the point of trying to get out of it this year, she suddenly remembered that Ian always went; she'd seen him across the ballroom.

Did Jon know that? Gazing at her brother's veiled eyes, she had the uneasy feeling that he did. It would be insane for her to think she could be in the same room with Ian—even a crowded ballroom—without giving her feelings away. And she hadn't yet told him about the baby, wanting to be with him for that, to see his face when he heard; how could she stay away from him when the longing to be in his arms tortured her?

"Come on, Michele," Jon repeated. "You promised, and I'm holding you to it."

"Is Dad going?" she asked slowly.

"No. He said he had things to do."

It was madness, but she wasn't surprised to hear herself give in. "All right."

Jon's eyes flickered, but that was his only reaction. He rose to his feet. "Get your coat, and I'll walk you to the car."

Michele didn't argue. Even with herself.

A few hours later, she stood before the dressing mirror in her bedroom, fastening her earrings. A long, hot bath had eased some of her physical tension, but she knew she was still edgy. She had tried to disguise at least the outward indications of that, applying makeup to soften her face and shade her eyes, and wearing a gown that was made up of flowing lines and soft material.

She wore her hair in a style less severe than usual; it was piled high on her head in a mass of loose curls, with a number of long curling strands allowed to trail over one shoulder. The gown she wore was a shimmering gray; long-sleeved and with a deep V neckline, it had a full skirt falling from a high waist.

She'd been too busy to pay much attention to her own appearance these last weeks, and for the first time, she could see the signs of strain in herself. With no excess weight to spare, the lost pounds had left her obviously thinner, but despite that she looked neither ill nor exhausted. Her eyes seemed larger, her cheekbones more prominent, but it was a finely honed look as if some drastic alteration had taken place inside her, leaving her starkly different and yet curiously more focused, more centered than she had been before.

It was too early in her pregnancy for that to cause such outward changes, but Michele thought the child she carried was at least partly responsible nonetheless—because of her emotional awareness. There was a bond between her and Ian now that could never be broken no matter what happened. Their love had created a new life, a tiny scrap of humanity both Logan and Stuart. The bridge they had sought to build between their families had become in part a living connection.

Michele held on to that awareness, because it gave her strength. She went to her closet and got the cloak Jackie had talked her into buying back in the fall. The long, hooded cloak was pale blue and trimmed in ermine; it was both exotic and dramatic, and Michele hadn't yet worn it because she hadn't been able to get up the nerve. Tonight she swung it around her shoulders automatically with no more than a faint inner shrug and went downstairs.

Jon didn't say very much during the drive downtown to the hotel where the event was being held, but he did tell her something that made her believe he was well on his way to being convinced someone other than a Stuart was working against them.

"I played a little hardball with one of the electrical inspectors this morning."

Michele looked at him, worried. "What did you do?"

Jon smiled thinly. "Since we weren't having any luck finding my guy at city hall, I went straight to the horse's mouth. I took with me half a dozen signed statements from other builders who are positive he took bribes to delay their projects. They didn't have proof, mind you, but he knew damned well the statements alone would get him fired."

"He talked?"

"He sure did. He admitted he'd been paid to delay us. The arrangements were made by phone, and he was paid in cash, by messenger; half up front and half a week after our crews were forced to stop working. His employer didn't identify himself, but from what was said, he gathered the man was a Stuart."

"It wasn't," Michele said flatly.

"No," Jon said just as flatly, "I don't think it was."

"Why?" she asked.

"Because the inspector had a lot more to say. And he was surprised I didn't know." Jon snorted almost angrily. "Serves me right for being so damned convinced the Stuarts were behind it that I never looked for anything else."

"Tell me."

"He said there had been a lot of quiet talk these last weeks about somebody working against us and the Stuarts. Apparently, it's all over the grapevine: inspectors, suppliers, even the crews on both jobs. A hell of a lot of money's been paid in bribes and kickbacks, but nobody knows who's behind it. The thing is, it's as if this guy has inside information; he seems to know exactly when and where to cause delays that cost both us and the Stuarts in time and money."

"You think he's buying the information?"

"He's bought everything else." Jon sounded frustrated. He was handling the car easily despite the cast on his left arm, and scowling through the windshield.

After a moment, Michele said, "Have you told Dad?"

"I've tried. He doesn't believe it, Misha. He's convinced the Stuarts are behind everything. I've been able to hold him back only because both projects have been stalled. But I don't know how much longer I can manage it."

There was little she could say to that, but something else was nagging at her. "Jon, you said a lot of money had been spent in bribes and kickbacks. How much?"

"Can't know for sure. Tens of thousands. Maybe even hundreds of thousands."

Recalling all the data she'd collected on the last two possible rivals, Michele said, "That's too much. None of our rivals could spread that much money around even if they wanted to; all their capital's tied up, and their personal fortunes just wouldn't cover it."

"Then who the hell's after us?"

"I don't know. But we have to find out."

The remainder of the drive was silent. Michele tried to think of an answer, but all she had were questions. If not a business rival, then *who*? If not for the gain of the Techtron project, then *why*?

Ian had almost decided to skip the charity event. He was hardly in the mood to make polite social chitchat even for a good cause. He was here because he had suddenly remembered that Michele had attended last year.

The hardest thing he'd ever done was to stay away from her after they had agreed it was best. The brief daily phone calls had done nothing except heighten his desire to see her, to be with her, until he felt frustration gnawing at him. Simply not seeing her was bad enough; the knowledge that someone was intent on playing very nasty games with both families made him worry constantly about her safety. He wanted her with him, wanted her close, so that he could watch over her.

If anything happened to Michele, Ian knew he'd lose his mind. It was an icy fear that never left him now. He had never felt that kind of fear before, but he knew that it would always be with him, for as long as he lived. Because he loved Michele, he would never shake the terror of losing her.

But that was a fear that came from love, a natural result of giving a hostage to fortune. It was the other pressures that were so rawly painful. The pressures that came from a feud neither of them wanted any part of. He knew it was madness to come here tonight hoping to at least see her across a crowded room, because it would only be a glimpse that would torment rather than satisfy. And that aching knowledge made him all the more determined to stop the damnable feud.

The bitter legacy of his family's hate was this— that he was forced to steal glances at the woman he loved.

He saw her when she came in with her brother. He had positioned himself across the huge room at an angle where he could best watch the entrance. There was quite a crowd, and because this was a buffet dinner, most of the people were on their feet and moving around. A pianist in the far corner played music that was no more than unlistened-to background noise.

The instant he saw Michele, Ian forgot about giving himself away to anyone who could be watching. He couldn't take his eyes off her. She was wearing a gleaming gown the exact shade of her gray eyes, and as she moved into the room beside her tall brother she looked beautiful and delicate—and changed.

She had lost a little weight, and that made her appear almost fragile. Yet there was something about her that was stronger as well, an elusive intensity as if all the force of will that made Michele uniquely herself had been compressed and focused inside her. Rather than breaking from the stresses all around her, she had grown stronger and surer. Like a diamond, Ian thought, a thing of incredible beauty and unmatched strength born under unimaginable pressures.

He watched as she and her brother were joined by the red-headed Jackie and a tall, dark man who was apparently her date. It was almost impossible for him to think about anything except Michele, but gradually he became conscious of something nagging at him. There was a wrongness somewhere, something he saw or didn't see, and it disturbed him.

• • •

"Ian's here," Jackie said in a low voice, after pulling Michele from the group that had gradually formed around them. Jon and Cole Sutton were talking with a man about computers, and neither seemed to notice their dates moving away.

"I know." Michele hadn't dared search the room for him, but she knew he was here because she felt it.

Jackie stared at her, lips compressed. "It's still going on, isn't it? You and him."

Michele had avoided her friend since they'd returned from Martinique, partly because she'd been working so hard and partly because of Jackie's feelings about Ian. Now, steadily, she said, "I love him. And he loves me. Is that so hard for you to believe?"

"The explosion—"

"Ian wasn't responsible for that. And neither was his father. There's somebody else, Jackie, somebody who wants to destroy both families."

"That's insane."

"Yes, it is. But true. Even Jon can see that now."

Jackie was frowning, but her expression cleared as Cole Sutton slipped away from the group around Jon and joined them. "Did you sell him a computer?" she asked, slipping her arm familiarly through his.

"No luck. He's the old-fashioned kind." Cole was a tall, dark man somewhere in his thirties with a face so hand-some his features were almost delicate. He had deep blue eyes and a slow smile, and he reminded Michele of some-one although she hadn't been able to decide who it was. He was a sales representative for a high-tech company that had a flourishing office in Atlanta, and like many salesmen he was a charming man with an easy manner.

Jackie had been seeing him for only a few months, but she had fallen quickly and hard. Having finally met the man, Michele could see why, but he made her just a little uncomfortable. Something about the way he stood beside

Jackie gave Michele the impression that he was hardly conscious of her, and that was definitely odd considering that they were lovers.

"Better luck next time," Jackie sympathized, smiling up at him with unshadowed love.

Cole didn't appear to notice that look, since he was glancing around the room absently—but someone else did. Michele saw her brother coming toward them, and in the few seconds that Jon's eyes rested on Jackie's face, his feelings were as plain as neon.

He's in love with her.

For the first time, Michele understood why her undoubtedly handsome brother dated rarely and tended to throw himself into his work. Jackie had never shown the slightest romantic interest in Jon, treating him with casual friendliness and nothing more; she had even confided in him about her romantic problems with other men. And now she was glowingly in love with Cole, totally unconscious of Jon except as Michele's brother.

Michele felt a pang of compassion and wondered why she had been so blind to his feelings before this.

"I'm ready to eat," Jon said calmly as he joined them. "How about the rest of you?"

There was nothing Michele could say to help him, so she said nothing. They went to the buffet together and then found a table, all four of them talking casually. The noise level in the room increased, and Michele could feel her tension increase as well until she could hardly stand it. She excused herself softly and left the table, but instead of going to the restroom she retrieved her cloak from the attendant and slipped out a side door that led to the rooftop terrace.

In good weather, the glass doors of the ballroom were left open so that guests could wander out onto the terrace. The frigid weather tonight made that impractical, so the doors had remained closed and the lights on the terrace hadn't been turned on. Michele had been here more than once, and knew her way despite the darkness. She avoided the light spilling out from the ballroom as she made her way to the far corner of the terrace and stood looking out on the lights of the city.

It was bitterly cold, but the sleet had held off and there was no wind. Even high above the city, the air was still, the traffic noises from below only muted sounds.

Michele waited. And when he came to her, she turned instantly to burrow into his arms. "I couldn't stand it anymore," she whispered, all her senses flaring almost painfully at the touch of him against her.

"I know. I couldn't either." Ian turned her face up and kissed her, the first gentleness deepening rapidly to become intense hunger. He held her slender body tightly, knowing that this was the danger they'd faced by staying away from each other; the very passion that had drawn them together in the face of a centuries-old feud was literally too powerful to be denied, and the long separation had built pressure in them both like steam under a tightly closed lid.

It didn't matter that more than a hundred people laughed and talked only a few yards away, many of whom would have been shocked to see a Logan and a Stuart in each other's arms. All the reason and common sense and caution in the world couldn't lessen their response to each other.

Eight

"Michele. God, I've missed you." Ian raised his head at last, staring down at her, realizing with a jolt that it would be years before he knew her face the way he needed to; every time he looked at her she was new and different and more lovely. Now, in the faint lights of the city all around them, she was almost unreal, like something he had dreamed out of the night.

She laughed shakily, clinging to him. "I've missed you, too. I knew it was crazy to come here tonight, but I had to see you, even if it was just for a little while—"

Ian kissed her again, trying to satisfy the craving inside him and knowing it was impossible. "A little while isn't enough," he said huskily. "Michele—"

He broke off abruptly as she stiffened in his arms. Even though the light was too faint for him to see it, he knew she had gone pale. Keeping one arm around her, he turned slowly and saw a tall figure moving toward them across the terrace. All his instincts told him who it was, and even though the light from the ballroom was behind

Jon and left his features in shadow, Ian could feel himself tense warily.

"Ian." There was no expression in the even voice, no hint of emotion or reaction of any kind. It was the first time he had spoken to Ian in their adult lives.

"Jon." It was a peculiar feeling, Ian thought, a sense of knowledge without familiarity, of caution and understanding, affinity and distance. They had been set apart all their lives by the feud, but now the woman both of them loved was a connection between them.

Michele's brother came toward them until he was only a few feet away, then stopped. Still without inflection, he said, "They're paging you in the ballroom. An emergency call."

The apparent calm of Jon's reaction hadn't eased Ian's wariness, but he felt some of Michele's stiffness drain away as if something in her brother's voice had lessened her own fears. She looked up at him, clearly more worried by the message than by the messenger.

"Something's happened?"

"I left this number with the security service at the building," Ian told her.

"I'll wait here," she said. When he hesitated, she added quietly, "It's all right."

Ian knew from Michele's reports that her brother had been looking for evidence just as they were, but she hadn't been sure that he believed both families had a common enemy, which made Jon's calm now hardly reassuring. Still, Ian had to trust Michele's assessment, and he couldn't believe her brother had any violent intentions.

Not, at least, at the moment.

"I'll be back," he told her, reluctantly leaving her to cross the terrace. As he came abreast of the other man, he hesitated, then said, "I'd never hurt her, Jon."

After a moment, Jon's only response was, "Better take your call."

Ian glanced back at Michele, standing so quiet and still, then swore under his breath and left them alone.

When he had gone, Michele watched her brother cross the remaining few feet between them and stand by the low terrace wall gazing out on the city. Having been braced for a thunderclap, this mild reaction made her more than a little wary, but she wondered now if the combination of Jon's growing belief in their faceless enemy and his seemingly hopeless love for Jackie had made him examine his own feelings. All she knew for certain was that he hadn't been surprised to find her out here with Ian.

"Cold place for a tryst," he said finally in the same expressionless tone.

It was cold, but Michele was only now aware of it. She drew her cloak more closely around her. "Not a tryst. It wasn't planned. None of it was planned." Her voice was as quiet as his, almost hushed, as if they were both afraid of disturbing some fine, delicate balance of emotion.

He drew a short breath. "I think I always knew it would happen someday. From the time you were about fourteen, and your favorite story was *Romeo and Juliet.*"

"I'd forgotten that."

"Had you?"

"Consciously, yes. I loved that story. But I hated the ending. People shouldn't have to die for love, Jon. And they shouldn't have to hurt their families *because* they love."

After a moment, still without looking at her, Jon said, "When you came back from Martinique, I knew you were different. Then the day I got out of the hospital, you went out, and when you came home, I knew there was a man. I couldn't even accept the possibility that it was Ian Stuart, but you were fighting so hard to prove they weren't our enemies, and I couldn't get that out of my mind. I—finally called your hotel in Martinique to find out if he'd been registered there."

"When did you call?"

"A week ago."

He had known that long and had said nothing. She had done her brother an injustice in believing he'd react instantly and with hate, Michele realized. It seemed that Jon had given this a great deal of thought before facing his sister.

"Dad doesn't know." It wasn't a question.

"He isn't ready to hear that. I don't know if he ever will be, Michele."

She stepped close to him. "And what about you? How do you feel about it?"

An odd little laugh escaped Jon, a sound that wasn't amusement. "Hell, I don't know. I thought I hated him. But I came out here expecting to find you two together . . . and I didn't feel much of anything. I wanted to be suspicious of his motives, but I saw the way he looked at you. And the way you looked at him."

"We didn't want to hurt anyone. That's why we've stayed away from each other. We want to prove to Dad and Ian's father that someone else is working against the families, and stop the feud now before someone really gets hurt." Michele hesitated, then added quietly, "We're going to be married, Jon."

Without surprise, her brother said, "Dad can't stop you. But he won't accept it."

"Will you?"

Jon turned to look at her for the first time. "I have to, don't I? You wouldn't have gone this far without really thinking it through, not knowing all the risks you're taking. There's nothing I could say to you that you haven't already said to yourself. It can't have been easy for you. If you . . . love him after everything you've heard for twenty years, then it must be a pretty strong love."

"It is. The strongest, surest thing I've ever felt."

He half nodded. "That's why I have to accept it. Maybe

Dad can cut off his nose to spite his face, but I can't. You're my sister, Michele. I just want you to be happy."

Though she was still afraid of her father's reaction, Jon's acceptance lifted at least part of her dread. "I was so afraid you'd hate me," she said unsteadily.

He smiled crookedly. "No. Right now, I'm finding it a little hard to hate anyone. I've decided I don't much fancy being a lemming. You were right about that. Five centuries is too long to hate."

"Good," Ian said in a quiet voice as he rejoined them. "We can use your help. Our not-so-friendly bomber has struck again."

Michele half turned to him, instinctively reaching out until his long fingers closed over hers. "Not your building?"

"The elevators. All of them except one; apparently, the man was scared off by security before he could finish the job. The guards saw someone disappear into the stairwell, then everything hit the fan and they were too busy to chase him."

"Was anyone hurt?" Michele asked anxiously.

"No. But I'd like to know how in hell he got into the building."

She looked at her brother. "It wasn't Dad, was it?"

Jon shook his head immediately. "No. He gave me his word he wouldn't retaliate without telling me, and he doesn't break his word."

Accepting that, Michele looked back at Ian and told him what Jon had found out from the bribed inspector. He heard her out in silence, then said, "If that many people know someone else is involved, one of them may know something that can help us. I'll start questioning our men in the morning."

"I'll do the same," Jon said. "And our suppliers."

Looking at Michele, Ian said reluctantly, "I have to get to the building. Dad was notified right after I was, so he'll be there. I have to talk to him."

"Will he listen?"

"He'll listen." Ian sounded grim. "I'm not going to give him a choice about it."

"I'll wait for you inside, Michele," Jon said, leaving them alone on the terrace.

After a moment, Ian pulled her into his arms and held her tightly. "Was he being tactful? Or does it test his resolution to see us together?"

A bit wryly, she said, "Maybe a bit of both. It wasn't easy for him; I think he's a little numb. But at least he's on our side now."

Ian kissed her. "I'm glad—for all our sakes, but especially for yours. I know how much it would have hurt you if he hadn't been able to accept this."

Hugging as much of him as she could, Michele said fiercely, "I just wish it were *over*. I don't want to be afraid that something terrible's going to happen. I want to be with you. I love you so much . . ."

"I love you, too, baby," he murmured.

The endearment brought vividly to mind what she wanted to tell him, but there just wasn't time. It wasn't something meant to be related during a brief phone call or hurriedly in a stolen meeting on a cold terrace.

She drew away slowly. "You'd better go. I'll call you tomorrow."

Ian framed her face in his hands and kissed her, then again because it wasn't enough, it could never be enough between them. "Be careful," he warned tautly. "Whoever he is, this enemy's too bomb-happy for my peace of mind."

Michele nodded and watched as he crossed the terrace and went inside. For the first time, she felt very, very cold. And very much alone.

He had watched and listened from the deepest shadows of the terrace, his bitter rage growing. Damn them! They'd made peace among them, forming a solid union despite the odds and a lingering wariness between the men. He should have destroyed the love affair at the first sign, he realized, shattered it before bonds of trust could be formed. Now the three members of the younger generation had formed an alliance, all working to neutralize his attempts to disrupt the careful balance between their families.

And even worse. They knew about him. It was only a matter of time before they put all the pieces together an discovered who their common enemy was.

For an instant, as the woman stood alone near the edge of the terrace, he was tempted to leap across the darkness separating them and push her over. Just a quick shove, and she'd fall to her death. Problem at least partially solved.

But he resisted the hot impulse, watching with glittering eyes as she went slowly back inside. He had to get them all, the three of them. And he had to do it in such a way that their fathers would be utterly convinced who was guilty.

That, he thought with satisfaction, would certainly push them both over the brink of sanity. Their children engulfed by the feud, neither of them would stop until one or both of them was dead. With a little luck—it would be both.

The plan began forming rapidly in his feverish mind. They thought the feud should end—so did he. But he wanted a swifter, cleaner death than the whimpering peace they sought. He intended for the pure white flame of revenge to annihilate all the dark, twisted remnants of hate.

Even the ones inside himself.

He had to do it. They'd given him no choice. He had to burn away the darkness before it consumed him.

Ian looked at the damage, thinking that even if the security guards had failed to capture the culprit, at least they'd managed to prevent the spread of a fire that could have been a great deal worse. All the elevators except one had been locked off on the tenth floor, and that was where they'd been rigged to explode. The charges had been powerful enough to snap the cables and send the cars crashing to the bottom of the shafts, and the saboteur had covered his retreat by flinging a bottle filled with gasoline and a lit fuse against a wall as he fled.

The remaining express elevator had escaped destruction, either because it had been on the ground floor while the saboteur worked or because the man had simply run out of time. Following their instructions, the security guards had not alerted the police, and no one outside the building had reported the explosions; with the size of the structure, it was unlikely that anyone had even heard. Their elusive enemy, Ian thought, seemed to be careful not to call too much attention to his work; apparently, he wanted the fight to be between the families and no one else.

Ian had ordered the express elevator thoroughly checked, but there'd been no sign of tampering. The other elevators stood open on this floor, their bare, smoke-blackened shafts all that was visible, and since the doors had been jammed by the explosions, he had roped them off. He glanced aside where his father stood talking to one of the guards, and braced himself mentally for the struggle he expected to take place.

A few minutes later, as Brandon Stuart joined his son, he said bitterly, "Damn them."

"The Logans aren't responsible," Ian said quietly.

"Oh, for God's sake, Ian—"

Ian turned away from his father and walked down the hall to a lounge area that was partly furnished since this floor had been completed. Some of the security guards and a couple of the company electricians were still grouped around the elevators, and he had no intention of discussing the situation with too many listening ears; at this point, he wasn't sure whom he could trust. He sat down on the arm of a chair and loosened his tie, waiting for his father to join him.

As he did, Brandon said, "Surely you've given up on those fantasies of yours."

"They aren't fantasies, Dad. Someone else is stirring up trouble between the families. Someone who knows just how to use the feud to his own advantage."

"What advantage? Who would have anything to gain by such a scheme?"

"I don't know yet."

Flatly, Brandon said, "I've given you all the time I could, Ian, and you haven't been able to answer that question. So I will. None of our competitors would go this far. Except the Logans. And *they* have everything to gain."

"It isn't them."

"What makes you so damned sure?"

"Because Jon and Michele Logan are working just as hard as I am to prove someone else is involved."

"I don't believe it. No matter what you've heard—"

"Will you listen to me? It is not them. We've agreed both families have an enemy, and it's beginning to look like it isn't a business competitor at all."

"Agreed?" Brandon's eyes narrowed. "You've talked to them about this?"

Very quietly, Ian said, "I'm in love with Michele."

"What?" It was little more than a whisper, genuinely shocked.

Ian kept his own voice quiet and calm. "We met on Martinique. We're going to be married, Dad."

"You're out of your mind."

"No. We're going to be married."

"Do you know what you're saying? Marry a Logan? For God's sake, Ian, sleep with her if you have to, but I'd sooner have a painted whore in the family than that—"

Ian stood up.

For a long moment, Brandon Stuart gazed into the ice-blue eyes of his son, and what he saw there shook him badly. Softly, formally, he said, "I apologize for that remark."

Shaken himself by what he was feeling, by the white-hot rage that had swept through him, Ian turned away and walked over to the windows. He stood with his back to his father, trying to control his anger enough to speak.

"Ian . . . I'm sorry."

"Are you?" He heard the thick sound of his own voice, and cleared his throat harshly. "Sorry for what you said? Or sorry for hating a woman you don't even know?"

Brandon was silent.

Ian laughed shortly and turned to stare at his father. "I want you to understand something. Michele and I are going to be married. For her sake, I hope we can stop this insane feud and live here in peace. For all our sakes, I hope you can accept that. But right now, I don't give a sweet damn whether you do or not. She's the most important thing in my life. Everything else can go straight to hell."

"Including me?" Brandon's voice was mild, his eyes still watchful.

"If that's the way it has to be. I won't fight about this, Dad. And I won't hear another word against Michele. Ever. Accept it or not, it's up to you."

There was a long silence, tension quivering almost visibly in the air between the two men, and then Brandon said irritably, "Stop glaring at me, Ian." He hesitated, then added a bit dryly, "She must be some lady."

"She is." Ian forced himself to relax, knowing that the critical moment had passed safely, that his father was, at least, resigned. It was what he had hoped for when he'd made it plain he was prepared to sever all ties with his father; a genuine affection aside, Brandon Stuart's sense of family was too strong to allow him to risk losing his only son—no matter what.

"Does Charles Logan know about you two?"

"Not yet."

"It is," Brandon said, "an understatement to say he won't like it."

"That's one reason we're trying to find out who's behind the sabotage. As things stand now, he's convinced it's you and me; one whisper of my relationship with Michele, and she thinks he'll go right over the edge."

"She's right. In fact, I would have expected the same reaction from Jon. I assume he knows?"

"Yes. I think he's suspected for a while; he wasn't very surprised to have it confirmed. He's hardly . . . comfortable with the idea, but he accepts it. He loves his sister too much to lose her over this. And he agrees someone else is involved in the feud."

Brandon went to a chair and sat down, frowning. After a moment, he said, "Which brings me back to the original question. Who?"

Slowly, Ian said, "It's directed at both families, and the intent is apparently to set us at each other's throats. If it isn't a business competitor—and it's beginning to look like that idea was off base—then it has to be someone who hates both sides." He shook his head. "I don't believe either Jon or myself has made an enemy that rabid, and I know damn well Michele hasn't. Which leaves you and Charles Logan. The two of you must have an enemy in common."

"Besides each other, you mean?" Brandon said wryly.

"Think about it," Ian urged, sure he was on the right track. "There must be someone who has reason to hate you both, and very bitterly. Someone who would go to a great deal of time, trouble, and money in an all-out attempt to destroy you both, by using the feud to his advantage."

Shrugging, Brandon said, "I can't think of anyone I've crossed that badly. I may have been ruthless from time to time in business, but not enough to rouse the kind of hate you're talking about. Maybe he's after Logan alone, and using me as his weapon."

"Maybe. But I think he's after both families. And he's not just ruthless—he's deadly. Jon could have been killed in that explosion; God knows what'll happen next."

"More of the same, I'd guess. Whoever he is, he seems to favor explosives in elevators."

Ian sighed, the various kinds of frustration increasing until he thought he'd explode. "Michele traced the device used on their building to the West Coast, and got a list of buyers; the names don't mean anything to any of us, but one of them may have paid the seller to keep quiet. We're waiting for a description of that man now."

Brandon looked a little surprised, but then said, "I'd forgotten. She is an investigator, isn't she."

Ian nodded, frowning.

"You look worried," his father noted.

"I am. I've just realized a few things. Whoever he is, this bastard knows us. All of us. He has to assume that, given enough time, if Michele suspected a third party she'd have a good chance of finding out who it was; it's what she's trained to do. Now, he's going to realize sooner or later that his plan isn't working, and I'm betting on sooner. He's pushed both sides more than once, and we haven't struck out at each other."

"That isn't like us," Brandon murmured.

"No, it isn't. He could be getting nervous about that, especially if he suspects we're on to him. And the next time he hits . . . he may not aim at a building."

"Neither way is without tragedy."

Michele couldn't get that promise out of her head. She and Jon had spoken little during the drive home, both of them aware that what was important had already been said. Their father had been surprised to see them back so early, but neither of them had chosen to tell him about the explosion in the Stuarts' building; he'd find out soon enough.

Michele went upstairs and, instead of getting ready for bed, changed into jeans and a thick sweater. She took her hair down and washed away the makeup. She felt edgy and couldn't seem to get warm. Always, in the forefront of her mind, had been the awareness that someone could be hurt if the feud erupted, but it had occurred to her only tonight that if their common enemy lost patience with the stalemate between the families, he could abandon all caution. And, as Ian had said, he seemed too fond of explosives.

And elevators.

She paced her room restlessly, going over everything in her mind until she could hardly think straight. No matter how hard she tried to come up with answers, only the terrifying possibilities assumed a concrete form. He could decide to turn his attention to people instead of buildings, and if that happened, none of them would be safe.

It was almost midnight when Jon knocked softly on her door and poked his head in. "You have a call," he told her.

"Ian?"

"No. Said his name was Steve. Your contact on the West Coast?"

Quickly, Michele joined her brother out in the hall. "Yes. Where's Dad?"

"He's turned in for the night." Jon followed her down the stairs to the phone in the entrance hall, and stood waiting to hear if there was any new information.

She picked up the phone. "Steve?"

"Sorry to bother you so late, Michele." He sounded more than a little bothered himself.

"Never mind, I was up. Do you have the description?"

"No, that isn't it. Michele . . . I got a very weird message a little while ago. It's supposed to be from the man I've been trying to find again, the one who sold those timers, but I swear it doesn't sound like him."

"What's the message?"

"Got a pencil? You'd better write this down."

Michele found a pencil and pad in the drawer of the small table. "Okay. Ready."

"Here it is: I must warn them. Tell her this immediately. It is vital that she know. Sunday is dangerous. Story I told you was false. Unable to tell you the truth. The buyer is no stranger. Three devices, not one. Only they can stop him. Next days critical."

Frowning down at her neat printing on the pad, Michele said, "That's it?"

"That's it. Block-printed on unlined paper, and signed with scrawled initials. Michele, I never told the man why I was tracing the device, and I never mentioned a woman. But this message . . . it seems to be meant for you."

After a moment, Michele handed the pad to Jon and said, "How was it delivered?"

"Pushed under my door here at home. Which is another weird thing. I heard the bell, and when I went to answer it there was no one there. Just a folded sheet of paper. Since the message was damned specific about Sunday being dangerous, I thought I'd better call you right away."

"I'm glad you did." One statement on the message echoed in her head. Three devices, not one. And two had been used. "I really appreciate it, Steve."

"No problem. Hey—I'll mail the original to you first thing tomorrow. In fact, I'll express it."

"Thanks."

"And if you figure it out," Steve added wryly, "how about letting me in on it? I'm puzzled as hell."

Michele conjured a laugh. "I'll do that."

"Be careful."

"I will." She cradled the receiver slowly and looked at Jon, who was frowning over the message she'd copied. "Does that make any sense to you?" she asked him.

"Who's it from?"

165

"Supposedly, the man who sold the timer. But Steve says it doesn't sound like him."

"It sounds damned peculiar," Jon muttered. "She? Did he know you were behind the questions?"

"Not according to Steve." Michele picked up the phone again and called Ian's apartment, so worried that she felt almost sick with it. Three devices . . . band and there was no telling when—or if—that third one would be used. If the saboteur's patience was exhausted, he could have decided to strike twice in one night. The phone rang nearly a dozen times before she broke the connection and tried his office number. No answer. She hung up. "He must still be at the building."

Jon was making a second copy of the message. When he was done, he handed her the original, then glanced at his watch. "Midnight; we're already into Saturday."

"Sunday is dangerous," she murmured, staring down at the message as she read. "Next days critical. How would the man who sold the timer know what his customer meant to do—and when? And why warn us?"

"I don't know. But we can't afford to ignore any warning, no matter who it's from, or why."

"I have to see Ian," Michele said. She was thinking of the message, but that wasn't all that filled her mind. The brief moments they'd shared on the terrace had only sharpened her longing to be with him, and she was haunted by the knowledge that if something were to happen to either of them, he'd never know about their child.

Jon looked at her for a moment, then picked up the phone and called for a cab. "I don't want you driving," he said gruffly when he hung up. "If this bastard can wire elevators, he can wire cars; stay out of yours until I can have it checked over. And use the stairs at Ian's building." He hesitated, then added, "Don't worry if you aren't back by morning. I'll think of something to tell Dad."

She stood on tiptoe to kiss his cheek, but said fiercely, "I hate all this lying!"

"Better than the alternative," Jon pointed out. "At least for now. Besides, Dad may not have a chance to ask about you. It's way past time he was made to listen to a few hard truths. I'll tell him about the sabotage of the Stuarts' building and ask him who could have done it, since we didn't. And I'll hit him with everything else we know. Maybe I can finally get through to him, at least a little."

"We're running out of time."

"I know."

A few minutes later, in a cab heading downtown, Michele wondered for the first time if they were being watched. She wanted to reassure herself that the question was a paranoid one, but after all that had happened she knew it wasn't.

All around you are the shifting patterns of things seen—and unseen.

Odd how the fortune teller's predictions kept coming back to her so vividly. As if they had been somehow imprinted on her mind, stamped in her memory but prompted to surface only by some spur she had no conscious control over. She had tried more than once to remember all that had been said, but when she concentrated nothing would come to her except disjointed words and meaningless phrases; it was only when she least expected it that the whispers echoed softly in her mind.

She had no faith in either precognition or predestination; no belief in fortune tellers or fate. But she couldn't escape the uneasy feeling that there was a design to all this, that events were being carefully arranged for a specific purpose. And oddest of all was her impression that more than one hand was involved in the pattern.

She felt like a piece on a chessboard, involved in some obscure struggle for power and moved by the whim and the tactics of an invisible hand.

Roused from the unsettling thoughts by the arrival of her cab at Ian's apartment building, she paid the driver and got out, drawing her coat tighter around her against the cutting force of the rising wind. She hurried into the building, going straight to the security guard's desk.

"Is Mr. Stuart in?" she asked the same man who had been here on that night weeks before.

"No, ma'am. But he said you were to go up any time."

Michele glanced toward the bank of elevators, then located the door to the stairwell nearby. After a slight hesitation, she drew a pen and a small, spiral-ringed notebook from her purse, and jotted a quick note.

"I'll go up," she told the guard, then folded her note and handed it to him. "Will you give him this as soon as he comes in, please?"

"Yes, ma'am." The guard was blessedly incurious, merely accepting the note and saying nothing at all when she headed for the stairwell instead of the elevators. Still, she couldn't help hoping that the man was better at his job than he seemed, or that Ian was responsible for the total lack of curiosity or suspicion where she was concerned.

Ian's apartment was on the eighth floor, but Michele hardly noticed the climb. She let herself into his apartment, realizing only when she was inside that doors could also be wired to explode. It was a sickening realization.

She shrugged out of her coat and left it lying across the couch with her purse, moving restlessly around the neat, quiet living room. She had barely noticed how Ian's home looked the first time she was here, her attention wholly caught up with him and the feelings between them. Now she looked, trying to concentrate, trying not to worry because he wasn't here.

And gradually, as she wandered, she found a kind of peace in what she found. Ties. Connections between them. She found many of her favorite books on his shelves, her favorite music among his records and tapes, prints and watercolors and oils by her favorite artists on his walls.

The furnishings were in styles and colors she would have favored, their arrangements lending the spaciousness she preferred.

She settled on the comfortable couch at last, kicking off her shoes and curling up with her cheek resting on a pillow, the sense of him so strongly with her that she felt curiously content and just too tired to think anymore. The edges of fear retreated, and as quiet filled her mind she drifted off to sleep.

At first, she wasn't sure it was a dream, because why on earth would she dream of the striking old man who had stood outside the fortune teller's tent on Martinique? But it had to be a dream, because she knew she was asleep, and he certainly couldn't be here in the apartment even though she saw him clearly when he emerged from a shadowy corner of the room and stood looking down at her with gentle eyes.

"Have courage, child. It's nearly over now."

She wanted to ask him who he was and why he was here, but some part of her understood those answers without having to hear them. He was the hand of destiny, she realized, and his was both a kinder and a more compassionate touch than she had believed, guidance rather than compulsion. He was light and dark, yin and yang, creative and receptive, forever at odds, forever united, a divided force connected only by a fragile thread, seeking wholeness, struggling for harmony, fighting for love.

Are you? she asked, or thought she asked.

"How poetic you make it sound!" He was amused but kindly and with understanding. "I am Fortune, child. A roll of the dice, a turn of the card, a fork in the road."

Are you doing this to us?

"I only watch. And try to help. You have all the pieces now. The answers are within reach." He glanced aside, as if some sound had drawn his attention, then looked back at her with his gentle, unutterably sweet smile. "Courage," he repeated.

Michele opened her eyes with a start, feeling her heart thudding as she sat up. A glance at the clock glowing on Ian's stereo told her that less than an hour had passed. She looked around warily. Empty. The room was empty. It had only been a dream, of course, prompted by her own unsettled thoughts of fate and destiny. She drew a shaky breath of relief, but even then couldn't shake the sense of presence, couldn't totally dismiss the notion that he *had* been there, that strange old man, coming to her out of the night because he'd somehow known she was at the end of her rope and needed reassurance.

Of all the wild, impossible ideas . . .

"Michele?"

She hadn't heard him come in, but at the sound of his voice she jumped up from the couch and hurried to meet him. His arms closed about her instantly, lifting her off her feet as he held her tightly against him.

"I was so worried about you," she whispered. "He bought three devices, Ian. There's one he hasn't used yet."

"Three? Are you sure?"

"Steve got a message tonight from the man who sold them, and he called me at home—"

"Easy," Ian soothed, setting her back on her feet and kissing her gently. She was trembling, clearly strained to the breaking point, and he couldn't bear to see her that way. Even a diamond could be shattered if the blow fell in just the right place, and Michele had already withstood too much.

He guided her to the couch and sat down, drawing her into his lap and holding her. "You're tired. Just rest for a little while," he murmured into the soft, dark cloud of her hair. "We'll get through this, baby, I promise."

Clinging to him, she said unsteadily, "It just hit me tonight, all at once, that anything could happen now. Then the message came, and it didn't make sense, but I had to tell you about it. Jon called a cab for me because he wants to check my car out, and he told me not to take the elevator here—"

Michele broke off and drew a deep breath, trying to quiet her own surging emotions. But they wouldn't quiet. For the first time, she felt her own exhaustion, the strain of too much worry and fear held taut for too long, but it wasn't rest or sleep she needed, and she felt that, too. She needed to be with the man she loved, just be with him; she needed to draw strength from the certainty of their feelings.

Raising her head from his shoulder, Michele looked into his beautiful warm eyes, and her heart was thudding so hard she thought it would burst. "I don't need to rest," she whispered. "I need you."

Ian touched her cheek tenderly, and then his hand slid around to the nape of her neck, beneath the soft weight of her hair. He kissed her, the first gentleness disappearing rapidly as she made no effort to hide her own taut desire. Her mouth opened under his, her hands going to his neck as she moved restlessly in his lap, and a soft sound tangled in the back of her throat.

His concern for her had prompted gentleness rather than desire, but as always her honest need for him instantly ignited his own passion. It had been too long; no matter how urgent the worries and dangers surrounding them, once they were together nothing else seemed to matter.

He carried her to his bedroom, and to his bed. They were both too wound up to allow patience, too eager for one another to permit a slow joining. Clothing was flung aside carelessly in the lamplit quiet of the room, and they fell on the bed together.

"Love me," she whispered, trembling under the onslaught of his hungry caresses, burning with the feverish, all-consuming need to belong to him. The time apart had caged that necessity, but now it burst free like something alive and on the wing, and she gloried in the freedom of it.

He was murmuring to her, husky words of love and desire, his hands shaking as he touched her, and when he eased into her they both caught their breath raggedly.

Michele totally lost control in his arms, and she didn't care. The pleasure was so intense it was like being drawn into a whirlpool of sensation, a quickening spiral that wound tighter and tighter until she couldn't breathe, couldn't stop the sounds escaping her, couldn't do anything except cling to him wildly and cry out as all her senses shattered.

Nine

"Can you stay?" Ian asked quietly.

"Yes." She would have stayed even if it had been impossible, because she needed to be with him too badly to leave him. "Jon's going to have it out with Dad first thing in the morning, so he probably won't even notice I'm not there. If he does notice, Jon said he'd cover for me."

"I'm beginning to like your brother very much."

"He's been a bit of a surprise," Michele admitted. "I think he saw how badly I wanted to be with you right now, and he seems worried about how I'm holding up."

"You're too thin," Ian murmured, his fingers gently probing the tiny indentations between her ribs.

They were lying close together, and he was propped on an elbow as he gazed down at her. Michele opened her eyes slowly and looked up at him, relaxed now and feeling both stronger and more content than she had in weeks. She took his hand and guided it to rest on her lower stomach.

"I won't be for long," she said softly.

He actually paled, his darkening eyes fixed on their hands both resting over her slender body. His fingers moved slightly, almost compulsively, as if he were seeking signs that wouldn't be visible for weeks yet.

"You're sure?" he asked huskily.

"Yes. Do you mind?" She was watching his face intently, certain of his response but needing reassurance as any woman does at such a time. And she found it when his gaze lifted to hers, his eyes still dark and filled with tenderness and a moving look of wonder.

"Michele . . ." He kissed her, a slow, warm, drugging kiss that was love and delight and a purely male pride.

Understanding that last emotion made Michele laugh softly as her arms went up around his neck. "Didn't you think you had it in you?" she asked.

He chuckled as well, gathering her even closer against him. "I didn't know. You said there was a good chance, but that was weeks ago."

"As near as I could figure it," Michele said dryly, "that twenty-four hours we were together on Martinique was the perfect time for me to get pregnant. In fact, it was the only time all month I *could* have. My doctor once told me that he never recommended the rhythm method of birth control because it was so undependable, but that it would probably be as effective for me as the pill." Suddenly grave, she added, "It wasn't deliberate though, Ian. I hope you know that."

Just as seriously, he said, "There were two of us there, remember? I'm just as responsible for not taking precautions. In fact, when you told me it could have already happened, I wondered if maybe that's what I wanted. Now I'm sure. I love you, Michele Logan. And I want our child very, very much."

It was some time later before Michele could rouse herself from the blissful warmth that had surrounded them both, but she made the effort even though it cost her a pang to bring up what had to be faced. It wasn't over yet, and until it was the stolen moments with Ian couldn't be all peaceful ones.

"That message," she murmured. "You have to see it. There's a warning about Sunday. And next week. The copy I made is in my purse."

"I'll go get it," Ian said, clearly reluctant to leave her as he slid from the bed.

She banked pillows and sat up against them, absently drawing the covers higher. It was doubtful either of them would sleep before dawn, she knew, if then. And even though the last weeks had left her tired, just being with Ian gave her the energy and stamina she needed.

Besides that, their time together was too precious to waste in sleep, she decided.

While she waited for Ian to return, she thought about the strange dream she'd had, frowning a little over the peculiar things that had been said. Was her subconscious trying to tell her that all the pieces were there, right in front of her to see? She supposed that was the only explanation, but it still puzzled her that her subconscious had taken the form of an odd old man she had seen only once, weeks ago, outside a fortune teller's tent on Martinique.

Fortune teller . . . *I am Fortune.*

Well, maybe it made sense after all. Of a sort. She closed her eyes and tried to remember the predictions once again, but all she got were disjointed phrases. Two paths . . . neither way without tragedy . . . seeds sown . . . bitter fruit . . . cannot change what must be . . . the truth you feel. . . .

Opening her eyes and frowning across Ian's bedroom, she told herself yet again that it was absurd to look for answers in the meaningless words of a self-proclaimed psychic. She'd have better odds rolling dice.

A roll of the dice, a turn of the card, a fork in the road.

Twenty-six relatively blameless years, Michele thought

with a surge of rebellion, and now she was surrounded by a great deal too much cryptic nonsense. Fortune tellers and faceless enemies and mysterious messages.

"Why are you frowning?" Ian asked as he came in.

"Because nothing makes sense." She looked at him, and couldn't help but grin. "Although I must admit, being served a snack in bed by a naked man at three A.M. is certainly nothing to frown at. I could get used to this."

Chuckling, he placed the heavily laden tray on the bed and crawled in beside her. The tray held an assortment of cheese, crackers, fresh fruit, and various other snacks, as well as two tall glasses of milk. Ian handed her one of the glasses and clinked his against it very gravely.

"I was starving, and I noticed you didn't eat much at the party. Besides that, you can't tell me your doctor didn't scold you for losing weight."

"He just mentioned it in passing," Michele murmured.

"I'll bet."

Michele took refuge in her milk and wrinkled her nose after the first sip. "I never did like this stuff."

"Drink it," Ian said, and fed her a cracker before she could protest.

She laughed at him but felt warmed by his concern. Conscious of an appetite for the first time in days, she ate enough to satisfy him, and then they both continued to snack while he frowned over her copy of the odd message.

"As paranoid as it sounds," she offered after a few minutes, "do you think this could possibly be a ruse of some kind, a trick from the very man we're after? Or am I hearing the wrong kind of hoofbeats?"

Ian blinked, then nodded as he understood the reference. "When you hear hoofbeats, think horses, not zebras?"

"Right."

"The most likely explanation is usually the correct one," he noted thoughtfully. "It's a little hard to believe that whoever's against us would go to all the trouble of warning us, and putting us on guard. At the same time, I'm having a problem believing that the shady character who sold the timers would send a message like this one—apparently aimed directly at you."

"That's one of the things I can't figure out," she muttered, nibbling on an apple that Ian had cored and sliced. "Steve swears he never mentioned a woman, never even said he was trying to get information for someone else."

Ian studied the message. "The buyer is no stranger," he read slowly. "No stranger to the seller? Or to us? Sunday is dangerous, next days critical. Only they can stop him."

"Weird, isn't it?" Something else about the message was bothering her, something she couldn't make come clear in her mind. The sentences themselves were wrong, she thought, misleading in a way she couldn't put her finger on, as if there was a pattern that she was missing.

"What does Jon think?"

"That we can't afford to ignore any warning, no matter how enigmatic it is, or whom it comes from."

"He's right. We'll all have to be especially careful tomorrow, and somehow figure out why next week is critical."

Michele looked at him worriedly. "How can we be more careful than we have been? How do we guard against a lunatic with a habit of hiring middlemen to plant explosives? Whether we believe the message or not, we have to assume there's another timer—or some kind of device—that hasn't been used yet. Being on guard and having good security hasn't stopped him so far; he could booby-trap anything."

"About all we *can* do is take cabs and stay out of elevators." Ian shook his head. "Why elevators? First the one in your family's building, and then ours last night. If he just wanted to stall completion of the buildings—or make it look that way—then why choose elevators as his targets?"

Michele had been around the construction business long enough to see what he was getting at. "It is strange," she agreed slowly. "There are a hundred other things he could have done. Sabotage the electrical systems, the air conditioning, the plumbing—any of those would have taken a lot more time and money to repair, and the damage would have been more widespread."

"We're missing something," Ian said. "I don't know what it is, but there's a key somewhere. I asked Dad last night if he and your father had an enemy in common—"

A sudden chill shot through Michele, and she stiffened. "That's it," she breathed unsteadily as the words surfaced vividly in her mind. " 'Even now, the seeds sown decades ago grow twisted to bear a dark and bitter fruit.' *Decades* ago."

"One of the fortune teller's predictions?" Ian asked, guessing from the phrasing.

"Yes. And now it makes sense. Ian, you know the history of our families as well as I do."

"Probably. The point being?"

"For every generation, the hatred was an inherited thing, a family matter rather than a personal grudge. But somehow, it always *became* personal. And so the feud was maintained, each generation hating for their own reasons. Right?"

"As far as I can remember, that sounds right. Until we came along, that is."

Still marveling at the quirk of fate that had prompted her meeting with Ian on an island so far away, she leaned over to kiss him. "I'm so glad we came along."

"So am I," he murmured, touching her cheek gently.

Michele forced herself to think of less pleasant things. "But before we did—thirty-five years ago, to be exact—something happened between our fathers. I'm willing to bet that until then, they didn't feel much personal animosity, but after that they hated each other."

"Do you know what happened?"

"I got part of the story from Jon, but I don't think he knows all of it. You were right, it was a woman. Apparently, both our fathers fell in love with her. From that point, I'm not sure of the facts. She was with Dad for a while, then told him she loved your father more and went to him. But something happened; Jon said there was a confrontation of some kind, and she ended up without either of them."

Ian leaned back against the pillows and frowned. "You think this woman could be behind the sabotage?"

Michele drew a breath. "I think we'd better find out what happened to her. Maybe our fathers gave her a reason to hate. Maybe the *why* of all this . . . is revenge."

After a long moment, Ian said, "I'll get the story out of Dad. I have a feeling he'll be more willing to talk about it than your father. Besides that, Dad knows about us."

"He does?" A bit warily, she added, "How did he take it?"

"On the whole, fairly well." He smiled at her. "Not delighted—but resigned."

Ruefully, Michele said, "Then we've done better than I ever expected. Your father and my brother have survived the shock. If Jon gets through to Dad in the morning . . ."

Ian glanced at the clock on his nightstand. "It's already morning." He leaned forward to get the tray and set it on the floor by the bed. "You need to rest."

Michele cuddled up to his side, but as he reached out to turn off the lamp, she said thoughtfully, "I'm not all that tired."

Enough light filtered through the drapes for Ian to see the catlike gleam of her haunting eyes. "No?"

"Well, no. Maybe it was the milk."

He realized that his hands were stroking her delicate body, the soft flesh of her throat drawing his lips as if to a lodestar. Half groaning, he said against her warm skin, "I've said it from the first; you make me so crazy I can't even remember my own good intentions."

"What good intentions?" she murmured, but not as if the subject interested her.

"Letting you rest, baby." He lifted his head, looking down at her with burning eyes.

Michele wound her arms around his neck and kissed him. "I'll sleep late," she promised softly.

It was late when she woke up, Michele knew that even before she opened her eyes. She also knew that she woke reluctantly, and it took her several moments to realize that a ringing telephone was the culprit. She lay with her head on Ian's shoulder and listened drowsily as he talked, not really trying to figure out what was said until he moved slightly to replace the receiver in its cradle on the nightstand.

"Oedipus," she murmured. Her pillow shifted as Ian chuckled.

"What?"

"Or Electra. It's a complex. Psychology." She lifted her head and stared at him owlishly. "No. That's between parents and children. What is it between siblings?"

"I have no idea," Ian said politely. "No idea what you're talking about, and no idea what 'it' is between siblings since I don't have any."

Michele's drifting thoughts finally settled, and she made the connection. "Ah. My brother calling my lover while I'm in my lover's bed. It must have started a train of thought." She considered that, then added bemusedly, "I think the train derailed."

Ian was laughing. He raised his head from the pillow and kissed her. "You're very interesting to wake up with, you know that? I remember on Martinique you woke up once saying, 'When I haven't any blue, I use red.' When I asked you what you were talking about, you said Picasso."

She frowned. "I wonder what brought that on. There's usually a germ of an idea in there somewhere."

"As in Oedipus?"

"I guess. That was Jon on the phone, wasn't it?"

"Yes. And if he was feeling any brotherly jealousies, he didn't let on. I told him about your idea that this whole thing may have started thirty-five years ago, and that I was going to call my father and get the facts. He said once you had a name, you could probably trace the woman. Apparently his morning confrontation was less than successful, since your father hardly listened before storming out of the house in a rage. He also said your absence hadn't been noticed, and that we all needed to talk about the situation. I certainly agreed. He'll be here in about an hour."

Michele peered past Ian at the clock on the nightstand. "Eleven. Even after all that food in the wee hours, I'm starving. Can we eat while we talk?"

They could, although Ian was still preparing the meal when Michele went to let Jon in. She was staving off hunger with a slice of hot French bread, and at her brother's surprised look said lightly, "It's all Ian's fault; he primed the pump."

"Should I ask what you're talking about?" Jon wanted to know, looking around the apartment with wary interest.

"My appetite. Ian fed me at three o'clock this morning, and it seems to have triggered my appetite. For the first time in weeks, I'm hungry. Come on into the kitchen; lunch is almost ready. Have you eaten?" She kept her voice casual deliberately, aware that her brother was a little uncomfortable and trying to make it easier on him.

"Not since breakfast." Jon followed her into the spacious and well-equipped kitchen, and his faint amusement grew as he saw Ian skillfully at work preparing spaghetti. Nearby on the counter was an assortment of greens for salad, which Michele returned to as she finished her slice of bread.

Ian glanced at him, saying merely, "Coffee's over there by Michele; wine's on the table. Help yourself."

Jon chose wine, then sat at the table and watched the activity in silence. Even though he said nothing, the room wasn't silent, because Michele and Ian were clearly in the middle of an amiable discussion concerning his skills—and her lack thereof—in the kitchen. As he watched and listened, Jon felt a pang of envy. The relationship between the two was so close it was a tangible thing, as if they dovetailed perfectly.

He knew they were as worried about the dangers surrounding them as he was, yet they seemed curiously insulated, as if the love they shared was a kind of shield. His last misgivings about the relationship faded, and he could only feel something like awe at the knowledge that with all the generations of five hundred years ranged against them, they had found each other.

A few minutes later, Michele unconsciously echoed her brother's thoughts by proposing a wry toast before they began eating. "To destiny," she said, raising her glass.

The two men gravely touched their glasses to hers, and it was Ian who said, "Are you still thinking of the fortune teller?"

"Well, dammit, she's gotten more right than wrong." While they ate, Michele told Jon about the visit on Martinique, and how one of the predictions made had prompted her to think of what had happened thirty-five years ago.

"Right now," Jon said when she'd finished, "I can't think of a better idea. It's a long time to wait for revenge, though."

"Maybe it took time to plan. And to raise the money. This has cost somebody plenty."

Ian nodded in agreement. "Once we eliminate business competition, it pretty much has to be a personal grudge. And our fathers have hated each other as long as any of us can remember; if the beginning of that hatred hurt someone else, then that's a good place to look for a common enemy."

Jon looked at him. "Have you talked to your father about it yet?"

"No." Ian glanced at his watch, and then pushed back his chair and rose. "I'll call him now." He went out into the living room to use that extension.

He was a little surprised when his father resisted talking about the subject; no matter how he argued, he couldn't get anything out of the older man except the bare facts of the woman's name and when she had left Atlanta.

"We may be on to something," he told Jon and Michele as he rejoined them in the kitchen. "Dad sure as hell didn't want to talk about it; it was like pulling teeth just to get a name out of him."

"But you got that much?" Michele asked.

"Barely. Her name was Helen Gordon, and she left Atlanta exactly thirty-five years ago this past June."

"Any idea where she went?" Jon wondered.

"Not really. Although Dad did say he thought she was originally from somewhere on the West Coast. An interesting coincidence, isn't it?"

They looked at one another for a moment, and then Ian asked Michele, "Think you can track her?"

"There isn't much to go on but, given time, I think I can. Driver's license, social security number—most people have both those. If she didn't change her name or try to cover her tracks in some other way. But I'll need to use the computer in my office."

"Your office building's closed on Saturday," Jon noted.

"Security will let me in. It wouldn't be the first time I've worked during the weekend."

Ian and Jon exchanged glances, and the former said, "Then we'll all go."

Michele didn't object. With the threat against them all, she knew she'd worry constantly with Ian or her brother out of her sight. She was more than ever conscious of time ticking away, and was convinced that if they could only find out who was behind the attack on both families they would be able to find a way to stop the destruction.

"Where's Dad?" she asked Jon as they all rode to her office building in a cab.

"Where he usually is on Saturday. The golf course."

That relieved her mind somewhat. They were, she knew, tempting fate by being together downtown where they were known by sight to too many people. Even on a Saturday.

Tempting fate. The entire situation seemed to revolve around a fateful sequence of events, Michele thought. If they were right about what had happened decades ago, the beginnings were there; the old feud burned more brightly than ever after some conflict ended in hatred. Then a son and daughter of the right ages born to different sides, neither of whom was steeped in the bitterness of their families quite as much as they could have been. A lifetime of knowing each other from a distance, and an unexpected meeting on an island paradise far away from their homes.

What were the odds against that, Michele wondered, that she and Ian would meet unexpectedly in a place where their attraction could be nurtured? And, even more, the odds against love growing where so much mistrust and suspicion had been sown?

Was it fate, after all? Had the hand of destiny always meant her to love Ian, to forge a bridge between families at war for five centuries?

Michele was a sensible woman, her beliefs for the most part grounded firmly in reality. But it disturbed her to realize how many random factors had woven themselves into a pattern so complex and bewildering. If a single thread had snapped, the pattern couldn't have held. If she had not met Ian, not loved him enough to trust him; if Jon had not been able to at least see the possibility of a common enemy; if that enemy had not chosen to use a state of the art device still new enough to be traced with relative ease; if a fortune teller had not made predictions so uncannily appropriate that they seemed to Michele a set of clues to the puzzle . . .

If. If all those connections had not been made, the feud would now rage more bitterly than ever, probably with violence and destruction on both sides.

Michele didn't realize how long she had been silent until Ian helped her from the cab in front of her office building and asked quietly, "Are you all right?"

She looked up at him and Jon as they stood on the pavement, and managed a smile. "I was just thinking of . . . connections."

Ian squeezed her hand as if he understood, then said, "There's one connection we don't want made just yet; we'd better get off the street."

Michele agreed with that. With the fateful twists that had already taken place, it would be all too ironically perfect for some roving journalist to see a startling sight on a downtown street corner and make the right connection.

The security guard let them into the building, as unsurprised by Michele's appearance as she'd expected. He knew Jon by sight and accepted both Ian and Michele's offhand explanation of needed research without a blink.

By tacit consent, they took the stairs rather than the elevator, a minor inconvenience since Michele's office was on the fourth floor. The hall was deserted when they emerged from the stairwell, office doors closed and a high-countered reception desk near the elevators unoccupied.

Michele led the way to her office and got out her keys to unlock the door. But, with the key inserted, she suddenly went still.

"What?" Ian asked immediately.

"It isn't locked. Jon, didn't I lock up yesterday?"

He nodded.

Leaving the key in the door, she stepped back. "Maybe we should err on the side of caution."

"Definitely," Ian said grimly. "None of us is going in there until we're sure it's safe."

Michele took a deep breath and made herself think for a moment, then said, "I think my brain's in neutral. The security cameras. This way." She led them back down the hall to the reception desk.

"You have a camera in your office?" Jon asked as she went around behind the desk. "I've never noticed it."

"You weren't supposed to," Michele said. "This is an insurance company, remember? One of the things we do is recommend security systems to clients who want us to insure them; the better the system, the less chance we have of taking a loss. This building's full of gadgets, because the president thinks we should practice what we preach."

She pressed a button on an enigmatic keypad built into the lower level of the desk, and a panel opened to reveal three small monitor screens. The two men joined her as she activated the camera in her office by pushing another button, and the center screen came alive with a flicker.

The screen showed a neat desk at first, the camera holding steady. Michele pressed more buttons, and the image shifted slowly as the camera panned around the office. For several minutes, she maneuvered the camera remotely so that they were offered a clear view of the door and the walls near it. Finally, she straightened with a sigh.

"Nothing. The door's clear."

Even so, it was Ian and Jon who went into the office first, neither of them giving Michele a chance to argue. The small room appeared peaceful, but both the men began to search methodically. After a few moments, Michele began to think they were all being ridiculously paranoid, and had started toward her desk where Ian was looking when his voice stopped her cold.

"Michele, get out of here."

"What is it?" she whispered.

Ian had eased open the bottom drawer of her desk, where files were normally kept, and was staring down into it. "Another one of those damned timers. There's five minutes left on the clock. Get out of here!"

Her heart was beating so fast it seemed to echo inside her head, but she forced herself to think clearly. Five minutes. Five minutes could be a very long time.

It could also be no time at all.

Steadily, she said, "There isn't enough time to call in someone to disarm it. We'll have to do it."

"Great," Jon muttered, joining Ian to stare down at the deceptively innocent-looking device.

"If it's the same device he used before, I studied all the diagrams and specifications. It can only be detonated when the timer reaches zero; you could throw it out a window and it wouldn't go off until then. I know what to do." Her eyes held Ian's as he looked up, and she went around the desk to join them.

Tautly, Ian said, "When this thing gets to a minute, we're out of here—disarmed or not."

"Agreed," Jon said instantly.

Michele took a long look at the device and sighed in unconscious relief. "It's the same one. But all I see is the timer; where are the explosives?" That, she knew, was the critical question. If their enemy had gotten as fancy with his explosives as he had with the timer, they were in trouble. If, on the other hand, either dynamite or plastique had been used, preventing an explosion would be simple.

Ian carefully pushed aside the files still in the drawer, and they all saw two thin red wires extending from the timer toward the back and out of sight. He followed the wires by touch, reaching all the way into the drawer without pulling it out any farther. "Out the back of the drawer," he said. "I can't tell where they go beyond that."

"Under the desk," Jon said, and knelt to peer beneath.

An instant later, his voice strained, he said, "I can't see the wires, it's too dark. But there's something wedged into two corners. It looks like plastique."

Instantly, Michele said, "Find the wires and pull them out of the plastique; as long as the timer isn't connected to the explosives, nothing can happen." Unless, of course, there was another surprise planned. It would have been stupid to bank on anything where their enemy was concerned.

"Three minutes," Ian said.

Jon reached under the desk and probed. "There's one. Where the hell's the other one? Wait—got it." He emerged with the two red wires in his hand.

The LED indicator of the timer continued to count off the seconds methodically.

Jon rose to his feet, leaving the wires lying a safe distance from the plastique, and dusted off his hands precisely. "I suggest we wait outside," he said with unnatural calm.

"You won't get an argument," Ian said, taking Michele's hand and guiding her from behind the desk.

They picked the farthest spot from Michele's office— the stairwell—and waited there. Ian kept his gaze fixed on his watch, but held Michele close to his side as the seconds ticked away. "Three . . . two . . . one . . . zero," he murmured.

The silence was unbroken. After another eternal five minutes, Ian sighed roughly and hugged Michele hard.

Jon was leaning back against the wall with his hands in his pockets, his face as pale as those of the other two. He looked at his sister and said very politely, "I'll never again give you a hard time about your job."

Michele was trying to quit shaking, her face pressed against Ian's chest, but at that masterly statement couldn't hold back a watery laugh.

Sometime later, after the plastique had been removed from her desk and stored with relative safety in a thick metal box Michele found in the storeroom, she sat in her chair and watched as Ian and Jon examined the timer.

"What I'd like to know," Ian said, "is how the bastard activated the timer. He doesn't seem to have much trouble getting into security-conscious buildings, but how would he know when to set the clock? He couldn't have known we'd be here, or when we would be."

"He's watching," Michele told them. "That timer can be activated remotely. All he had to do was get in here to set the explosives, and then stand by outside until we came into the building. Or until I did."

Ian frowned. "You think he was after you alone?"

She drew a breath. "I think so. Because if he was after all three of us, then he expected us to be together, and that doesn't make sense."

"How do you mean?" Jon asked.

"Look at his apparent plan. Divide and conquer; he's been out to set the Logans and Stuarts at each other's throats from the start. Now, I could accept that he realized we were working together and decided to eliminate all three of us, but I would have thought he'd have asked himself first of all *why* we're working together."

"And if he did," Ian said slowly, "he might have found out about you and me."

"Oh, hell," Jon muttered as he realized.

Michele nodded. "If he knows, and if he wants to push Dad over the edge, he has a perfect weapon. Why bother to blow us up? Tell Dad about Ian and me, and then he can just sit back and watch."

"We're out of time," Ian said.

She turned on her computer and stared at the blank screen as the machine warmed up. "Even if he doesn't know for sure," she murmured, "the sight of us together might give him ideas. And it won't take any more than a hint to Dad."

Michele got to work. With so little information about Helen Gordon, it was a slow process, and since data storage by computer was a fairly recent thing, a large number of older records hadn't yet been converted into sophisticated electronics. Michele made several phone calls, but she had to resort to personal contacts made over the past few years because few record-keeping facilities boasted weekend business hours. And more than once, a computer hacker who owed her a favor—or wanted one owed to him—gave up an access code never meant to be public.

Around four o'clock, Jon went out and brought back food and drinks for them, and Michele ate while she worked. The men talked quietly at first, then later poured over the information that began chattering from her printer. Michele was tapping into every source she could think of, assigning some to the printer and some to her screen, but it wasn't until nearly six o'clock that the information began falling into place.

"I've got a record of a California driver's license. Helen Gordon, a Los Angeles address. It expired almost ten years ago, and was never renewed, but the address is the same going back more than thirty years." Michele looked up, frowning.

"Is she the right Helen Gordon?" Jon asked. They had already located and discounted several of that name.

Ian, who was studying a printout of students registered in the Atlanta area colleges and universities thirty-five years before, suddenly asked, "What's that address?"

Michele glanced at her screen and rattled it off.

"Bingo. You were right; she must have come out here to go to college. Listed as a transfer student from Los Angeles, and at just the right time. Dropped out in the spring quarter thirty-five years ago this past April. No reason given."

Within the next half hour, they found more indications that they were on the right track, and when Michele uncovered a coroner's report dated ten years previously, there was little doubt they had found the right woman.

She read the information on her screen, then sat back

in her chair feeling a curious little chill. She looked at the waiting men and said flatly, "Helen Gordon died ten years ago, in an accident. An elevator cable snapped."

"So at least now we know why it's been elevators," Ian said tiredly. "But if she's dead, who's after us? A husband? Offspring?"

Michele stared at him for a long moment as a final connection was made in her mind, then muttered, "Oh, damn . . . " and began very quickly typing commands into her computer. With the right question finally asked, the answer came through in minutes. Even so, Michele couldn't believe the answer though it made all too much sense.

"Michele?" Ian leaned forward, his eyes concerned. "What is it? You've gone white."

"Oedipus," she said dully. "I must have already known. I just didn't make the right connection this morning."

Jon looked totally bewildered. "What?"

"The love of a boy for his mother, his jealousy of his father. And a hundred times worse for him if she was bitter." Michele drew a deep breath and said, "We know Helen Gordon left here in June of that year. Six months later—exactly thirty-five years ago on this coming Monday —she gave birth to a son. She wasn't married; maybe that was why she combined two family names for his. According to his birth certificate, he was named Nicholas Gordon South."

"Our mysterious buyer," Jon said, then realized that Michele and Ian were thinking along different lines. It was in both their faces. "What?" he demanded.

Softly, Michele said, "Six months later, Jon. That's when her son was born. Six months after leaving here, after being involved with both our father and Ian's. I wonder if Nicholas Gordon even knows which name is rightfully his."

After a long moment, Jon said, "You mean we could have a half brother who's trying to destroy us?"

"We could. Or Ian could. I find it a little unlikely that she could have been involved with a third man at just that time. One of them must have fathered her son."

Jon began to swear steadily in a low voice and without inflection.

"What about Gordon?" Ian asked Michele. "Can you trace him? He's still faceless as far as we're concerned."

Michele set to work, forcing herself to concentrate because the alternative was too painful. But she couldn't help thinking that the fortune teller's warning had been all too terribly accurate. The seeds sown decades ago *had* borne a dark and bitter fruit.

The only cause for Helen Gordon's son to have launched such an all-out campaign to destroy the Logan and Stuart families had to be that he hated them both. Michele was convinced that the blood of at least one side of the feud ran in his veins, and he was prepared to destroy both sides in his bitterness.

Ten

Within another hour, Michele knew she'd lost the trail. Nicholas Gordon South had simply ceased to exist when his mother died ten years before. The family home she had lived in until her death was sold, and her son vanished. If he changed his name, he didn't do so legally in California; if he held down a job or dealt with any of the myriad institutions requiring valid identification, he did so under another name.

"It's no use," she said finally, leaning back and rubbing her tense neck slowly. "He might as well have dropped off the face of the earth."

"Enough," Ian said, going around the desk to take her hands and pull her gently to her feet. "You're exhausted. You haven't taken a break in hours."

The telephone on Michele's desk shrilled abruptly, interrupting Ian and making her jump. After an instant, she leaned over and picked up the instrument.

"Hello?"

"Michele, it's Jackie. Jon said you might have to work on something today, so I thought—"

"Jackie, what's wrong?" Her friend sounded shaken, as if she'd been crying.

"I—I went by your house a little while ago. Your father was—I've never seen him like that. He was storming around yelling at Leona to pack your things because you weren't coming back to his house. Michele . . . somebody told him about you and Ian, that you were together on Martinique. Leona said there was a call, and he just went crazy—"

The phone slipped from Michele's nerveless fingers, and Jon quickly reached over to grab it and ask Jackie what was wrong.

Ian pulled Michele into his arms and held her gently, his face grim. "Baby . . ."

"I knew it would hurt," she said quietly, looking up at him. "I knew that. But not like this." She felt shattered, wounded, as if someone had reached into her and opened a vein. "How can people . . . hate so much? He's my *father.*"

Ian wanted to reassure her that it would be all right. He wanted to wipe away the lost anguish in her haunting eyes, shield her from a blow she should never have had to bear. But he couldn't. All he could do was hold her.

Michele clung to him, not crying because the hurt went too deep for that easy release. This was the risk she had faced, that the cost of her bond with Ian would be the severing of the ties between her and her father. She had known it was possible, even probable, but she had hoped from the beginning that it wouldn't happen. Even now, she couldn't quite believe it had happened, and some part of her refused to accept it.

Jon hung up the phone, his face pale. Speaking directly to Ian, he said, "She'd better stay with you. From the sound of it, Dad's really gone over the edge." With suppressed violence, he added, "Dammit, this time he's going to listen to me if I have to knock him down and sit on him."

Michele turned her head to look at her brother, though she didn't draw away from Ian. "Be careful."

Nodding, Jon said, "I'll call and let you know." Then he hurried out of the office.

There was a moment of silence, and then Michele looked at Ian and said fiercely, "I love you. No matter what happens, that isn't going to change."

"I love you, too, baby." He held her a moment longer, then reached out to get her coat. "Come on. There's nothing else we can do now."

For the first time, Michele realized that it was night, that darkness had fallen while they'd worked. She was very tired, and the pain of her father's reaction had been encased in numbness. It occurred to her that if it had to happen, better this way; if she had looked into her father's eyes and seen what he was feeling as he disowned her, it might well have been a sight from which she would never have recovered.

Ian took her back to his apartment, and took care of her. He warmed soup and insisted she eat it, then put her to bed and joined her even though it was still early. And this time, it wasn't a matter of good intentions. She was exhausted and numb, he was weary, and the comfort they found together was in simply holding each other.

"Will you *listen* to me!" Jon demanded, having to raise his voice just to be heard over his father's roaring.

Charles Logan wasn't making sense and hadn't been for some time. The pressures that had been building inside him over the last weeks, pressures contained by Jon's own persuasion, had finally escaped. Being told by a whispery voice on the telephone that his daughter had acquired a lover on Martinique would have been enough to upset him terribly; the additional information that the lover was none other than Ian Stuart had been a bone-jarring shock so devastating and enraging that he was in serious danger of suffering a stroke.

He was pacing his study, his movements violent and uncontrolled, so wrapped up in his own bitter fury that he was barely aware of Jon's presence. "I won't have it," he muttered, his voice hoarse from all the yelling. "I'll ruin the bastards, both of them. I'll see them lose everything they have. And *her!* How could she do this to me? . . . She knows what they are, she *knows.* I've taught her—"

Jon grabbed his father's arm and quite literally pushed him into a chair near the big desk. "Taught her?" His voice was bitter. "Oh, you did your best. You did all you could to teach both of us to hate. And you almost succeeded. I hated Ian so much it was like a sickness, eating away at me—until my bright, beautiful sister had the guts to make me wonder *why.*"

Charles stared up at him, a flash of bewilderment momentarily showing in his eyes. "Why? For God's sake, Jon—"

"God had nothing to do with it," Jon snapped. "And Ian had nothing to do with it. Just you. Just you and five hundred years of hate. Before I was even old enough to understand what hate was, you were filling me with it, making the Stuart name a curse so dirty it burned in my throat."

"They're our enemies!"

"*No.*" Jon grasped the arms of his father's chair and leaned down, no more than a foot separating two furious faces. "We pick our enemies, Dad. And we choose our friends. Only our families are chosen for us. But you couldn't stand that, couldn't bear to think I might not hate where you did. So you didn't wait to find out if your enemy was mine—you made sure of it. And I'll forever regret the fact that I *let* you, even though Ian has never done one single damned thing to make him my enemy."

"He's trying to stall the project, him and his father—"

"Are you so blind with hate that you can't see the truth no matter how big it is? Who sabotaged *their* building, Dad? Who planted a bomb hours ago that just missed killing Michele, me—*and* Ian? Do you have an answer for that?"

For the first time, Charles Logan was silenced, bewilderment growing stronger in his eyes because he didn't have an answer.

Jon straightened slowly and stared down at his father. With his first real chance to get through to the older man, he made every word count. "For weeks, I've been trying to convince you there was someone after us and the Stuarts, but you wouldn't listen. Even when it was so obvious there was no other answer, you still wouldn't listen. But you're going to listen now, Dad. And when I'm finished, if you still intend to disown your only daughter because she had the courage to fall in love with Ian Stuart even though she knew what it would cost her— then you'd better get ready to disown me, too."

"What? You can't mean—"

"I've never meant anything more. I couldn't live with myself if I turned my back on Michele just because she fell in love. And I sure as hell couldn't stay here and watch you pretend she didn't exist. There's been too much hate, and I'm tired of it. I don't give a damn what started the feud. All I know is that it's over. Ian and I won't fight."

"You'll fight," Charles said harshly. "When he hits, you'll hit back. And he will. It's in his blood. It's in your blood. Neither of you can escape it."

Jon heard a hollow laugh and realized it was his own—a sound of defeat; he didn't know what it would take to end his father's hate, but he doubted now that words would ever be enough. He leaned back against the desk and spoke quietly, without force or emotion.

"You want to talk about blood? Fine. Let's talk about

that. Let's talk about the older half brother I probably have."

Charles stiffened, his face flushing suddenly with a new anger. "What are you talking about?"

Studying his father dispassionately, Jon said, "Yeah, I thought so. You knew. You knew Helen Gordon was pregnant when she left Atlanta."

"Pregnant with *his* bastard," Charles muttered, "not my child."

"His bastard—or your child? That's a fairly useless distinction considering that neither one of you married her. Did it ever occur to you in all these years to wonder whatever became of a son that *might* have been yours? Did you stop and think just once that the hate you and Brandon Stuart poured all over that poor woman might possibly come back to haunt you one day?"

For the first time, Charles couldn't meet his son's flat eyes. He was a little pale, clearly disturbed that Jon was quite obviously scornful of his behavior. A proud man, he had never received anything but respect from his son, and it shook him now to see and hear the contempt Jon didn't try to hide.

"You don't know how it was," he protested, attempting to work up the righteous anger that had never failed to accompany that bitter memory. Until now.

"I'm listening," Jon said evenly. "And you're going to tell me exactly how it was. Because we're out of time, Dad. What goes around comes around. Unless we find a way to stop him, there's a good chance we'll all be destroyed by a man who doesn't seem to give a tinker's damn which one of you is his father."

Michele was awakened by the phone for a second morning, and just as the day before, she again lay sleepily listening to the rumble of Ian's voice without really hearing the words. The last echoes of some kind of rhyme were fading in her mind, and though she felt an impulse to concentrate on it, the effort proved too much.

When her pillow moved, she murmured, " 'The Lady of Shalott,' " and frowned because that couldn't be right. She lifted her head and stared at Ian.

He was smiling a little, his eyes warm.

"It's a poem," she clarified.

"Tennyson," he agreed gravely. "What's the connection?"

She thought about that, but if there was a connection, it totally escaped her. "I wish," she said ruefully, "my subconscious would talk louder."

Ian raised his head and kissed her. "I love you," he murmured huskily.

"I love you, too." She smiled at him, but then her smile faded as the events of the day before surfaced in her mind. She felt a throb of loss inside her. "Was that . . . Jon on the phone?" she asked.

Nodding, Ian said quietly, "He sounded pretty exhausted. Apparently, he and your father were up most of the night."

"And?" She wasn't sure she wanted to hear.

"And—by the time Jon got through with him, he was quite a bit calmer about you and me. The subject of Helen Gordon seems to have taken most of the fight out of him, at least for now. I got the feeling Jon was pretty rough with him."

Michele wasn't surprised. "I always figured one day Jon would have to fight Dad about something important. What your father told you about strong-minded men breeding strong-minded sons is true, but Dad's never had to oppose that strength in Jon."

"He has now."

"I wonder what the result will be." Michele sighed. "And I wonder if Dad'll be able to accept us."

"He's at least accepted the fact that what happened thirty-five years ago has come back to haunt us all. Jon got the story out of him, but he thinks I should get Dad's side of it before we compare notes."

"I'll bet both sides are radically different," she mused wryly.

"No doubt of it. Anyway, I need to talk to Dad face to face and pry it out of him. He usually works in the office on Sunday, catching up on paperwork. I can see him there." He paused, then added, "Will you humor me and get some rest while I'm gone?"

Michele looked at the clock, and said, "I've been sleeping for nearly twelve hours."

Ian had obviously expected a protest. "I know," he said patiently, "but you've been under a hell of a strain, and one good night's sleep isn't going to ease that. I know you're worried; I am, too. But until we get all the facts, there's really nothing we can do about Nicholas Gordon."

Steadily, she said, "The message said today would be dangerous."

"Baby, every day is going to be dangerous until we stop this. I'll be careful. But I'd feel a lot better if I knew you were here watching a dumb movie on television or reading a book."

Michele was reluctant, but she saw the sense of what he was saying. Though he hadn't used the argument of her pregnancy, she knew he was concerned about that as well, and since she still felt tired despite the sleep, taking things easy was a good idea.

By the time Ian left the apartment a couple of hours later, she was ensconced on the couch with soft music playing and several books within reach. At first, it was peaceful, and she managed to concentrate on the novel she was reading. In fact, she became aware of her tension only when the phone rang and she jumped a foot in surprise.

"And it's not even a horror novel," she muttered to herself, picking up the receiver from the endtable. "Hello?"

"You sound annoyed," Ian noted.

"I am. The phone made me jump." She glanced at the clock, adding, "You've been gone an hour."

"Dad's being difficult," he explained. "He's talked a lot and hasn't said a damned thing. Now he wants to go over to the building and take another look at the damage. I didn't want you to worry if it took longer than I expected."

"Just be careful," she pleaded.

"I will."

After she'd hung up, Michele sat staring into space for several minutes, conscious of something nagging at her. No matter how hard she tried, she couldn't focus on it. It was like having a tune running through your head and *knowing* there were words to it lurking just out of reach.

Deciding that it wasn't going to come to her because she was trying too hard, she returned to her book and concentrated on absorbing those words. It was nearly half an hour before she got back into the story, and she jumped when the phone rang again.

"Hello?"

"Hi, Michele." Jon did sound tired, though a faint thread of amusement ran through his voice. "I just wanted you to know that your clothes are back in the closet."

The relief she felt was almost numbing. "Jon, what on earth did you say to him?"

"A lot. A hell of a lot, in fact. He isn't happy about it, Misha. That would be too much to hope for. The idea of Ian Stuart as his son-in-law makes him choke. But once I convinced him that being disowned wouldn't make a dent in your determination, he was pretty well forced to accept the idea." Gently, he added, "He loves you, you know."

Michele had a sneaking suspicion that it had been as much Jon's loyal support as anything else that had swayed her father, but she was too grateful at the results to care. "I never wanted to hurt him. I hope you told him that."

"I did."

"Thank you."

"Don't mention it." Jon sighed, then said restlessly,

"As for the rest, it's not a pretty story. Has Ian gotten his father's version?"

"He's working on it now. At their building."

"I think I'll go over there. If Brandon Stuart's reluctant, maybe the shock of a Logan in his building will jar something loose."

Michele had to laugh. "Just be careful."

After she hung up for the second time, she caught herself brooding again. Even with her father's grudging acceptance of her relationship with Ian, she knew there were still likely to be storms from him; Charles Logan had hated too long to be able to put all his bitterness behind him, not overnight anyway, and not without a great deal of reluctance. Michele realized that, and she was prepared to face trouble when it came.

She wanted to hear the details of what had happened thirty-five years ago, but she thought she already knew enough to guess what had happened.

What occupied her mind now was the same nagging feeling of something overlooked, some vital piece of information that she had seen but not really taken notice of. She found herself on her feet, pacing the room, a tune in her mind she couldn't find the words for.

When the phone rang a third time, she answered almost absently. "Hello?"

"Michele, it's Jackie. Are you all right?"

"I'm fine."

"Your father—"

"He's calmed down. Jon talked to him. Did you just guess I'd be here at Ian's?"

"It made sense," Jackie said dryly. "Besides, I called your house this morning and Jon told me where you were. He also said you'd gotten some kind of warning that today wouldn't exactly be a good day. Is Ian with you?"

The warning, Michele thought. That was it. Steve had said he was going to express the original of that enigmatic message, and he would have found a carrier that would deliver it even on a Sunday; the guard at her office building would have it by now. Something about that message had bothered her, and she wanted to see the original.

"Michele?"

"What? Oh—no, he and Jon are both at the Stuarts' building. There's something I have to do, Jackie; can I call you later?"

"But, Michele, this warning—"

"I'll call you later. Bye, Jackie."

She took time only to jot a quick note for Ian on the chance that he returned before she did, then grabbed her purse and coat and hurriedly left the apartment. She couldn't have said why it seemed so important for her to see the message; she only knew that the tune in her head was louder and more emphatic.

Traffic was light, and her cab driver was more than willing to wait while she went inside her office building. The express delivery had been made, and she carried the flat envelope back out to the taxi.

"Where to, ma'am?"

She gave him Ian's address automatically, occupied with opening the envelope. As she gazed at the single sheet of unlined paper in her lap, her first realization was that Steve had taken no notice of the *way* the message was written. Block-printing, he'd said, and it was; but the sentences had been arranged with care and precision, one to each line, with clear breaks after the first two and second two lines.

She had copied the sentences as Steve had read them aloud, never realizing that how the message looked was even more important than what it said. But some part of her mind had sensed a pattern even so, and now she could see it clearly.

I must warn them
Tell her this immediately.

It is vital that she know
Sunday is dangerous

Story I told you was false
Unable to tell you truth
The buyer is no stranger
Three devices, not one
Only they can stop him
Next days critical

For a long, cold moment, what she saw made no sense. But then everything came together in her mind. She knew what had nagged at her, knew why she had awakened this morning with the title of a poem on her lips; her subconscious had been prodding her, because it had been there all along. The answer.

Unsteadily, she told the driver she'd changed her mind, and gave him the address of the Stuarts' building. While he uncomplainingly changed direction, she stared down at the warning in her lap. Now that she saw it, the hidden warning stood out clearly. The first letter of each line spelled out a simple message: IT IS SUTTON.

There were no men downstairs in the lobby. No evidence of security. Michele knew that wasn't right, Ian wouldn't have reduced security. She hurried across the lobby, sparing only a glance for the single elevator standing open; it would have been quicker, but she took the stairs.

The tenth floor. Ian had said the damage was on the tenth floor, so that's where they'd be. It took an eternity to climb the stairs, and with every step her fear grew. He couldn't have gotten here already, surely? Not from Jackie's. But perhaps he hadn't been with her, perhaps he'd only called her and said something casual like, "Find out from Michele where Ian and Jon are, I'd like to talk to them about better security."

And Jackie, poor Jackie, wouldn't have thought twice about the request. She'd been Cole's pipeline for months, feeding him information without ever realizing that was what he was after, more than willing to talk about the bitter hatred of the feud because she'd been raised on all the stories. She'd told him about Ian and Michele, their meeting on Martinique. Michele knew now why Jackie's attitude had changed so suddenly on the island; because she had called her lover, and Cole had convinced her that her friend needed someone on her side. The last thing he'd wanted was a rift between the two women—even with the chance of a dangerously strong tie forming between Michele and Ian.

Michele reached the tenth floor at last and, breathless, pushed open the heavy fire door.

They were all there. Ian, Jon, and Brandon Stuart were standing in a loose group just a few feet away across from the elevators. Before Michele could realize they weren't alone, a strong hand grabbed her arm and flung her into the group.

Ian caught her before she could fall, and pulled her into the shelter of his arm so that she was standing between him and Jon. And even though she would have chosen to be with him no matter what happened, the anguish in his eyes as he drew her close to his side made her heart ache.

"It's a pity everyone isn't here," Cole said conversationally. He was holding a wicked black automatic in one hand, and it was obvious he knew how to handle guns. He looked at Michele, and the easy, charming smile quirked his lips. "Didn't happen to bring Pop along, did you?"

Michele thought she had never seen anything as empty as his eyes. His gray eyes, she realized. He must have worn tinted contact lenses until now. *A strange, but familiar face, eyes veiled against you.* It made so much sense now.

"So you've guessed Charles Logan is your father?" Jon asked in an even tone.

Cole laughed, his empty eyes flicking to Michele again. "Once I saw her, it was fairly obvious. I look more like her brother than you do. Not that it matters, really. I don't care which side of the feud spawned me."

"Then why destroy us?" Brandon asked quietly.

"You destroyed my mother," Cole told him in the same eerily conversational tone. "Both of you. When she found out she was pregnant, you threw her out, because you thought I wasn't yours. And Logan wasn't about to take her back after that, even though she loved him, too. He didn't give a damn whose kid she was carrying. She told me. She told me how both of you called her those ugly names."

Cole's expressionless face quivered for an instant, raw hatred flashing hotly in his eyes. The emotion was like the dank air of a tomb; something shut up in darkness and silence for too long. "And she told me—*I* should have had a real name instead of one she had to make up. She told me we'd get even one day. She found a book about the feud, and we read it together. We made plans. It was poetic justice that the feud should destroy you both."

"But it won't," Michele said softly. "You're going to do that."

"That's your fault," Cole snapped. "It would have worked perfectly if only you'd believed what you should have. I thought you understood the feud." He nodded toward Ian. "You should have hated him when I made it look like he'd hurt your brother. Why didn't you hate him?" It was almost a plea.

Michele felt so cold she could hardly keep her teeth from chattering. He was insane, lost somewhere totally beyond their reach.

"Why?" Cole repeated the question, though this time it was in a voice crackling with hostility.

She held her voice steady with an effort. "Because I love him."

Abruptly calm again, Cole said chidingly, "That was a stupid mistake. Now you'll have to die with him." He stepped back, carefully moving around the roped-off area in front of the ruined elevators. "I have this last elevator all ready for you. I'll send the car to the top of the building, and then the charges I've set there will snap the cable." Holding the gun trained steadily on them, he pressed the button to summon the functional express car.

"You won't get away with this," Brandon told him harshly.

"Oh, I think I will," Cole replied with a smile. "This time, I've planted careful evidence. Everyone will believe that Charles Logan is responsible. I've thought it out, and I think that's best. I'll be able to watch him suffer while people say he killed his children as well as his enemies. One day, if I think he's suffered enough, I'll kill him, too."

From the corner of her eye, Michele saw Ian and Jon exchange quick glances, and she knew that neither of them would walk meekly into the elevator. Ian's arm tightened around her, and she realized he was getting ready to push her aside in the instant before he leaped toward Cole.

She was frozen, unable to move or make a sound.

The prosaic ding of the arriving elevator car didn't distract Cole's attention from them, but as the doors opened a furious voice succeeded all too well.

"What the hell is this all about?" Charles Logan demanded wrathfully, stepping out of the car. His fierce gray eyes swept the paralyzed group a few feet in front of him, almost jerking away when they encountered the sight of his daughter in the shelter of Ian Stuart's embrace.

He saw Cole then, and in the eternal moment that they

looked at each other face to face for the first time, it was obvious that Charles Logan recognized this man as his son. The expression in his eyes was pain and regret—and acceptance.

For a long time afterward, Michele wondered if, in the end, that was the one thing Cole was unable to bear. Because if there was any sanity left in him, it must have been the most bitter blow of all that after the long years of hatred, he looked into his father's eyes for the first time—and knew without a doubt that he could have claimed his birthright.

Cole let out a hoarse cry and stumbled back, the hand not holding the gun lifting as if to ward off some horror. Maybe he forgot about the gaping elevator doors his own handiwork had left jammed open. Or maybe he just lost his balance.

Ian and Jon tried to reach him, but they were too late.

It took hours to explain what was necessary to the police, hours of questions and statements. A past buried for too long had to be exhumed and minutely examined even as Cole's body was extricated from the bottom of the elevator shaft and carried away in a coroner's wagon and a bomb was safely defused. The security men, told to leave the building by Brandon Stuart after Cole had forced him to give the order, returned, a bit sheepish that they hadn't realized the order was made under duress.

The police were, to put it mildly, upset to find that sabotage had gone on for several weeks without being reported, and they had a number of harsh things to say about the matter. But the Logan/Stuart feud was as real—if incomprehensible—to them as it was to the principals, and so they were less severe than they might have been.

Or their almost unwilling compassion might have sprung from a different source. The feud had caused a death for the first time in more than a century, and though the result of that was never alluded to, it was obvious that the haunting final battle had ended that war forever.

Michele knew that. She sat close beside Ian in the lounge where the police had taken their statements, and though it hurt her to see her father's face she couldn't stop looking at him. As the entire sordid story had been pieced together in this quiet room, she had watched those fierce eyes lose their fire and that strong face slacken and go gray. It had taken a series of near-tragedies and one final one to bring home to Charles Logan the devastation of hate, and it wasn't a lesson he could ignore.

He had fathered a child thirty-five years ago, but his worst sin hadn't been disclaiming that fact; he was just as responsible for the seeds of hate as those of life.

The feud was over, but the cost had been terrible. There was no way of knowing what Cole might have been, and though Michele couldn't grieve for the man who had fallen to his death, she was saddened by the waste of his life.

And then there was Jackie.

"Somebody has to tell her," Michele said to Jon when the police finally began putting away their notebooks.

Her brother looked at her for a long moment, then said simply, "I don't know if I can."

Michele understood his reluctance. Of them all, Jackie had been the innocent pawn, ruthlessly used and sacrificed. She had been taught to hate, her mind filled with tales of treachery and worse, then she had lost her heart to a man who had set out to seduce her for his own mad purpose.

Jon knew only too well how Jackie would feel when she discovered the truth about Cole. And he knew there was every chance she would never forgive him for his part in what had happened to her; if she had never been taught to hate, she might never have been a tool for Cole to use.

"I don't know if I can," Jon repeated.

"You have to," Michele told him gently.

He knew that, too. "Yes. I'll . . . take Dad home and then go to her."

Brandon Stuart, who had been listening to them in silence, said to Jon, "You go ahead. I'll take Charles home. He shouldn't be alone."

The shocks of the day had had a numbing effect, and Michele felt only faint surprise as she looked at Ian's father. "You?"

He smiled just a little. "Why not? We're going to have to make peace or risk losing our children—and grandchildren. We might as well start now." He rose and went over to Charles Logan, who watched his approach with grim eyes.

Michele almost held her breath; she could feel both Ian and Jon waiting with just as much tension. And it was somehow ironic that the first words spoken by the two old warriors directly to each other in more than three decades were both prosaic and completely in character.

"If you came in the Mercedes," Brandon Stuart said, "you can drive us."

Charles Logan got slowly to his feet, still frowning. Irritably, he said, "I'll be damned if I will. My car's never had a Stuart in it."

"There is," Brandon said, "a first time for everything. Come on, I'll buy you a cup of coffee."

"I'll buy my own," Charles muttered, but he was moving with the other man toward the hallway.

The two policemen still in the room stared after them as if they couldn't quite believe their eyes.

Hours later, curled up beside Ian on his couch, Michele was still finding it hard to believe. "Just . . . walked out together," she murmured. "Two nice men going for coffee."

Proving that he understood what shock could do to

people, Ian mused, "Think they'll still be speaking to each other at our wedding?"

"They're both numb, I think. That's bound to wear off eventually. But . . . after today, I can believe in almost anything."

They hadn't talked much about Cole, not because either had forgotten the final sight—and sound—of him, but because it was still too much with them to be discussed. Michele had explained her sudden arrival at the building, showing Ian the original of the warning and telling him about the other realizations she'd had. First had been her nagging awareness that it was unlikely their enemy could have known she had gotten involved with Ian on Martinique; so busy stirring things up in Atlanta, how could he have known? Unless, she had realized, he was in touch with the only "friend" on the island—Jackie.

The "Lady of Shalott" her subconscious had prodded her with that morning had been perfectly clear once she had made the proper connection. It hadn't been the poem itself, but a few words of a single line that had floated around in her mind.

"Which words?" Ian had asked.

" 'The mirror cracked.' I must have been thinking of a reflection that wasn't quite right. I'd thought before that Cole looked familiar, but I didn't know who he reminded me of."

"I knew when he popped out of nowhere waving that gun," Ian had admitted. "But at the party Friday night, all I knew was that something bothered me about the four of you standing together."

Michele didn't like to think about the frightening moments before Cole's death, but she couldn't help but wonder about her father's timely arrival.

"Did you hear what Dad told the police about why he'd come to the building?"

"He said he'd gotten a call warning him that you and Jon were in danger," Ian remembered.

After a thoughtful moment, Michele said, "We've had a lot of helpful warnings, haven't we? Almost as if somebody was watching over us."

"Like you said, after today, I'd be willing to believe in almost anything. All I know for sure is that I love you, Michele Logan."

Glorying in the one certainty that had never wavered despite the odds against it, she murmured, "I love you, too, Ian Stuart." And gave herself up to the wonder of that.

Epilogue

Snow fell on Christmas Eve. It wasn't totally unheard of in the Deep South, but it was certainly unusual enough to merit considerable comment. And though Northerners innured to harsh winters would have considered the scant few inches of white stuff no more than a minor inconvenience, snowplows were rare birds in Atlanta, and the city had come to a virtual standstill.

Michele loved it.

She thought it was apt that after meeting Ian on a hot island paradise and then struggling with him to preserve their love through weeks of cold rain and sleet, they should be married while an uncommon snowfall blanketed the ground outside the tiny church they had chosen. Apt and curiously symbolic of the starkly different stages of their relationship: the tropical heat of passion, the cold rain of worry and anguish, the soft snowfall of peace and contentment.

Michele felt that peace, and it grew even stronger to merge with an almost overwhelming wave of love as Ian slipped his arms around her from behind and rested his chin on top of her head.

"You're very quiet, wife," he murmured.

She smiled, still gazing out the window of their bedroom at the falling snow. "I was just thinking how confused some of the newspapers seemed to be. They didn't know whether to headline the first Christmas Eve snow in ages, or the first wedding ever between a Logan and a Stuart."

The last couple of weeks had been decidedly hectic, not the least because Charles Logan's (reluctant but resigned) announcement of his daughter's engagement to Ian Stuart had created more than a nine-days' wonder.

Ian had gotten impatient at one point after being badgered by a newsman, and had demanded to know if there weren't more important stories going on in the world. With a somewhat comical frankness, the journalist replied that the world was pretty quiet just now and, besides—five hundred years!

Remembering that day, Ian chuckled. "We may have lost part of the headlines today, but I caught a glimpse of that pesky reporter peering into the church, and he had his notebook. And since even a blind man could have seen how much resolution it took for your father to give you to me, I'll bet our fifteen minutes of fame aren't up yet."

Michele couldn't help but laugh, grateful that they could at last find humor in the final remnants of the feud. "I was about ready to turn around and glare at him when he finally sputtered the right answer. Jon told me later that he poked Dad in the ribs just to make sure he got his line right."

Sobering a bit, Ian asked, "What about him and Jackie? I was surprised to see her in the church."

"She's still pretty shattered, and Jon's sticking close. If she comes out of this without blaming him . . . then maybe they have a chance together. It'll take time, though."

Turning in his arms, she lifted hers around his neck, smiling up at him. "And maybe . . . a little good fortune."

Ian, who knew by now about the odd dream Michele had experienced while waiting for him to come home, gazed down on her lovely face and admitted silently that sometimes fortune was so astonishingly good that it *had* to be a little magic. Aloud, he said only, "The hand of destiny?"

"A roll of the dice, a turn of the card, a fork in the road. Maybe it was fate that my car stalled that day. Or fortune."

"Or fortune," Ian agreed, bending his head to kiss her.

In a lamplit study a considerable number of miles north of Atlanta, an old man with a full white beard and wise dark eyes sat at a massive desk. He put a file folder aside, his benign face smiling, then drew another from the stack near the blotter.

He opened the file and studied the contents, nodding to himself from time to time. A difficult case, he mused silently, his elegant hands sifting through the papers. But not impossible, of course.

Nothing was impossible.

Coming next month...

MAGIC by Tami Hoag

Tami Hoag is a rising star on the LOVESWEPT horizon. Her special brand of humor mixed with sensuality has won her a large and devoted following of readers, and her novels consistently place on the romance bestseller lists. Tami's distinctive characters come to life on the pages of her novels and are truly memorable.

In MAGIC, Tami tells the heartwarming story of parapsychologist Brian Hennessy, who sets out to capture the noted ghost of Drake House on film but instead finds the woman of his dreams, Rachel Lindquist. In the following excerpt Brian meets Rachel for the first time. He doesn't want to like her, but he soon finds he has no choice.

Her eyes widened at the sound of her name issuing from the stranger's mouth. His voice was husky and warm, but the fact that he knew her name sent chills down her back.

Bryan nodded decisively. "You're Rachel Lindquist. You're Addie's daughter. I should have recognized you right off. You look a lot like your mother."

He stared at her hard, his straight brows drawing down low and tight over his eyes. He was damned attracted to her, and it came as a very unpleasant surprise. The warm curling sensation in his body was something he hadn't felt in a long, long time, but he was too strongly, basically masculine not to recognize it for what it was — desire. The primitive male in him was responding to a pretty female and he heartily resented it: he resented *her* for stirring that long-dormant need in him.

"So, you decided to come back after all," he said coldly, trying to distance himself from her emotionally as well as physically.

Rachel willed herself to stand still while Bryan Hennessy's scowl bore through her. He moved back and a little to her left and the tarnished light from the old chandelier above them fell more fully across his face. He looked as if he'd just awakened from a dead sound sleep. He looked annoyed more than anything. More than anything except male. He looked very male, big and brooding and sexy with his rumpled hair and beard-shaded cheeks.

The silence between them swelled with unspoken messages, messages Rachel didn't want to hear or understand. All the same, she felt a strange fluttering deep inside her and she pressed a hand to her stomach as if she could push the sensation away. It was probably just hunger. Most of the day had passed since she'd eaten.

Tearing her gaze away from Bryan Hennessy, she gave herself a mental shake. She was hungry, all right, but it wasn't the kind that would be satisfied by a sandwich. If she had learned anything over the last five years it was to be honest with herself. The kind of hunger coursing through her had little to do with prime rib and everything to do with primal attraction.

The realization jolted her. She had lived to the ripe old age of twenty-five and had never experienced such a strong physical reaction to a man, not even to Terence, whom she had once loved. She hadn't expected to ever feel it. It simply wasn't in her nature. She certainly hadn't expected to feel it for a complete stranger, especially one who was suddenly regarding her with a subtle kind of disdain. She didn't like it, didn't want it, and she most definitely didn't need it.